The Virgins of Venice

ALSO BY GINA BUONAGURO

CO-WRITTEN WITH JANICE KIRK
The Sidewalk Artist
Ciao Bella
The Wolves of St. Peter's

WRITING AS MEADOW TAYLOR
(CO-WRITTEN WITH JANICE KIRK)
Falling for Rain
The Billionaire's Secrets
Midnight in Venice

The Virgins of Venice

A NOVEL

GINA BUONAGURO

HARPER**AVENUE**

The Virgins of Venice
Copyright © 2022 by Gina Buonaguro.
All rights reserved.

Published by Harper Avenue, an imprint of HarperCollins Publishers Ltd

First edition

HarperCollins books may be purchased for educational, business or
sales promotional use through our Special Markets Department.

HarperCollins Publishers Ltd
Bay Adelaide Centre, East Tower
22 Adelaide Street West, 41st Floor
Toronto, Ontario, Canada
M5H 4E3

www.harpercollins.ca

The author would like to acknowledge the support of the Canada Council for the Arts.

Library and Archives Canada Cataloguing in Publication

Title: The virgins of Venice : a novel / Gina Buonaguro.
Names: Buonaguro, Gina, author. | Description: First edition.
Identifiers: Canadiana (print) 20220269114 | Canadiana (ebook) 20220269122
ISBN 9781443468398 (softcover) | ISBN 9781443468404 (EPUB)
Classification: LCC PS8603.U65 V57 2022 | DDC C813/.6—dc23

Printed and bound in the United States of America
LSC/H 10 9 8 7 6 5 4 3 2 1

*For my daughter, my mother, my grandmothers, and my great-grandmother,
and for all the matriarchs of my family whose names I do not know.*

I can live neither with you, nor without you.

—OVID, *AMORES*

I prefer love to wedlock, freedom to chains.

—HELOISE, *THE LETTERS OF ABELARD AND HELOISE*

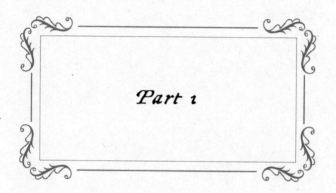

Part 1

Chapter 1

Venice, April 1509, Easter Monday

Bastard!"

"Son of a nun!"

Coarse insults bursting from passing gondoliers intruded on my peaceful nap, where I dreamt of writing poems and exchanging drowsy kisses. I sat up from my chaise with a wince, the opened book of Seneca tumbling from my knees to the ground with a thud, a page of my scribbling floating to the terrazzo floor like a forlorn flower. Mama would not be pleased my younger sister Rosa and I were exposed to such filthy language, but what could she expect with us cloistered on the terrace within earshot of the busy Grand Canal, its fetid smell wafting upward? Our little white dog, Dolce, twitched his ears and sat up straight on Rosa's lap.

"What is it?" The heat was having a soporific effect on Rosa as well, although a fast-moving dark puff from the northwest bullied the otherwise blue sky and cast shadows on the nearby palazzi, dimming their facades from pearl white to dove grey, from ripened apricot to rotten brown. She peered over the stone rail.

I placed a hand on her arm. "Just some foul-mouthed gondoliers. Nothing to be alarmed about."

It was late morning the day after Easter, and Rosa was bleaching her hair using an old family recipe that Mama called alchemy and I called a fruitless exercise in vanity since Rosa's hair was already so blond. For me, my hair reddish-brown with nary a yellow tress, it would be a waste of time I would much rather spend on my literary endeavours. But I could only indulge my dear sister. I was pleased to keep her company and enjoy the warmth and sunshine, guiltily delighted with the unusual amount of freedom we were enjoying. We had been home from our schooling and postulancy at the San Zaccaria convent since early February, when Mama almost died from a debilitating stillbirth and needed us with her.

Still, as a concession to Rosa, who would be alarmed if my face sprouted a freckle, I wore a wide-brimmed sunhat similar to hers, her bleach-soaked mane pulled through the purposeful hole on its crown and spread out behind her to dry.

She lifted the hat's brim and surveyed the palazzo opposite, then the bustling canal below. "Look, there's Papa. He procured a new uniform for Teodor." She pointed to our gondola, gliding on the azurite waters.

"You know Papa likes to keep up appearances. Although I'm sure it's second-hand livery." Our father, wearing red robes as befitted a member of the Senate, sat seemingly lost in thought while our gondolier navigated the boat through the traffic, the richness of his black skin contrasting with the bright red and white stripes of his stockings and new jacket. A jaunty yellow feather topped his matching red hat, making him appear even taller.

After Teodor rowed the gondola out of view, I reached to pick up the fallen paper that held the poem I had been working on. It was sodden, having landed in a puddle, the ink now smudged and illegible. Probably for the best. I thought not for the first time that I was hardly a female incarnation of Virgil.

Rosa sat back and closed her eyes, a charmed expression on the face I knew so well. While God had clearly marked us as relations, He had seen fit to arrange our appearances quite differently. In Rosa, already embodying a ripened woman's figure at age thirteen, He had sculpted her features into perfection, with wavy golden tresses, a pert nose, clear blue eyes, lush lips, naturally blushed cheeks, and a perpetually angelic expression, so when she lay in bed at night she was as beautiful and serene as St. Ursula. Her demeanour matched her sweet, petite visage, for she was as good and wholesome as the peaches we looked forward to indulging in by the Feast of the Assumption of the Blessed Virgin Mary.

In me, older by three and a half years, He had chiselled a plainer arrangement, a longer nose, greyish-blue eyes, thin lips, and a small birth-mark on my forehead that had the fashion been different I could have hidden with my hairstyle. In truth, I did need to pay more attention to my appearance than Rosa. I needed any assistance God could grant me. The good Lord had also given me brains as clever as any man's and a body that strove to match our brother Paolo in height, allowing me if I wished to forgo the raised heels preferred by the female patriciate as well as by the courtesans who consorted with patricians.

I settled back into my chaise. From below shot up more obscenities from the boatmen, the slap of water against stone, the shrieks of seagulls. In my mind's eye was the rough sketch his lordship Luca Cicogna had made for me just a few days before, inspired by Barbari's woodcut, the whole of

Venice unfurled on paper. Luca was no artist, but he wanted me to be able to perceive the unique vantage. Smiling, I imagined myself a bird, looking down on our city, the Grand Canal like a snake slithering through stone, the city on either side like two hands clasped in prayer.

My imaginings drifted from the woodcut to the nearby church, perfumed with copious flowers and ornately decorated with paintings, perhaps new ones by Giorgione, hundreds kneeling in the pews, looking on approvingly as a veil was lifted from my face and I turned to my new husband, Luca Cicogna . . .

I dared a private smile.

"If only Lord Cicogna could see you now!"

I was startled out of my reverie by the arrival of our older brother, Paolo, Dolce excitedly yapping at his feet.

Paolo stepped onto the terrace with a bowl of dried cherries and a yawn, still wearing his bedclothes, his chemise open to his navel. Even I as his sister could appreciate how fine a manly specimen he was. He knew it too, and took advantage of his opportunities every chance he had, a veritable Mars conquering the battlefield of Venetian bedchambers. "Justina, your suitor is coming over shortly for a meeting of our new society. We're calling ourselves the Inamorati. What do you think?"

"I think it's sweet." Rosa, the sweet one, would of course say that about a fraternity of virile young men calling themselves the Sweethearts. She always thought the best of everyone, naturally assuming their goodness.

"Oh, the irony." I snorted. "None of you wants to be anyone's sweetheart, just bed the first willing girl to flutter her eyes at you."

"How can you say that about your Luca?" Paolo popped two cherries in his mouth, then spat one over the stone wall and nearly hit an unsuspecting boatman ferrying a load of dead animals. We all wrinkled our noses at the stench, far worse than Rosa's dye.

I tried to whisk the stink away from my nose with my lavender-scented lace handkerchief. "While I would like to think *my* Luca has eyes only for me, I daresay he is like most other men in his appetites. But so long as I alone have his heart, his mind, and his legitimate children, I can be at peace."

"The first two you do, my dear sister, that is perfectly clear, and the third hopefully soon to come. Even so, he seems the sort to be faithful to you." Paolo was uncharacteristically serious for a moment, then shrugged. "Anyway, Luca and I and a few others are organizing this new Inamorati fraternity, and our first order of business is to plan our inaugural festa. I'm so glad you two are still home from the convent, since Papa has given me permission to hold it here and soon. That means, my dear sisters, that Rosa's bleaching exercise is not in vain."

Rosa screeched with childish delight. Across the canal, the Pizzamano sisters were also taking advantage of the day for a similar bleaching project, and at Rosa's outburst, they looked over with interest. Even from such a distance their widened eyes clearly noted Paolo in his intimate apparel and open shirt.

Paolo did not seem to notice as he settled himself on the foot of my chaise. "Moreover, Mama indicated I could work with the lovely and charming Madelena on the menu. My God, that accent of hers! And those eyes! It's all I can do to control myself. I don't know how I'll ever plan a menu with her. Anyway, my aim is to outdo the recent festa given by the Sbragazai. Baggy pants, my backside, they looked like buffoons in those costumes. Acted like them too."

"Well, do control yourself." I took a handful of dried cherries, mindful of my pristine dress. "You know she's the best slave we've had in years, and Mama would be furious if she had to leave because of your lack of discipline."

"Have you seen Mama this morning?" Rosa used a handkerchief to wipe away some bleach that had started dribbling down her temple.

Paolo frowned. "I thought she was out visiting already. Is she all right?"

I shook my head. "Madelena went in to help her dress but found her still in bed, saying her head aches quite badly and she did not want to break her fast."

Paolo stood up with alarm. "We should check on her then."

I put a hand on his arm. "Madelena said she expressly forbade any of us from going to her. It apparently is not related to her health. She just wants to rest. She plans to come down for the evening meal."

Rosa sighed. "Mama is so stubborn."

Paolo sat down again. "Justina and I are stubborn too, so just say the word and I'll fetch the doctor or midwife."

A demure clearing of the throat, and we three looked up to see Madelena standing in the terrace doorway, her dark hair smoothed under her white caul, an uncertain expression on her face. Dolce barked again, and Rosa scooped him up and stroked his ears.

"Lord Luca Cicogna has arrived for Lord Paolo." An Ottoman accent tinged Madelena's mellifluous voice.

Paolo broke into a wide grin. "My dear Madelena, send him right up here."

I gave Paolo a thwack on the thigh. "Don't you dare do such a thing!"

"You look wonderful, Sister." He doffed my hat and threw it aside, while Rosa bolted upright in bewilderment.

"But *I* don't!" Acrid bleach still coated her hair, and she was wearing an old, too-small dress.

Paolo wrinkled his nose as he munched on another cherry. "True, and you've just unfortunately reminded me that one of the ingredients in that disgusting concoction is Dolce's piss."

I giggled as Rosa rushed inside, shrieking, past Madelena, who looked from me to Paolo with a tremulous query.

"Send Lord Cicogna up, then attend to Rosa," he said. Madelena gave a small curtsy before disappearing inside, Dolce at her heels. "Do not fret, Sister." Paolo patted my knee. "This is the perfect excuse for your paths to cross. We can blame me and say that Madelena did not realize."

"My hair is all wrong." I fretfully combed my fingers through the tresses that flowed to my waist. "It is not proper to be down." At least I was wearing a clean, well-fitting, if third-hand, dress.

Paolo scrutinized me, then spoke with sincerity. "You look lovely, Justina. Your hair is truly your best feature, your crown like a true crown. Luca will thank me for allowing him to see you thus. And I will be your chaperone the entire time."

I took a deep breath. "I hope you are right." The clouds had grown thicker, and the breeze smelled like rain. The sky above the northernmost *sestiere* of the city was smudged with black, and distant thunder growled.

"Of course I'm right. The only reason Luca indulges our new fraternity is so that he has a legitimate reason to come here and talk to you. He's much too serious and studious otherwise."

I picked up the Seneca from the ground, tucked my ruined poem inside, and settled it back on my lap, my fingers drumming the closed cover. "Paolo, do you honestly think our fathers will ever allow us to marry? For love, and at such a tender age for him?"

"I do not know, Justina. But I do know this. Luca's heart is true, and he is a legitimate nobleman from a good and wealthy family, albeit a newer one, only one hundred years in the patriciate. But that is certainly hope to cling to. Our own father was not immune to such a match. You are well aware the reason he married Mama was for her newer family's fortune and connections."

"Fortune is not something we can offer, only a very long pedigree."

"True, and our current dearth of ducats does seem to be giving Luca's father some pause. But Luca is very persuasive. He will convince him. And ours is only a temporary state—I am sure of it and remind him at every opportunity."

I remained doubtful. "What about Luca's youth? You know it is almost unheard of these days for a nobleman to marry at twenty-four. Too green to be on the Great Council even. So much to learn, about government, trade, law, philosophy. Although I would do everything I could to help his political and mercantile enterprises."

Paolo stroked my hand. "I know you would, more than any other wife, I venture. I will reiterate Luca's finer qualities to Papa after Luca has obtained his own father's permission. Remind him what an upstanding nobleman he is, how well he would care for a wife, his Paduan legal training, the path rising before him. Not to mention what good allies his family would make at the doge's palazzo, and excellent trading partners too. They seem to have the Midas touch, with money to burn."

A soft knock on the door, and Madelena appeared again at the terrace threshold, Lord Luca Cicogna beside her.

Chapter 2

"Luca!" Paolo strode over to greet his friend, while I rose uncertainly, grateful to Seneca, as his words in book form gave my twitchy hands something to do, and also grateful to Papa, one of the few patrician fathers who had permitted his daughter to learn to read Latin. "My sister Justina has unexpectedly joined us for a moment." He glanced at Madelena, who was giving me a wide-eyed look as my hair rippled in the strengthening breeze. "Madelena, fetch my clothes." She nodded, then scuttled away.

Giving a little bow, Luca stood before me, his brown hair in waves past his ears, his easy smile more meaningful to me than the Lord's Prayer, although I would never admit such heresy aloud. "Signorina Justina, I hope I find you in good health."

Despite the admonishments to myself, I could not extinguish my glee at his elegant presence, his gentle voice, his deep brown eyes, his utterance of my name like the plucking of a lute. I wished to launch myself into his arms but knew decorum was paramount if I ever wanted his arms around me permanently. "I am well, Lord Cicogna, although please excuse my appearance. I was not expecting you. How fare you?"

"Think nothing of it—you look lovely. And I am excellent now." He gestured to the book in my hands. "What are you reading?"

"Seneca's *On the Brevity of Life*."

"Ah yes, one of my favourites. A superb reminder to make the most of one's days and not squander time. I think your brother would benefit from a perusal." He flashed a grin at Paolo, who could not hold back a guffaw.

I smiled. "The Roman philosophers never did much interest Paolo."

"No, courtesans, Roman or otherwise, interest him much more."

Paolo looked comically indignant, then laughed again. "I cannot deny it. Ottoman maids too."

I shook my head as Luca turned serious. "It is, however, heartening to see the philosophers interest you, Signorina Justina. *O how many noble deeds of women are lost in obscurity!*"

"I'm not sure reading Seneca is a noble deed, but it certainly is done by me in obscurity."

Paolo yawned. "This conversation is beyond me. Never did like Latin. If you'll excuse me, I should get dressed before our fraternity meeting."

I felt stricken. "Must you, right now?" It was improper for Luca to be alone with me, and in full view of the Grand Canal.

As if to save my honour, fat raindrops began punctuating the terrace floor, and the three of us hurried inside to the *piano nobile*. I set the Seneca on a nearby side table, brushing the droplets off the cover.

"Better now." Paolo raked his fingers through his dampened hair. "I think I hear Madelena already with my clothes." And he left Luca and me staring at each other. I knew Paolo was doing his brotherly duty and standing just outside the door as both guard and alarm, yet far enough away to give us a moment of intimacy.

Luca smiled and dared to step closer. "Paolo is a remarkably loyal brother to you and friend to me, is he not?"

I nodded and looked up at him, my resolve to remain decorous dissolving quickly. Taller than most Venetian noblemen, he was one of the few men I had to look up at, given my Amazonian stature. Although somehow I knew he would not mind even if we were the same height.

"And *you* are remarkable, Justina." He took my hand and kissed it gently. "Tomorrow morning, my father has at last agreed to speak with your father before the first meeting at the doge's palazzo, to broker our marriage terms."

"It is to be, then!"

"Shhh. We don't want anyone to discover us." He took my other hand and held them both tight against his chest, and while I trembled at his closeness, his heart beating fast beneath my fists, I also felt at peace. "My father knows your father must reach a decision very soon, given your seventeenth birthday is in early summer. Time must not be wasted."

"Seneca could have told you that."

"Your wisdom is your most attractive quality." He studied my face. "And you do not blush at the compliment."

"*I wish to go beyond the fire that burns me.*"

"Petrarch. You will be better than Laura for me. For Petrarch loved her only from afar." He leaned in closer.

"And we can marry." Our lips were but inches apart.

"Will you let me finally read your writings once we are wed?"

The thought of showing Luca my poems and essays scared me as much as the wedding night, but still I nodded. He would be my husband. I would trust him and keep nothing from him.

"I cannot wait." He threaded his fingers through my tresses, and I involuntarily shivered.

Outside the room Madelena gave a soft exclamation as Paolo cleared his throat, and Luca and I hastily drew back from each other. It was best if no one saw me alone with him, for honour, my own and our families.'

Still, Luca dared a quick peck upon my cheek, sending a spark through me. "One night's sleep until we begin our lives together," he whispered before stepping back, leaving me aflame.

Paolo traipsed in, buttoning his doublet. He clapped Luca on the back and gave me a friendly punch. "To the library, Luca, to wait for the others and formulate our festa." He swung his arm around Luca's shoulders, then said under his breath, "And to cool you off. You're lucky I don't toss you in the canal."

Luca gave me an embarrassed smile, and the pair of them departed the room to make their plans.

Outside, rain pummelled Venice in great sheets, smacking the terrace stones and pockmarking the water in the Grand Canal. I stood frozen with joy, hardly able to comprehend what Luca had just told me, listening to the rain for I don't know how long until Rosa rushed in.

"Sister! What happened?" Her hair, the slightest shade blonder, was rinsed of bleach and tumbling damply down her back, and she was now dressed in a proper gown.

"Luca said his father will speak to Papa tomorrow."

Rosa squealed. "That is too perfect! Oh, I hope Papa will allow me to stay to help prepare for the wedding, and not just let me leave the convent for the ceremony."

"Thank you for being happy for me." For we both knew one of us was to marry and the other to take the veil, the only viable paths for all women of our class.

"Of course I am. You are my dearest sister. Although I'm already a postulant, I wish I didn't have to return to San Zaccaria. I don't even have to marry, so Papa wouldn't have to raise a second dowry. Just live at home and take care of Mama. Or with you and tend to your children with Luca. I would not even care whether I had the opportunity to don the latest fashions and attend festas."

"We both know that living at home is not a choice. And that the nuns at San Zaccaria adore wearing the latest fashions and attending festas."

"You know me too well. I shall look forward to that." Rosa laughed as she shook her head. "Imagine, being able to marry for love!" Her gaze drifted out to the terrace. "I wonder when Papa will return."

Certain it wasn't Papa's return that mattered to her as much as that of the gondolier who conveyed him, I frowned. For while I had reason to believe I could be one of the fortunate few whose father arranged my marriage into a love match, Rosa would never have such luck with a man from a low class.

The Most Serene Republic of Venice—let alone our father—would never permit it. And the sooner she accepted that, the sooner she reconciled herself to life in a cloister, the better.

Chapter 3

O ur family all sat down for supper at the gloaming hour. Before us was our usual meal of fresh fish and vegetables of the season, in this case artichokes, followed by something sweet. We each also had a cup of white table wine. I wasn't very hungry, and I only hoped I could regulate my excitement and emotions to display my usual demeanour. Tomorrow would be the day my love marriage was arranged!

Our father had only recently returned from the doge's palazzo. A man given to commanding silences and preternaturally calm arguments, Papa was tall and slim, with high cheekbones, an aristocratic nose, and clean-shaven pale skin, his hair long, formerly auburn, now grey. He was not indulgent with his children, but he insisted we be educated and was fierce in his fealty to us. He had been married to Mama for more than twenty-two years, romantic love never in evidence but the pragmatic bond between them indubitable.

Mama sat across from him at the table, her dress peacock blue, her white neck bared to the top of her bosom, her blond, silver-streaked hair stylishly fashioned into two soft horns atop her head. Looking at her pale face, bloodshot eyes, and tight lips, I worried about her headache.

"Mama, I'm so happy you finally feel well enough to join us." I smiled to mask my concern. She nodded without meeting my eyes and took a sip of wine as Papa cleared his throat.

"I am very pleased to see our entire family dining together, that my wife is back in good health after her recent trials, and that my son Paolo has seen fit to join us this evening." Father and son both laughed. It was true that many evenings Paolo was absent at social engagements, and he always brought welcome levity to the otherwise sombre meals we had taken with our father over the past two months. "I am also pleased to see we have no guests, for I have important information to convey." He looked at each of us in turn, although my mother stared at her dish.

With my concern for Mama's health now allayed, her refusal to meet my eye made me suspect this announcement had to do with me. My stomach churned. Had Papa arranged another marriage before Luca's father had a chance to meet with him? Could it not wait one day more?

Rosa reached under the table to slip her hand into mine, but her touch only made me feel worse. I became surer that my love match was turning from gold to lead.

"I have made two decisions, one concerning each of my daughters."

Rosa's hand tightened around mine, for neither of us had anticipated a second development. Even Paolo raised a brow.

"First, my sweet, beautiful, younger daughter, Rosa. I have arranged a marriage for you."

Her eyes widened, and she drew in her breath. Paolo and I did too. No one was expecting her fate to be announced first, and we'd always assumed as the younger she'd be the one to enter the convent.

"The name of your husband is Zago Zane. He comes from one of the old houses in Venice, and his family is extremely wealthy. I know him well from our governmental proceedings, and I find him to be a very upstanding noble with a bright future ahead of him. He will care for you, give you a good home, and provide you with many luxuries. You may have already met him when he visited his sister Zanetta at San Zaccaria."

Rosa didn't say anything. I knew she couldn't: she was so shocked that she would be marrying so unexpectedly soon. I was shocked too. For one thing, she was very young, just thirteen, and knew her fiancé in no capacity whatsoever. Even though we had seen him at the convent visiting Zanetta Zane, neither of them took any notice of us. She also had an affection for our gondolier, which was an impossibility, but still, her heart would require some mending. And did this news mean our family's fortune was in a better state then we children had realized, that Papa could afford two dowries?

"What say you, Daughter?" Papa commanded, though not unkindly.

"Thank you, Papa." Rosa, ever obedient, looked down at her lap. She could not meet his eyes, perhaps because her own were filling with relief at not having to spend the rest of her life in a convent, mixed with fear of marriage. But she could not say anything to object. Her duty, our duty, as noble Venetian daughters, was to fulfill our father's plans and society's expectations.

"Congratulations, Rosa," I said in what I hoped was a comforting tone. "You are lucky to have him." I squeezed her hand, hoping she could deduce my underlying message: *And he is lucky to have you.*

Mama took another gulp of wine as Papa raised his goblet. "To your health, my dear Rosa. May you bear many sons and unite two fine patrician houses." Rosa's eyes widened again as she gulped down some wine.

"What about Justina, Papa?" Paolo was never shy, and I knew he had our mutual friend on his mind. "Perhaps it is hasty to plan two marriages at once. How will Mama manage such large events simultaneously?"

Papa smiled as he turned to me, and I felt my heart lurch. "For my wise, studious, older daughter, Justina, I have made a different sort of match, one I believe will allow her ample time to read and write, two pursuits I know she holds quite dear." He elevated his goblet again. "Justina is to take her vows at San Zaccaria."

Rosa gasped. Paolo looked stunned. My mother swallowed the rest of her wine and wiped her cheeks with her handkerchief. I realized then that she had known of my father's decisions. Her headache had had nothing to do with any womanly troubles.

I could not say a word. I could not comprehend what I was hearing.

My father had indeed pledged me to marry, just not Luca, nor any mortal man. I was to be a bride of Christ, cloistered in a convent until my soul departed this world.

My heart broke at this double loss. Of Luca and of marital life.

"Papa, is there no other choice but to place Justina in a nunnery?" Only Paolo dared question our father, as the only other male in the room, the only one with any measure of authority. Even so, we all knew it was impudent and risked reprisal.

Papa did not look pleased. "Paolo, you of anyone know best the financial straits our house is in, and you also are aware of how inflated dowries have become for our class. Two thousand ducats at least, not to mention a further thousand for a *corredo* that you well understand your future brother-in-law keeps for himself, never to return it to our family. And what about your future? If both your sisters marry with the requisite dowries, you may be left with nothing by the time you marry in a decade or so. A judicious match has set many a young man on the path to prosperity. You have a promising career ahead of you, and I need to budget for it. Besides, as my only son, you need to produce heirs." He cleared his throat. "*Legitimate* heirs."

"But Papa, as the eldest daughter, Justina always thought she'd be the one to marry. And maybe something else can be arranged for Rosa."

"I admire your brotherly devotion, but you realize as well as I that noble marriages are a strategic affair. I had both girls become postulants to hedge our bets. If Justina married down into the citizen class, she would lose her noble status, and that is impossible to contemplate for any of my heirs, given we are one of the oldest houses in Venice. Thus I want to make the best noble alliance possible, and marrying into the Zane family is precisely that. I suppose Justina could fulfill that role, but your mother agrees with me that Rosa is capable of making a far superior marital match."

Rosa cried out as I nearly retched at this impolitic statement, but I held my peace outwardly, saying nothing as Mama continued to avoid my gaze.

Papa wiped his lips with a cloth. "I have thought quite long and hard about what should happen to you three, whom God has trusted me to provide for and see to adulthood. After much consultation with my sister's husband as well as even your mother, I have decided that this is the best course of action. You each will have a life suited to you and in which I believe you will find contentment, and I will be able to care for you in the best way possible, secure upon my deathbed that I have fulfilled my duties to God, our republic, your mother, and you. Now, please excuse me."

He pushed his chair back and exited the room, leaving the rest of us in a bewildered state.

"You knew, Mama?" Paolo's voice was terse.

She nodded, tears flowing more freely now. "I'm truly sorry, Justina. But after much reflection, I felt this would be best for all my children. None of us want you sequestered in a convent, and we will miss you desperately. But we will visit every chance we have. And I thought you might find a measure of happiness there, able to study your precious books and write poetry and essays, although I suppose the subject matter will now need to be of a religious nature. You care for those pastimes far more than Rosa, and they are feasible in a convent. And Rosa is so agreeable and deferential. I know she'll make the better wife. You would chafe under the marital yoke. Trust me. We are more alike than you realize." With that, she too rose and left the room.

Paolo dashed to my side. "Justina, I had no idea that Papa was this close to making a decision. I knew he was thinking about it, which is why I kept stressing to Luca the necessity for haste. But his own father would not be rushed."

"Luca just told me that his father would negotiate the match tomorrow morning."

He hung his head. "I know. He told me too. I'm very sorry. I know how much you care for each other. To have made a love match . . ."

"Luca—you must forewarn him now! Tell him his father mustn't humiliate himself or his family."

"Yes, you're right. I'll do that straightaway." He kissed my hand before running out, and I envied him his freedom. Freedom to marry, freedom to walk the streets of Venice by himself, freedom to say what needed to be said.

I slumped in my chair, weary and bereft, my heart broken and my mind whirring. Madelena hovered in the doorway, ready to clear the dishes but clearly hesitant to intrude.

"Justina?"

I had nearly forgotten Rosa was in the room. My dear little sister, whom I'd played with since we were babies, comforted while being educated at the convent, read with every afternoon, slept with every night. Since her birth, I had never spent a day apart from her. I knew she was in as much pain as I was. For me not being able to marry Luca. For fear of marrying a man she'd never met, of what would occur in the marital bed, of having to bear children and perhaps dying while doing so. For our sisterly separation. I needed to save my own heartbreak for the shadows of night.

"I'll visit you every chance I have." She buried her head in her hands.

I caressed her blond-bleached hair as she wept, seeking to bring her comfort even though my own heart was anguished. "Shush now. Everything will be all right, for both of us. I promise."

It was a promise I knew I would not be able to keep. That was up to Zago Zane and my new sisters at San Zaccaria. Rosa and I would have very little to do with it.

Chapter 4

And so that day, which had dawned with such promise in the sun's rays, died with despair in the dark. Rosa and I lay in our bed holding hands, neither of us able to sleep, although Dolce did between us. Our lancet-arched windows were open to let in any hopeful breeze rippling off the side canal now that the rain and clouds had been replaced with more stifling air and a touch of hazy moonlight. The canopy above us sometimes fluttered, as did the fronds of the palms in their urns under the windows. It was very quiet outside, just a few stragglers scraping through the streets or paddling along the canals, trying to make it home before the curfew bell rang and the fires were extinguished. Curfew was never a determining factor for Paolo, who had still not returned from his errand. I would have heard him rattling around the darkened palazzo, cursing every time he stubbed his toe. I half wished him to return instantly to tell me everything and half wished he would never come home, for I dreaded hearing of Luca's reaction.

Luca. I had fallen in love with him. Outside the convent walls, I had the freedom to love him, perhaps even marry him. Inside, I had to love only Jesus Christ, my Saviour. Of course I loved Him too, but to the exclusion of all others? In the deepest part of my heart, I could not say yes, even though I dared not express these heretical thoughts aloud. Could I risk committing them to parchment? The very idea seemed sacrilegious.

But it would be lying to say I loved the Lord as my husband, and such equivocation was a sin. I loved Luca. I wanted to perform all wifely duties for him only. And I knew, given my ordinary appearance and unique female cleverness, that Luca was the rare sort to love me back, to allow me—nay, encourage me—to continue reading and writing, to respect me—dare I say it?—as something close to an equal. That was likewise a heretical thought.

My heart splintered as I tried to calm my racing pulse with deep breaths. Never to be with Luca . . . It was too much to bear. But bear it I must, along with my new life, which stretched endlessly before me like the lagoon to the horizon.

Could I live the rest of my days cloistered in a convent? San Zaccaria was the one I knew best, having been educated there. Livia Nani, my mother's sister, a lively, wise woman who thought of Rosa and me as daughters, would welcome me and encourage my studies as best she could within the structure of the religious day, a day I knew well from all the years I'd already spent in it. I adored her. I knew too Zanetta Zane, Zago's sister, though not well. I had been far beneath her notice as a sheltered boarding girl and postulant, but now I would be her peer. Given the way she always sneered at Auntie Livia and her dear friend Elisabetta, I had no affinity for Zanetta, and I knew Livia would do her best to protect me from her.

But would such protection be enough? As a young noblewoman, I certainly had no freedom to walk the streets of Venice, but I did have some freedom within my own home. Freedom from constant prayer and the timetable of the convent. Some freedom to read whatever I wished, and to write too, I had to grant that to my father. Freedom to be with not only my mother and sister and aunts, but also my brother and uncle and cousins, and I suspected my life was richer for the men in it. Family visited, and we could even glimpse Papa's and Paolo's friends and associates, which is how I had come to know Luca in the first place, after we returned from San Zaccaria on Candlemas to nurse Mama back to health.

Luca. As my thoughts returned to him, my heart shattered a little more.

I sighed and turned on my side to face Rosa. She was wide awake, staring at the ceiling, looking so very young.

"Do you think I'll make a good wife?" Her voice was toneless and small.

Whatever I was feeling, as her elder sister I needed to strengthen her mind, to ease her into her new life with her head high. "I think you'll make a wonderful wife. You are beautiful and dutiful and trained well by Mama and the nuns. Lord Zane will adore you from the moment he lays eyes on you."

"I'm scared."

"What of exactly?"

"Of what I'll . . . have to do with him. Of giving birth. Look what happened to Mama and our newest sister. Mama almost died, and our sister went to God before she drew her first breath. What if I die? What if the baby dies?"

I would have been thinking these same questions if Papa had arranged any husband for me but Luca. I could not be afraid with him. But I would be with Lord Zane. And he might have been my husband, had my father not designated the convent my new home. Rosa's fears were well founded from what we saw around us. Marriage—for the wife—was a game of chance. Would he be gentle and kind, or harsh and boorish? Would he make Rosa's life sweet or sour?

"You won't die. The baby won't either." I spoke with conviction although I didn't truly know what would occur. I just knew I had to reassure Rosa.

"How can you be sure? Mama lost five babies so far. I know you remember them all. And this last was the worst for Mama. It's only due to God's intervention she survived that one."

"And the midwife's. We were lucky she's so knowledgeable."

"But Signora Benedetta said she's getting too old to be a midwife now, so I will probably die!"

I moved Dolce to my other side and gathered Rosa in my arms, her body trembling against mine. "We'll find someone new then, someone just as good as that old wise woman, someone even better."

"Do you promise?"

"Of course I promise. I would do anything for you."

"I would do anything for you too, Justina. But what if Lord Zane is cruel to me? We both know his sister Zanetta is not the kindest to Auntie Livia. What if that nature runs in their family?"

"True, but we have not really met the man, just crossed paths with him a few times in the convent parlour. So we should give him the benefit of the doubt. Papa would not have chosen him without proper appraisal, and Papa wants what is best for us. Lord Zane must be cunning and good at governance and wants a beautiful wife able to host important visitors and diplomats. He will rise high, may even be the doge someday.

And you would be the dogaressa. And when that happens, we'll both be very old and wrinkly and you'll come visit me at San Zaccaria, just like you always have. And I will say many prayers for you as both my sister and the dogaressa."

"And you will be abbess?" Rosa smiled, then sniffled. "I can't imagine sleeping without you every night."

"You will sleep next to Lord Zane, and he will be warm and will protect you."

"What if he snores?"

I laughed softly. "Then we will find a wise woman to brew him a tea to help him stop."

"You never snore." She smiled again as she become sleepier, her eyes flickering shut. I caressed her eyebrows and stroked her nose and sang a song from our childhood to help her along, one a former slave from the east had sung us.

I, however, stayed awake, alternately looking at my slumbering sister in her innocence, gazing at Dolce, and staring out the window at the moon through the clouds.

I am not going to marry Luca. I am going to be a nun. I am leaving my home forever. Farewell to all . . .

So absorbed in my own thoughts, numb from shock, I did not hear Paolo's quiet knock at first.

"Justina? You still awake?"

I padded over to let him in. He gathered my hands into his own.

"How did he take it?" I tried to keep my voice flat.

He shook his head. "Not well. He is, fair to say, distraught."

All I could do was nod.

"Oh, Justina, I am very sorry. I wish I could do something for you."

"Thank you for saving his family from humiliation. That is something."

"It is nothing."

"At this point, it is everything."

He hugged me tightly. "I will visit you all the time at San Zaccaria."

"And take the opportunity to flirt with my new sisters." I made a show of smiling, but he did not return it.

"You only have one sister." He pointed his chin in the direction of our sleeping sibling.

"That is not how Venice thinks, as you well know." I shook my head, knowing I must not let myself think his way either. "Go to bed now, Paolo. Thank you again."

Kissing my forehead, he finally let me go, retreating to his room as I closed the door. Rosa slept on, one hand on her heart.

I returned to bed as noiselessly as I could, then turned my back to her and let the tears flow.

Chapter 5

The next few days swirled by in a rush of preparations and shopping. Paolo's festa, its planning sessions now held at the other members' palazzi instead of ours for my sake, would serve as the engagement party for Rosa and Lord Zane as well as the couple's first meeting. This was an unusual season to marry, since most weddings occurred during Carnival, but our father had finally been repaid on a small loan and, at his sister Leonarda's urging, did not want to waste this dowry opportunity. More critically, one of Venice's ambassadors in Rome had hinted in his latest dispatch to the Great Council that His Holiness Pope Julius II was strongly considering excommunicating all of Venice, which might prevent Rosa and me from taking our respective holy vows. Both our ceremonies were therefore arranged to be held as soon as possible, just ten days away, Rosa's on the day before the Feast of San Marco and mine on the day after.

When the morning of the festa arrived, Paolo was up unusually early and frenzied. The main event would be a secret mummery for which he had written a script with Luca. This might have been the first occasion in his life he'd ever taken seriously. Rosa was nervous and barely ate breakfast. Papa was busy putting together the final pieces of the two-thousand-ducat dowry. The dowry would return to our family upon the death of either spouse, the exact details to be specified more clearly when Rosa wrote her will, which, according to Venetian custom, noble wives did with their first pregnancy. At the same time, Mama fretted over the final items our family would contribute to the *corredo*, the portion of the wealth and property that would become Lord Zane's solely. Much of the *corredo* of course included actual coinage for Lord Zane to do with as he wished. The rest was mainly clothing and jewellery Mama had purchased for Rosa, which Lord Zane would keep and could resell. Papa had instructed Mama to spend wisely but freely up to three hundred ducats of the *corredo* amount agreed upon, so that Rosa would be adorned and beautified as befitted her noble status. Since Venice had a vibrant market of barely worn frocks on offer, many of her dresses had been purchased second-hand, due to both haste and economy.

Late morning, I awaited my mother's and sister's return from the seamstress, where they had gone for final alterations on Rosa's engagement gown. I paced up and down the sun-splashed *piano nobile*, peering out the tall windows to see the moment Teodor moored our gondola at the water entrance.

"Coming round." I heard Teodor's sonorous voice through the open windows and hurried down to the ground floor so I could greet the retinue. The gondola glided along the stone steps, and Teodor hopped out to stop and secure the boat. He then helped my mother onto the landing, and she swept inside without a backward glance, holding some packages. Madelena jumped out by herself, and Teodor loaded her arms with even more before she too headed inside. She, however, did glance behind her, and her concerned eyes momentarily met mine.

I turned to the source of our mutual worry. Rosa was busy removing the veil from her face, draping the fabric artfully around her head and neck. Teodor tried to avert his eyes but could not resist looking at her. He then held his hand out, and she took it, never taking her eyes from his as he assisted her out of the gondola. She wobbled, he touched her at the waist to steady her, and a veritable conflagration passed between them. It was unmistakable. He held her hand for a moment too long before releasing her. She finally cast her eyes toward me, and I hurried her inside the storage room as Teodor watched her go, his dark brown eyes filled with longing. He took a handkerchief from a pocket, removed his hat, and wiped his brow before returning the hat and adjusting its yellow feather.

"Rosa, what are you doing? Right on the Grand Canal, in full view of the world?"

"What do you mean?" All innocence, but her cheeks were pink.

"You know exactly what I mean. You are a noblewoman engaged to a nobleman, and Teodor is our gondolier. Not to mention you removed your veil before coming inside. You play with fire."

She looked downward. "I cannot help it. I admire him. I've admired him ever since we returned home at Candlemas."

"Shhh." I glanced up the stairs to ensure no one lurked within hearing distance. "I have suspected your feelings for him run deep, but you know it can never be. Our class can never, ever mix with servants."

Her eyes welled with tears. "I know. But the pull I feel toward him . . . And I know he feels the same way. He says nothing, but the way he looks at me . . . I admire him so. I could lose myself in his eyes. His features so finely arranged, the sound of his voice . . . Help me, Justina. I don't know what to do."

I hugged her. "You must put him out of your mind. You are to marry a nobleman, and you must be pure and virtuous and produce a legitimate heir. You are meeting your husband this very evening."

She sniffled. "I know. I feel as if I'm marching to a pyre."

"You must be strong. For Papa, for our family, for our state. It is our duty as noblewomen of Venice." I said this as much to convince myself as her.

She nodded and wiped her cheeks, which still retained a vestige of her childhood. "What will I do without you?"

"You will still have me, just not every day. Remember what the philosophers say: *Every new beginning comes from some other beginning's end.* You must find a way to conclude your feelings for Teodor and do your duty to your husband. You are a woman now." But my words rang hollow. Even in urbane Venice, a thirteen-year-old girl was basically a child.

"Rosa, Justina, come now. Time is running low to prepare," our mother called down the stairs, sounding irritated.

Rosa took a deep breath and looked at me.

"Coming, Mama," I called, taking my sister by the hand and leading her up the steps, neither of us saying another word about our gondolier. But we were both lost in thought, me trying to quell the images of Luca that kept creeping in unbidden and Rosa looking distressed, fearful of the impending meeting with her new husband.

Mama, Madelena, and I spent the afternoon dressing Rosa in a sky-blue silk gown woven with golden thread. Second-hand and a frugal price it may have been, but it was in impeccable condition, worn only once or twice, mended, laundered, and altered to fit Rosa exactly. Her blond hair styled to perfection, her cheeks rouged and lips slightly reddened, she wore pearls borrowed from Auntie Leonarda around her neck, and a gold chain of Mama's circled her waist and fell to her knees. She refused to eat even though Madelena brought in the cook's best offerings, but she did deign to drink some wine.

When Mama deemed Rosa sufficient, both Mama and I went to dress, Madelena bustling after our mother since, through cold calculation, her beauty mattered more than mine. "And don't pick up that dog!" Mama instructed on the way out. "You mustn't allow a speck of fur or spit on that gown."

"Yes, Mama." Rosa shrugged at Dolce, who whined at her feet.

There had been no shopping excursions for me. Papa saw no point in buying anything new for the convent, even if the nuns of San Zaccaria were known to keep up with fashion. My practical mind could only agree, although it was disappointing. So I donned one of my own better frocks, a third-hand rose-coloured damask Mama had bought me for Easter that the seamstress had lengthened through some clever needlework. I wondered if even then Mama had known the plan to return me to the convent. I sighed as I attempted to style my own hair, knowing that was the simple truth—she had known—as per Occam's law of briefness. Still, this dress flattered me. I tried not to think about Luca attending the festa tonight. I did not know how I'd react when I saw him, and I dreaded it.

Rosa helped me with the finishing touches, turning my hairstyle from poor to pleasing with a few expert brushings and putting on some putty to diminish my forehead's beauty mark. We looked at our side-by-side reflections in the small Murano mirror that graced one wall.

"You are beautiful, Rosa."

"As are you, Justina."

"Just do what Mama told you."

"I know. Bow my head. Don't meet his eyes. Don't smile."

"And the dancing maestro will guide you too. He says you have progressed nicely in just the few days you've met with him."

"I hope I can dance as nicely with Lord Zane as I do with the maestro."

"You are a beautiful dancer. Much better than I could ever hope to be. All I do is trip over my own feet."

Rosa gave me a hopeless smile, and I caressed her cheek, brushing away a tear.

"Luca will be here tonight, Rosa. I might need you to assist me."

"I will do whatever I can, my dear Justina." She stretched out her hand to hold mine, and a few tears escaped my own eyes.

A knock on the door, and Madelena cracked it open as I brushed my tears away with my fingertips. "Ready?"

"Is Lord Zane here?" Rosa asked.

"He is, Signorina."

Rosa turned to me, stricken. I took her hand firmly and led her out the door, through the hall, down the stairs, to the library.

To her husband.

Chapter 6

Rosa stood at the threshold, paralyzed at the sight of Lord Zane. He was thin and not particularly tall, with very blond, almost-white hair, pale skin, and a posture as straight-backed as a church pew. His green eyes were not kind, yet neither were they mean. Just very serious. His whole expression was unreadable, and I felt I was trying to translate Ancient Greek, never my best subject.

"Rosa, my dear, come!" Papa beckoned her over, and I nudged her forward until she stood beside him and Mama. Paolo came over to my side and put his hand briefly on the small of my back. "Rosa, this is Lord Zago Zane. Lord Zane, my youngest daughter, Signorina Rosa Soranzo."

Rosa lowered her head and gave a small though perfectly executed curtsy.

Lord Zane bowed deeply in response. "Signorina Rosa, I am pleased to meet you." His voice was deep but conveyed no emotion. We had to take his word that he was indeed pleased to meet her. The men and women around

him smiled, and I surmised they were his family, confirmed when he introduced his parents, two married sisters, and their husbands. Zanetta was
there too, dressed much like her secular sisters for her excursion outside
the convent walls. She looked over at us imperiously, her green eyes and
white-blond hair very much like her brother's, and I immediately tried to
extinguish the flare of dislike that rippled through me.

Rosa curtsied again.

Zago's mother, her face lined and blond hair seasoned with grey, held
a small wooden box, ornately decorated and carved with the words *Nessta
fa bella donna*. She handed it to her son, who presented it, more to Papa
than to Rosa.

Papa smiled. "Integrity indeed makes a beautiful woman. Petrarch said
it well. What do you say, Rosa?"

"Thank you, Lord Zane." She was barely audible. She took the box and
stared at it as if unsure of what it was or what she should do with it, even
though Mama had repeatedly briefed her on all aspects of the proceedings.

"A gift. For your personal effects," Signora Zane said, not unkindly.

Rosa nodded as Papa cleared his throat, his signal to Madelena to take
the box away.

A man in black robes stood next to a small table that held an array of
parchments—the notary and his documents. The man nodded slightly at
his audience, proffered a quill, and gestured toward the ornate iron inkwell
that had been my grandfather's. Papa, Lord Zane, and his father stepped
toward the table. Both Zanes wrote in meticulous penmanship while Papa
signed his name with a bit of a flourish.

I could not bear to look at Rosa, who stood almost entranced, and instead
glanced around at my familiar surroundings. Several dozen volumes, all

published by local Venetian printers, lined the library shelves. Luca had told me once about visiting the Aldine Press, its intoxicating smell of ink and whirlwind of workers and scholars, and I had vainly tried to tamp down my desire to see it, knowing I never would.

Then Papa came toward Rosa and held her by the shoulders. "Congratulations, Daughter." He took her hand and placed it in Lord Zane's. As tutored, she looked demurely at her feet while Lord Zane brushed his lips against the back of her hand. I knew that despite her apparent composure, terror consumed her as Lord Zane appraised her more closely. I could not decipher whether she passed his inspection, and I felt a trickle of distaste toward my future brother-in-law, a companion to how I felt about Zanetta, who observed the proceedings as if she had just bitten into something rancid. At least Signora Zane and the married sisters seemed more pleased.

"And now we dance!"

Rosa seemed bewildered by this instruction, glancing at Lord Zane, who wrinkled his nose when their eyes met. But he had not issued the cheery command—it was her dancing instructor, foppishly bedecked in feathers and satin, who swept over dramatically, took Rosa firmly by the hand, and led her from the library to the *piano nobile*, which had been transformed into an enormous dining room. Ten tables, each surrounded by velvet-cushioned chairs, sat upon silk carpets. Three enormous glass chandeliers hung from the ceiling, their colourful arms like a rainbow of dancers, while from their bottoms pale green imitation grapes hung heavy, jostling slightly.

At least one hundred pairs of eyes turned their attention to my sister: our relatives and important members of the government, including several senators and even the ambassador from Bologna, while against the side walls stood Paolo's friends dressed in the regalia of their Inamorati fraternity. Luca was somewhere among them—my heart beat a little faster at the thought—but I did not seek him out as I made my way through the room to my seat, focusing my attention solely on Rosa. She might glance at me at any moment for courage. I needed courage from her too, for I could not hide from Luca and was yet unsure how I'd react.

At the back of the room, opposite the tall windows, the servants had erected a large platform, and it was here the maestro led Rosa. Several musicians struck up a song, with the lute player leading a popular melody. Maestro smiled as he whispered something to her, a jape perhaps, for he was known for his gaiety. Her eyes smiled warmly for a moment as they began to dance, and everyone clapped.

She danced superbly, much more gracefully than I ever could, although she'd had just a few days to learn. At one point, I could tell she was concentrating on the sequence of steps, because her brow furrowed in the same way as when I asked for her thoughts on one of my poems. I knew she was feeling nervous. I had to admit some relief that I was not the centre of such attention.

My father's sister, Auntie Leonarda, settled beside me, and she remarked how pleased Rosa's match made the entire Soranzo clan before telling me about the birth of her latest granddaughter, whom she hoped I could meet before too long. My aunt was dressed spectacularly, all red silk and lace with plenty of gold and rubies, and her grey-streaked auburn hair was swept up in the latest style. Given her stoutness, she reminded me of a bejewelled old apple, and her intellect was on par with a piece of fruit. Of course, I could only be gracious and agreeable, saying I looked forward to meeting my newest baby cousin at the first opportunity while thinking darkly that I hoped the poor girl wouldn't follow me into the convent. The one person from a convent I would have liked to see was Auntie Livia, but alas she had sent regrets that the new abbess-elect of San Zaccaria was hosting a celebratory dinner she could not miss, not to mention she needed to aid her friend Elisabetta with an ailment. I knew Elisabetta from my time at San Zaccaria, my aunt's faithful companion since they'd both taken their vows some twenty years prior. I did wonder why Zanetta did not have the same obligation to attend the dinner in honour of the abbess-elect, about whom all I could recall was my fear of her steely demeanour.

The dance concluded to a spasm of applause, and Maestro swept Rosa over to the head table beside Lord Zane, to whom he bowed with flamboyance. Lord Zane stiffly nodded and only glanced at Rosa, whom the Maestro prompted to take her seat. She flushed as the people around her nodded indulgently, and I wished I could squeeze her hand.

The notary made his way to the little stage. "It is time now for the presentation of the dowry."

Papa nodded at Paolo, who stepped outside the *piano nobile* and returned holding what was clearly a very heavy chest, aided by Teodor, who wore a grim expression along with his new livery. They set the chest down on the terrazzo floor. Teodor went to sentinel the door, clearly wishing he were anywhere else. Torture lined his eyes as he glanced at me—beseeching me?—before staring at the floor, and I was at a loss. Rosa blushed more deeply as she noticed this exchange, and I gave her a resolute smile. Lord Zane only had eyes for the notary, who accepted a large parchment from Paolo. This was the legal documentation for some real estate my father was also bestowing to flesh out the dowry to a respectable amount.

"Is it true the dowry actually totals two thousand and the *corredo* one thousand?" Auntie Leonarda whispered to me, although it felt as if she were screaming. "It is a miracle my brother was able to arrange such an auspicious match for such a pathetic sum, and that he was even able to accumulate such an amount. I know he's always tight for ducats. He's not the most astute investor. He was lucky that loan he extended was paid back early, especially since his latest ship has not come in as expected."

I was saved from having to respond to this humiliation, for it was then that my father started his speech and my eyes met Luca's.

Chapter 7

All my determination to avoid him dissolved. I desperately wanted to speak with him, even just be near him, but knew the stupidity of my desire. Moreover, someone, like my inquisitive aunt Leonarda, might notice if I did.

He indicated with his eyes the room to the side where his compatriots had filed out to start dressing for their mummery, which was going to be an enactment of the *Iliad*. He was already dressed as Paris, wearing skins over one shoulder and around his waist and a laurel crown, looking absurd, though I did not care.

I gave a slight shake of my head, for I could never get away and keep my honour intact. His eyes darted around until he found my brother. Luca went to Paolo and whispered something, then disappeared, taking any hope I had with him.

Without noticing my stupor, Auntie Leonarda listened to Papa drone on about how Rosa's marriage would strengthen the Venetian state, until

Paolo appeared at my side. She adored Paolo, as did most mothers, perhaps because he flagrantly flirted with all the older matrons. "Auntie Leonarda, how wonderful to see you! You must excuse my sister, for I require her assistance. You see, I am to be Helen, shhh, and I need feminine aid for my dress." They both chuckled before Paolo whisked me across the room. I avoided meeting the eyes of anyone from the Zago family as we passed their table.

"I don't need any help, the costume is well planned," he whispered, "but someone else requires you."

"No! I can't. I mustn't." Still, I followed my brother with trepidation into the side room. The Inamorati players all grinned knowingly as Paolo took me to a curtain that served as their makeshift changing closet. Perhaps they were such good friends of Paolo and Luca they could overlook my conduct, or perhaps they didn't worry so much about the behaviour of a future nun.

"He must speak with you. And knowing you as I do, you must speak with him too. I will stand right outside to guard your honour. I need to change anyway. I will make a most ravishing Helen." Flashing a cocksure smile, he pushed me inside.

"Justina."

I stared up at Luca, unmoving.

And then he did something he'd never done before, could never have done before. Without any hesitation, he pulled me close, so close I could smell the sandalwood he wore, my heart beating wildly as he pulled me into a kiss. It was nothing like the hasty, restrained lip brushing we'd exchanged on prior stolen occasions. My hands were on his bare shoulders, his skin so warm, and his hands roamed my face and neck and bosom. And I let them without thinking twice, wishing they could roam even further, uncaring that God could see me, even if no one else could.

Finally, he pulled back, his breath heavy. "Justina, my heart is broken."

I panted as well. "Mine too."

Our lips met again in a rush, his laurel crown falling to the floor. Then he broke away once more, his face anguished.

"My father has arranged another marriage for me."

I nearly fell, and Luca held me up.

"So soon? I thought surely he would wait until you were the traditional age."

"It seems that once I approached him about marrying you, he had wedlock on his mind. He has made a very lucrative match. We will marry next Carnival."

I almost vomited at the thought.

"I'm so sorry, Justina. I only wish to marry you. You must know that."

I removed his hands from my body and forced my own to their sides. "She is a lucky woman. I'm sure she will make you very happy."

"She will do nothing of the sort. She is from a very wealthy family, and our fathers decided it was a fortuitous strategic alliance to further advance both our fortunes. I have met her once, and she is a silly girl. She is your age, true, but nothing like you."

"You must treat her well." I thought of Rosa, my dear silly sister, and how she felt to be marrying a stranger, a dismal one by the evidence thus far. Luca would never be like Lord Zane, I would not let him. "She will be scared."

"I will treat her fairly, but I shall never, ever love her. And she seems anything but scared."

"Regardless, you must do your duty to Venice and your family and produce an heir and care for your wife and children." I took a deep breath. "What is your bride's name?"

"Elena Paruta." He looked pained to utter the words. I knew the family name of course, a newer and very rich house, but had never met her.

I forced calmness into my voice. "Ah, the beautiful Helen to your Paris, and your home will be Troy before the fall."

"Do not jest, Justina. You are my only Helen."

"I am not beautiful."

He took my hands again, and I let him, my resolve softening at his touch. "You are Aphrodite, the most beguiling woman I have ever laid eyes on. And your intelligence surpasses that of Athena, so you are like two goddesses." He leaned down to kiss me again, more slowly this time, and my lips trembled against his.

Paolo poked his head, sporting a long blond wig, behind the curtain, and Luca and I parted slightly. I was embarrassed and worried Paolo would judge me. He contorted his painted face, as if trying to tame his tongue. "I can only give you two a moment longer. The *Iliad* will start at the ringing of the next bell." Then, with raised eyebrows, he withdrew.

Luca drew me close again. "Justina, this cannot be farewell. I must see you again."

"I will only see you once more, at Rosa's wedding. I am taking the veil two days later, and you will be married thereafter."

"I swear on my honour this will not be the last time."

"It is my honour, and Venice's, that we must worry about."

"We will find a way. I swear it." He kissed me again, with ferocity.

Paolo pulled the curtain back, and we separated with reluctance. Luca bent down to retrieve his crown and placed it upon his head. I straightened it for him, savouring every moment that I touched him, willing myself to remember how it felt, for I would have only these memories to sustain me for the rest of my days at San Zaccaria. I did not see how we would ever find a way.

"Sister, you must make your way back to your seat by yourself. I must not ruin the surprise with my costume. Luca, you're in the first scene with the three goddesses."

Luca shook Paolo's hand. "Thank you, my friend. I wish I could call you my brother. Or should I say my sister?" And he gave a small laugh at Paolo's appearance, in vibrant linen robes of the Greek fashion altered to fit his physique but unable to mask his virility.

"Me too, Brother." And he laughed as well, then turned around to give us one final moment of privacy.

Luca kissed the back of my hand, then left to await his cue.

After allowing a few tears to escape, I bit my lips to compose myself. When I emerged, Paolo inspected me. "Your honour does not appear too sullied. You must keep your eyes downcast though, so Auntie cannot see you've been crying. We'll douse all but the stage torches, so that should camouflage you well."

"Thank you, Paolo. I can always say I'm sad to be separated from Rosa."

"That too, but I know this is different. I wanted to give you this moment even though I knew Papa would kill me if he discovered I was derelict in my fraternal duty. Will you be all right?"

"I am not sure I will ever be all right. But what choice do I have?"

He hugged me, and as I felt the false hair along his back, I could not suppress a giggle. "If you were my sister instead of my brother, you would join me in the convent. You are a beautiful man, but you make the ugliest woman I have ever seen. No bridegroom would want you."

He wiped away the tears that lingered on my cheeks, then kissed me on my birthmark. "You are a strong one, Justina. Now go." The servants were extinguishing the candles on the tables, and he pushed me back in the direction of my seat among the crowd.

This time as I passed the Zago table, Zanetta was staring straight at me with her piercing green eyes, and I could only duck my head and hurry to resume my seat before the mummery began.

Chapter 8

The *Iliad* was a grand success, and Luca performed admirably as Paris, blossoming from selfish shepherd to heroic warrior, dying with much dignity and honour as Helen my brother looked on through melodramatic weeping. There was much applause, followed by more dancing and a feast of pine-nut cakes, gilded partridges, and other opulent dishes.

I found myself drifting into fantasy as Auntie Leonarda, her husband and children, and the other guests guffawed and talked through the rest of the evening. I didn't like the symbolism of Helen and Paris, which ended in tragedy. I preferred Luca to be Odysseus and I the devoted Penelope, finally recognizing her beloved husband after his return, and the passion of our reunion . . . Or I was Aphrodite, falling in love with Adonis . . . Or we were betrothed, and I was sitting in Rosa's seat and Luca in Lord Zane's, stealing secret glances at each other . . . And then our wedding night, in Luca's bedchamber, in his bed, my gown falling to the floor, Penelope in Odysseus's strong arms after twenty long years . . .

"Farewell, my dear girl." Auntie Leonarda jolted me out of my reverie. "I will come to see you take the veil of course."

"Yes, Auntie. And I look forward to meeting your new granddaughter."

"I'll bring the baby to visit you after you've entered San Zaccaria. You can bless her then."

I could only nod as she left to bid farewell to my parents. It was time to find Rosa and discuss every aspect of the evening.

Instead, I faced Zanetta. "Signorina Justina, how lovely to see you." Her words were polite but her tone disdainful. "I look forward to you joining San Zaccaria as a holy sister. Our paths did not cross much when you were a boarding girl, but I am sure we will get to know each other much better in the coming months."

"Thank you. I look forward to it too." I spoke warily, knowing Auntie Livia might have a contrary opinion.

"I trust you are in good health?"

I cocked my head quizzically. "The very best, as is my sister." I wondered if she was concerned whether Rosa would be able to breed straightaway.

"I noticed you suddenly left the room before the mummery, and I was distressed that you might have taken ill."

I did feel slightly ill at that pronouncement. Had she seen something between Luca and me? "I thank you for your concern, but I am quite well. My brother just needed some assistance with his costume."

"Ah. Excellent to hear. You looked perturbed upon your return to your table, but perhaps your brother is quite demanding when it comes to fashion." She pursed her lips into a smile.

"Oh, not at all. He just said something quite teasing to me. I'm sure you know how brothers are."

"Your brother, I suppose. Zago has been nothing but refined to me and our sisters ever since we were small."

I smiled and nodded, having no idea how to respond to this cut against Paolo.

"However, I will say your brother possesses much more theatrical skill than Zago, so there is that."

I knew I would have to live with Zanetta for the rest of my life as spiritual sisters, but I was beginning to understand Livia's distaste for the woman.

"I was surprised to see His Excellency Luca Cicogna playing a role. He always struck me as a serious young man, with no time or interest for frivolous fraternities."

I tried to stifle a gulp. "I thought Lord Cicogna did an admirable job as Paris."

"I am sure you did. I agree. He is an exceptional young man. I quite enjoyed speaking with him this evening. Much better than enduring a dreary dinner hosted by San Zaccaria's new abbess—if we can truly call her that. Last month's election was corrupt, if you ask me." She sniffed. "I must take my leave. My mother is signalling me to depart. Her gondolier will be returning me to San Zaccaria. I will be sure to send your well wishes to your aunt. Evidently she was too engrossed with pandering to our new leader to witness her niece's engagement to our family." She gave the barest minimum of a curtsy and glided off toward her clan, me staring after her with slight horror.

Only noticing Rosa mixed among the rest of the Zanes forced me from my own state of anxiety. My sister appeared stricken as she said farewell to her new family. Lord Zane kissed her hand perfunctorily, and Rosa dipped her head in deference as I hurried over.

"Sister, praise God you are here!" Rosa's voice shook as she spoke, but she retained her composure in front of the other guests who had yet to leave.

"Come, Rosa, it is time to retire." I took her firmly by the hand and escorted her out of the *piano nobile* to our bedchamber, anxious to tell her about what had transpired with Luca and Zanetta and hear about her experiences as well.

I shut the door behind us and helped Rosa disrobe. She stood as still as a stone lion, or perhaps an effigy was a more apt comparison, allowing me to move her arms but not helping or talking. She seemed almost comatose, devoid of emotion. I sat her on the bed and started untangling and brushing out her hair.

"I cannot do it." Her voice was a whisper.

I stopped mid-brush. "Cannot do what?"

"I cannot marry him."

I knew what I should say. What my parents would say, what Auntie Leonarda would say, what Paolo would say. *You are just having wedding nerves. It's normal and to be expected. Every bride has them.*

But I knew Rosa would never believe me. We were too close for that.

So I held her to me.

"Help me, Justina. Help me get away from him." The vehemence in her voice surprised me.

"I wish I could."

"You can. Let me join you at the convent."

My mind processed that idea, but I could see no way to fulfill it. "You know that Papa just signed the marital contract today. It is binding. I do not see how—"

"Then I shall kill myself!"

"Can it be that horrible to marry Lord Zane?"

"You met the man! It is that horrible. He has mean, dead eyes."

Yes, his eyes had no sparkle or liveliness, as if he were going through the motions. "I will be honest with you, Rosa. I agree that Lord Zane did not present a favourable first impression. But you barely exchanged three sentences with him. Dozens of people surrounded you. You must give him the benefit of the doubt. His character may be more melancholic or phlegmatic. Once you get to know him and he you, I can only imagine his eyes will come to life and things will be better." I had been telling myself the same thing about taking the veil. Maybe it would not be as horrible as I imagined. After all, our Auntie Livia did not seem miserable, and I had seen her every day for years at San Zaccaria. I needed to convince both Rosa and myself that our new lives would be tolerable, if not what we wanted.

"I shall kill myself." She started moaning softly, as if in physical pain.

Afraid that someone might come to the door at her noise, I grabbed her wrists, and was finally able to soothe her, her breath eventually coming in uneven guttural snatches.

"You must put such thoughts out of your head right this instant. You know taking your own life is a mortal sin and moreover will break Mama's heart." I held her tightly. "Not to mention mine. Surely the trials of the seventh circle will be worse than any trials here on Earth. Dante's *Inferno* tells us so. Let me help you. I will be your confessor. I will be a nun, and you will pray with me, and I will help you bear any suffering you may be enduring."

We lay down together on our bed, and she sniffled against my chest.

"And God in His mercy and infinite wisdom may even allow you to flourish, once past this initial period of fear and uncertainty."

She nodded into my bosom, and I breathed a small sigh of relief that I had been able to calm her. At least for now. My own worries would have to wait—only Rosa mattered at this moment.

She sat up to reach for the gift that Zago Zane had given her, the ornately carved wooden box with Petrarch's words upon them. It was quite beautiful; clearly the carver was a master craftsman. Madelena must have brought the box up for safekeeping during a lull in her duties at the festa.

"Integrity makes a beautiful woman," Rosa whispered, as she opened the box, lined with rose-coloured satin.

"You will do our family proud."

She nodded as she snapped the lid shut and then closed her eyes without another word.

I don't know how long it took her to fall asleep, but she pretended to do so until eventually she was. I stayed up for much longer, my prayers braided with the pain of losing Luca, the disbelief at having to spend the rest of my life in the convent—with Zanetta—and the worry over what Rosa might rashly do.

Chapter 9

When Rosa and I arrived in the dining room the next morning, both of us bleary-eyed, our mother greeted us with the news that France, a papal ally, had invaded Venetian territory near Bergamo. "The pope threatens Venice with not only spiritual punishment, but physical as well." She sighed. "Teodor has already taken your father to the doge's palazzo." Paolo was still sleeping, as the festivities had gone late into the night, and he was too young for formal governmental duties yet. "Do not fret though, girls, the Great Council has the situation well in hand. The city of Venice has never been invaded in our thousand-year history and never will be."

So it was just the three of us at the table, warm sunlight spilling across the wood and platters of food as my mother outlined the upcoming days before the wedding. "Given the escalating political situation and the Holy See's threats to excommunicate the city, it is excellent that your father has already accelerated all the required steps for both of your ceremonies.

Rosa's declaration of matrimonial vows will be published tomorrow, and then we will begin the rounds of visiting. First to the house of the groom, then to the palazzo of Auntie Leonarda, and then to the convent to visit Auntie Livia and let her share in the joy of your nuptials. Then the wedding will take place the day before the Feast of San Marco. Fittingly, I would say, as your marriage, between patricians, only strengthens the republic. We plan to have several barges towed along the Grand Canal to celebrate."

Rosa nodded mechanically. "Yes, Mama." I squeezed her hand while simultaneously worrying if my father could really afford such ostentatious displays.

"We still need to purchase your wedding gown fabric, of course, and pay extra for the rush of it being made in less than a week, although Justina will also be able to wear it when she takes the veil, and I believe it will then fetch a good price on the second-hand market. So there will be fittings, and more dancing lessons, although you did wonderfully last night. And we will need to pack your trousseau and belongings."

"Yes, Mama." Her face was downcast.

Mama's eyes softened. "Rosa, I know you are nervous. This is all so new for you. You are young, and your reaction is to be expected. Give yourself time, and eventually you will be content."

"Yes, Mama." She tried to smile, but it was joyless, and I squeezed her hand again.

"I have one more item of note." Mama hesitated, then cleared her throat. "Lord Zane has made an unusual request, and your father has agreed to it. It's not unheard of. I was speaking with several relatives about it, and even your aunt Leonarda was hardly scandalized."

Rosa looked stricken, and I could not help but interject. "Please just tell us, Mama, what Papa has agreed to."

Mama cleared her throat again and could not meet our eyes. "Well, your father has agreed that when we visit the Zane palazzo tomorrow evening, Rosa will stay behind."

Rosa's face lost all colour. "What do you mean?"

"I mean that you will stay behind until the next morning. You will spend the night with Lord Zane."

"No, Mama!" Rosa's face crumpled. "I'm not ready."

"Mama, how can you allow this? They will not yet be married." I could not disguise my confusion and anger. "Will it not compromise Rosa's honour and that of Venice?"

"I told you this is not unheard of. It has the blessing of those who matter. You know I have no say. It is for men to decide. All I can do is prepare Rosa for what is to come. Is it better she be surprised?" My mother sounded more sad than angry.

"Of course not. But—"

"No, Justina." Again, Mama's voice was tinged with resignation. "Rosa, although only thirteen, is a woman now, with everything that entails, and she must face her duty as such. She is far from the first noblewoman to marry according to our ancient Venetian customs, and she will certainly not be the last."

My anger did not dissipate, but I was just able to control my tongue. Tears ran down Rosa's cheeks.

"When Teodor returns from the doge's palazzo, we will have him bring us to the draper to choose your wedding gown fabric. Then we will go to the dressmaker to discuss the design." Mama spoke gently. "Justina, please join us. I know Rosa will appreciate your guidance. And your company. Let us make this a pleasurable excursion." She did not add that this would be one of our last times alone together as mother and sisters.

Mama arose, then came and laid a hand upon each of our shoulders, Rosa grabbing hers in return. "I am keenly aware that this is a time of much change for you both, and that you will soon be separated." She spoke with compassion. "I am also aware choices have been made for you that you do not agree with. That is our lot as noblewomen of Venice. I speak from experience, remember. I married your father when I was fifteen years old. Livia became a nun at San Zaccaria two years later when she was fourteen, something she did not want to do. It was," she cleared her throat yet again, "difficult. But we knew we had to do our duty, to restore honour and chastity to our city. Especially in the aftermath of what happened at the convent of San Anzolo di Contorta when we were babies." She made a quick sign of the cross. Whenever anyone mentioned this nunnery, they always crossed themselves, but neither Rosa nor I ever knew exactly why. We just knew it was something terrible. "We have made peace with our lives as we matured. If I had not married your father, I would not have you two and Paolo. And I would not trade that for anything. And Livia has told me she is grateful that her path lay in a most prestigious nunnery, one with a beautiful new church and a long, illustrious history. Over time, as you know, she has made dear friends. She values that now, as an older woman. So please trust that we are doing what is best for you and for our republic." She bent down to give us each a kiss on the tops of our heads before leaving.

"Justina, what am I going to do?" Rosa was still crying, and I wondered if her face would lose its puffiness in time for tomorrow evening.

"I suppose you should think of the children you will have." My words rang hollow even as I said them, but perhaps she would take some comfort in them. This certainly did seem the case for Mama, as we three surviving children all were quite close with her.

Madelena bustled in to clear the dishes, stopping short when she saw Rosa in such distress. "I'm sorry to disturb you."

"You do no such thing, Madelena." I gestured to the table. "Please carry on. We must prepare for our outing anyway."

She began her work but then I had a thought. "Madelena, would you stop for a moment and tell us something?" Rosa looked at me quizzically.

Madelena put down her tray. "If I am able, Signorina."

"Mama has outlined the nuptial events over the coming days. She wants Rosa to be prepared." I took a deep breath. Paolo might be more appropriate to ask, but I was not sure I dared query my brother about such a thing. Besides, we required a woman's perspective. "Rosa is to stay a night with Lord Zane. Before the wedding ceremony."

"Oh!" Madelena's expression conveyed her immediate understanding. "And you would like me to tell Rosa what to expect."

"Oh," Rosa echoed. "Yes, Madelena. I have no idea. Please tell me." I did not know either. And while I would never experience the marital act, I thought I might as well educate myself on the matter, if only to discover what I'd be missing.

Madelena looked from Rosa's face to mine and back to Rosa's. "Are you certain?"

"Quite, Madelena," I said with Rosa nodding beside me. "Please do sit down. I promise we will not tell our mother."

"All right," Madelena said, glancing at the door. "It is probably a wise idea."

With a blush, she began talking. Both Rosa and I were wide-eyed and horridly fascinated by the details, and I could not help but marvel at the carnal knowledge our maid possessed and of which we were so ignorant.

Chapter 10

We met Paolo on our way to the water entrance. He yawned a hello, although a still-reeling Rosa could barely reply in kind. He looked at her with pity, then raised an eyebrow at me. I just shook my head, as he could not imagine what we'd just learned, and he entered the dining room where Madelena had resumed cleaning up. I could hear the smile in his voice as he greeted her.

In truth, I now found being with Paolo painful, for he only reminded me of Luca. I envied the trouble-free friendship they had, their ability to see each other when the mood struck, their masculine freedom. Then I chided myself for my deadly sin, reminding myself envy was not very becoming behaviour for a future nun.

But I did not want to become a nun.

I could only groan at my predicament.

Mama was awaiting us with a wary smile as Teodor glided in. Rosa threw her veil over her head as Mama nodded approvingly, but I suspected

Rosa was less interested in modesty and more in not having Teodor see her looking so distraught and puffy-faced.

The gondola's *felze* was adorned with wine-coloured velvet curtains that shielded us females from public view. We settled ourselves inside the little compartment, and Rosa and I removed our veils. The day promised warmth, and snippets of water like diamond shards glittered through the gaps in the curtains, as did the gondoliers' decidedly less-glittering calls. Occasionally Teodor's voice, muffled through the velvet, rang out with a stern boating warning or friendly greeting to his brethren, but mostly he hummed quietly to himself a tune I did not know, his voice resonant as a choirmaster's. Smells assaulted us at every turn: canal dredge, spices, chimney smoke.

Mama tried valiantly to distract Rosa by chatting about some fashions she had seen on brides over the past winter and fabrics she thought Rosa would admire. "In addition to your wedding dress fabric, we must find something for tomorrow night. Not the dinner, we have the dress already, the one you wore for Mass on Easter Sunday, but for the later part. Something very beautiful. Something to make your husband fall in love with you. To start your marriage off on the right footing." Tears welled up for Rosa, and I handed her a perfumed handkerchief. She dabbed her eyes, inhaled the sweet scent, then intently studied the intricate Burano lace as Mama talked on and I nodded encouragingly. Rosa did adore discussing fashion, at least in ordinary times.

The fabric shop sat in Campo Santa Margherita. Teodor steered us off the Grand Canal through two smaller canals and found a spot to moor on the Rio de Santa Margherita. Rosa and I threw on our veils, and he escorted our trio out of the vessel and along a narrow cobblestone street.

As a well-dressed merchant on horseback squeezed by us, I grabbed Mama's arm, helping her balance on her low chopines. Just behind us trailed Teodor, gingerly assisting Rosa with a hand on her elbow. They exchanged a few words that I could not decipher, and I fretted about their proximity to each other.

A lattice of spring sunlight streaked through the lace veil that covered my face. The street hawkers in Campo Santa Margherita, who sold everything from fruit to used clothes, were swapping laughter with their colleagues and negotiations with their customers. Just before we entered the draper's shop, I dared to throw back my veil so I could feel the sunshine on my face and see the clouds like cherubs floating dreamily in the azure sky—but I also caught the leering eye of a fishmonger. Mama pushed me inside before grabbing Rosa. Teodor remained stationed outside, a hand raised to shade his eyes, and perhaps his expression too.

Up a flight of stairs in a room stuffed with bolts of cloth in every hue and material, Rosa obediently held up varying fabrics in shades of white as Mama discussed dress styles with Portia the draper, a skinny young woman with several blackened teeth who clearly knew the latest noble nuptial fashions. I forced myself to push aside daydreams of what I might look like getting married to Luca and concentrate instead on Rosa. The copious cloth muffled the noise from outside, giving the room a church's hush.

Finally Mama was satisfied with a perfect swath of ivory silk. This was to make Rosa's wedding dress, trimmed with San Zaccaria lace, and would thereafter be quickly altered into the frock I would wear to become a bride of Christ. I smiled brightly at Rosa, but she did not return it. She was displaying no pleasure at any part of this, and I worried she might make good on her threat of the night before.

Mama turned to Portia. "Before we go, might you have anything ready-made that would be suitable for a young bride's wedding night? Something that will make her feel as beautiful as she is?" Mama laid a hand on Rosa's shoulder as she spoke, Rosa shrinking slightly from her touch.

"Indeed I do, Your Ladyship." Portia nodded, assessing Rosa. "Let me have my assistant Agnese wrap your fabric while I show you." A girl of about nine, the kind who if she weren't working would be scurrying in the gutter like a canal rat, hurried forth to do her mistress's bidding while Portia led us to an adjacent windowless room. On a wooden rack hung dozens of gauzy nightgowns.

Mama glanced at me, perhaps remembering my impending vow of chastity. "Rosa, you stay here with Portia to find something. Justina, this is not a sight for you." She led me back to the main room where Agnese was packaging our purchase.

Footsteps came up the stairs, and in burst a very elegantly dressed woman with the confidence and smooth stride of a lioness. Her hair was bleached very blond, and she wore liberal amounts of face paint and olean-der perfume. She looked ready to attend a wedding, with gold and jewels decorating her bare décolletage, her areolae just peeking out, and a lace collar spread like a fan behind her neck.

She seemed almost gleeful to spy Mama and me. "Well, hello there, most serene noblewomen of Venice. And how are you on this fine spring day?" The woman's voice was like a hymn, although I suspected ecclesiasti-cal sounds did not frequently emanate from her mouth.

Mama paled, clearly shocked at this woman's breach of manners in so brazenly addressing patrician women, and stood a little in front of me, as if to shield me. But she could not cover my eyes or my interest: I was meeting a real-life courtesan. Of course I had seen them at church, but that was from afar and through a veil and with my upstanding father at my side. Here was one right before me, all pleasing smells and pleasant sights, with everyone's attention attuned to the presence of such a magnificent creature.

"Enchanting to meet you both. My name is Veronica da Spin, although most people, including the many noble senators and husbands who frequent my establishment, call me La Diamante. And Agnese, darling, how do you fare?" The little girl blushed at the effusion from such a spectacular lady.

Before Mama could respond, Portia came bustling in holding a bundle of satin and lace, evidently having found something to Rosa's liking, although, given Rosa's expression as she followed, I took it she hadn't truly liked a single thing in that room built for seduction. Portia stopped short upon seeing La Diamante. "Agnese!" Little Agnese was hardly within shouting distance, but she scampered over to receive the next item to package.

Portia forced a smile as she loaded Agnese's spindly arms. "Your Ladyship, I'm sure you have much to do regarding the upcoming wedding, with no time to linger here. The item you desired is well fitted for your daughter. I will drop off your purchase and personally collect my payment this evening at your palazzo, and we will deliver your fabric directly to the dressmaker. Will that suit you?"

"Perfectly, thank you." Mama straightened her posture. "Come, Daughters. We must make our leave." She swept out of the room, and Rosa threw me a confused look.

As we exited the shop, Teodor was laughing with two burly men in livery but snapped to attention upon seeing us, his face returning to his usual serious expression, befitting a gondolier out with his master's wife and daughters. Were the men La Diamante's personal guards? They looked the type who wrestled for entertainment.

After reminding us to don our veils and follow closely behind, Mama took Teodor's arm to steady her balance.

"What was that all about?" Rosa whispered as she clutched my hand. "Justina, was that a courtesan?"

"Yes, I believe so."

"Her dress was exquisite. And just for a shopping expedition!"

Rosa was right. The style was the very latest and suited La Diamante perfectly, accentuating her best features of bosom and face.

"She must have need of new dresses often. To entertain her . . . guests." I groped for the word, not knowing what such men were called.

"Remember Paolo telling us once about courtesans? How men visited them for music and rhetoric and poetry?"

"Given what Madelena just told us, I think there might be more to courtesans besides such intellectual and musical pursuits."

We were nearing the gondola now, so Rosa's voice took on a more urgent tone. "Do you think anyone we know has visited a courtesan for more than . . . musical pursuits? Given Paolo's knowledge of such matters, I suppose he must have."

"Yes, Paolo certainly." Had Luca? I could not picture him doing so. But maybe any woman who truly loved a man and believed him to reciprocate would naively feel that way.

"I guess Lord Zane might very well do the same," Rosa murmured as we approached the canal. I could not tell if the thought of Zago in the arms of another more experienced woman disgusted or comforted her.

Teodor assisted Mama under the *felze* before helping me inside with a few polite murmurs, while Rosa awaited her turn. Mama began discussing the dress designs, so I could not hear what Teodor and Rosa said to each other before she too entered and lifted her veil. But her cheeks were pink and she was smiling, a genuinely happy smile, the first I'd seen on her since Papa had announced her engagement.

At our evening meal, Paolo not unusually absent, Papa regaled us with tales from his day of important work at the doge's palazzo, describing the decaying relations with the pope and his League of Cambrai, the continuing aftermath of the fire at the Arsenale last month, and a widowed patrician named Marin Sanudo who perpetually hoped to become Venice's official historian by chronicling every scrap of government news in his daily diary.

"You should be glad, dear Rosa, that I did not arrange for you to marry Lord Sanudo. You would perish from the monotony! The way he goes on and on about governmental proceedings. It's all he ever talks or thinks about. His prospects are limited at best too. No, I am more grateful every day not only that Lord Zane was the right choice for our family, but that I was able to arrange the match so quickly, given the pope is breathing down our necks with an interdict that would prevent the sacrament of matrimony from being conducted." His expression turned grim.

"Yes, Papa." Rosa said it in the mechanical way that was becoming her trademark when around our parents, while I could not help but fleetingly wonder if Lord Sanudo also visited courtesans. Mama patted Rosa's hand, looking as concerned as I felt.

Papa wiped his lips. "I am retiring early tonight, as is your mother. Tomorrow is critical, with the publication of your banns and then the evening, when we bring you to the Zane palazzo for the next official function of your engagement. Please go directly to your room, so you are both well rested. Maid!" Madelena swiftly appeared. "Leave these duties until later. Signora Soranzo needs your assistance with some mending for tomorrow's outfit."

Madelena gave a small curtsy and followed my parents out, with Rosa and I trailing silently behind. The shadows were growing long, and the air was turning heavy with impending rain.

In our room, we helped each other into our nightclothes and climbed into our bed.

"I will not be here tomorrow night, Justina."

I nodded, although I wasn't sure she could see me in the dark. What was there to say? It was the truth, whether we liked it or not.

"It will be the first night we've ever spent apart in our whole lives."

I nodded again. Also true, and not a thing we could do to alter it. I would have to become accustomed to sleeping alone in my own cell. Not with Rosa, not with little Dolce, and never with Luca.

"I'm scared of what Lord Zane will do to me." Her voice was barely audible, and I did not know how to respond.

So I took her hand, until finally I entered the darkness of slumber.

Chapter 11

When I woke up the next morning, Rosa was neither in bed, nor the room. Outside, the world was a wall of grey. A fog had moved in with the stealth of a lion, and I could not even see across the Grand Canal. It was as if our palazzo were its own island, I the last human in Venice. The only visible object was a faint orange disc overhead, the sun struggling to burn off the mist. The quiet was absolute.

Until I heard Mama scolding Paolo into awakening and joining us for breakfast. I threw on a dressing gown, knowing I would be suitably preened later in the day, and headed to the dining room. Rosa was already sitting there, looking dazed, and not yet properly dressed. Her mussed hair would require special care today, and the traces of tears on her cheeks were not so unsightly that Madelena could not mask them with the judicious use of paint. Papa brought the papers announcing the matrimonial banns, which we all admired—or in certain cases, played the part. Mama smiled sympathetically at Rosa, who kept her eyes on her barely eaten breakfast.

Jovial Paolo had eyes only for Madelena as she worked, serving platters and taking away plates, while she pretended not to notice his attentions. I fretted that my brother would disregard my father's advice about legitimate heirs, leading our family to court scandal. I decided to pray for him and Rosa daily once I entered the convent.

Mama issued instructions, saying she'd splurged on an extra maid to assist her for the day to allow Rosa Madelena's full ministrations, and then everyone departed to ready themselves.

Paolo grabbed my wrist to keep me behind. "I saw Luca last night, and he wants to know how you are."

I swallowed hard. "You may tell him I keep well and prepare in earnest for our sister's wedding and my own conventual ceremony."

"I will tell him you said so." He studied me. "But you don't keep well, do you?"

I stared at the table. "I am managing. But I will admit to you that I may very well end up on my knees in perpetual prayer, for God to soothe me. I cannot absorb all the things that are happening. To make the convent my home forever, to be governed by a prayer schedule, to be under the rule of the new abbess. She was so stern from what I remember. And to be separated from Mama and Rosa and you ..."

"I too dread the day you are to leave us." He hugged me before turning to go. "I'd better get dressed, or Mama will have me strung up between the columns of San Marco and San Teodor in the Piazzetta like a common thief."

"Paolo, wait." He looked at me expectantly. "I see the way you look at Madelena. You must heed Papa's advice and control yourself. You know what will happen to her if you do anything."

He laughed. "Is that all? It's not *if* I do anything. It's whether I do anything and am caught. You know I am well versed in the amorous arts."

I snickered. "So I observe. But remember that while she is just a slave, she too must eat. Not to mention she has a heart."

"Yes, a heart. And those eyes. And the way her neck meets her shoulder, like Leda."

"You must not be the swan."

He grinned. "You've never seen Palumba's engraving, have you? You've only read about the myth in Ovid, right? My God, that picture . . ." He fanned his face with exaggeration.

"Enough, Paolo! I cannot hear any more. You know I am soon to take my vows, and my purity must not be tainted." I covered my ears, only half in jest. I both did and did not want to hear more, wondering how much would resonate with what Madelena had told us.

He chuckled. "Unfortunately for God, with me as your brother, I fear it is too late."

"Paolo . . ."

"Does your purity require further contamination?"

"Be serious. And tell me what you know about La Diamante."

"Ah yes, one of Venice's finest courtesans. She is renowned for her lute playing, her poetry, her intellect, and her ferocious guards whom she pays handsomely. Those are not the only attributes for which she is well known, although I have not had the pleasure to assess them for myself just yet, a fact I should soon remedy. Now pray tell, how has one of Venice's virgins heard of La Diamante?"

"We made her acquaintance at the draper's yesterday. She seemed . . . affable."

Paolo pushed aside a wisp of hair that had fallen upon my cheek. "Sister, you are very dear to me, and one of God's more intelligent specimens of the weaker sex. But for the sake of your virginity, I will spare you. Just know you must steer clear of such creatures. Some things are better left unknown to the women of our class." He kissed my forehead before we parted ways, and I took a deep breath as I forced my thoughts to return to holier subjects.

Chapter 12

That evening, the five of us crammed into the gondola, along with a small trunk containing Rosa's overnight belongings. All of us wore our finery, but Rosa looked exquisite in green silk. She wore her lace veil as Teodor escorted her first into the *felze*, so her expression was hidden, but I had never seen Teodor look more serious. I thought his hand held hers longer than necessary, but no one else seemed to notice in the chaos of departure.

Under the *felze*, Rosa did not raise her veil once during the journey up the Grand Canal. My mother too seemed lost in thought, her gaze fixed upon the gondola bottom. My father and Paolo sat outside the *felze* in the open air, discussing the business ventures they would soon embark upon in co-operation with the Zane men. Papa hoped these would permit him to finally emerge fully from his debts. The fog had taken all day to dissipate, and the sun came out only in time to set.

While its exterior was constructed of light yellow marble and brick, the interior of the Zane palazzo was as sombre as its inhabitants. Everything was a dark hue, the frescoes a swirl of muted browns, greens, and blues, even the terrazzo floor primarily black and grey marble. It felt almost funereal, though perhaps that had more to do with my overwhelming sadness. Rosa played her part well, smiling when required, curtsying when expected, demurely contemplating the floor precisely as instructed by Mama. The shy, blushing bride, nervous around her fiancé. It was a role, I now realized, that had been repeating for centuries, handed down from mother to daughter, a Venetian patrician woman's birthright.

Unless she became a nun, of course.

Lord Zane was less aloof than he'd been upon our first meeting. But this time, he looked more critically upon Rosa. There was some warmth there, but more so curiosity. In my mind he seemed akin to a merchant inspecting his property, which in a way I suppose he was.

Far too soon it was time for our family to depart, leaving Rosa behind with Lord Zane. The Zane family discreetly left us all in their *piano nobile*, Lord Zane stiffly telling Rosa that the maid stationed outside the room would escort her to him after she said her goodbyes. Rosa wore a mask of stoicism. First Paolo bid farewell, whispering something to her. Her eyes widened in alarm, but he did not notice as he kissed her cheek and swept out. Then Papa embraced her, telling her to be brave. Her eyes grew increasingly horrified as he left her with Mama and me.

"Don't leave me here, Mama, please!"

"Shush, you mustn't create a stir, my darling." Mama tried to put her arm around Rosa's shoulders.

She wrenched herself away. "Justina, please, do something, anything! I cannot stay here!"

"Keep your voice down, Rosa," Mama implored. "Justina, we must go. Your father will not be pleased." I was frozen by indecision.

"No!" It would be impossible for anyone in the palazzo to ignore Rosa's shriek. She threw her arms around me. "No no no no no no! I cannot go through with this." I held fast to my sweet little sister and gave Mama a pleading glance.

"You can and you must." Mama used her most authoritative tone, to no avail. She looked around desperately, her eyes finally settling on the doorway. She cracked it open, summoning the Zane maid posted outside as Rosa wailed again, like the scream of a crow, and I attempted in vain to soothe her.

"Hold her." The maid looked bewildered at Mama's tearful command. "You heard me, woman, hold her."

The maid, a cathedral of a woman older than Mama and double Rosa's size, did as instructed, looking pained as Rosa screeched so loudly I wondered what the Zanes would think. Mama then tugged Rosa and me apart, my cries now joining Rosa's in a chorus of despair. Mama pulled me away, telling me this was what had to happen as she struggled to control her own crying. "There is nothing we can do, Justina. Leave your sister to her fate. You are only making this harder for her."

"No!" We both yelped again as Rosa strained to wrestle out of the maid's grip and Mama dragged me out the *piano nobile* door and closed it. I banged on the wood with my fists, Rosa shouting for me in return, until Papa came over and slapped me. I stopped banging, stunned, my cheek stinging.

"That's enough." He was furious, his voice lower and slower than normal, and I had to strain to hear him over Rosa's moans, like those of a trapped animal. "That is quite enough. What the Zanes must think of us. You two girls are an utter embarrassment. You should be ashamed of yourselves. You bring shame to our family and our republic." He grabbed my arms and yanked me down the stairs to the water exit as Mama sniffled behind us and Paolo looked on sheepishly.

I made no pretense of covering my face in front of Teodor, who stood waiting with the gondola, his own eyes shining, his hands shaking as he helped Mama and me under the *felze*. When Papa and Paolo boarded, Teodor pushed off.

Mama closed the *felze* curtains, and we both silently cried in each other's arms.

Chapter 13

In my bedchamber, cuddling Dolce for comfort yet so very alone, I put prayer to paper.

God, I am to become Your bride. Please, for me, Your new wife, please help my sister. Please make Lord Zane gentle and kind behind closed doors. Please help Rosa adjust to her circumstances, so she can accept her new position as loving wife and helper to her husband. Please God, please.

Trying to shove the image of a miserable Rosa with Lord Zane out of my mind, I slept as fitfully as a baby with a fever.

The next morning, wrenched awake by a scream nearby on the side canal, I did not break my morning fast but kept to my chamber, staring out at the sliver of blue sky. Someone knocked on the door, but I ignored it. I heard voices in the house, and more outside. Teodor's deep rumble, calling to another gondolier. Madelena's softer timbre, issuing instructions. Seagulls, boats, bells, the comings and goings of the city. I cracked the door to let Dolce out so he could eat and relieve himself. Another knock on my door just after the *tierce* morning bell, Paolo cooing my name, but I just stared at myself in the glass, the ghost of Papa's slap still imprinted on my cheek. I knew Papa was doing what he truly thought best, but how could he ignore his own daughter's obvious distress? I was having trouble reconciling the two.

Finally, after I didn't know how long, yet another knock came, and Madelena gently announced she had brought Rosa back. I opened the door this time, not knowing what to expect, and Madelena passed me a look of misery as she escorted Rosa in and helped her onto the bed.

I had never seen Rosa like this, had never seen another creature like her. She was silent, and her eyes were swollen almost shut from crying. She curled into a ball with her back to me as Madelena began to unpack her belongings. Her beautiful gown had a long tear in it, as did her underclothes. I began to quietly weep, and Madelena did something she'd never done before and I normally would never have allowed: she encircled me in her arms. I clung to her for a long time, staring at Rosa's hair, which had escaped its pins and fallen onto the linens like a mournful nest.

Reluctantly I let go as Madelena said that Mama had convinced Papa to delay Rosa's visit to our aunt Leonarda's palazzo with Lord Zane. She promised to return as soon as she could with washing supplies and said she would try to slip out to see if the first cucumbers had arrived at the market, to help with the swelling around the eyes. As she left with Rosa's dress in her arms to mend it later, it occurred to me that Rosa and I had little more freedom than our slave girl.

I crept over to Rosa, sat beside her on the bed, and eventually laid a tentative hand on her shoulder. She shuddered and pulled away.

"Rosa?"

No reply.

"Let me help you." I cautiously touched her shoulder again, and this time she did not pull away. I dared to lie down beside her and drape my arm around her. I could feel her shaking. "Tell me what I can do."

Finally, she said something imperceptible.

"I cannot hear you, my dear."

"Take me with you to the convent." A barely audible whisper now.

"Oh Rosa, I wish I could."

"That's the only thing . . . you can do . . . to help me."

My heart felt chopped in two, for that was what I could not give her. It was not up to me. Anger flashed through my body, hatred toward Zago Zane for hurting my sister, toward my father for his decisions, toward Paolo for not convincing our father otherwise—he would eventually be in Papa's position, making decisions for his own children, no matter their opinions—hatred toward Venice itself and the impossible duties it commanded of its sons and especially its daughters, hatred toward God even, for ignoring my prayers.

And then I was awash with guilt for my wrath, for letting myself give in to such a sensation and committing a sin. I had to try to be a dutiful nun, to offer soothing words to the afflicted. I might even help myself in so doing.

"Rosa, let us pray together the Ave Maria to the Holy Virgin. She will understand and she will help us." Maybe only she could help us, as another woman and a mother.

Rosa kept her own counsel, but she did let me continue to hold her, and

I tried to tame my passion as I spoke the words, not the Latin version, but the ones I'd learned as a child before I'd studied at the convent, the very one I'd soon be entering forever.

> *Hail Mary, full of Grace, the Lord is with you.*
> *Blessed are you among women,*
> *And blessed is the fruit of your womb—Jesus.*
> *Holy Mary, Mother of God,*
> *Pray for us sinners now and at the hour of our death. Amen.*

I murmured it again, and again, and again, praying to perhaps the only one who could hold our pain in her own heart, until I knew Rosa had slipped into sleep, and soon my own head drooped next to hers and I slept too.

Chapter 14

Madelena left us undisturbed until early the next morning, when she came in lugging a bucket of water to find Rosa and I both awake but still in bed, holding each other, Rosa clutching her old doll. She had spoken no further, and I hummed a mindless tune as I stroked her hair.

Madelena set the bucket down and stacked some linens next to it. "I'm very sorry to have to tell you this, but your mother has sent me to help you dress for a visit to San Zaccaria later this morning, with a visit to your aunt Leonarda this evening." She took a deep breath. "She also asked me to convey that it will be just the three of you this morning, and she is very sorry but Lord Zane must join you at your aunt's as planned."

Rosa nodded vaguely. I shook my head, swallowing my wrath, offering my anger up to the Virgin.

"Now," she said briskly, directing her words to Rosa, "let's put some cucumbers on your eyes, to reduce the swelling, and after you wash I'll paint your face. You will look as beautiful as ever, I promise." Madelena helped Rosa shift onto her back, then placed two green discs of cucumber over her eyes. She was coaxing but firm in handling my sister, as if she had some experience in the matter. And perhaps she did. "I'll lay out frocks for the both of you and be back in a bit to help with the finishing touches."

I nodded as she left, then looked at my sister and the cucumber circles upon her eyes. As she lay there, I decided it was time to wash and dress myself. What choice did either of us have in anything? Better and easier to just follow instructions. That at least required no thinking.

Madelena had left out plain dresses fit for a convent visit, and I did my own hair, ineffectually but well enough for today's purpose. I knew all the effort would go toward Rosa, as the bride-to-be.

When I finished, I removed the cucumbers from her eyes, and she stared at the wood-panelled ceiling, barely blinking. "Rosa," I cajoled, helping her into a sitting position. She would not do anything of her own accord, neither washing nor dressing, but she allowed me, and then Madelena, to assist her, primping, styling, painting, beautifying. She even allowed me to feed her a few pieces of bread.

By mid-morning, we were at the water entrance with Mama and Madelena. Teodor looked as if his mother had died, so out of sorts that Mama herself asked him if he was feeling poorly as he helped her into the gondola. He shook his head.

Inside the closed curtains of the *felze*, Mama held Rosa's hand and kept glancing at me with worried eyes. Teodor rowed faster than normal to our destination, out of the Grand Canal, past the magnificent doge's palazzo, and just past Luca's family's terracotta-coloured palazzo. As Teodor tied up the gondola on the *fondamenta*, the street that ran along the canal, and escorted us up the lane to Campo San Zaccaria, I tried to ignore God's cruel trick that placed the Cicogna palazzo in such close proximity to my future cloister, then chastised myself for doubting God's plan, even though I could not decipher His reason to test me so. Whatever the reason, that adjacency was clearly to be my trial, the test of my love and fealty to my divine husband.

I took a deep breath and forced my fists to unclench as I paused next to the white marble cistern in the square, the site of the assassinations of two doges. Mama and Rosa walked toward the adjacent stone building that was the convent itself. As familiar as the place was, I was having trouble accepting that this was going to be my home for the rest of my life.

The church's soaring facade was clad with white and some pink marble in Gambello's architectural style, the towers guarded by sculpted angels, and I allowed myself a momentary surge of pride. I would be a nun within that holy and beautiful place named after the father of the humble John the Baptist, the home of so many noble nuns, and the benefactress of many doges.

A few workers entered the church's small wooden doors, loudly straggling in, defying the plaque in the campo that commanded no arguing and cursing. Their supervisor would surely not be pleased by their unholy behaviour.

"Signorina." Madelena grasped my arm and led me to the cloister entrance, a white carved-marble doorframe within the apricot-coloured walls, over which weeping flowers prettily hung. Teodor gave a brief nod before heading toward the cistern to wash his hands and take a drink of water.

In the sumptuous convent parlour, Mama, Rosa, and I sat silently on a green velvet sofa, Madelena standing guard, and waited for Auntie Livia.

Maids in simple dresses and aprons scurried back and forth, carrying linens or platters of fruit or trays of buns or baskets of eggs. One even held a little dog that reminded me of Dolce, though not nearly as charming. Faint choral singing came from far away. A bark, then terrified meowing, and excited female chatter. A servant placed on a small table in front of us a silver tray bearing four small glasses of wine and a plate of pine-nut cookies.

As we sat waiting, Zanetta swept in, her white-blond hair pulled severely back. Rosa blanched, while Mama rose. "How lovely to see you again. I trust my sister Livia told you of our visit."

"Yes, I heard my brother's bride-to-be was coming today," Zanetta said, brushing back a few stray wisps that had escaped from her coiffure with a haughty sniff.

Mama just smiled and nodded. "Rosa, dear, please rise and greet your new sister-in-law."

With my guidance on her elbow, Rosa did as commanded, not meeting Zanetta's eyes, which inspected her from head to toe.

"She is looking a bit pale." Zanetta addressed Mama, and I wondered how much she knew about what had happened with her brother. "I hope she is in good health."

"Most excellent health. Just a little tired perhaps. So much excitement." She gave a brief nod to Rosa, who sat down and stared at her lap. "You know my other daughter, Justina. You might recall that she will very shortly be joining your ranks here at San Zaccaria." I hastily rose and curtsied.

"Yes, and we talked at the engagement festa." Zanetta curtly nodded as she appraised me.

I made a point of looking her right in the eye. "A pleasure to see you again."

Her own expression belied any reciprocal pleasure.

We all sighed in relief as Auntie Livia entered the parlour, and Zanetta took her leave with only a word of goodbye.

Rolling her eyes, Livia rushed over to give us all hugs. "My darlings! What a joy to see you on such a happy occasion!" Behind her was Elisabetta, of the Marcello noble family, Livia's dear friend and someone both Rosa and I knew well from our schooling at the convent. Livia and Elisabetta wore the subdued hues befitting patrician nuns, but their low-necked dresses were of the latest style and the finest fabrics, and their heads were bare, their hair styled quite similarly to Mama's, into soft horns.

Mama took Livia's hands. "Thank you, Sister. How do you fare?"

"I am well, very well, although I'm terribly sorry I cannot offer you more than a small refreshment. The kitchen is in tumult, baking cakes and cookies. Later today, as you may well know, our new abbess-elect is giving us nuns another special feast. Justina, Rosa, you remember Marina of the Marcello family? A distant relation of Elisabetta's." Having forgotten the two were related, I was struck by the contrast between how warm Elisabetta always was and yet how cool the abbess-elect seemed. "The election was close and sadly disputed. She received just five more votes than Angela Riva, who was far from pleased. I already wrote your mother with the news, but I know much is going on at the Soranzo palazzo and you cannot be asked to recall all the details of our conventual politics." She hugged Mama again.

Elisabetta came over to kiss both Rosa and me in greeting. Mama dipped her head regally and asked her if she had returned to full health. With a tight smile, Elisabetta replied that she had. Mama had never really liked Elisabetta, merely tolerating her for Livia's sake, and I wondered if she were jealous of the sisterly affection the two nuns clearly exhibited. "I wished to greet the girls and tell Justina that I very much look forward to her joining us here at San Zaccaria." She gave me another kiss before excusing herself. "I must see to our students." Those would be the children in the convent's care, orphans, boarding girls, and postulants.

"I'll join you as soon as our visit is over." Livia nodded happily as we all settled on the sofa. "Justina, you will not be able to enjoy tonight's event, but you already know that San Zaccaria makes the best sweets in all of Venice and serves only the finest wines. You'll miss the main celebration too, when Mother Marina is officially given control of the convent in just a few days, but you will be installed here in time for the next celebratory feast in early May. You should have been here the day after Easter when the doge came. The cooks outdid themselves." She beamed at me, her eyes pale blue and jolly, her face plump and relaxed, looking far younger than my mother, even though just a few years separated them. I smiled in return, reaching out to squeeze her hand. She had always been my favourite aunt. "And here is the bride, the beautiful Rosa," she continued, turning to Rosa, who could muster no smile but only gazed at the floor.

"Chiara?" She addressed Mama, who cleared her throat.

"Rosa is having some . . . ah . . . trouble adjusting to her new future, as many young brides do. But nothing she will not learn to become accustomed to, with a little time and God's grace."

Auntie Livia crossed herself. "Not yet fourteen years old. How could she feel otherwise? She is a child asked to be a woman before she is ready. I will pray for her, that her mind may be eased." She clasped her hands together and murmured an inaudible prayer. "Rosa, dear, please come here."

Rosa did as commanded, coming to sit beside our aunt.

"Let me tell you something. Before your mother married your papa over twenty years ago, she was fifteen years old and frightened too by what awaited her. When she came to this convent for her blessing, our own auntie promised to pray for her daily, which I can attest she did until the day her soul departed this earth and joined her divine spouse in paradise."

Mama nodded. "Yes, and knowing my auntie was praying for me every day gave me the strength and courage to face my fears."

Auntie Livia put her arm around Rosa's shoulders. "And I will do the same for you, Niece, you can depend upon it. Come any time you wish to visit Justina and me, and tell us what to pray for and we will do that. And your mind will be serene again."

Rosa glanced at me doubtfully but said, "Thank you, Auntie Livia."

"And you must ignore your new sister, Zanetta. She is a lemon of a woman, and happily you will not be marrying her. Now, tell me all about the engagement festa. I was so sorry to miss it, but Betta was feeling poorly as you know and the abbess-elect needed me at that dinner. I know you must rush everything through in case His Holiness makes good on his threats of an interdict, but nothing will stop me from attending the wedding itself." Auntie Livia helped herself to a glass of wine, indicating that Mama, Rosa, and I should do the same, as Mama described the festa Paolo had put on and the upcoming nuptial plans. I noticed she did not tell the tale of the extra duty Rosa had been required to perform.

As the clanging from the nearby church bell reverberated in our marrow, Mama said it was time to prepare for our evening visit to Auntie Leonarda's. As she, Rosa, and Madelena took their leave, Auntie Livia said she wanted to speak to me privately for a few moments. Mama nodded, saying they'd pray in the church while they waited.

"Is Rosa all right, truly?" Auntie patted the seat beside her on the sofa.
I moved closer, and she took my arm. "I don't know."

"You can tell me anything, Niece. The convent affords much discretion."

I was relieved to finally be able to tell someone. "She was asked to fulfill
her wifely duties . . . in advance, and the experience was clearly . . . difficult.
I believe she is in some sort of shock in the aftermath."

Auntie's brow creased with concern. "She is such a tender child, so obedient. Beautiful too, thus I'm not surprised to hear that was requested. But
I am surprised that my sister allowed it, and even more so that she did not
mention it. Perhaps your father felt he had no choice in such a request,
with him scraping together every ducat for the dowry. Do you feel this
Lord Zane is a good man?"

I hesitated.

Auntie Livia pulled me close. "We will not have any secrets soon, you and
I, once you take the veil. And I may be able to serve as some influence on
Chiara. She visits often to seek my counsel, although interestingly she has
not on Rosa's marital matters. I suspect she knows I would not approve of
how things are being handled and is even embarrassed. For while we women
are trained to shoulder our lot in life, cruelty is not necessary."

"Well then, no, I'm not at all sure Lord Zane is a good man, although
Papa and Paolo seem to think so." I took a deep breath. "I believe Rosa also
may feel an attachment to another, which only compounds the problem.
She knows it cannot be, but I'm not sure her heart agrees."

Auntie sighed deeply. "It is as I suspected upon seeing Rosa's face. Even
Chiara could not hide her distress behind her jabbering about marital festas.
And what of Paolo? He has visited several times since Carnival, though I
fear I am just an excuse so he can meet my beautiful younger sisters." She

hinted at a smile, and I could hear what I thought to be a kitten mewling from behind a closed door.

"Paolo is his usual self, but I do wonder if he might find himself in trouble, although not with a San Zaccaria nun."

"Your maid who was here, Madelena?"

"You are certainly observant, Auntie!"

"She is just his kind, young, dark, and beautiful, and I have much time to think as well as keenly observe my visitors. And you are not the only one to suspect of course. Your mother . . ."

"Ah. Although I'm not certain she'll be able to keep him away if he truly desires."

"That is true. I suppose the worst that can happen is paying a fine and a dowry, a pittance I'm sure, even for your father."

"Do you not think they might sell her? She was given to Papa as a slave just after the Epiphany in lieu of another loan repayment, remember, not hired as a servant."

Livia's eyes narrowed. "I had forgotten. I do not know. Your papa is not a cruel man, but he has more than his fair share of financial problems." She shook her head. "I don't think so. Anyway, it's the bastard everyone worries about, especially if it's a male child. But boys will be boys, and Paolo will be Paolo, despite any interventions we may attempt." We held hands the way we used to when I did my schooling here. "I know you must leave soon, so I will finally ask after you. Are you ready to join our ranks here at San Zaccaria?"

"Of course, Auntie."

"No secrets?" She raised an eyebrow. "Paolo did let slip . . ."

I blushed despite myself. "Then you know about Lord Cicogna."

"I do. Lord Luca Cicogna. And when I got word of your father's decisions regarding you and Rosa, I realized that your fantasy did not come to fruition."

I tried in vain to replace any melancholy that my expression may have conveyed with a pious look instead.

"Do not despair, my dear niece. Many patrician girls take their vows with much trepidation. But with Christ as your husband, you will find a way to acceptance. Besides," she gave me an extra squeeze before letting go, "you might find our prison more pleasant than you imagine. It is quite different being a full nun, versus a boarding schoolgirl or postulant. You will see. I will help you navigate Zanetta and her ilk. And you will find time for reading and writing, which I know you so enjoy."

I dearly hoped she was right about that, as that would make my situation at least slightly more tolerable. "Do you worry about Venice being excommunicated?"

She waved her hands dismissively. "Venice can handle His Holiness. And while such an edict may perforce alter some of our rituals, we nuns can handle His Holiness as well, especially with Mother Marina at the helm."

We kissed each other on both cheeks before I left to find Mama, and Livia returned to the cloister's sanctum, her dark blue dress swishing at her silk slippers.

Chapter 15

The possibility of a papal interdict lent a frantic pace to the ancient Venetian wedding rituals we continued to honour, albeit on a more compressed schedule. Rosa performed her role as if in a trance, doling out subdued smiles and small curtsies whenever required, linking arms or holding hands with Lord Zane for the various ceremonies but never looking him in the eye or anywhere in the vicinity of his face. Every night she fell into bed without an extra word beyond *goodnight* for me, and she awoke early each day with a gentle shake from Madelena to start on her preparations. I sometimes tried to cheer her up, but I was consumed with my own worries over being separated from her and what life in the convent would be like, as well as mourning Luca. I chastised myself for my selfishness, but I could not help it.

The morning before the wedding, Paolo asked me for a weaving lesson, for accuracy's sake. He was playing Penelope in the *Odyssey* mummery his Inamorati fraternity was performing at the final nuptial festa the next night. I did my best to show him a few authentic movements and to ignore him when he mentioned Luca's upcoming performance as Odysseus, but I was distracted thinking about what the day would bring, how Rosa was doing, and how I'd react upon seeing Luca. Today was the official installation of Marina Marcello as abbess of San Zaccaria, and I also wondered what role she would play in my own life. Auntie Livia seemed pleased, which was encouraging, but as a husband controls his wife, so an abbess influences her daughters.

Finally the wedding day dawned, bright and warm, the palazzo imbued with a spirit of both honey and vinegar. Rosa's dress was exquisite, edged with intricate lace as delicate as gossamer that had been specially purchased from San Zaccaria to honour my holy vocation. Madelena had styled Rosa's hair to perfection, and she wore a gold and diamond necklace of Mama's that had not yet been sold to cover the cost of the nuptial barges. She was stunning, although her expression unsurprisingly conveyed no joy whatsoever. The only thing she said upon seeing her reflection in the mirror was that she hoped when I wore the same dress, without the necklace, for my own conventual ceremony two days hence, I would feel a measure more happiness. And yet I could only imagine what it would be like to marry Luca in it.

The ceremony took place at the nearby Church of San Vio, with several hundred people in attendance. Our mild-mannered parish priest, whose eyes flickered to my sister throughout the ceremony, seemed perturbed by her obvious distress but unsure what to do about it with my father staring unblinkingly from the front pew. Rosa took her vows in a hushed voice while her betrothed spoke clearly and very solemnly.

Finally my sister was married, two days before I was to take my vows, our lives changed forever. It was almost anticlimactic after all the earlier events, and anyway in my eyes she had been as good as married the night she spent at the Zane palazzo. Still, I could not help quietly whimpering beneath my veil throughout the Mass, knowing Rosa was unhappy and that finally the separation we had both dreaded was here and permanent. In contrast, Rosa displayed as much emotion as the wooden statue of the Virgin displayed near the front of the church. Auntie Livia, given leave from the convent for the day, sat beside me, stroking my hand. Zanetta, similarly freed for the festivities, sat across the aisle with the Zane family, but I did not see Luca. I knew he must be sitting somewhere behind me, could sense his presence, and wondered if he was looking at me. I half hoped he was and half hoped he wasn't.

After the ceremony, we all processed through the sun-baked campo with much fanfare and boarded the enormous barge that was to sail up and down the Grand Canal the rest of the afternoon and evening. Workers had already brought on board all the items necessary for a feast and festa, having decorated the barge with pennants, tapestries, and enormous bouquets of fragrant flowers, while a quartet of musicians played with much merriment. Pulled by six boats oared by common men hired from San Vio parish, the barge was led by a fishing boat, also from our parish, carrying three exuberant trombonists, and the canal-side walkways were smattered with humble people cheering.

The afternoon was beautiful, the air clear and warm. The turquoise canal waters dreamily reflected the peach- and cantaloupe-coloured palazzi, and as evening deepened the stars honeycombed the indigo sky. The servants lit wax torches in preparation for the mummery, which was when I finally saw Luca, dressed as Odysseus, resplendent with sword and shield—although I found that odd since the *Odyssey* took place mainly at sea. But I supposed that fact wouldn't have made for as interesting a costume, and the Inamorati, like all the patrician fraternities in Venice, revelled in their pomp. Luca made an excellent Odysseus, though I was quite partial, and I could not help but think he was speaking to me when he spoke these lines: "Be patient, my heart, for you have endured things worse than this before." Yet again my own heart fought the reality of my predicament. There could be nothing worse. *Jesus is to be my husband.* I knew I had yet another mortal sin to add at the confessional and prayed God would be merciful.

After the mummery, Auntie Livia regaled me with stories about the installation of Abbess Marina—how marvellous the ceremony had been, how perfectly everything was arranged for the patriarch, how absolutely divine the food was, how wonderful the volume of poetry published in her honour—and said she could not wait to have me with her. I nodded and smiled, glad for her welcome, although my mind felt leagues from my body. Auntie Livia then pressed me to join her in dance, but I politely declined, not feeling very festive.

Instead, I resolutely exchanged pleasantries and accepted congratulations on behalf of both my sister and myself for our good fortune and endured Auntie Leonarda, too old and fat to dance, with the patience of Leah awaiting the birth of a daughter. But I was only half there in mind as the festa whirled around me, focused on keeping Rosa in my sights should she need me.

The torches burned low, and I knew the evening would soon end. My dread mounting in anticipation of Rosa's departure, I turned to see that my dining companion Auntie Leonarda had been replaced by Luca. My eyes widened as the flame within that I'd kept so low resurged in intensity.

"Hello, Signorina Soranzo, and how are you this fine and joyous evening?" Luca dipped his head in a sort of sitting bow, and I did the same in return. He now wore the colourful costume of his fraternity. Would I ever find him unattractive? If anything, I found him more handsome than before, despite my frantic but unfulfilled prayers to quell my desires. He looked quite serious and a touch thinner since I had seen him last.

"I am well, thank you, and yourself?"

"In good health, thank you. Congratulations to your family on your sister's marriage and your own impending conventual vows."

All I could manage was another polite word of gratitude.

Luca glanced around. No one appeared to be taking the slightest note of us as the musicians played louder and the dancers danced faster and the laughter crescendoed and the servants poured more wine. "I see I can talk plainly to you, though I must keep my hands to myself."

I nodded slightly and dared to raise my veil for him. His breath caught as he looked me full in the eye.

"In fact, I am not well at all." He roughly combed his fingers through his hair. "All I can do is think of you."

I bit my lower lip. "Do not tell me this. I cannot bear it. There is nothing we can do. Our parents have set our course, and we must obey." I tried to smooth my voice's trembles.

His brow creased. "I do not want to cause you further pain. But I am in agony. My own nuptials have been moved up to two weeks hence due to the possible papal interdict."

So soon? Not that it should matter to me, for I would be well ensconced in my sisterhood by then. But it did matter, and I felt exquisite pain sear my heart. "You are so young. Might you not have more leeway?"

"I wish I could remain a bachelor with all the freedom that commands, but my father is insistent. Once marriage was in his head, he forged ahead, and the alliance he has brokered is simply too good to pass on at this delicate financial moment, with Venice on the brink of war with His Holiness's army. My fiancée's generous dowry will give us ample capital to carry on our family's trade if there is a war and the city is excommunicated, and even allow me to join the Great Council this year, before I turn twenty-five."

I swallowed hard. "That is quite an honour. You must do your duty then, to your family, to Venice, and to God. With God in your heart, you will find your way to acceptance." I was echoing Auntie Livia and hoped her wisdom was as helpful as she proclaimed.

Luca bestowed on me a half-hearted smile. "Look at you, already the devotional nun."

"I will pray for you." My tears barely obeyed my command not to spill.

"Please do. I will need all the prayers I can receive, and I fear no one will pray for my happiness as well as you."

I forced myself to smile. "Every day." I saw Madelena out of the corner of my eye and knew she had come to take me to Rosa.

Luca inhaled deeply, clasped my hand, and kissed it with a sacred tenderness. A jolt ran through me deeply, but I closed my eyes and tried not to convey it.

"Goodbye, Justina. I hope you keep writing."

I gave a slight nod. "Goodbye, Luca."

I knew this was not farewell for the evening or the week, but forever.

He rose, bowed, and strode into the crowd, taking my heart and hope with him. As he walked away, I noticed Zanetta among a knot of Zane family members, eyeing him and then me.

Before I could start to worry about what she may have seen, Madelena reached my side and covered my face with my veil, for propriety and my own privacy. "Are you well, Signorina?"

"I will have to be, Madelena. I must find a way to be." Through the veil's sheer fabric, I took in her appearance more fully. "I should ask the same of you." Madelena was slightly dishevelled. It would not be apparent to anyone else, but by now I knew our slave well. She was always meticulous in her plain albeit pleasing appearance, and I could understand why Paolo admired her so.

"I am well enough, Signorina." She did not meet my eyes. "Your sister will be leaving any moment with Lord Zane."

I glanced up and realized the barge was docking in front of the Zane palazzo. "And you are concerned."

"I am." She caught my eye, then again looked away.

"Tell me, Madelena. I can see you wish to say something."

"It is difficult. I do not wish to speak ill of my owner."

"Papa."

She nodded.

"Speak plainly, Madelena. I will not betray your confidence. Please consider me a nun already."

She took a deep breath. "Your father … threatened Rosa. To not make a scene when she leaves. I was there helping her freshen her appearance right before we boarded the barge."

I digested this piece of information. "Did he hurt her?" I could not imagine Papa doing so.

"No, no, not physically. She just nodded."

"Papa must not realize what . . . happened to Rosa that night at the Zane palazzo."

Madelena shook her head. "Besides your mother, you, and me, as well as that one Zane maid, I don't think anyone does. Except Teodor. He didn't say anything, of course, but I don't see how he could not have noticed when he took her home the next morning. And I know how loyal he is to your family." I knew this to be so, but I also recalled the fiery way he looked at Rosa. I prayed that either his love or loyalty would protect Rosa's reputation.

"Thank you for telling me this." She curtsied and rushed off in her usual manner as I scanned the barge for my sister, locating her staring at the floor as she stood beside Lord Zane, who was conversing with a clutch of black-robed patricians of his own age. Now officially married, Rosa no longer wore a veil, and though her face was the most familiar thing in the world to me, I was unaccustomed to seeing it revealed in public.

I headed right for her, nearly reaching her side when a trombone melody cut through the night. Someone announced, "It is time for the bride and groom to take their leave." A cheer went up from Paolo's fraternity as well as some passersby along the canal.

"You mean their pleasure!" shouted another male voice. Laughter and tittering rippled through the crowd, even Zanetta curving her thin lips into a smile. Rosa blushed while Lord Zane chuckled, and his friends clapped him on the back with jocularity.

My parents stepped forward, my father grinning broadly, my mother smiling tightly, to hug Rosa. This was the formal moment when she was no longer of our house but Lord Zane's. Paolo also came over, more subdued than normal, but Rosa managed to be stoic.

Until she turned to me. I held her close, and I could feel her distress against my chest and neck.

"Please don't make me go," she whispered in my ear. "Please let me come with you to San Zaccaria." The jubilation rose in volume, allowing us to murmur to each other.

I clutched her tightly. "I would like that more than anything."

"Please. Or I will kill myself."

"Don't say that. It will not be that horrible; it just can't be. You must be strong."

Papa came over to pry us apart, giving Rosa a black look with a meaning I now fully comprehended. Rosa obeyed, tears streaming down her cheeks, but meek and compliant as my father pushed her toward Lord Zane, who grabbed her hand to lead her off the barge to the water entrance of his palazzo.

He turned back toward his audience and lifted his hand with Rosa's. More cheers and applause arose, sprinkled with hoots and not a few crude comments about what was to transpire. Lord Zane looked happier than I had ever seen him, and I reminded myself that he was my new brother, Zago, as I was now encouraged to call him.

Rosa looked more miserable than she had allowed herself to show in days, her face streaked with tears, despair in her eyes.

Lord Zane—*Zago*—whispered something to her and her expression turned stricken. Then the couple turned away from the barge and entered the carved wooden doors of the palazzo.

Chapter 16

The Feast of San Marco, a most joyous day in Venice, dawned as grey and foul as my mood. After a fretful night of sleeping alone, the bed so empty with only Dolce for company, I was more than a little anxious to hear news of my sister. But neither news nor rain came, and Mama would not send Madelena, seeing as we required her assistance at home. The Zane maid did not appear, nor did Rosa herself, which I had thought was not entirely out of the question. At mid-morning I looked out the window to see a slightly bedraggled Teodor rowing back through the gloom toward our water entrance, and I could not help but wonder where he'd been. Might he have tried to uncover information at the Zane palazzo? But it was impossible for me to decipher his expression, and it would have been quite improper for me to inquire as to his whereabouts.

However, it was not improper for Madelena to ask him, and in between packing my chest with the belongings Mama thought suitable to take to the convent, she dashed down to talk to our gondolier. When she returned, giving me a meaningful look, Mama and I were in the library, where she was encouraging me to pack a few precious books, with my father's permission. Only in the aftermath of our midday meal was I able to steal a few moments alone with Madelena.

"Teodor did row over to the Zane palazzo this morning. He did not see Rosa, of course, but he talked to their gondolier. The gossip among the servants is that the marriage was consummated and that Rosa is . . ."

"What? Rosa is what?"

"A little worse for wear, but according to that maid Maria, not nearly as bad as before."

I gave a small cry of agony, and Madelena hugged me.

"I wish Mama would let me go to her."

"But there's no time. You must prepare for your own ceremony tomorrow. As soon as you are in San Zaccaria, your mother and I will visit her, and then I will come and tell you."

It was all I could ask for, though I wanted to curse the rapid timing of our ceremonies forced upon us by His Holiness the Warrior Pope. "Thank you, Madelena."

"Of course, Signorina." She turned to leave but stopped as soon as Paolo entered. An unmistakable look passed between them before Madelena exited, and even more worry swelled inside me.

Paolo smiled exuberantly. "Ah, Sister! Sit with me while I sup. It is the last time we will have such an opportunity to be alone together. Not that you'll have time to miss me. I plan to visit you frequently at San Zaccaria." He took my hand, and we headed to the kitchen. The cook was absent, likely at the Rialto market, so Paolo scrounged around for something to eat, then plunked himself on the worktable.

"Paolo, don't try to distract me with talk of the convent."

"What do you mean? Distract you from what?"

"From what is going on between you and Madelena. You risk a bastard with our slave, and you also probably risk Papa selling her to another family, on much worse terms for her."

Paolo's jovial disposition slumped. "It is that obvious?"

"Yes," I said harshly, then softened my tone. "I certainly can understand her appeal. But you will ruin both your prospects."

"Well, I'm not sure I'd go that far. A delightful little bastard wouldn't be so horrible. But I do see your point about selling her. Papa would have no compunction about that these days. He would say she was bringing shame to the noble house of Soranzo."

He was likely right. As Livia had said, Papa was not a cruel man, but he was practical. Moreover he was a senator and also financially desperate. "Yes, but I say you and she both would be. And you had better not be visiting me at San Zaccaria just to further sully our family's honour by flirting with my new sisters."

"Upon my word, I intend to visit because I shall dearly miss *you*." He looked for a moment so contrite. "However, enjoying the company of a beautiful and innocent handmaiden of God will not be a bad side benefit."

I rolled my eyes. "You are incorrigible."

"Perhaps I should keep up the trend among friends and family and marry myself, then ask Papa to give me Madelena as a wedding present. Then I can sully my own house instead of his. Not to mention the sheets." His smile this time was mischievous.

"You are truly wicked, Brother."

"In all seriousness, it will not be the same around here after tomorrow. Both my sisters gone and never returning to this house. I shall be lonely."

"I doubt that very much, but it's nice of you to say so. Speaking of sisters, would you please visit ours at the Zane palazzo this afternoon and bring me word of how she is? I worry about her, Paolo. I know Mama says not to, but I worry all the same. Madelena says she will go herself, but that won't be for at least two days."

"Rosa will be fine. All wives are eventually. It just takes time. That's what everyone says, and so it will be for her. But all the same, I can read the concern in your face, and so I shall go now and report back to you." He finished his last bite, wiped his mouth, and arose. "I feel quite confident you will be able to rest easy tonight. And you must. It is the biggest day of your life tomorrow."

"I hope you are right, Brother." But for every confident and manly word he uttered, I as a member of the fairer sex only felt more dread.

The grey chill that matched my melancholy lasted the entire day, past sunset, past supper, past the final packing and preparations—the noise from the San Marco festival filtering through the windows, the crowd undeterred by the evening drizzle—and still Paolo did not return. I was so distracted by thoughts of Rosa and dread about taking my vows the next day that I could only blindly follow the instructions Mama set out for me. The only happy diversion came when she said I could take Dolce with me to the convent, and I thanked her profusely for the kindness. Dolce, two books from Papa's library, Rosa's old doll, my thick stack of writings from the moment I could hold quill and parchment, Luca's inexpert copy of the Barbari map—all would be like bringing a piece of home with me.

Finally it was time for my bedtime preparations. I could hardly believe Paolo had not yet returned. I feared he had gotten waylaid by the festivities on his return from my mission, or far worse, never arrived there in the first place, forgetting entirely about his sisters amid the celebratory mood of the city. Disappointed in my brother's thoughtless behaviour, of which I knew him to be quite capable, I had just changed into my nightdress when a knock came upon on my door and I tore it open.

"Finally! How is she?"

Paolo looked dreary. "I won't lie to you. She is not happy. She says Zago has terrible breath and is horribly mean. But of course she's only thirteen. Those are the kinds of things she would focus on. She is admittedly very young and Zago not the most buoyant, thus it cannot be expected to be otherwise. But I see your look and can assure you she is no unhappier than she was before, and I'm sure she'll grow accustomed to her husband." He cleared his throat. "I do think Zago is working her quite a bit more than she would like. He let drop he needs an heir as soon as possible, as the only son. You know how it is."

I nodded. I did not feel better at the thought of what Rosa was experiencing, as if she were merely a vessel for a male child, but I was not naive enough to think that such desire in a husband was unusual. She was a married noblewoman now, and compliance and breeding were entirely expected of her.

"She did send you her love as well as a letter." He handed me a folded paper sealed with the Zane crest. How odd to see that instead of our own.

"Thank you, Paolo, for going to see Rosa and bringing this to me." While part of me wanted to spend my last evening distracted by my convivial brother from thoughts of San Zaccaria, most of me preferred to scrutinize Rosa's letter immediately and in private.

"This isn't everything I bring." He looked quite pleased with himself as he produced a book from his cloak. "Gifts for you. From Luca."

"Luca?"

"Yes, that's what took me so long. I had an inkling I should visit him, and it is good that I did so. He insisted I give this to you." He handed me the brown leather volume. "He says it's the latest printing out of the press of Joannes Tacuinus de Tridino, a grammar by Valerius Probus. Doesn't mean anything to me, but I knew you'd appreciate it." As I fondled the book, he added, "And clearly Luca knew too."

I flipped through the pages lined with Latin, trying to hold back my tears. It seemed all I ever did of late was weep, but I didn't know what else to do when so moved, this time in the most bittersweet of ways.

Between the last pages Luca had inserted a sheet of paper, like Rosa's folded in thirds, and sealed with the waxen Cicogna crest, my name written on the front in his meticulous script. Two letters to read tonight, from the two people I held most dear.

"Luca wanted you to have one more thing." This time from his cloak he extracted a long-stemmed rosebud, handing it to me.

"For the Feast of San Marco." I drank in its fragrance, the red petals soft and velvety. "He shouldn't have."

Paolo smiled. "I will take my leave. You need your rest now for tomorrow. The word on the canal is that the pope's interdict will come down any day now, so Papa's timing of your vows is fortuitous. Good night, Sister, sleep well." He hugged me with warmth, as if he truly might miss me.

Despite my recent misgivings, I knew I would miss him dearly—how he could always make me laugh.

Eventually he departed, leaving me alone with a new book, two letters, and a perfect rose.

The book I tucked with the others in the open chest that I was to take with me on the morrow. The rosebud I placed upon my pillow. The letters I held to my lips, thinking I could inhale the scent of either one or the other writer, but all I could smell was ink and wax. I opened Rosa's first. I could tell she had scrawled quickly in her childish hand, probably in a rush to give it to Paolo before he left.

> *To my dear sister Justina,*
>
> *It has been only one night since I left you, and it feels like a lifetime. I wish I could say that it was a blissful night, but it is more akin to torture. My husband—how strange to write those two words—seems both disinterested in and enamoured with me, meaning that he has no interest in sweet lovers' talk upon the pillow but did take his pleasure three times without a word, falling asleep in between. Papa can rest assured that Zago consummated the marriage. With any luck, his first grandson will arrive in less than a year. If I can survive that long.*
>
> *I know you enter San Zaccaria tomorrow. I did ask—nay, beg—permission from my husband to attend your ceremony, but he refused, saying we were still celebrating our nuptials. I am sorry, but I will visit as soon as I can. It may be for a long visit. I would not rule out the possibility. I realize that, just like mine, your fate is not as you wished. I pray you will find peace and tranquility in the convent and that it will eventually feel like your home.*

Tonight when I go to bed, after my husband has performed his marital duty and I mine, I will turn my back to him and pretend it is you I am sharing my bed with, in our chamber together, and that when I wake up, things will be as they were when we were children, the happiest days of my life.

Your loving sister always—Rosa

I read the letter three times, feeling increasingly troubled about Rosa and correspondingly helpless at the little I could do besides perhaps being a reason for her to leave the Zane palazzo to visit. I had held out some hope she would come to my ceremony, but I was not too surprised Zago did not grant her permission, and I tried to refrain from cursing his cold heart. All I could do was take comfort in Paolo's judgment of Rosa. He seemed only mildly agitated by our sister's words and behaviour, believing she would become accustomed to her marriage and new life.

Still, I knew her best and wondered if Paolo was truly naive in female matters, despite his constant assurances of his experience and wisdom to the contrary. As I inserted her letter within Luca's book in my chest, I could not help but let escape a guttural cry for my dear young sister.

After the worst of the pain had passed, I broke the seal on Luca's letter.

Dear Signorina Soranzo,

Please accept this book as a memento of my admiration for my friend Paolo's sister and a pleasant memory of the scholarly love we shared. I hope it may also further inspire your own literary ambitions. Every day I will pray for you, as you promised to pray for me.

Luca Cicogna

This letter too I read several times. I felt there was more to it than the actual words on the page, but perhaps I was just searching for meaning that wasn't really there. *Admiration* and *scholarly love* seemed like much cooler words than the heat we shared in person, but he likely fretted that my mother would read it, and he was right to be concerned about that. A new worry leapt to the forefront: as of tomorrow, I would have many more mothers and sisters who might take a keen interest in any letter addressed to me from a man not my relative.

I wondered whether I should take the letter or leave it behind, burn it perhaps or ask Paolo to save it for me. But the thought of Luca's letter staying at our palazzo proved unbearable. After further study of the letter's nuances, I decided Luca had been wise to be so cool. Still, I buried the letter within the folds of a dress I was taking with me, at the bottom of the chest, alongside his sketch of the Barbari map.

Knowing I should get into the habit of praying on my knees before bed, I shrugged and instead huddled under the bedcovers, the rose clasped in my hands close to my heart. The stem was very long, with all thorns removed, and an old Venetian saying came to mind: *The longer the stem, the greater the love.*

The bed felt oceanic again in Rosa's absence, and I found myself praying anyway, for her safety and health if not her happiness, for Luca to be able to find a measure of contentment in his own marriage, and for me to find some joy in the convent and not abject misery.

Chapter 17

By the ringing of the midday *sext* bell, I was standing inside the nuns' choir at the Church of San Zaccaria, so cool in contrast to the day cooking up outside. I was not the only one taking my vows; two other girls from patrician families were there as well, the younger only eleven years old and with a noticeable limp. I did not know either of them well, as they had become postulants quite quickly. With the worries of papal interdict, the city's spiritual fathers were turning a blind eye to the compression or outright forgoing of the usual ceremonies.

After Papa brought me to the choir and kissed my forehead, he went to stand in the pews with Mama and Paolo alongside Auntie Leonarda, her husband, a few cousins, the families of the other postulants, and several benefactors of the convent. The most conspicuous absence was of course Rosa. My brow wrinkled at this glaring deficiency.

San Zaccaria was a breathtaking church—although not as magnificent as San Marco Basilica, as described to me by my father, of course; that was to be expected. I knew San Zaccaria well from my years attending Mass here as a boarding girl, the highlight being Bellini's altarpiece, its colours vibrant and fresh, installed just a few years before. But now I was seeing it with new eyes—a nun's eyes. I knew how many tens of thousands of ducats my sisters had collectively contributed in recent decades, and the result of their efforts could only be described as gloriously inspirational.

The altar sat within an apse with pointed arches, Gothic windows, and intricate carvings. Some said the whole design was in the French style, although the paintings in the vaulted ceilings were by Castagno. The black-and-pink-tiled floor was ancient, with some of it going back as far as the ninth century. Several tombs contained our order's holy relics, including the bones of San Zaccaria himself, which pilgrims from all over Christendom came to worship. The ornately carved wooden choir stalls lining the walls were polished to a shine, and in them sat nearly forty nuns, Auntie Livia among them smiling beatifically at me, waiting for Mass and the ceremony to start. Zanetta sat a few seats over from her, her expression sour. Perhaps it was her permanent disposition, as I had never seen her pleased.

Underneath the church was the crypt, which held the tombs of eight doges, the floor often covered in lagoon water that reflected the low vaulted ceilings. An elderly nun had a few times taken us fidgety youngsters there on a rainy day, Rosa and me and some others, and we'd spent our time ostensibly learning the history of the dead doges while gleefully splashing around, soaking our shoes and stockings. I remembered Rosa's babyish shrieks of delight and the nun's indulgent smiles at her charges.

A bride of Christ, I wore Rosa's wedding dress, complete with its San Zaccaria–crafted lace and threads of gold, and I pushed away thoughts of marrying Luca in it. I was taller than my sister, but the dressmaker had fabricated it such that Madelena had been quickly able to let it out to suit my height. Rosa and I were of similar frame otherwise, and only some spot cleaning and hasty mending had been required. I would barely wear it today, and then Papa would have Mama sell it to the second-hand clothing merchant.

Paolo was holding a velvet purse that contained a hundred-ducat contribution to San Zaccaria's coffers, my own much less expensive but equally required dowry. Papa had also promised me a twenty-five-ducat annuity for any expenses I incurred while living at the convent, plus the exclusive use of Madelena one day a week. Not as much as some but still a dignified amount for a noble nun.

I was jerked back to the undeniable present by the sweet chanting of the nuns and then the intoning of Patriarch Contarini, who wore scarlet bishopric robes and hat. Beside him stood iron-haired Mother Marina, the new abbess of San Zaccaria, who watched us as the patriarch spoke. I could not read her expression and had few memories of her from my time as a boarding girl. She had always seemed intimidating, although upon reflection she had always been cordial to me.

This went on for some time, with me hardly registering what was being said. As I dug my fingernails into my palms, all I could think was, *This is really happening to me, this is really happening to me, this is really happening to me.* I felt incorporeal, as if I were old, ghostly, bearded San Zaccaria himself in Castagno's painting on the ceiling, looking down on three brides poised to wed some spectral groom. With pity? I chided myself to think any saint, particularly one who sacrificed his own life to protect his infant son from Herod's murderous soldiers, could feel pity for a trio of young noblewomen dedicating their lives to Christ in a convent that many described as luxurious.

Eventually the patriarch approached us, placed a plain gold ring upon the third finger of each of our left hands, and proclaimed that we were married to Jesus Christ, our protector, and that we accepted this ring as a sign of faith from the Holy Ghost to be the wife of God.

Even as I assented to this with my words, within my mind I uttered snatches of Seneca, ignoring the heresy therein as I wedded God. *Sometimes to live is a courageous act.*

It was only when the patriarch commanded us to kneel on the hard floor and then lie prostrate with our lips touching the stone that I began to break down, and I registered that others in the church were already weeping. My fellow novices and other women, it seemed. Our mothers?

Then the patriarch threw a large black cloth over me, muffling the crying in the church and leaving me in utter darkness. The ethereal female voices chanted the *De Profundis*, the fact that it was a funeral hymn not escaping my notice. *Out of the depths I cry to you, O Lord. Lord, hear my prayer!*

I beat my palms upon the stone until they hurt. *Lord, hear my prayer. Lord, hear my prayer!*

Lord, why are you not hearing my prayer?

Chapter 18

After my new sisters offered to the heavens the last echo of *De Profundis*, Patriarch Contarini instructed us to rise and go through the door that led to the convent parlour, used only by us nuns.

Sister Elisabetta greeted us and had us remove our gowns, which the servants would return to our families, and don our habits, all except for the wimples and veils. Instead on our heads she placed wreaths of thorns. Yes, it hurt, the pressure on my skin imploring me to remember Christ's ultimate sacrifice. But all I could think of was my own.

"Forget your father's house, my new sisters, forget your families." Elisabetta said these harsh words as kindly as she could. The youngest novice, whom I would soon know as Santina, started crying again as she limped back toward the church door, though I and the other novice, Viena, more my age, managed to keep our composure.

Clad in our new black habits, we returned to the church, clutching our wimples and veils. Elisabetta escorted us, brandishing scissors, and asked us to kneel. This was the last part of the ceremony.

Our thorn wreaths were gingerly removed, and I felt my forehead for pricks, licking a speck of blood off my finger. We all unpinned our hair, allowing our locks to cascade down our backs to our waists, mine auburn, Santina's dark brown, Viena's golden. Elisabetta, her touch gentle, started by cutting my hair off just above my shoulders, the fallen strands tangling in a small pile next to my feet. I managed to grab a stray hair as it fell, and I entwined it in the palm of my hand, clutching it tightly, the final vestige of my old life, as I tried to banish thoughts of Luca marvelling over my tresses, my best feature. Auntie Livia had told me not to fret, that, unlike the stricter convents, San Zaccaria's required haircutting was symbolic rather than complete, and we would be allowed to grow our hair long again after the ceremony. But I still felt naked, as if I were wearing next to nothing, as exposed to the elements as an ecclesiastical criminal strung up in the *cheba* cage in Venice's main bell tower, left to starve to death. Viena was also outwardly stoic, but Santina was hysterical by the time her dark hair littered the marble. Elisabetta reverently placed each nest of hair on a silver platter with a crucifix on top, all three to be left on the altar overnight as a sign of our sacrifice, then burned in the morning.

Mother Marina approached us. In turn, she took the wimples from our hands and placed them on our heads, tucking in the remaining hair as tenderly as a mother putting her child to bed, then arranging the veil on top with pins counted out beforehand. My knees on the cold stone floor were screaming with pain, but even that torture was less agonizing than the shrieking inside my heart. Tears rolled down my cheeks in a steady cascade despite my best efforts to contain them.

After what seemed an eternity, the abbess asked us to stand as the bells rang. She came over to me first and embraced me. "Welcome, Daughter," she said, wiping my tears away with a small lace handkerchief. "You no longer bear your father's name. Welcome again to your new home where you will be reborn."

"Thank you," I murmured as she moved to Santina. How strange and awkward I felt, dressed in a habit, wearing a wimple and veil, a nun at last. I felt like a player in one of Paolo's mummeries, if women had been allowed to partake in such activities.

Mother Marina and Elisabetta ushered us toward the door to officially enter the convent parlour as the nuns sang the concluding hymn. I glanced back for one final look at my family, Mama crying into Paolo's chest as he vainly tried to soothe her, Papa standing silent beside her, Auntie Leonarda waving her lace handkerchief at me.

Resigned, I was about to turn to my new life when I noticed someone at the very back of the church. I could not believe it at first, but then those brown eyes locked with mine, and I felt that familiar fire.

Luca had come to see me marry Christ.

Santina gave my arm a pull, forcing me to keep moving. As Angela Riva clanked the door shut on the parlour, filled with my new sisters welcoming us, Auntie Livia ready to whisk me into a hug, even Zanetta deigning to acknowledge me, tables studded with platters of sweetmeats and pitchers of wine, a celebration ready to start, I wished I were as dead as my old self.

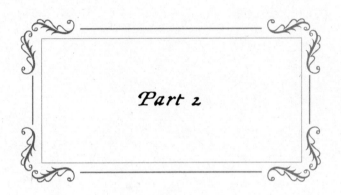

Part 2

Chapter 19

J ustina, wake up!"

I rolled over, still immersed in a dream, one that involved lying under soft sheets in a feather bed, Luca with me, keeping me safe from the papal army that was ransacking Venice outside his palazzo walls in pitched battle with Venetian mercenaries. Luca had barred the doors and windows, and we were both without care or worry, ensconced in our own little protected world. He had just been pulling my nightclothes up, starting at my ankle, lifting the fabric to my knee, like a butterfly on my skin, and then further . . .

"Justina, you must wake up!" Viena's urgent voice combined with the clanging of the church bells and the yips of Dolce to penetrate my sleep-addled mind.

Somewhere far inside popped a kernel of realization: there was no Luca, I was not in his bedchamber, and even though Venice was now officially at war with Pope Julius II and his League of Cambrai, the only battles fought thus far had been on the mainland, while Venice remained secure behind its watery fortress.

I bolted upright, my nightclothes gathered around my waist. I was safe, for now, but alone in bed. "Mass!" I ran my fingers through my shoulder-length hair, still unused to its shortness. It seemed to have hardly grown in the last month.

Viena peered at me with her big blue eyes, her own shortened hair covered by her veil. "You mustn't be late. It's Ascension, and Mother Marina made a point of saying we all need to be on time today. Here, let me help you dress." She pulled my habit off the hook on the wall.

I groaned as I rose and acquiesced to her ministrations. I wasn't sure I would become accustomed to such an early arousal, just before the sun broke through the night. Auntie Livia assured me it was just because of the recent calamities and that things were laxer during normal times.

Still, to be wrenched from such a dream . . .

After barring Dolce in my cell, Viena and I rushed through the corridors to the church. Our sisters were silent. The singing that usually reverberated within the marble walls, a glorious symphony of voices united in praising Jesus Christ, had been forbidden by the Warrior Pope, a particular blow for our chorally oriented convent as we attempted to properly celebrate the fortieth day of Easter, when Our Saviour ascended into Heaven to take His place at the right hand of Our Father.

Viena and I pressed our way to our assigned position as mute altos by Auntie Livia and Elisabetta. In addition to the dozen or so boarding girls, postulants, and foundling babies and toddlers left on the convent doorstep, all my sisters seemed to be there. I tried to ignore the wrinkled noses and harrumphs of those irritated by our tardiness, particularly the black looks thrown by Zanetta and Angela Riva, whose infrequent smiles revealed several rotted teeth. Auntie Livia had urged me to disregard them, but I still found any ill will directed at me difficult to discount. At least Mother Marina remained expressionless. I was so new, a lamb among both sheep and a few wolves, and I needed to prove my place in the meadow. Viena had become my only other friend and ally, as little Santina had been absorbed by her aunt Angela Riva and their relatives. The rivalry between these two growing factions, split by the contentious abbess vote, had seemed only to harden further with our induction.

Normally a joyous feast day, the Ascension service today was tinged with sadness. One baby inconsolably wailed throughout the entire service, symbolic of what we all had been feeling for the month since the interdict had been announced. The day after that announcement, Paolo had written to tell me that just before Venice received official word of her excommunication, Luca had married Elena Paruta in a rushed ceremony. And while I had known both events were coming, the news still hit me like two blows to the stomach. So while my fellow sisters wailed over His Holiness forbidding them to sing at a mass that was no longer official and the loss of all sacraments except confession, I wept for the final loss of my love.

Our sorrow had been compounded just over a week ago, when we Venetians learned of our shocking and ignominious defeat to His Holiness at the Battle of Agnadello, the first ever loss on Venetian soil in the magnificent near-millennium history of our Most Serene Republic. The defeat also accounted for our perfect mass attendance in the last few days. No one dared missed a precious opportunity to pray for our salvation, aided by the Senate's generous donation of two hundred ducats to each observant convent that prayed for our city's victory.

The dispatch had arrived, covered in gallows hastily drawn by the author, at the doge's palazzo on May 15, the day after the rout. An immediate cry of despair arose from the assembled patricians, Papa included. Not a few of them even wept at the loss, so panicked were they about Venice's future. They hoped to keep the news secret for as long as possible, a futile effort in our city, where secrets and gossip spread faster than the plague. Within hours everyone knew, including the convents' inhabitants, all of us wondering how long until the Warrior Pope himself rowed across the lagoon with his army, sacked our city, and allowed his soldiers to defile our women.

We nuns had all cried, and Mother Marina called for an emergency prayer session immediately, women and girls running to the church in various states of dress: habits with veils askew, nightclothes and bare hair, a few in fancy gowns with fancy hairstyles, the servants in simple dresses covered by aprons. We all fell to our knees and wailed to God until the choir mistress forced order upon us, and we began to recite, not sing. *In this valley of misery, we call on you for help. You are our lady of perpetual aid. Holy Virgin, pray for me . . . Pray for us.*

Pray for our families. Pray for our convent. Pray for our city, that the pope's army does not sack it.

Pray for Rosa. Pray for me. I don't want to be raped . . .

Two days later, Papa came to visit, holding court in the convent parlour for the many nuns who squeezed in to hear his details, just as they did for every patrician father and brother who brought precious news. He provided as much updated and accurate information as he could to counteract the absolute terror that had descended upon the canals, streets, homes, and churches like a miasma worse than the thickest fog. There had been much anger at the generals and—Papa told my aunt and me privately—at our doge, Leonardo Loredan, none too illustrious, whom some accused of being half-dead in his response, with no plans to visit and rally the troops. The government was dazed by indecisiveness, worried about food supplies and internal turbulence. Papa told me that, not surprisingly, none of the patricians were planning their annual summer exodus to the country. Being on the mainland was much too dangerous a proposition, especially since typically their wives and children would remain there while they travelled back and forth. No, this season all members of the patrician class were staying firmly in well-defended Venice.

The foul mood had continued unabated for days, even forcing the last-moment cancellation of today's much-anticipated Feast of the Ascension, when the doge married the sea in a splendid celebration replete with golden barges festooned with red and yellow Venetian flags, and polished gondolas filled beyond capacity with merry spectators. Mother Marina announced this cancellation at the conclusion of the service, and I tried to hide my disappointment and subsequent immediate guilt for feeling so. Ascension had always been one of my favourite days, and I had been looking forward to attending with my fellow sisters, finally released from the cloister for a few hours. But it was not to be, despite the Council of Ten pledging to add more security measures to ensure the city's safety.

At least Madelena would be coming shortly. It was my day for her, and she had missed last week due to the pandemonium. After Mass I changed out of my habit and into one of my old silk gowns to await her in the parlour. I brought my recent poetic attempts to consider, but I could not concentrate, and they all seemed trite anyway.

Madelena arrived later than normal with a basket and profuse apologies.

"The city is in complete chaos," she said as I ushered her into the privacy of my chamber, where Dolce greeted us both excitedly. I had missed the soothing lilt of her Ottoman accent. "The booths were already set up in the Piazza San Marco, but early this morning the Council of Ten ordered all the merchants to pack up their wares. They cursed and grumbled, but they're doing it." She set her bulging basket down on my bed. "I could see into the piazza from the gondola, and Teodor told me what he knows. There are armed soldiers everywhere."

I exhaled. "I worry about you roaming around. Paolo and Papa too, although they are men. At least I know Mama and Rosa are safe inside. What news of them all? I haven't seen Papa for nearly a week, and no one else from the family has come to visit since word of the battle arrived."

"Your father is barely at home, always at the doge's palazzo in endless meetings. He has your brother go to the piazza every day to mingle with the other men of the city and monitor what the commoners are saying. Even with all the extra men at the disposal of the Lords of the Night Watch, plus the maritime guards now patrolling the canals, the government fears an uprising."

Sitting on my bed, I wondered if Luca was with Paolo in the piazza. Or had he already joined the Great Council and so spent most of his time in the doge's palazzo? I pushed away such painful considerations. "So the worry is that Venice will fall, either by external or internal forces."

Madelena nodded, fear etched on her face. "It's terrifying to be out and about, even with Teodor mostly conveying me and a most capable defender at that. No one knows what will happen one moment to the next. Everyone fears the worst. And the worst can be beyond your imagination. My grandmother told me about the fall of Constantinople. Murder and suicide, plunder and rape, thousands taken as slaves, houses destroyed, families torn apart."

"Oh, Madelena." I hugged her, as had become our custom. Papal forces sacking Venice, slaughtering men, and assaulting women was simply unthinkable.

"Your mother has taken to her room, crying and saying endless rosaries. She is frantic about all of you. You know how her nerves have not recovered since the stillbirth. And now with you and your sister both out of the house, and your father and brother barely there, she has no one to comfort her."

"Poor Mama." How I wished I could tend to her, knowing her fragile health. Our separation gnawed at my heart. "And how fares Rosa? I have not had a visit from her since I took my vows, and the way you describe the city now, I don't suppose I will any time soon. Zago will never permit her to come."

"I did bring you letters." She produced three from her basket, along with a new undergarment, several ribbons, a bundle of blank paper, two bottles of ink, three goose quills, and a small square drawing of the Madonna and Child to hang on my almost-bare cell walls, which I had requested from Papa soon after I took the veil. Besides a large crucifix, I had tacked up only Luca's Barbari sketch, to remind me of the world beyond the thick convent walls. "Here's one from your mother and two from your sister, one from before the battle, and another from just two days ago, when your mother finally gave me leave to see her. I must admit she does look even more miserable than before Agnadello, but then again we all feel that way."

I tore open the missives. Mama's was short, more a prayer for my welfare and a desperate wish to see me. Rosa's first, dated the day before the battle, was filled with small anecdotes about life in the Zane palazzo and a few complaints about Zago. The second was full of laments for the future of Venice and wishes for safety for our family, plus a mention of how sick to her stomach she had been feeling for the past few days.

"I need to see her." Like a caged animal, I paced back and forth. "Mama too. I cannot bear to be away from them."

"Is that possible?" Madelena looked doubtful. "Teodor is waiting for me, if you think you can leave. It is chaotic out there, but with Teodor I think we will be safe enough."

"I must consult with Auntie Livia. She will know how to obtain permission from Mother Marina. She'll likely be in the garden at this hour, and I need to take Dolce outside anyway." He yapped at his name, and the three of us headed to the garden.

In the corridor, we passed Zanetta, Angela Riva, and little Santina. Since we had taken our vows at the same ceremony, I had initially hoped Santina and I might be friends, despite our age difference. But her mind was so poisoned against me and my circle, she stuck her tongue out and made a grimace any time she saw me or Viena. This time was no different, and her aunt Angela did not help matters. "Now, now, dear niece, we mustn't waste our efforts on such tramps and shrews." She patted Santina on the head indulgently, then turned to me. "I hope you are not about to find trouble, Sister Soranzo." She dipped her head, knowing full well the insult. *Signora* was the term of respect for a bride of Christ; calling a woman of equal status *Sister* was demeaning. I was incredulous at such talk and hurled a glance at Zanetta, but she merely stayed silent, suspicion in her eye, as if she were convinced I was on the verge of some crime.

Keeping Livia's advice to turn the other cheek against such antics firmly in mind, I led my motley crew to the nearer of the convent's two courtyards, a garden redolent with rosemary, pine, and oleander. It was one of my favourite places to retreat, Dolce's too, and it felt especially peaceful today, perhaps because of how much disorder reigned outside. The oleander bloomed red, pink, and yellow, its scent intensified by the heat, and Dolce did his business under the blossoms. A magnificent wisteria crept along one of the stone walls all the way to the roof, only a few purple flowers remaining among the green leaves, and a fig tree and a magnolia were planted diagonally to each other. The other walls were covered in thick ivy in verdant shades.

Elisabetta and Auntie Livia were on their hands and knees, immersed in conversation as they weeded the herb portion of the garden: lavender, basil, oregano, chives, ginger, and many more I could not identify. Several chickens pecked their way among the shrubs. Dolce barked wildly at them, stopping only when I shushed him, though he still growled. The chickens took no heed.

Livia smiled as she looked up. Then she noticed my expression. "Justina, my dear, what's wrong?" She removed her work gloves as she stood.

I told her my worries about both Mama and Rosa, and her own face mirrored my concern. "Auntie, do you think Mother Marina would give us permission to visit them?"

"Given my sister's health woes of the recent past, she might. Except for the servants, she has not let anyone leave in the past week. But you said we had access to the Soranzo gondolier, so I will inquire immediately. So sorry, Betta, to leave you stranded with the work half-completed."

Elisabetta came over to us and put a comforting hand on my aunt's arm. Ever since I'd known her as a boarding girl, Elisabetta had always struck me as lovely and kind, with reassuring hazel eyes and a thick brown

braid laced with silver strands that fell down her back to her waist. She'd
been my aunt's closest friend ever since I could remember. "Don't give it
a second thought, Livy. You must tend to your sister and niece, if Mother
Marina will allow it." One of the chickens, a russet brown with a bright
red comb, wandered over and gave Livia's shoe a peck, while Dolce glow-
ered menacingly.

Livia scooped up the bird and smoothed the silky feathers on its head.
"Will you make sure Enrica is returned to my room later? I'm not sure how
late we'll be."

"Of course." Elisabetta accepted the bird Livia passed on to her, cooing
as if it were her own pet instead of Livia's. "I'll bring Dolce back to your
room too, Justina."

"Thank you, Elisabetta."

"Yes, thank you, Betta." Livia turned to me. "I'll speak directly to Mother
Marina, and then meet you in the parlour. Assume we'll be granted permission and put on your habit and veil."

I nodded, relieved by her confidence. And, I had to admit, despite the
fear that gripped our city, despite my grim mission to check the welfare of
mother and sister, I was selfishly thrilled to be leaving the convent for the
first time. I just hoped Zanetta wouldn't see us.

Chapter 20

Outside in the campo, I inhaled deeply. Not that it smelled particularly nice here. It was just pure instinct, the feeling of release, after a month of cloister. Such freedom was something we San Zaccaria nuns were allowed in special circumstances, but not with great frequency, and this was my first experience of it. I luxuriated for a moment in my liberty, however supervised and circumscribed.

Quickly though, reality and worry beat down like the sun, which was as hot as the San Zaccaria ovens churning out sweetmeats for a feast day. A group of soldiers marched through the campo brandishing swords, while near the church a white-haired monk in a simple brown robe and dirty bare feet preached to a small crowd of beggars and servants who clearly came from all corners of Christendom. "Our sisters, the brides of Christ, must repent for their egregious sins, the breaking of their sacred vows, their unnatural fornication, since their unholy behaviour risks the shame and destruction of our Most Serene City by the Warrior Pope!"

"Ignore him," Livia intoned under her breath as we threw our veils over our hair and followed Madelena to where Teodor had tied up the gondola, so close to Luca's palazzo. I could not help glancing around in search of him but saw only soldiers and gondoliers.

Teodor bowed to both Livia and me, taking our hands to gingerly transfer us into the swaying vessel. He gave me the smallest smile before his expression slipped back into seriousness as he untied the gondola. We three women settled ourselves under the *felze* as the Marangona work bell rang, signalling the midday meal for the Arsenale shipbuilders. Back in business after the recent fire, their work seemed especially urgent these days, the pace at the shipbuilding yard known to be nothing less than frenetic.

After a final glance at Luca's palazzo, hoping in vain to see him at the balcony, I turned my gaze to the fishing boats and naval ships bobbing in the lagoon along with one trading vessel and the solemn workers stripping the forlorn barges of their colourful decorations.

Before I knew it, Teodor was pulling up at the water entrance of my former home, and I felt a surge of nostalgia and an urgent longing to be with Mama. After disembarking, I ran upstairs, Livia trailing behind me in a more dignified manner, and Madelena bringing up the rear.

Bursting into Mama's darkened and stifling room, I found her prone in bed under the covers, clutching a rosary. She seemed truly startled to see me, as if I were an apparition. I stroked her face, the skin clammy and pale. "Mama, you must eat something, drink something." I gestured at the strawberries and watered wine Madelena had left on a tray by the bed, and a small swarm of fruit flies scattered in all directions before resettling themselves.

"Dear Sister." Livia pushed open the shutters and a sunlit breeze flooded in, helping to disinfect the stale air. "You must sit up and do as your daughter says. You must build your strength."

Mama's eyes seemed to come into focus as she peered at us. "Justina? Livia?"

"Yes, it is us," Livia said briskly as both she and I pulled back the heavy covers and helped Mama into a sitting position. I took the cup and brought it to Mama's dry lips for a sip.

"They let you out of the convent? But what about the war? It's not safe!"

"Shush and don't fret." Shooing away the flies, Livia proffered her a strawberry, and Mama took a tentative bite. "Mother Abbess was less worried about the papal army accosting two innocent nuns on their way across the Grand Canal and more about the health of our family."

"Besides, we had Teodor to guard us," I added, forcing her to take another swallow.

Mama's lips curved into a weak smile. "He is a loyal servant."

"We are lucky to have him and Madelena both."

Mama nodded and finished the strawberry.

"Mama, does your ill health have anything to do with the baby? Should we send for the doctor or midwife?"

Her eyes welled. "I mourn for her still, and I do miss you and Rosa terribly. But no, my affliction is not of the body this time." She wiped away the tears that trickled down her cheeks. "It does me good to see you both."

"There has been much to become accustomed to, Sister, in a very short while." Livia caressed her forehead, much as I used to with Rosa, and I felt a pang at this sisterly bond. "Shall we pray together?" She made a sign of the cross, then took the rosary that had slipped onto the bed and held it, along with Mama's hands. "*O Lord open my lips, O God come to my help, O Lord hurry to help me . . .*"

I grew restless and instead began tidying, something I could leave for Madelena, but I suspected Mama had forbidden our maid to touch the contents of her room in the last few days. I folded the unneeded warm blanket Mama had been using, leaving her covered with just a light linen sheet more appropriate for the weather, and straightened her toilet items. I then neatly stacked a pile of letters and papers that had accumulated like scattered leaves on the floor.

Curiosity overcame me, and I shuffled through the letters to see who had written them. Some were from Livia and me of course, and many were from Rosa. A skim of their contents revealed similarities to the missives she sent me, nothing new or unusual.

The one at the bottom was in a hand I did not recognize, although the script was clearly feminine and inscribed on heavy, expensive paper. I glanced over at Livia and Mama, chanting the prayers of the rosary in unison, eyes closed. A seagull screamed outside and a puff of hot air rustled the letter, emitting a faint floral perfume.

Signed at the bottom by Veronica da Spin, *La Diamante*.

Why would any courtesan be contacting Mama? I felt guilty reading her private correspondence, but I could not help myself and started from the top. The letter was dated two days prior. However, it was not as I had thought addressed to Mama, but to Papa.

> *Your Most Excellent Lordship Soranzo,*
> *Nicolo, I will skip the usual pleasantries and not delay in telling*
> *you what I require. As you are well aware, you over several years*

and more recently your son Paolo owe me an impressive amount of money for my services—one hundred ducats. You certainly have been reliable clients, and I do remember you both with fondness.

However, I sadly must set aside such warm thoughts and conduct business. In light of recent events and Venice's uncertain future, my lawyer has advised me to expedite my collection efforts. I know governmental affairs preoccupy you, which I suppose is why my previous letters to you have gone unanswered.

The time has come. I require immediate payment—in full. If I do not hear from you in five days' time, I shall be forced to escalate matters, and I think we both would agree that would not be welcomed.

Knowing something of your family's ongoing financial troubles, compounded I can only imagine by war and disruption of trade routes, I realize funds may be difficult to obtain so quickly and thus can offer you an alternative arrangement to discharge the debt. I know your eldest daughter has recently taken the veil at the convent of San Zaccaria. While she is not a conventional beauty, I do believe there are certain men who would pay handsomely for the privilege of deflowering her. If you agree to such an arrangement by the specified date, I would consider your debt to me satisfied.

I look forward to your imminent reply and remain faithfully yours,

La Diamante

She had signed her name with a flourish.

Like an anvil, the letter dropped to my lap, along with my hands. Livia and Mama prayed on, innocent of my alteration. Now I knew why Mama was so upset. It went beyond grief and concern over the fate of our city, beyond an unfaithful husband, which was common enough. It involved the whoring of her daughter, a new nun. Me. Would Papa even consider such an arrangement? I was horrified to realize that he might if he were financially desperate enough. Mama would know the same. And yet he clearly had not been replying to La Diamante, which gave me a modicum of hope.

Could Mama sell her jewellery to save my virtue? I knew that over the years and for Rosa's wedding she'd had to pawn her gems and jewels down to the bare minimum to be respectable in noble circles. Would what remained add up to a hundred ducats?

Might she be able to raid her dowry? No. That was tied up in real estate and other illiquid assets, so not accessible enough.

La Diamante had intimated she would involve others. Those muscled men I'd seen outside the draper's? Whom would they hurt exactly? Papa and Paolo? What about Mama? Rosa?

And her lawyers too. Would she sue Papa? Could he lose the palazzo, our ancestral home? Although Papa had already used it as collateral for the latest shipping venture he had gambled on, so that would not even be feasible.

And so would Papa agree to whore me to repay his debts? This was a horrific thought in so many ways.

No wonder Mama was so stricken. Looking at her and Livia continuing to chant the rosary, I shared her sentiments but felt no compulsion to unite with them in prayer. It seemed far too late for that.

Chapter 21

Knowing my aunt and I must return to the convent by night-fall, I left Livia with Mama so Teodor could take me to see Rosa, Madelena accompanying me. The Grand Canal was still busier than on a normal workday and nothing like the festive day it was supposed to be. Many of the boats were overflowing with goods and wares that would go unsold, and more than a few merchants seemed especially surly, presumably due to the money they would lose, not to mention the extreme heat and generalized fear, embodied by the presence of so many soldiers.

In a state of numbness, I dabbed the sweat from my brow with a lace handkerchief as the gondola glided to a stop at the Zane water entrance. Teodor hopped out, tied up the gondola, and then assisted both me and Madelena onto the landing. His grip on my arm seemed exceptionally firm, as if he were trying to control his strength.

Maria, the large Zane maid whom I recognized from the night Rosa had been forced to stay here, greeted me, if it could be called a greeting. Thankfully the Zane men were at the doge's palazzo with my father and the other government officials, and even Signora Zane was not in, ironically having just departed for San Zaccaria to visit Zanetta. Rosa was here, but Maria said she was not to be disturbed.

"And why not?" I attempted to keep my voice calm as my eyes adjusted to the dim interior light. I needed to see my sister now more than ever. "I've gotten special dispensation from my abbess to visit Rosa because she wrote to tell me she is ill."

"Ill? She's not ill." Maria laughed harshly.

"My maid was able to visit her just two days ago, so if you'll permit me to see for myself . . ." I forged ahead, Madelena at my side, but Maria, with the bulk of a basilica and the strength of stone, held fast to my shoulder, and I tried unsuccessfully to wrench myself free.

"I'm sorry, Signora, but I have been given strict instructions that your sister is not to be disturbed."

"But she will need me if she is unwell!"

Maria did not relent, but her expression turned from firmness to something resembling pity. "I cannot let you up or I'll be fired, and I can't afford that, especially in these troubled times. But I can tell you this." She looked askance and lowered her voice. "If I know anything about women's woes, I'd say your sister is with child."

"With child?" Madelena and I repeated in unison. I blinked, stunned to my core for the second time that day.

"She's vomited every morning this week, and she's pale and dizzy. I've seen it dozens of times over the years. And she's young, and Lord Zane, if you'll pardon my crassness, beds her just about every night. It's not at all surprising. A maid knows." She threw a nod at Madelena, who bobbed her head in return. "It'll be obvious soon enough."

"Is she . . . all right?" I had to find out what I could, and Maria seemed to be softening.

"She needs to adjust to being a wife and now a mama. She's younger than most, but she'll get there. We women do, even you noblewomen, if you don't think me impudent to say so. Easier to just give in, or pretend to. Men are the only ones who can partake in mummery, but I'd say women are by far the better players."

"You said she wasn't allowed to see anybody today. Why? What changed in the last two days?"

"I imagine it's because Signora Zane is out today. Every other time your maid or someone from your family comes, Signora Zane is nearby. Can't keep an eye on her this time." A bang echoed through the palazzo, and Maria looked around guiltily. "You'd better go. Can't let it be known I was telling you all this or they'll have my head."

I wanted nothing more than to dash up the stairs screaming Rosa's name, but that course of action did not seem likely to help anyone. And getting Maria into trouble would not be wise either. She might be our only conduit to Rosa. "I'll go, but I beg of you to tell Rosa I was here, that I tried to see her. Will you do that for me?"

She looked dubious, her arms folded over her ample bosom, inspecting both me and Madelena. Finally, she nodded, and when she spoke, her tone was surprisingly gentle. "I had a sister. She died in childbirth a few years back, and now I help support her brood with my wages. Miss her terribly. We were very close. I'll tell your sister you were here, for the sake of sisterhood."

"Thank you so much."

She smiled what seemed a genuine smile, if only for a moment, then opened the doors to let us out onto the landing before quickly shutting and bolting them.

Madelena and I stood in the sunlight, blinking from the brightness. Teodor looked at us expectantly. "That was fast. How is Signorina Rosa?"

It wasn't Teodor's place to ask, and he should have called her Signora, but at this point I hardly cared about decorum. "We weren't allowed to see her."

With a puzzled expression, he seemed to want to say more, but then resumed his workmanlike demeanour. "Where to then, Signora Justina?"

"Back home. I need to say goodbye to Mama, then Livia and I must return to the convent before sunset."

Under the *felze*, Madelena and I drew the curtains as much for shade as for privacy.

"With child. I do not know what to think. I know I'm supposed to be happy, but I'm not. And I certainly don't want to tell Mama just yet. What do you think?"

Madelena nodded. "It's only speculation on the maid's part, and even if Rosa is, many girls lose them early, especially ones so young. Best not to worry your mother before it's necessary."

The gondola rocked suddenly, and another gondolier hurled a string of insults at Teodor. Madelena poked her head through the curtains, throwing a ribbon of light onto the bottom of the boat. "Everything all right?" I could not make out his response over the other boatman's shouting about Teodor's ineptitude.

Teodor rowed away with vehemence, water slapping against the side of the gondola.

Madelena nearly lost her balance as she closed the curtains and resettled herself. "Apparently Teodor almost rowed into him by accident. He was none too pleased."

I could not fret about Teodor's conduct, my mind consumed with other worries. There was too much to absorb. Could I help raise the funds to preserve my honour? Did Livia have some money stashed away? And now Rosa with child. "I need you to keep trying to visit Rosa, to make sure she's all right, and to let me know. I wonder if they're reading her letters too. Why are they being like this?" Tears welled up in anger.

"Of course I will. I'll find out everything I can."

The gondola pulled up by our water entrance, and Teodor jumped out to tie it up. His mouth was a thin line as he assisted me out. The late afternoon light cast long shimmery shadows on the canal water, and I saw my own reflection break apart as another gondola disturbed the water and disgorged a tall young man onto the stone steps, one I'd believed I'd never see again.

Chapter 22

Teodor, Madelena, and I all froze. I from the emotion that overcame me, stronger than the thick heat, Teodor and Madelena, I could only assume, awaiting my reaction.

Luca broke the silence. "I wasn't expecting to see you. How do you fare, Signorina Justina?" He gave a small shake of his head, the sunshine catching the caramel, umber, and tawny strands that made up his hair. "I mean, Signora."

I could not help but smile. "I am unaccustomed to that honorific myself."

My words unlocked action in my servants. Teodor bowed to Luca and exchanged words with Luca's gondolier as he attended to a matter at the back of the gondola, while Madelena remained ever vigilant of propriety. "Perhaps, Signora Justina, you should come in from the sun? You've forgotten to raise your veil."

My hands flew to the veil that clustered around my shoulders. Far from sun damage to my skin, Madelena was correctly worried about the damage to my honour. Not that my honour might matter for much longer. But I would not waste my time with Luca thinking such thoughts. "Yes, it is quite strong." Perhaps due to my own desperation, I was struck with a bolt of boldness as Luca eyed me uncertainly. "Would you join me, Lord Cicogna, for a moment in the shade?"

Relief flooded his features. "I would be delighted."

Teodor, rope in hand, watched with wide eyes as Madelena held open the door to our main floor storage room, and Luca followed me into the damp coolness. He cleared his throat. "I came to tell your brother that a Cicogna ship arrived this morning." That must have been the trading vessel I'd noticed in the lagoon. "It was most unexpected. That means some traffic is still coming through, so the Soranzo one might arrive soon."

"That is most fortunate news for your family, especially given the current situation." I was pleased for Luca but could not help but feel a shudder of jealousy that it was not my father's ship, just in time to repay La Diamante.

"I shall check to see if Lord Paolo has returned during our absence." Madelena gave Luca a small curtsy and me a *be careful* look before heading up the stone steps.

"I'm here to see your brother," he said, "but I thank the Almighty that I'm seeing you instead." He picked up my hand. "May I?"

I nodded, a shiver running through me as his lips met the skin of my hand.

"Have you been praying for me as you promised?"

"I have." I inhaled deeply. "For your new bride as well. And for all of Venice."

He did not let go of my hand as he raised his head to look into my eyes. "Thank you. And likewise. I pray the Lord keeps you safe, especially during these dark times."

I knew I would have to confess my sin of lust, and yet I wanted to keep it to myself, like the coordinates of a buried treasure.

Luca kept looking at me, and I felt he could read my thoughts. "Nowadays, I walk the long way to the doge's palazzo. The way that takes me through Campo San Zaccaria." He caressed my palm gently with his thumb, and I quivered. "I touch the wall of the convent as I pass, and I imagine it is you: the stone your skin. I close my eyes and imagine it is your cheek that I am stroking, your neck . . ."

He took his other hand and did just that, his fingers upon my face as gentle as a dove, wings brushing away the tear that escaped. I knew I had to stop, stop him, stop myself, from the wanting and the sinning, but I was powerless as perhaps the devil himself pulled me closer to Luca's body.

"We mustn't," I whispered as he took me in his arms. "It is a sin."

"I know. And I no longer care." He leaned down slightly. Our lips brushed, and it was like the sun bursting. I started shaking, and he shook too.

A throat cleared, and I jumped away from him. He looked as guilty as I felt. Madelena stared at her feet. "Lord Cicogna, I'm sorry to report that Lord Paolo is not yet home. Signora Justina, your aunt prepares to return to the convent with you."

"Thank you, Madelena." Although I wasn't sure if what I felt toward my maid was gratitude or anger. "Would you please prepare a refreshment for Lord Cicogna? I will be up shortly." I needed more time, just a few moments longer. It might be the last.

She curtsied slowly and returned upstairs.

"I am so sorry, Justina." Luca looked stricken. "I do not know what I was thinking. I have caused you to sin."

"And I have caused you the same. You are married now." If I had to sin, let it be with Luca and not the highest bidder. I shook my head, forcing such thoughts away.

He dipped his head. "And a miserable existence it is."

"You mustn't say that. She is your wife and will be the mother of your children."

He exhaled. "I do not mean to speak ill of my wife, but you are the only one I can be truthful with. I do not love her and never will."

"Love comes with time. Everyone says so." The image of a distraught Rosa flitted into my head. Love was not coming for her. Was love even possible with a man such as Zago? Although Luca was nothing like my brother-in-law.

He nodded but looked unconvinced. "Yes, everyone does say so. My parents, your brother, the priest. Even Elena herself." He ran a hand through his hair, mussing it until he looked even more handsome, if possible. "However, she knows far less than she thinks on many other matters, so I am not certain I can believe her on this one."

"I am sorry. I hope"—I swallowed hard—"I hope you can come to love her, or at least find peace with her."

He groaned, his expression etched with misery. "I feel as if I am going to crack." He took a step toward me again, but this time I was prepared and retreated a step. "I apologize again," he said, his eyes tormented. "I should not be telling you any of this. It is unfair to you. It's just . . . It's just that I did not expect to see you here. Or ever again. And to see you on the steps, the sun lighting your hair, your hair so short now, but still beautiful—" He put his hands against his lips as if in prayer. "It was too much. I could not help myself. Forgive me."

"There is nothing to forgive." For I was as much to blame. I was drawn to him like a hummingbird to a flower, my heart beating as fast as those wings, but I had taken a holy vow. I so wished I could tell him my troubles, about La Diamante, but it was not proper to share them outside of family. Especially not with him.

He stepped back, his hands dropping to his sides. "I will go now and see Paolo later."

I knew he should go, and yet I did not want him to. "Would you leave him a message?"

He shook his head. "Perhaps it is better that only your maid and gondolier know I have been here. I will see him soon enough. My own gondolier awaits." He brought his long fingers back to his lips as if about to blow me a kiss and then thought better of it, wiping his cheek instead. He turned to go, then stood in the doorway, the sunlight casting a halo around him. "Farewell, Signora Soranzo." He spoke very formally.

As did I. "Farewell, Lord Cicogna."

And then the doorway was empty. As Madelena arrived with two cups of wine, I brought my own fingers to my lips as if to forever press the memory of his kiss against them.

Chapter 23

After bidding Mama farewell, her eyes listless despite our pleading smiles of encouragement, Livia and I sat in the gondola for the short journey back to San Zaccaria. The shadows had lengthened, and the lagoon had emptied of all but the naval ships. Teodor rowed strongly, clearly mindful that he still had to return Papa home from the nearby doge's palazzo.

Livia confided her puzzlement at my mother's turn for the worse. "I know everyone shares the worry over Venice's defeat, and I know too that my sister is still fragile, but I do not think either of those things accounts for her depth of despair." Livia wrung her hands, her veil loose around her neck. "I have found that in her darker moments, prayer always soothed her, but my holy remedy did not work this time."

As Teodor slowed down just past the doge's palazzo, I fretted over whether to tell her, over exactly what to tell her. I was not sure I could keep any news from Livia, and besides, she might be able to contribute some ducats to cut this Gordian knot.

"What say you, Niece? You are very quiet." Livia opened the *felze* curtains as Teodor tied up the boat to a red-and-white striped pole, and the cantaloupe-coloured facade of the Palazzo Cicogna slapped me in the face. It was a beautiful building with lancet windows, white trim, and green awnings that shaded two small balconies. And on one of the balconies stood Luca. I could not tear my eyes from him, wondering at the cruelty of God to continually test me.

Luca did not notice me at first, his gaze far into the darkening lagoon, the clouds black splotches on the purple- and pink-streaked sky. And then a woman came out to stand beside him. Not a woman, but a girl truly, not much older than Rosa or me. His wife, Elena, who companionably hooked her plump arm through his. I did not think she was pretty.

Livia's concerned eyes followed mine, and she grasped my shoulder to turn me away from the sight and throw my veil over my face.

But it was too late. Out of the corner of my eye, I had seen Luca take note of me, his posture stiffening, his wife emitting a loud girlish laugh and then nattering on.

Teodor too noticed the scene, and he marched Livia and me in the direction of San Zaccaria. Tears streamed down my cheeks under my veil, and Livia held me tightly by the arm. The gondolier bid us an uncertain farewell at the convent entrance as Livia thanked him and the late evening *compline* bell rang. After bowing, he dashed off.

When I had left the conventual edifice earlier in the day, I had been relieved to escape from its confines. And yet here I stood on the threshold hours later, deeply grateful to return to its substantial sanctuary. I wiped away my tears with the backs of my hands as a tabby cat lurking nearby stared at us with its yellow eyes.

As was our convent's custom, two sisters guarded the entrance until everyone in the convent retired, although such a feeble defence would be completely ineffectual against an actual threat such as armed papal troops, a ritual of theatre rather than true security. Inside the parlour the guards tonight were Zanetta and Angela Riva, the last two people I wanted to greet me. *Greeted* is not an accurate way to put it, however. *Sneered* would be more apt. They sat with an empty wine bottle on the table as well as the remains of a fragrant *torta greca*.

Anger flared through me at the sight of them. Or it was the sin of wrath: hatred. At them and their gang, who despised Livia, Elisabetta, Mother Marina, Viena, and all whom I held dear in my new home. At Zanetta's brother, for making Rosa so miserable. At her mother, for keeping my sister hostage. Horror at the thought of having to whore myself to some rich old man eager to take a virgin's virtue, and bitterness at being separated from Luca for eternity.

Zanetta smirked as she raised her cup and took a long swallow. "How was Rosa? We all heard you received permission to visit her and your mother. Only the Lord knows why our abbess would permit such an indulgence, now of all times."

I opened my mouth to say something, I didn't even know what, but Livia simply stated that we were tired and wished them both a good slumber before guiding me through the otherwise empty parlour and directly to Mother Marina's office.

"You've got to ignore the termagant. I've been doing that ever since the day we took vows together, Zanetta, Elisabetta, and I. I've despised her ever since, but I knew even as a young girl that the best way to tame her was to ignore her." She knocked on our abbess's door and entered.

Mother Marina looked up from writing at her desk and crossed herself. "Thank You, Lord, You who has seen fit to bring my sisters safely home."

"Yes, Mother Marina," said Livia. "Thank you for allowing us this visit." I stared at the terrazzo floor flecked with pink and green, still in a stupor, trying to rein in both my anger and my despair, thinking I was too cowardly to confess my sins of lust and wrath. "My niece is very fatigued, so please excuse her."

"Of course, my dears, of course. It has been an exceedingly long day for you both." She arose to cross the room and lightly touched each of our heads. "May God bless you with a sound night's sleep." She was being so kind. I bitterly doubted that Angela Riva as abbess would have even considered permitting us to leave the convent.

I anticipated only nightmares if I were to welcome slumber at all as Livia led me to my cell, where she shut the door firmly. Dolce barked with joy at our arrival. "Hush, little one." She took out a treat I had stashed in one of my trunks, and Dolce gnawed on it contentedly.

Then she turned to me as I sat on the edge of my bed and started again to cry. She put an arm around my shoulders and handed me a handkerchief.

"Are you all right? I think this is not over Zanetta but rather Luca."

Luca, Rosa, my father's debt, and what seemed like the only solution to discharge it. It occurred to me that if Luca were my husband, his family's wealth could help pay for my father's bad business sense. Tears shuddered my breathing, and my face contorted to stem them. Finally I shook my head and dabbed my cheeks, the lace feeling rough despite its fine quality. "Seeing Luca again . . . it just brought it all back . . . What I have lost . . . I am trying to fulfill my vows, truly I am, to remember my true husband is Jesus. But . . ."

She brought me closer. "There, there. You are not the only nun in this convent to feel this way, you realize that? Many of our sisters had hoped to marry, had attachments at least, and some left an *inamorato*, or one they hoped to be such a sweetheart, behind. We know it is our duty as the daughters of Venice. But that knowledge does not make it any easier."

I shook my head again and sniffled. "No, it does not."

"One's heart does ease with time, from my observations. I've been in this convent for twenty years, and I've seen . . ." She smiled with what seemed nostalgia. "Well, I've seen much. I've even seen it all. Some of our sisters give in and find salvation in the rhythms of conventual life. Some find the satisfaction of attachment in their friendships, as I have. Many busy themselves with the day-to-day work of running our abbey, which allows us to use our minds and skills and even hands and political acumen in a way we never could as wives and mothers. I suspect you will fall into the latter category, and so you must discover the gifts you will bestow upon your sisters."

"Like you have, helping Mother Marina become abbess?" For I realized she'd done just that, behind the scenes.

"I am not sure I would state it so baldly." She smiled ruefully. "Better to develop such a productive ability than do nothing and fall prey to the petty, useless gossip in which many of our sisters sadly indulge. Though I am sorry to see our sisterhood fracturing in two in the aftermath of the contentious abbess vote. I'm not sure Angela Riva and Zanetta will ever forgive me. But that is the reality of politics, I suppose, whether at the Great Council or in a humble nunnery."

I nodded. Yes, I needed to bring my own gifts to my new home, not resist them, not sway to and fro like the tidal waters of the lagoon, but rather chart my own course through the shallows like an experienced boat-man. But what gifts?

"Auntie, do you hope to become abbess someday?"

"I will admit to only you and Elisabetta that I do harbour such ambi-tions. I am still young, but if I have learned anything at all here it is that one must position oneself early to rise to the top of the convent's hierarchy. Mother Marina has been a most formidable teacher on whom to model myself. It is not unlike those young noblemen who strive to join the Coun-cil of Ten someday. Even to become doge."

"You know I will wholeheartedly support you in such endeavours."

"I have not a doubt, as my loyal kin."

I took a deep breath. "Auntie, there is more I must tell you. I am vexed beyond Lord Cicogna and Zanetta. For I learned several things on our outing, and I cannot bear all these family burdens on my own."

"Of course. Tell me everything. You need not bear anything alone." She looked at me expectantly.

"First, Rosa is with child."

Livia arched a brow. "Well, that's to be expected. Many a wife becomes big with child soon after marrying."

"I realize that, but I still feel uneasy about it. I'm not sure she herself even knows, and when she does, whether she'll know what to do or be properly cared for. She is so very young."

"That she is. But what do you mean, if she knows? How could she not?"

"The maid speculated. Apparently Rosa has been sick every morning for the last week."

Livia tsked. "Poor dear. She is as sheltered as any new noble bride."

"Perhaps I would feel better if I had actually seen Rosa."

"You did not see her?"

"The maid would not allow me in."

"But you're her sister!" My aunt seldom betrayed any emotion beyond happiness and serenity, but I could tell now that anger simmered behind her eyes.

"Signora Zane was here, visiting Zanetta, and evidently Rosa can see visitors only if she is in the palazzo."

"That is indeed troubling. And would explain why you looked even more ready than usual to strike Zanetta." She patted my arm. "I do not think we can tell your mother yet, in her state. And your father is not the right one at this point either. Perhaps we can enlist Paolo to assist us. I shall pray over what to do."

I took my aunt's hand, warm and soft, glad she had agreed with my own assessment and would share the worry. "Thank you, Auntie."

"You said you learned several things. What else?"

I exhaled loudly before telling her about Papa's letter from La Diamante and her proffered arrangement. By the end of my tale, Livia's eyes were bulging and her mouth agape.

Her mouth contorted with vehemence before spitting out her words. "She's a common whore. And my brother-in-law Nicolo! To distress your mother so, and to consider such a devil's bargain with your virtue!"

"In fairness, we do not know what Papa is planning."

"I apologize, Justina. He is your father, and the Bible does command us to honour our parents. But I have known him a long time, and sometimes . . ." She did not finish that thought.

"Auntie, might you have the money?"

"Oh darling, if I had that kind of money, I would give it to you before we finished reciting the Lord's Prayer. I will contribute what I can, but I don't have much with me here at the convent. And I'm not sure telling any other members of the Nani family of my brother-in-law's financial woes would be prudent. He owes my father and cousins much already, and they are none too pleased about it."

"What about my aunt Leonarda?" I felt a momentary surge of hope, although I hadn't seen her since she'd brought her grandchild for me to bless in the days after I took the veil.

"Your father's sister?" She sighed. "I'm sure she would love to help her brother, but I know her husband feels much like my Nani relatives—he's been called on one too many times and thus does not think too highly of your father's mercantile sense. Besides, she has a mouth bigger than the Piazza San Marco."

My shoulders slumped. "You're right, of course."

She rubbed her eyes, clearly exhausted. "I have much to pray for tonight. Do not despair. We will help your mother and your sister and you, I promise. I just need to think. We'll talk again in the morning."

I felt lighter for having shared my burden with Livia, although I still could not see a path forward. Despite my troubles, I yawned as she kissed me on both cheeks. The corridor was quiet as she hurried toward her room. I shut the door, donned my nightclothes, and ran a brush through my hair. I could barely keep my eyes open, and I sank onto my bed with gratitude that this long day was at last over, come what may on the morrow.

Too hot for covers, I curled up on top. As I drifted off to sleep, I heard a soft rumble from what seemed so close. *God laughing before the rain*, I thought absurdly.

Chapter 24

I woke to the ringing of the Marangona bell. At first I thought it was the first one, signalling the ship workers to start their day at the Arsenale. But then I saw from the slant of sunlight on my face it was the bell that signalled the midday meal. As if on cue, my stomach rumbled.

Sometime in the night, or maybe it was morning, Dolce had leapt onto the bed, and he was still snoozing beside me, right next to Rosa's old doll. As I wafted back into wakefulness, my nose wrinkled at the faint malodour that permeated my cell. Dolce had joined me in bed because he had made a mess next to his cushion. I could only blame myself for being too tired to take him out last night.

Sighing, I rose from bed and cleaned up, leaving a small bundle of soiled cloth in the basket outside my room that the laundresses collected daily. The corridor was quiet, with the clinking of cooking and conversation from the refectory just audible in the distance. The rest of the convent was now at the midday meal, and clearly nobody had missed me at morning

Mass. Or Livia may have urged Mother Marina to give me special dispensation to allow me to rest. Whatever the reason, I felt the strange sensation
of gratitude for being in—what was becoming abundantly clear—a fairly
lenient convent. Still distressed by the previous day's events, I decided to
play truant for a little while longer and then find Livia. If she had already
come to any conclusions, she would have returned by now.

I was hungry, however, and so I went to the dwindling stash of refresh-
ments in my cupboard. I was down to two almond pastries. I placed one
on the floor for Dolce and nibbled at the other one. Slightly stale, it was
still delicious. San Zaccaria was renowned for its baking with good reason.

I poured the remainder of a bottle of wine into a cup, added some water,
and sipped at it. The items Madelena had brought me lay on the small table
that sat against one wall, and I took another look at the Madonna drawing.
It was by Carpaccio, just a simple sketch really, something he had probably
dashed off in an hour and given my father while he had worked on the hall
of the Great Council in the doge's palazzo with Bellini. Papa admired the
man, and I took heart that he saw fit to pass on the drawing to me. It was
a meaningful gesture. I shook my head slightly at the many facets of my
father, how I could both adore him and despise him simultaneously.

I wondered fleetingly if I could sell the drawing. But to whom? And for
how much? Surely not even close to a hundred ducats.

The hall of the Great Council I had never seen of course, but Papa had
once described it to me: the largest room in all of Venice, grander even than
anything in Florence or Milan or Rome, every inch of the walls and ceiling decorated with elaborate paintings and gold, the russet-brown wood
floor polished to a gleam. I tried to picture Luca in that room, the Great
Council's youngest member, mingling with hundreds of other noblemen,

helping to defend, safeguard, and administer our republic. I imagined he must be nervous, but I did not think he would show it. He exuded an easy and comfortable confidence. Yet he was far from arrogant. He had the temperament to be doge someday, although that would be decades off when his hair was long grey. I entertained a brief fantasy of me as his dogaressa, silver-haired too, before saying "No" out loud, startling Dolce.

"No, you mustn't, Justina," I said, again aloud. I wiped my hands and lips with a napkin and then briskly stood up. I leaned Carpaccio's Madonna against the wall in the middle of the table, pulled up a chair, and took out a sheet of paper. I cracked open an ink bottle and sharpened the quill with a penknife. I was not sure what compelled me, but I started writing, quite furiously. It was not a poem this time, or a formal essay, or a letter, at least not a letter to anyone I knew. More like a letter to myself, or a diary.

Papa had once spoken of a patrician who was chronicling the governmental proceedings of Venice. What was his name? I absentmindedly brushed the quill feather against my chin. Marin Sanudo, that was it. Well, if Lord Sanudo could write about what went on in the doge's palazzo, I could do the same for what transpired in San Zaccaria, although I had no aspirations to be an official historian. So, since this would be for no audience but myself, I decided to be scathingly honest about what went on. My sisters, particularly the Angela Riva circle, would not appreciate my frankness, nor would the priests and patriarch admire what they would likely conceive as sacrilege, but I did not care, for they would never see it. I would write for the first time with a purpose, beyond my childish literary forays and petty poetry. I would write for myself, to make sense of my position, of my days, of what was to be my life, stretching out endlessly before me.

꙳

I wrote until hunger knocked insistently at my stomach and Dolce nipped my ankle in anger for being inside so long. After corking the ink bottle and cleaning the quill with an old cloth, I stood up and stretched. When the ink had dried, I gathered my pages and put them at the bottom of my chest, along with the letter Luca had given me before I took my vows. My soul next to my heart.

I would ask one of the servants to bring me bathing supplies later, but first I would take Dolce for a walk and stock up in the kitchens before supper. Then I would need to find Auntie Livia. I was starting to worry that she had been unable to think of a solution for me. Just over two days of the five La Diamante had originally given remained.

Dolce zipped into the hall in front of me, anxious to visit the garden. At the same time, leaving Viena's room next door was a workman. I thought I recognized him as a young carpenter labouring on the church. Viena stood in the doorway beaming before catching my eye and briskly thanking him. He bowed deeply to her, gave me a slight nod and smile in acknowledgement, then whistled his way along the corridor, toolbox in hand. Dolce barked at him before whining at me.

"Hello, Justina." Viena ran a brush through her shoulder-length golden hair. "That was Jacomo. He was repairing one of the shelves in my room. He's an excellent carpenter, if ever your cell needs anything."

"Thank you, Viena, and good to know." As much as I enjoyed my conversations and burgeoning friendship with Viena, I knew Dolce would not last much longer, and I smoothed my skirts as a signal of my rush.

"His workmanship is quite unparalleled. And it doesn't hurt that he's quite handsome, does it?" A signal that Viena did not seem to understand, as she was in a garrulous mood. "Just waking up now? You must have had a very tiring visit with your family yesterday. I hope everything is all right."

I grimaced. "News travels quicker in this convent than a mouse running from a cat."

Viena smiled, then turned thoughtful. "Indeed. It is wise to remember that."

"It was a rather exhausting day. But I do need to take Dolce outside, so please excuse me. Let's talk later."

"Of course." She blew me a little kiss. "Your brother was here this morning, by the way. He was quite deep in conversation with your aunt."

I furrowed my brow. Paolo was here and no one had summoned me? "I had better take care of Dolce quickly then and find Auntie as soon as possible."

Viena nodded as she watched me go. "Bye, Justina."

Bidding her farewell, I whisked along the corridor and down the stairs, Dolce at my ankles, and out to the garden. Dolce ran to do his business, scattering chickens, sparrows, and Viena's prowling cat in his haste and delight, while I helped myself to a few new peas and strawberries. Despite my hunger, a visit to the kitchen would need to wait until after I spoke to Livia.

Where to find her? Many afternoons when Mother Marina did not require her, she could be found helping to tend the younger girls and foundlings, so I headed to the convent schoolroom, where indeed Livia was wrapping up a lesson in letters, the older girls chattering and putting away their quills and papers. Elisabetta was also there, softly chanting a nursery rhyme to a laughing baby on her lap, several toddlers at her feet singing along in sweet little voices.

"And now time for some cakes in the refectory!" The girls cheered, and

Livia and I exchanged smiles, my unhappy stomach wishing I could join the children in their refreshment. All the ambulatory girls noisily exited, the oldest ones, not more than ten or twelve, scooping up the babies who could not move on their own. I was reminded of myself and Rosa, who just four months ago had fulfilled similar roles, and I felt the all-too-familiar pang of grief that had infused me since Rosa's engagement had been announced.

I sighed and turned back to Livia, who had been murmuring something to Elisabetta. Elisabetta nodded, then squeezed my shoulder in farewell as she followed her young charges.

"I heard Paolo was here this morning."

Livia gathered her teaching supplies. "He was, and he and I had a good chance to converse about Rosa. When he left, he promised to go right to her and return on the morrow with news."

"That's a relief, and I suppose why you did not rouse me for his visit."

Livia stroked my hair and spoke soothingly. "I knew how fatigued you were and how trying yesterday was. Sometimes the best solution to a problem is sleep, even if only to face that problem afresh."

"What of the financial matter?" Sleep had provided no fresh perspective on that.

Her expression morphed from motherly to meditative. "I spoke frankly with Paolo about the letter. He did not know your father had not ... repaid his debts. He said he personally had only been to La Diamante twice and quite recently."

"And assumed Papa would also pay for it?"

Livia cleared her throat. "Yes, exactly." She clearly saw the anger starting to rise on my face like an *acqua alta* in November. "He had no idea about

La Diamante's . . . proposal and was clearly stricken at the thought. He said he'd see if he could raise the funds himself and asked me to give him the day. He'll bring news of that tomorrow as well."

My rising anger flooded out. "They run up such a debt, and now he can finally figure out a way to raise that sum? Those ducats could have been put toward my dowry, for a proper marriage."

"Calm yourself, Justina."

"Calm myself! How can I calm myself? I could have married Luca!"

"Shush, you must pacify yourself." She shut the schoolroom door and took my hand. "We do not want to draw attention to our family matter."

"Why should I care if anyone hears us?" I still spoke too loudly, and Livia frowned.

"Hush and settle yourself so you can think. First, you know Lord Cicogna's father would never have accepted a dowry of that amount plus your conventual dowry—it still would have been much too low, too insulting, for someone of his status. Second, we don't know Paolo can actually raise that sum. What collateral does he have? I'm sorry to say the Soranzo name is tainted when it comes to money.

"And you should care because you don't want Angela Riva or Zanetta Zane or any of their kind to know our family's business. We don't want them to know anything at all about any of us because they will find a way to use it against us, any who oppose them. Yourself, me, Elisabetta, Viena, Mother Marina, Teresa of the infirmary, all of us. They will find a way to harm us. Not to mention if outsiders catch wind of what is happening inside these convent walls, and at such a sensitive time for Venice." She gripped my hand harder, and I wrenched it away. "You are young and cannot be expected to fully understand yet. But everyone is looking for someone to blame for Venice's ignoble defeat at Agnadello, and already there are rumblings to blame us."

"Us, the nuns of San Zaccaria?"

"Not just San Zaccaria. All the convents the city's fathers believe might be exhibiting immoral behaviour punishable by God. They are looking for an excuse, any excuse."

"An excuse to do what?"

"To limit our freedoms."

I snorted at this assessment. "Our freedoms, ha. How can you say we are free?"

"Oh, Justina." Livia sat heavily in a wooden chair and smoothed her hair, and for a moment the old woman she would become flashed across her face. "I know this place feels like a sort of prison to you. Yet you do not see how free we are. Just look at your mother. For the sake of the Holy Virgin, look at your sister!"

"It is true that they are not happy. Imprisoned, you could even say. But that would not have been my case."

She shook her head. "Perhaps not. But I've seen far too many marriages end up exactly where your mother's is, if not as severe as Rosa's. The best of intentions, caught up in young love, or more likely lust . . . And then, well, a man asserts his authority, and the honeymoon is over."

"It would not have been that way for me." My voice was low and fierce. "Luca is not like that."

"How well do you really know him, Justina?" She appraised me, then her expression softened. "Perhaps you are correct. And if you are, then I am sincerely sorry, for you would have been the only truly unfettered woman in all of Venice. But as that is not the case, you must learn to live within the strictures of the convent. And when you do, as I have, you will feel as free as a bird, as happy as Dolce, as true in your convictions as Mary Magdalene knowing that Christ was resurrected." She crossed herself, inhaling deeply.

"Do you genuinely feel that way, Auntie?" I tried to memorize what she was telling me, with the aim of writing it all down in my new diary, to try to understand it more fully. I remembered too my lazy morning. As the mistress of a palazzo with a prominent husband, such truancy would be a rare luxury indeed.

"I do, Justina." Her beatific smiled bathed me in its tranquility. "Now, let us see if the children have left any cakes, and prepare for Paolo's visit on the morrow."

Chapter 25

The *tierce* bells the next morning found Livia and me in the parlour with a jug of watered wine and a platter of pastries, my anger still seething and my worry still simmering. As La Diamante's deadline edged closer, I could do little more than fume in my new diary and await Paolo with impatience.

Most visitors came in the afternoon, so the parlour was blessedly quiet. Livia suggested we say a rosary while we waited, and chanting in Latin was a momentary salve for my troubled mind.

We were on the second decade when Paolo appeared. He stood in the doorway, irritating me with his felicity. Only when he strode forward did we see its source. Two women stood behind him. One was Signora Zane, Zago's mother, wearing silk and a sneer, but the other was Rosa! Looking pale and thin but cautiously joyful, pawing the ground, clearly anxious to be in our arms but unsure of the propriety.

Livia gave a small curtsy. "Here to visit our dear sister Zanetta, Signora Zane?"

Signora Zane returned a vinegar face. "If you would be so kind as to let her know I'm here. She is not expecting me."

I believed only I could detect the slight purse to Livia's lips, she was so outwardly amiable. "It would be my pleasure." She turned to Rosa and gave her a quick embrace. "Niece, it is most excellent to see you. Justina, please offer the good signora some refreshment." Then she glided into the convent's inner sanctum.

"May I?" I asked awkwardly, gesturing toward our food and drink, anxious to be rid of her so I could speak with Rosa.

"No, thank you. I'll await Zanetta by myself. I'm sure you would enjoy a few moments alone with your sister." She peered down her nose at Rosa, who cowered under her scrutiny. Such a far cry from the first time she'd met Rosa, when she'd seemed almost kindly. I supposed Rosa was falling far short of her expectations, and my antipathy toward the Zane family flared again. What could they have expected from a veritable child?

I forced politeness into my voice. "Thank you, Signora." Rosa dipped her head, but Signora Zane had already made her way to the sofa furthest away, and I could only make haste toward my dear sister.

She gave a little shrug before I enveloped her in a hug. We had not seen each other since her wedding day a month before. I held her at arm's length to inspect her from head to toe. She looked beautiful, dressed in sage-green linen befitting the hot weather, but I was dissatisfied by her appearance. Unsure of what to do, I enfolded her again. Paolo looked on, clearly quite pleased with himself.

"Brother, how did you manage this?" I spoke quietly to afford us some privacy, while Rosa attempted to compose herself. It was hard to stay angry with Paolo when he had succeeded in bringing Rosa to me.

"Well, I used my manly charms to entice Signora Zane to allow me to also escort her to see her daughter. Given how busy the patrician menfolk are, and thus their gondoliers, and that it seems everyone in this city wants to declare their love for their relatives as frequently as possible these days, this was no small offer, and she took me up on it gladly." He glanced at the signora, sitting ramrod straight and studying a large painting of the Transfiguration, executed by one of my more talented sisters from a previous era. "Well, as gladly as such a woman can take anything. Christ, pardon my language, the Zane family has no sense of humour at all."

"Well, thank you, Brother, truly. How fares Mama?"

"A bit better, I think. She came to the dining room to break her fast this morning with Papa and myself. She did not say or eat much and looked fatigued, but I took her presence there as a good sign."

"That is promising. It must be Madelena's doing." Embarrassed, I could not bring myself to ask in front of Rosa whether he'd been successful at raising funds, thinking I should leave such a difficult conversation to Livia.

Paolo's smile shone brilliantly at the mention of our maid's name. "Yes, she truly is an angel of God."

I tried to ignore that knot of worry as Rosa and I settled on the sofa, arms linked, while Paolo plopped himself in a chair and helped himself to a pastry. I stroked Rosa's hand, wondering if I should bring up her possible pregnancy. "How are you, dear Sister?"

She whispered, "Miserable. I hate it there. I hate them all."

My face crumpled. "I am so sorry, Rosa. How is . . . how is your health?"

"I am so worried about what will happen to Venice that I have been sick to my stomach every day for the last week." She did look as if she might be sick at any moment, and I glanced around to see what might help her.

"Would a pastry ease your indigestion?" I knew from Mama that some-times bready foods soothed an expectant mother.

She shook her head. "I'm too queasy to eat. Do you think the pope's army will sack the city?" Her wet eyes were earnest, and I took out a hand-kerchief to dab her cheeks.

I peeked at Paolo, who was now yawning as he poured himself a cup of wine, clearly only half listening as he kept glancing toward the convent interior, no doubt hoping one of the more beautiful younger nuns would make an appearance. "I don't know, although I do know the Great Council will do everything in its power to prevent such a horror. But do you think your malady could be anything else?"

She shrugged as she rubbed her eyes.

I hesitated, then came to a decision. "Do you think . . . you could be with child?"

Paolo sat up straight as she blanched, becoming even whiter as her eyes widened. "I hadn't thought of that—"

Whatever else she was going to say was interrupted by the entrance of Zanetta, who greeted her mother like a peacock in heat, taking great pains to ignore our clan. I did not mind, for Rosa's sister-in-law's theatrics obscured our conversation.

Paolo grinned as Livia hurried over to us. "It sounds like congratula-tions are in order."

"What congratulations?" asked Livia.

"I am to be an uncle, and you a great-aunt!"

"Shhh, Paolo," I said, my eyes signalling to the Zane women still in the throes of their greeting. "We don't want them to know yet."

He scoffed. "They'll know soon enough."

"He's right, Justina." Livia sat on Rosa's other side and put an arm around her. "But not too soon, Paolo. We must first ensure Rosa writes her will, free from any . . . influence." She lowered her voice, so we had to lean in close. "I know this is paramount, for an expectant mother must be ever mindful of the dangers of delivery. But I hope we can mitigate those by being able select the midwife, an experienced one our family completely trusts rather than of the Zanes' choosing."

Paolo sat on the table before us and stifled another yawn. I supposed he'd had another late night, oblivious to any papal threats. "I could have Madelena visit Mama's midwife. I know she is aged, but she delivered us all and may still be willing to assist. And I will personally consult our family's usual notary for the will."

"The key will be allowing Rosa unfettered access to that notary."

"I will help there too. As the husband, Zago cannot be the executor. That would be against Venetian convention. It should be me as her blood brother. Ensuring the Soranzo dowry money is returned to her bloodline is even more important than choosing the midwife."

Her head swivelling between speakers during this conversation, Rosa whimpered at Paolo's declaration.

"Paolo, how can you be so cruel!" I interjected, and the two Zane women looked over, then both rolled their eyes and resumed their conversation. Taking a deep breath, I modulated my voice. "We will ensure Rosa has the best midwife if ours cannot manage it, and I for one cannot wait to bless the child."

Livia patted my knee. "You are quite right, Niece, and I too look forward to his baptism. However," and she rubbed Rosa's thigh, "it is still judicious to be prepared for all eventualities, even remote ones. Rosa must write a will. We must also ensure she has a beautiful painting of the Virgin and Child upon which to gaze in her chamber."

"I'm sure even Zago will agree to that," Paolo said. "No doubt he would like a son, and a handsome one."

"Do you think it will be a boy?" Rosa murmured, her hands exploring her flat belly. "Zago so wants an heir. Otherwise he will be the last of his line. He said the reason he agreed to marry me was because I was so young, so I would have time to bear him at least one son."

Livia and I exchanged looks, and I felt a wave of revulsion, not at all infrequent when it came to considering my brother-in-law.

Paolo took no notice as he helped himself to another pastry. "Indeed. And with any luck, the first will commence a male trend."

Rosa gave a wary smile. "Yes, that is my wish."

Paolo licked the powdered sugar from his fingers, then brushed the crumbs from his hands and arose. "It is decided then. I will return Signora Zane and Rosa to their palazzo, then I will have Madelena summon the midwife while I hasten to the notary."

Livia cast me a quick glance. "Before you depart, Nephew, a private word."

"Of course, Auntie." His smile faltered as he escorted Livia to a quiet corner of the parlour.

Rosa leaned her head upon my shoulder. "I'm hoping after I have a son Zago leaves me alone for a while."

I forced myself to cluck sympathetically. "I'm hoping the moment he learns you're with child he leaves you alone." I patted her hand. "For the health of your unborn son, of course. That is something the Soranzo midwife certainly can assist with."

Rosa nodded and produced the tiniest of genuine smiles. "I wish I could visit longer. Are you sure I cannot stay? Forever?"

"I wish you could, dear Sister. The bed in my cell is only made for one, but I wouldn't mind you nuzzling close beside me every night."

"Me neither." She swiped the tears from her cheeks with the back of her hands. Livia returned to us while Paolo spoke briefly with Signora Zane, to inform her it was time to go. Livia gave me the slightest shake of her head, my heart sinking as she embraced Rosa.

Rosa sniffled in her arms as Paolo approached. "I'm sorry to break up this *festa* of my favourite female relations, but duty calls."

"We have not even had a chance to discuss the latest in city matters," I said, stalling, hoping perhaps to beg Paolo to try harder to help me.

"True. Next time I call, I will give a full accounting, or perhaps Papa will find time to visit to relate the details. Suffice it to say that matters are still precarious, but perhaps a sense of normalcy is returning." He raised his eyebrows rakishly.

Livia put her hands upon Paolo's shoulders, and his expression quickly turned sober. "Do be prudent, Nephew, and circumspect in your behaviour."

"Always, Auntie, always," he said seriously, before smirking as Signora Zane deigned to come over, Zanetta at her side. He leaned over to kiss Livia on the cheek, at the same time whispering something in her ear. She nodded in response as the prospect of sisterly separation overcame me again.

"Rosa?" He put his hand out for our sibling, and she took it with reluctance.

"Thank you, Brother, for bringing Rosa," I said. "Please do so again soon."

"We shall see about that. I'm sure your brother is a busy man." Signora Zane grimaced at me before kissing Zanetta tenderly on both cheeks.

Paolo ignored her, bowing to Livia and me. "I will return as soon as I have more news."

Livia, Zanetta, and I, an unlikely trio, waved goodbye to our loved ones as they exited the convent, Rosa blowing me kisses, her face streaked with tears.

After the convent door to the outside world closed, Zanetta flashed us a contemptuous look. "I hope your sister earns her keep before too long," she said before flouncing off.

Livia rolled her eyes at me in her wake and spoke loudly. "Let us rejoice in having seen Rosa after all this time."

"Yes, I will pray to our heavenly husband to thank Him for her visit." The door shut behind Zanetta with a thud. "Now tell me, Auntie, exactly what Paolo said."

She sighed. "As I suspected, he visited several banks, and all of them laughed at his request when they heard his family name. He asked a few friends and did raise a few dozen ducats, but given the worries of the city, no one is willing to part with much." I wondered if he'd asked Luca, then decided he probably hadn't to spare me the shame. "He also spoke briefly to your papa, who apparently is frantic with worry and embarrassment but also besieged with government duties due to the war, and he tasked Paolo to take care of it. He did manage to sell an inexpensive bracelet of your mother's, but unfortunately she'd already sold off the more valuable items."

"So this could happen. Papa could truly give my honour to La Diamante if Paolo cannot raise the money."

"He has not given up yet, though, and neither have I. I wrote a few letters yesterday and will write more today. Elisabetta has also given a small contribution."

"That is very kind of her. I may be able to sell a small drawing by Carpaccio that Papa gave me, but I'm not sure for how much. Perhaps five or ten ducats. How much does all that add up to?"

"About forty ducats, forty-five or perhaps fifty if you can sell the Carpaccio. I am reluctant to approach Mother Marina, but she is another possibility of funding."

My heart sank at these revelations. "Given what you told me about the need to keep the convent's reputation spotless, I can see why you'd rather not go to her."

"Not yet, but I will if I must. I believe in the end our mother abbess would rather forestall a scandal and keep it quiet than see it come to fruition and be made public. But I still hold out hope we can raise it all, or enough to hold off La Diamante and buy a little more time."

"We only have another day," I replied mournfully.

"We will do everything we can, Niece." She crossed herself.

"Amen to that." I imitated her, with less conviction.

Chapter 26

I spent the afternoon tidying my room and frantically trying to think of other ways to raise more funds, with Livia promising to do the same. I even considered whether it made sense to discreetly give in to La Diamante's wishes, whether I could go through with it. I swallowed hard. Would it be worth the potential scandal to my family name and convent? I groaned at the impossibility of the situation. The stakes were much too high for too many parties, not even counting myself. We would just have to scrounge up the money.

When a knock came at my door, I assumed it was Auntie with news, so I was startled to see Viena, come to fetch me back to the parlour. From the slant of the shadows and the growl of my stomach, I could discern it was close to the evening meal, an unusual hour for a visitor.

"Has my brother already returned?" I inquired as we threaded our way through the corridors. I was not expecting him until the morrow. "Or my father, perchance?"

Viena only grinned knowingly until we reached the parlour threshold, where a few of my sisters were finishing visits with their families.

Near the Transfiguration painting stood Luca in his black robes, a troubled smile on his face. He would only be here if something were terribly wrong and no one else could deliver a message. I clenched Viena's arm as we walked over to him.

"Lord Cicogna, what are you doing here? Is everything all right? My mother . . . ?"

"Your mother asked me to come here, in fact. She is agitated but in otherwise adequate health, as is your father. It pertains to your brother, actually." He glanced around, clearly not wanting to be overheard, so I led him to a quiet corner, asking Viena to locate Livia, and quickly. She dashed off.

"What about Paolo?"

His mouth was set in a grim line. "He has been arrested by the Council of Forty."

The highest criminal court in Venice. "Oh my heavens!" I felt faint. Luca, alarmed at my reaction, guided me to a sofa, his touch sending energy throughout my body despite my discomposure. After settling me, he pulled up a chair so he was sitting across from me, able to look me straight in the eye.

"What did he do?"

Luca cleared his throat. "Apparently he, along with several other young noblemen who were also arrested, are guilty of staying overnight at the convent of Santa Maria della Celestia."

"Overnight at a convent?" I repeated his words in a kind of stupor.

He nodded, his face a knot of concern. "I do not mean to offend you, as I know you are a newly consecrated nun."

I took a deep breath and waved my hand in front of my face, trying to create a draft of fresh air. "I need to know. You will not offend me."

He still seemed discomfited but acquiesced. "As you may be aware, Celestia's newly elected abbess has been holding the usual ceremonial suppers. On at least one recent occasion, after most of the guests departed, apparently a few young noblemen stayed behind, locked in overnight, and danced with some of the nuns to a wind band until the sun rose."

I looked at him in disbelief. "And Paolo was one of them."

"Apparently so. Lord Bembo, the state attorney, brought the case to the Forty, and sixteen young patricians, your brother among them, were arrested this afternoon."

"Where is Papa? Does he know?"

"Yes, and he's already speaking with the lawyer defending them. I was at the doge's palazzo when Paolo and the others were brought in, and your father asked me to tell your mother, who subsequently requested I come here to inform you and your aunt. Many of us were surprised at the arrests, given the current political situation. God knows this is not the time to stir up such matters, even if it is technically against the law to fraternize with nuns in this manner."

I let my breath out in a long sigh, attempting to digest this information. Paolo arrested, just when we needed him so urgently, with La Diamante threatening our insolvent family, Mama not well, Rosa with child, Papa distracted by political turmoil and clearly desperately fighting off bankruptcy. "If they weren't caught in the act, how did the Council of Forty discover these transgressions?"

He clasped his hands together in a clear attempt to halt his fidgeting. "Apparently a courtesan heard the tale in her salon and thought to inform the Forty."

"A courtesan?" I asked weakly. "Who?"

Luca looked at me doubtfully. I was certain he was calculating the chance I knew the name of a single courtesan in our city and whether there would be harm in informing me. "She is known as La Diamante. I believe she was richly rewarded for her intelligence, for the Forty has said quite publicly and forcefully that Venice must root out any stains before God at such a critical juncture." He rolled his eyes. "She is avaricious, not to mention hypocritical."

La Diamante. I could hardly register the name. Did she know Paolo would be implicated, or was that coincidence? Did she have something against our family, or was her motive merely greed?

Luca peered at me with concern. "I know it is much to absorb, Signora Justina. But your father has assured me the lawyer is quite capable. While the transgressions were too blatant for the government to ignore, the man is convinced the Forty will come to their senses soon enough."

"What is the penalty for staying overnight at a convent?"

Luca ran his hand across his cheek, a muted rasping sound coming from the faint afternoon beard that was growing along his jaw. "A fine of a hundred ducats and up to a year in prison for a first offence. Two years if fornication can be proved, the act being hurtful to God."

I gasped, and the remaining visitors looked over at us with curiosity. I hadn't noticed before, but Angela Riva was there wishing her sister farewell, and she arched an inquisitive eyebrow at Luca, clearly not recognizing him as a member of my family. I smiled painfully at Luca to deflect attention, and his eyes filled with compassion. The words of the monk in Campo San Zaccaria came back to me: *Our sisters, the brides of Christ, must repent for their egregious sins, the breaking of their sacred vows, their unnatural*

fornication, since their unholy behaviour risks the shame and destruction of our
Most Serene City!

Had Paolo fornicated with a nun? Knowing him, likely. What would
happen if the Forty convicted him, even for the lesser charge? Besides
being jailed for a year, he would be fined one hundred ducats, the exact
amount we were already attempting to raise to save my honour. The shame
on our family might be too much for Mama, who was already grappling
with La Diamante's threats, lingering health problems, and fear of Venice
being invaded. And the news would soon be all over the city, if it weren't
already. It might inflame Zago. Not to mention the scandal beyond my
kin's involvement in it: noblemen staying overnight in convents, dancing
until dawn. Their behaviour threatened our republic. It did sound like
something Paolo would do, but how indiscreet of him, how selfish. Men
were of course welcome in convent parlours, just as Luca was here with
me now, and certain men like priests and labourers could go beyond the
parlour, but staying past curfew? The brazenness astounded me.

"Lord Cicogna, you said the punishment for men is a fine and imprisonment. Pray tell, what is it for the nuns?"

"That is under the control of the Church, of course, and, depending on
the denomination, the abbess herself, but I have heard it can range from
simple penance to banishment or excommunication, depending on the circumstances and the severity of the crime."

I exhaled slowly. From saying a few rosaries to being permanently
ousted from the Church. In our abbey, Mother Marina would decide, the
abbess being the final authority in a Benedictine order such as ours. Would
she be so harsh as to excommunicate a noble nun? What would become of
such a woman? If her abbess cast her from her convent, could she return

to her parents? Would they receive her back, when such a tainted patrician daughter would upset the delicate order of the republic? Could she ever marry? Never another patrician, since her noble status would be irrevocably tarnished, although perhaps a commoner would have her if her family had enough money. Or perhaps she must find a different path in life, perhaps one that led to the palazzi of women like La Diamante and thus further intimate transgressions. I shuddered, and Luca appeared concerned.

Auntie Livia rushed over just then, raising Angela Riva's eyebrows even further, and Luca quietly related the particulars to her, emphasizing that the Forty had only arrested Paolo and not yet put him on trial. She seemed less shocked than resigned, asking Luca a series of questions on how the defence would be handled, and he spoke of legal nuances of which I was quite unaware.

"Thank you, Your Lordship, for keeping us apprised of my nephew." Livia leaned back in her seat, deflated. "I hope we can further impose upon you to deliver us information as it unfolds. Although I suppose we'll hear about it second- and third-hand soon enough."

"Of course. It would be my privilege." He glanced at me with what I interpreted as yearning, a glance I knew that my sharp-eyed auntie would not miss and hoped Angela Riva would.

I felt I must speak as my family's representative. "Yes, thank you. Our family is in your debt. My mother will be eternally grateful."

He shook his head. "Not at all. Since I joined the Great Council, I have gotten to know your father, and Paolo is my dear friend. You are . . ." He trailed off uncertainly. "You are his sister. It is as simple as that. I will return as soon as possible tomorrow with whatever news I obtain." He arose then, first giving Livia a kiss on her hand in farewell, then doing the same for me, lingering a moment too long. Angela Riva was openly staring, her brows now furrowed, and I felt yet another worry knot inside me.

After Luca departed, I walked beside Livia on our way to the refectory, and an idea came to me. Livia agreed it was the best among an array of bad choices, if I were brave enough to see it through.

I had to speak to Luca again. I could not do what I hoped to do without his help.

Chapter 27

The refectory was its usual beehive of chatter, although I barely heard it. We sat on cushioned benches along long tables, divided into the two general convent factions. Along one wall, at the table with Livia and me, were Elisabetta, Viena, and several other like-minded relations and friends. The Riva coterie that included Zanetta and Santina was on the opposite side of the room, while the mother abbess sat at the head table with the other senior sisters of San Zaccaria, including the prioress, Teresa the infirmarian, the choir mistress, and the librarian.

The servants laid the food before us, and after a quick formal prayer, we began to sup with silver cutlery. An elderly sister read to us from the Holy Scriptures throughout the meal as required by our order, but she spoke softly, allowing us to converse freely, as was our convent's custom.

Opulent frescoes decorated the refectory walls to enlighten and inspire us, painted by both sisters and artists from outside the convent specially commissioned during the previous century. The largest and most beautiful was a rendition of Christ's final supper created by one of our more artistically proficient sisters a few years before. Its majesty and perfection never failed to awe me, and more than once I had imagined what it might have been like to break bread with Our Saviour—my husband.

Not tonight, though. I was too absorbed by happenings outside the convent walls, and I barely spoke to my tablemates. I was anxious to confer further with Livia, but Mother Marina had asked Livia to meet after supper for her counsel on the revelations out of Celestia.

"You must overcome any embarrassment you feel and ask Lord Cicogna to act as your intermediary tomorrow, as soon as you see him," Livia whispered before she headed to Mother Marina's office. "I believe he is your best chance. Your only chance, if I am being honest with you and myself, given we are almost out of time. But if he will not help you, come to me right away, and if we must tell Mother Marina, then we must. With the Celestia fiasco, I am fairly confident she will want to help avoid any potential scandal."

Nodding, I retired to my cell. As I changed into my nightclothes, cleaned my teeth, and brushed my hair, I agonized over the day. Had I seen Rosa only that morning? It felt a lifetime ago. We had made plans for her pregnancy, so many of them dependent on Paolo. Then to learn of his arrest—for staying overnight in a convent! The fresh wave of shock was enough to almost fell me again. And if convicted, he would owe the exact amount needed to ransom my virginity—a hundred ducats. I could see why my father would choose Paolo's freedom over my virtue. It would have to be one or the other, for how would our family ever raise double that sum? And so it seemed I would have to whore myself to save my father and brother, reputation be damned. At least Rosa was already married off.

Unless I could convince Luca, my only conduit to a courtesan. I hated the idea of asking him for help in such a humiliating situation, and taking advantage of his affection besides, but I could see no other way if I wanted to keep this scandal private and not let all of Venice know. News of Paolo at Celestia would be awful enough for my family.

I briefly entertained the idea of asking Luca to bid for me. That way I'd at least sin with him while helping my family. Knowing his own integrity, he would spend a chaste evening with me, despite the inevitable gossip that would ensue. Regardless, even the thought of asking him to do this made me blush and want to fall on my knees in penance.

I tried to untangle all this in my diary, Dolce dozing contentedly at my feet as I scribbled away. I was in such a state of concentration that I heard the knocking only after it escalated in insistence.

Viena. "Come over, Justina. I have some goodies fresh from the ovens."

She would not take no for an answer, and soon I found myself in her cell with a slice of fragrant, warm cake and a glass of bubbly white wine before me. She wore a violet silk dressing gown. She was very beautiful, petite and shapely, perhaps not the most quick-witted, but that was not a negative quality in a noblewoman. I felt overly tall and gawky beside her. It was a wonder she had been sent to the convent, given her charms, but then I remembered she had a much older sister, married before Viena was even born.

I sat down and took a bite, while she did likewise. "You have much to tell me, and you can start with why that absolutely magnificent man was here to see you this evening. One of God's finer incarnations of a Venetian nobleman, I must say."

I felt the blood rush to my face. I agreed of course, but I had been sure never to speak of Luca and my almost marrying him to anyone at San Zaccaria. Only Livia knew.

"Come now, there is clearly a story there." She giggled.

"Lu—I mean, Lord Cicogna came bearing urgent news about my brother." She looked intrigued, but I shook my head. "I cannot speak of it. Not yet anyway. You will likely know soon enough."

She sighed. "All right, but you must not spare any details when you can. We need all the information from the outside world we can obtain to enliven our dreary lives. Besides, I am not referring to any urgent family news. I'm referring to the spark I saw between you and him. The flame that connected you was unmistakable."

Was our mutual attraction that obvious? I did not know how to respond and was grateful when she changed the subject to herself.

"You know, I do so hate being a nun." She, like me, had made it known all along that becoming a handmaid of God was not her calling, but I had believed her as resigned to her fate as I was.

"Well, everyone says it takes time to settle in." Viena's fluffy grey cat leapt up on the table and sniffed at my half-finished plate.

"No, Leo." She pushed him off abruptly. He landed on his feet on the fine carpet and sauntered over to a pot of catnip she kept in the corner. "I hate being a nun," she repeated, then took a final bite of her cake and a long swig of wine, "but I am becoming accustomed to the freedoms it provides."

Livia had alluded to much the same. "What do you mean? I can't say I've found much freedom yet."

"No?" She smiled conspiratorially. "I have."

I could not help but smile back. "Go ahead, tell me. I can plainly see you have something to say."

She grinned. "I'm in love."

I was shocked yet again, this time by her boldness. "Did you leave a sweetheart behind?"

She shook her head coyly as she swallowed more wine. "Guess again."

"Oh, a game, is it?" I laughed uncertainly. "Not Father Hieronimo!" He was the elderly priest with white hairs sprouting from his nostrils and ears who came to say the excommunicative version of daily Mass.

"That old coot? Ha ha, never! No, I have someone much younger and comelier in mind."

I racked my brain. "A visitor? Someone's brother? Not my brother!"

She shook her head, snickering at my speculations. "Someone who is skilled with his hands. *Very* skilled."

I stared at her in horror. "Not the carpenter who fixed your shelf?"

She looked positively gleeful as she nodded. "Jacomo," she said dreamily. "Those hands. Those very long and deft fingers . . ."

"You cannot be serious."

"I am deadly serious." And she certainly looked it, a satisfied expression lacing her lovely features. "And he loves me too. He told me today."

My head swam with this revelation. After what had just happened to Paolo and Celestia, I was terrified. "You must tread carefully these days." Then another horrifying thought struck me. "He's not even a patrician."

"Who will know or care about that? I already can't marry a nobleman, what does it matter with whom I . . . exercise my freedom?"

"But it is a sin." I could barely breathe. Fornication, right here in San Zaccaria, right next to my own cell. What would the Council of Forty do?

Would the punishments be even harsher for a second convent accused of transgressions while the Warrior Pope threatened Venice's security?

She shrugged and topped up our glasses with the last of the wine. "I do not think God cares what we do here. We're locked away and forgotten, even by Him."

"God might not, but our families do. The Council of Forty certainly does."

She cocked her head at me. "What do you mean?"

I did not want to reveal what had happened to Paolo, but I felt it necessary to warn her of the possible consequences of her transgressions. "In addition to the, er, family news, Lord Cicogna told me something else. Several young patricians were arrested today for spending a night at Celestia."

Her eyes widened, less with worry and more with interest. "Is that so?"

"They were noble. Imagine if commoners were found cavorting with patrician nuns."

"And what has happened to the nuns?"

"I do not know. Anything from penance to banishment or excommunication is possible. We convents fall under ecclesiastical control, not the Council of Forty."

She drank more wine, looking pensive. "I will have to tell Jacomo to be very discreet. Although it's not as if he's in here for a festa or even breaking curfew." She conveniently glossed over the fact that he was just a commoner. "He's here every day anyway, working on the convent and church, and goes home every night to sup with his parents. He's not even married. It's a perfect situation. No one will be the wiser." She wiped her mouth with a lace napkin. "Right?"

"I will not say anything, Viena." It was not in my nature to gossip, which put me at odds with most of my sisters at San Zaccaria, who twittered hearsay like so many flocks of birds. "You can trust me. But can you trust our other sisters? Think of Angela, Zanetta, Santina. I do not trust them at all, and I worry for you. For Jacomo too, if he is caught. He could face a fine and imprisonment, let alone loss of his livelihood." I crossed myself, unable to refrain from adding, "Not to mention your soul if you do not confess."

She scoffed. "Let me have a little amusement. What other diversion do I have from this tedious life stretching interminably ahead of me? And now with the loss at Agnadello? Who knows how long Venice will even last?" She gestured around her well-appointed little cell. "How long any of this will last?"

I sighed. "I don't know. That is how everyone seems to be feeling these days. And it's not strictly amusement, is it?" I could not begrudge her love.

"No." She picked up Leo and rubbed his back with long strokes, her large blue eyes thoughtful as he started to purr. "Jesus may be my husband, but Jacomo may be my only chance at earthly love."

My heart wrenched at the thought of Luca and his wife. I did not have any such chance at all.

I rose to leave, then had a second thought, eyeing Viena's lovely silk dressing gown. It looked newly purchased. I gathered my courage, for I had little choice. "Viena, do you have any ducats I may borrow? I would pay you back, although I must admit I don't know when."

"Not much with me, but I could lend you five for now. Would that help?" She extracted some coins from her trunk. "My papa has a few ships held up due to the war. They are somewhere near Crete, I think, awaiting word of peace. Only a handful of ships are coming through these days."

I sighed. The Cicogna ship seemed like the only one. "Yes, five would help. Thank you very much."

"Of course, Justina. We're friends now, right?"

"Yes, we are, aren't we?" I smiled genuinely and thanked her again as she chatted about the spices and wares on her father's ships.

Half the amount raised, or just a quarter if I were to include Paolo's fine too, but only a day to go. I wondered if La Diamante might agree to payment in parts, then groaned at what seemed to be her insatiable greed.

I left Viena's room long after the Realtina bell that signalled the city's nightly curfew. The convent was quiet, the hush interrupted only by an occasional giggle or chair scraping along the floor. Most of my sisters seemed to have retired, but I felt wide awake with anticipation. I knew sleep would not come easily.

I tiptoed down the corridor, aware of my every footfall on the floor and every creak in the building, toward the garden. In the courtyard, the air was cool, at least relative to the thick afternoon heat that had descended upon Venice for the season. The moon was not yet visible, but stars honeycombed the wedge of bruised sky above me.

I sat on a stone bench, inhaling the floral perfume, listening to the singing cicadas, then looked up and began to pray. *Father, forgive me my sins. Of lust, of gossip, of envy. Please help my family. My mother in her frail health, my sister with child, my brother in prison, my father to aid the future of Venice and his own children. Protect them all from the wrath of La Diamante. Aid Viena too, that she may avoid sin and live a holy life.*

And Luca. May he find joy in his marriage. May he have children. May he care for his wife. May he find it in his heart to help me.

And please, I beg of You, help me resolve my love for him. For yes, I still love him. My lust too. Every time I see him it pains me. Please help me turn to the only husband I have, your Son Jesus Christ. Amen.

As I finished my prayer, probably futile, I became aware of a clucking sound. A chicken, russet brown with a bright red comb, staggered over to me and pecked my slippers. "Enrica, what are you still doing out here? Auntie Livia must be worried about you." Enrica stared calmly at me with beady eyes as I scooped her up, tucked her under one arm, and headed toward Livia's room, her feathers tickling my hand.

At Livia's door, I knocked softly. No one answered, and I suspected my aunt was already deeply asleep. It had been a trying day, and I could not blame her. I considered keeping Enrica in my cell overnight. But anticipating the difficulty of trying to keep Dolce's excited barking from wakening the entire convent, I gently pushed on Livia's door to see if I could open it.

It swung silently inward, and I crept in, Enrica emitting a contented cluck. A candle burned low in a holder on the bedside table, casting a soft glow around the cell and onto the bed. And in the bed was Livia, sleeping as expected.

But she was not alone. Entwined with her, the covers twisted around them, was Elisabetta. Both unclothed, their skin glowed alabastrine peach in the candlelight, their long hair enmeshed in a luxurious tangle of brown and silver. Their white nightgowns and undergarments trimmed with lace lay in a heap on the floor.

I stared at them in a state of utter stupefaction. Our husband Jesus on the large crucifix above the bed did the same.

Livia adjusted herself slightly, and Elisabetta murmured something incomprehensible before settling herself back upon Livia's breast with a satisfied smile.

I placed Enrica on the floor, then reversed my path, my heart beating wildly, my mind not comprehending, and closed the door firmly behind me.

Chapter 28

I tossed all night and woke at dawn feeling more tired than when my head had lain upon the feather pillow. *Unnatural fornication . . .* Perhaps the preaching monk was not referring just to conventional sinners like my brother and Viena. While I had heard whispers about men who loved their own kind and knew the punishment for sodomy was death, I had never heard before of women in such a state and did not know what penalty they would face.

I opened my bleary eyes, uttered a rare morning prayer, and cuddled Dolce for comfort. By this time, knowing some of my family's affairs would quite soon be very public, I was determined to keep two secrets: Livia's and Viena's. They were my family, an aunt like a friend and a friend like a cousin, and I had a loyalty to them. Livia did not even know I knew. She had only ever been good to me, so it was difficult to judge her too harshly.

However, I did resolve to record my thoughts on the matter in my diary, not using any names and referring to events as obliquely as possible. I wrote for myself, to help me sort through my conflicted feelings, but it was more important than ever to ensure my diary stayed hidden. The next time I saw Madelena, I would ask her to procure a lock for my chest. I could hide the key elsewhere in my room.

Feeling pious, I attended morning Mass, the excommunicated version. Father Hieronimo droned through the reduced and sparsely attended service by rote, my mind spinning like a polychromatic wheel among Livia, Elisabetta, Viena, Rosa, Paolo, La Diamante, and of course Luca, darting among confusion, pain, worry, fear, and love, both familial and carnal. Father Hieronimo became enlivened only when he gave his sermon, when he exhorted us nuns to do our part for our Most Serene Republic, staying true to our vows and praying ceaselessly for Venice's inhabitants to prevent dire consequences descending upon the innocent populace. I wondered if he'd already heard of the transgressions at Celestia. If he hadn't yet, it was only a matter of time.

As he yammered on, I felt a flicker of doubt in my pledged loyalty to Livia and Viena. Was I condemning them to Hell by not encouraging them to repent their sins? Was I condemning all of Venice to ruin? Was it already too late given the licentious behaviour of my brother and his friends? And what could I do about my own virtue if La Diamante would not accept my meagre offer? Did I owe a higher fealty to God or to my family?

For the rest of the dreary service, I attempted to focus on the priest's hairy nostrils to banish all thoughts of Luca, using the disgust I felt at the sight like a mental hair shirt to maintain my holiness. If I could have gotten my hands on such an unpleasant garment, I might even have donned it, but no one in San Zaccaria ever deigned to wear one to my knowledge, and I would not even know where to find such a wretched vestment.

My renewed dedication to my vows was tested immediately after the service, when I was summoned yet again by Viena to the parlour. Although I wished my father might swoop in to rescue me, I knew from her sly smile that Luca was awaiting me next to the Transfiguration painting.

I attempted to moderate my pace to the parlour, not rushing with excitement but striding with pure purpose as I thought a nun would. My heart involuntarily twisted at the sight of him, but I took a moment at the threshold of the otherwise empty room, inhaled deeply, and crossed myself before facing him, my eyes cast demurely first at his neck, then his chest—I would allow myself to descend no further—finally focusing just beyond the slope of his shoulder. I inhaled again, catching a waft of the myrrh soap he'd evidently used, and my resolve to be unaffected began to falter.

"You look tired." Concern etched his face, his jawline perfectly clean-shaven. "Still beautiful of course. But I am not surprised, given the news I delivered yesterday."

You don't even know the half of it, I thought wryly as I sat down and he joined me. Unable to keep my gaze away from his face, I gave up, hoping God would forgive me, and met his eyes. Another unforeseen twitch occurred behind my breast, much to my consternation. I thought quickly of Father Hieronimo's nose hairs. "I am coping as well as can be expected, Lord Cicogna. What news of my brother?"

"No new developments with his legal case yet, I'm afraid, and the news has unsurprisingly spread throughout the city already." So Father Hieronimo likely did know. "But do not despair. I managed to speak with your father, who is most unfortunately unable to detach himself from the Senate meetings for any real length of time, and then only to speak with

Paolo's lawyer and the other fathers. He sees many reasons for optimism."

"That is something then." I was nonetheless crestfallen at my father's seeming lack of urgency regarding my own prospects.

Luca placed his hand on mine. "He also asked me to convey his deepest apologies to you." Clearly Luca did not comprehend the mystery behind this request, and I momentarily closed my eyes. I wanted more than I could bear to continue feeling the comfort of his skin against mine, but, glancing at the door, I forced myself to withdraw my hand, and he returned his uncertainly to his knee.

He went on. "I was able to visit Paolo in prison just now. He is in excellent spirits. His usual self, you might say." He gave a slight laugh, and I returned a small smile. We both knew my brother well. "He has every confidence the charges will be dropped. I pray he is right."

"I do as well." We had come to the point in the conversation where I needed to take a leap of faith in Luca, or at least in the friendship he had with my family.

"Are you all right?" He took both my hands firmly this time, his warm ones heating my cold ones, which I did not, could not, withdraw this time. His touch felt too good, too reassuring, and I needed all the reassurance I could get. "You have gone quite pale." His own face flushed, and a tangle of attraction and nerves ran unbidden through me once more, followed by immediate remorse.

I nodded, unable to speak.

He looked dubious. "There is so little I can do to assist you, ah, your family regarding Paolo, save bring you any news. I do wonder if there is anything else I may do for you in place of your brother and knowing how preoccupied your father is."

La Diamante's deadline tomorrow morning, the notary, the midwife, the money. I took a deep breath, grateful he'd given me the opening. "As a matter of fact, there is, Lord Cicogna."

He lowered his voice but not his eyes. "Luca. Please call me Luca. It would mean much to me."

"Luca." And just saying his Christian name, as intimate as a kiss, gave me courage. "Would you help me arrange a meeting for tomorrow morning?"

"Of course. Who with?"

I took an enormous breath. "The courtesan La Diamante."

He quirked an eyebrow, clearly perplexed. "Whatever for?"

"I know it is an unusual request. But my family has business with her." I exhaled. "Business of an urgent nature."

He studied me for a moment, a sort of comprehension blooming in his expression. "A business that Paolo cannot attend to while imprisoned, and your father is unable to, or too busy, or perhaps both."

"Yes." I was grateful he did not ask me to elaborate. My father and my brother were no longer of any help to me, and I did not need to ask their permission to act. Without intending to purposely hurt me, they had created this mess, and it clearly was now up to me to find our way out.

Luca's brow wrinkled. "Surely I cannot bring a courtesan to a convent parlour, nor a nun to her premises."

I inhaled. "I have been considering how best to arrange it. I thought we could meet in the campo by San Zaccaria. I will be there giving food to the poor who frequent the square." The barefoot monk and his threadbare followers flashed through my mind, and I wondered if the preacher would accept some of San Zaccaria's delicious pastries.

Luca let go of my hands as he kneaded his chin in thought. "That could work. But are you certain this meeting is the best course of action? Is it truly necessary?"

"I can think of no other way." I forced myself to remain calm. "I must try to conduct this business as best I can, for my family's honour."

He finally nodded. "All right then. I know finances are difficult for your family and have been for some time. Although I do not fully understand, of course I will help you. I will arrange it. I know her palazzo. I will bring her first thing tomorrow, without her guards, so as not to draw too much attention. Though I think it best if you are there alone too. La Diamante might feel cornered if there are too many on your side."

"Thank you, Luca." I did not want to inquire as to how he knew her residence, hoping it was common knowledge among young noblemen. But he was positioning himself on my side, which gave me fortitude.

"You are welcome." He smiled gravely. "Is there anything else?"

There was—Rosa. I wasn't sure when Madelena would return. Had Paolo seen Madelena before his arrest? Still, I shook my head. "It is not right to impose upon you any further."

He lowered his voice even though we were alone in the parlour. "It would be no imposition, but rather my pleasure. I know your father is consumed with the unknown whereabouts of his incoming ship, not to mention all the urgent governmental proceedings. All the senators are. The doge has commanded them to spend every waking moment at his palazzo, and now with Paolo . . . Lord Soranzo is very little even with your mother, just home to sleep for a few hours. He told me he would not be able to visit you for several more days at least. He was quite troubled but has certain duties to the city due to his rank, and he knows Paolo trusts me. And I truly would be honoured to aid the noble and ancient house of Soranzo. Please, allow me."

In fact, he likely was the only noble left in Venice willing to aid our house. I worried about taking another obligation from him. But Rosa mattered more. "Paolo was going to locate our family notary to draw up a will."

His forehead furrowed. "For whom? Is anyone ill? Your mother?"

"For my sister Rosa. She is newly with child."

"I see. A natural request for a mother-to-be. I can locate him. Where does he live?"

"Near the house of Gritti." I gave him the man's name before pausing. "But—ah, I ask too much."

"Go on. I said I would help you, Justina. I did not say that idly. I am a man of my word."

I knew that about him, knew it in my bones, and I nodded. "But it is not as simple as locating him. Paolo was going to bring the notary to Rosa at the Zane palazzo and help her draw up the will, providing her guidance. My parents do not yet know about her condition. We did not want to worry my mother, and now with Paolo, clearly my father can contend with no more."

"I think I understand. I will ask the notary to accompany me to visit Paolo for specifics, and then I will take the man to see Rosa myself. I will then visit La Diamante and arrange to bring her to San Zaccaria tomorrow. You should plan to be in the square by tomorrow's first Marangona bell."

I exhaled. "Thank you very much, Luca." It was much to ask.

He dipped his head. "It is not only my pleasure but my honour, Justina."

Just as I contemplated how I could ever repay him, Zanetta and Angela Riva strolled into the parlour, and I nearly threw up in fear at their daggered glances, relieved Luca and I were no longer holding hands. I needed to change the subject, and quickly. "I'm afraid I completely neglected my manners, Lord Cicogna. How fares your wife?"

He looked at me sharply, then glanced at the women, who were a little too interested in our conversation. I recalled Angela Riva had noticed me talking to Luca last night and wondered what she thought of our strange pairing a second time in as many days. "She is in good health, thank you for your inquiry. As you may well understand, I will not be sending her to our summer palazzo on the mainland, as would be the usual custom, due to the uncertainty with this war. She is not ... pleased. She had been very much looking forward to it."

So her temper flared at being denied her amusements, even though there's a war on, I mused, recalling how Luca had said she was little more than a silly girl.

I nodded sagely as Santina limped in and began speaking to Angela Riva, while Zanetta still gazed in our direction. "I have heard all the summer houses will be empty this season. It is for the best."

"We truly have no choice, with the pope's army gathering strength. Well then, I will take my leave. I have much to do today." He eyed me meaningfully, not daring to say more.

"Of course. Thank you so much, Your Excellency, for bringing word of my brother." I stood and curtsied, and he mirrored me with a formal bow. "I am not sure how I will ever repay your kindness."

"I will return when I have more news. I am pleased to assist your family at your father's request." Before exiting the convent, he nodded in the direction of Zanetta, who acknowledged him with a bright smile and slight dip of her head.

I had time to consider neither my obligations to Luca nor my feelings as Zanetta sidled over, cheeks flushed. "I heard your brother was arrested last night. I knew Zago marrying into your family was a mistake. And now you

will taint our good name by unfortunate association. The Soranzo clan—
as poor as San Cassiano whores and as sinful too." She shook her head
in disgust as she returned to Angela and Santina, and I, open-mouthed,
took my leave as quickly as I could, praying she would not hear tell of me
meeting with a courtesan.

Chapter 29

My heart banging from Zanetta's harsh words, I practically ran to my favourite courtyard. The day was still and grey, and I peered up at the sky, wondering when the rain would begin to fall. The courtyard was empty except for a few chickens, Enrica among them, and I found a brown egg under a plant in the strawberry patch, the fruit red, plump, and ready for picking. Having missed breakfast, I helped myself to a few and was pocketing the egg to bring to the kitchen when Livia entered the courtyard. I had not seen my aunt since my discovery the previous night, and I knew not what to say.

She beckoned to the stone bench. "Did you have a chance to talk with Lord Cicogna? I went to your cell earlier and Viena said you were speaking with him."

"I did, Auntie, and he agreed to help. He will arrange for me to meet La Diamante and assist with Rosa's will."

She exhaled and crossed herself. "Thank you, Jesus."

I sighed. "But as you know, we have not even half the required amount in hand."

"True. But you will now be able to meet La Diamante face to face. When you explain the situation and promise to continue to raise the funds, I'm sure you will find even a whore has a heart."

I frowned. "I hope you are right. I still don't know where the rest will come from, but hopefully it will buy us some time. Maybe Papa's ship will come in soon. It can't stay away forever, can it?"

"Precisely. It is all about the art of negotiation."

I was quite deficient in such arts and wished fervently Auntie could come with me to help bargain with the courtesan. But I recalled Luca's words about meeting La Diamante alone, saying she wouldn't want to feel cornered, and I imagined a trapped animal baring its fangs and claws.

Livia patted my hand. "Your Lord Cicogna is a good man."

"Most unfortunately he is not mine, but I am exceedingly grateful he will help save my family from further scandal."

"Yes, Celestia was the talk of the refectory this morning, and the noblemen's names are known, Paolo included. Zanetta was livid, and it was all I could do not to slap her over her ravings about the Zane name being sullied."

"She said the same to me in the parlour, as Luca was leaving." I shook my head. "I cannot even report the words she used to slander my family name. I can only imagine Zago's reaction and hope Rosa does not suffer. But we both knew this would be all over the city come first light, Venice being how it is."

"This republic does love a good scandal, and to lay the blame wherever feasible."

"I suppose these days such gossip distracts us from the dread of being sacked."

"In this case, however, it does nothing to raise the esteem of the convents. For many, this will be further proof that our sins contribute to the insecurity of our city, and we will be scrutinized more than ever."

"I suppose so." I hoped that didn't mean Luca could no longer visit as a non-relation, but clearly I would have to be more circumspect, with Zanetta searching for further reasons to hate my family.

Livia straightened herself. "Still, we do have freedoms within these walls, if we are careful."

She must have been talking about herself and Elisabetta. They certainly were discreet, my having had no knowledge of their liaison until last night. How long had it been going on? They'd known each other for two decades. Nor had I known of Viena's intrigue, right next door, until she herself told me. As I considered both these affairs, I found myself decreasingly scandalized and increasingly envious. "Yes, it matters whether one flaunts those freedoms with a festa or tells not a soul."

"Exactly. One must exercise supreme discretion. For instance, you must by now realize that not all the children we care for are foundlings, boarding girls, and future postulants. One of the toddlers we currently care for is the son of a nun."

Of course. How could I not have realized it sooner? "It is easy enough to mix such a child among the others, although clearly with Mother Marina's tacit acceptance."

"It is not something Angela Riva would have allowed. How she would have run the convent, much more strictly and I feel without heart, was part of the reason for such a contentious vote. I believe such compassion and

prudence is good politics on the part of Mother Marina. If our convent
cannot be completely virtuous, better to give the appearance of being so.
Thus she keeps her nuns happy as well as the government and the Church.
She learned this from the abbesses before her, and I do not take the lesson
lightly."

"But what about what God thinks?"

"I believe God understands that good governance is a virtue. As it says
in Romans, *Pay to all what is owed to them: taxes to whom taxes are owed,
revenue to whom revenue is owed, respect to whom respect is owed, honour
to whom honour is owed.* Respect and honour are necessary for harmony,
and for love. And of course, there is always absolution through confession.
Besides, God is love incarnate. Love, I have come to realize, is the point of
everything. Love is not always sinful. Or at least would not be if one were
of a different class, or circumstance, or time."

My sidelong glances at my aunt turned into more of an open stare.
These were heretical thoughts indeed, with a clear classical influence, and
certainly suited her own attachment. They were also undeniably appealing.
I made notes in my head to sort them out in my diary as soon as I returned
to my room.

A gust of warm wind blew in from the northwest, bringing with it some
leaves and the scent of rain, and Livia brushed the stray hairs away from
her face. "Lord Cicogna is doing much for you today."

"True. Although I know he respects my father and is doing it for Paolo
too. Their friendship runs deep." A raindrop smacked the stone in front of
us, but neither Livia nor I made a move to rise.

She scoffed. "His love for you is clearly what is deep. You certainly
seem to be quite right in your assessment of his character. He is truly

an uncommon nobleman. I wonder what made him so." A smattering of more raindrops. My cheeks were wet, whether due to tears or rain I was unsure. "Surely you can see for yourself his affection. It is obvious enough to anyone who observes the two of you together for even a moment."

Viena had said much the same. Clearly I was a terrible player, despite my frequent prayers to alter my sentiments. "But what can I do about any of this? I cannot act on my emotions, and he is married besides. That would be foolhardy, particularly since you said the convents will come under increasing scrutiny. Not to mention the scrutiny of Zanetta and Angela Riva."

The rain spat down more persistently, and Livia arose now, as did I. "You are right, Niece. We must simply be thankful for his generosity, whatever the inducement, because it aids your honour, your family, and my sister." Her hair was matted to her head now, and I realized I must look similarly bedraggled. "Let us dry off before meeting at the refectory for the midday meal. Though I will warn you that you must be strong. The gossip is new and tantalizing."

"I may skip another meal, Auntie, if you do not mind taking the blow for the family."

She patted my arm and smiled wryly. "I do not mind in the least, Niece. That is what aunts are for." Scooping up a sodden Enrica, she went back inside, cooing to the chicken and leaving me to the elements and my thoughts. I was thoroughly drenched as well as disconcerted.

Reflexively I put my hand in my pocket and found the egg. With a yelp of frustration, I threw it at the courtyard wall, where it splattered against the stone, broken shell dripping down along with the yolk and white, mingling with the streaks of precipitation.

Chapter 30

After drying off back in my cell, I scribbled furiously in my diary as the rain beat down, trying to untangle my conversations with Luca and Livia.

Five pages I devoted to Livia's ideas on what made a good abbess, especially amid trouble and gossip—the political as well as spiritual nature of the role. That was something I'd never considered before, the abbess being like the doge of the convent, or perhaps the doge and Council of Ten combined into one, with the sisters making up a Great Council.

On another page, I sorted my web of feelings about Luca. I could not deny the obvious connection between us, noted by both Viena and Auntie Livia. Nor I could fathom his marriage to his wife. I knew most patrician men wedded with purpose and sought love outside the official union. Would Luca ever consider doing the same? His integrity might prevent him, and that was something I respected deeply about him. I certainly thought he would not if he were united with me, with love within our marriage. But he was not with me, I seemed to remind myself as often as the Marangona bell had rung throughout Venice's thousand-year history.

Would I be content to be his mistress?

But how could I dare such a thought when the government had arrested my very own brother for making merry with nuns? How could I expose Luca to such scandal? Let alone San Zaccaria, my auntie, Mother Marina, my own mother? Myself?

Auntie Livia's words echoed in my ears: *One must exercise supreme discretion.*

Could I exercise such discretion? To satisfy a whim?

But it was not merely a whim. The love I felt for Luca was beyond my power. I even wondered if God had something to do with it, then just as quickly dismissed such an apostate thought. God and Venice would consider me little more than a whore, no better than La Diamante, if I sinned with him. Though would any of this matter anyway if soldiers invaded the city and raped me?

I took a deep breath. I did not have to sin with Luca. To spend time with him was not a sin. Was it? I need not damn myself to eternal Hell. Just be with him, alone, in broad daylight. It certainly was a tempting thought.

Would such a meeting bring me peace, or just increase my desire?

If Luca were willing, could we manage it, with supreme discretion? How could we evade notice? And if we couldn't, would he be arrested like Paolo?

What would be my punishment?

I had no answers, just a never-ending list of questions that I scrawled out until my hand ached, knowing I was searching for a loophole that increasingly felt like a noose.

Dolce eventually nudged me, reminding me it was time for his walk. I put down my writing and took him to the courtyard, hovering in the doorway with a towel in hand as he gambolled in the puddles, although the rain had let up and sunrays peeked through the clouds as if God Himself were making His presence known. The broken egg had slid down the wall, the liquid innards now barely visible, remnants only I knew were there, just like my love for Luca.

As I stood there in contemplation, gazing at Dolce's frolics, a hand patted my shoulder. Elisabetta. "Your maidservant has come," she said. "I would be happy to dry Dolce and return him to your cell so you can speak with her."

Elisabetta was always so thoughtful, and I murmured my thanks, feeling awkward as I passed along the towel. Knowing her secret, I was unable to look her in the eye. She seemed slightly puzzled by my distance but merely smiled.

I hurried to the parlour to see Madelena. She was breathless and pale, having rushed here on foot from Piazza San Marco, where Teodor awaited my father's emergence from yet another senatorial meeting. I hugged her quickly, then, seeing the array of visitors in the parlour, suggested we return to my cell for privacy.

Upon our entry, a dry Dolce, already delivered by Elisabetta, wagged his tail in greeting. I shoved my burgeoning diary into my trunk. Madelena could not read, but better I formed the habit of stowing it away when not in use.

She petted Dolce. "I saw your brother just before his arrest and so was able to visit your mother's midwife, Signora Benedetta. She is now in worse health than at your mother's delivery a few months ago, but she said as long as she could she'd be happy to look after anyone associated with the Soranzo family, Rosa in particular since she delivered her herself."

"That is a relief." I sat on the edge of my bed, feeling a bit lighter at this disclosure.

"She and I went to see Rosa this morning. I simply told Signora Zane she was a special friend of your mother's, and surprisingly she allowed us in, although she grumbled quite a bit about your brother sullying their family's name. She was probably happy it wasn't your brother visiting, so felt an old crone wasn't a threat. Besides, you know how prudent Signora Benedetta can be. Anyway, Signora Benedetta confirmed Rosa is with child." She cleared her throat, and I worried how taxed she was by her various duties. "In fact, the signora seems to be able to tell just upon looking at a woman."

"I guess it's her half century of experience. So now we wait until Lord Cicogna visits Rosa with the notary."

She raised an eyebrow at the name, and I filled her in on all that had transpired, leaving out the part about La Diamante and her demands.

"I am sure you welcome such assistance from Lord Cicogna," she said, and I ignored her obvious double meaning. "I gather as soon as your sister writes her will, she can break the news to the Zanes?"

"Yes, and then Signora Benedetta can tell my brother-in-law to give Rosa a rest."

Madelena stroked Dolce, who had curled himself on her lap. She seemed fatigued, and I wondered if she was becoming infirm. "I hope so. Your sister appeared very tired and pale. She feels quite queasy most of the time. And it didn't help when I told her what has happened to your brother. Signora Benedetta had luckily brought along some mint and even had some fresh ginger. Very good for nausea. She said the added benefit of ginger over mint is that it spices the breath, not always pleasing to a man. So that may help for now."

"I'm hoping Lord Cicogna will take the notary to her later today. He can reassure her about Paolo too, as he will have seen him this morning. Though I'm not sure how he'll manage getting past the Zane guards."

"Your Lord Cicogna is an intelligent man. He will think of something."

Someone else calling Luca mine. But I needed to push away such thoughts and take advantage of Madelena's brief presence. "How fares Mama?"

"That is the second reason I have come to you today. Your mother is not well at all."

"Oh no! Because of Paolo's arrest?"

"Ever since your visit on the Ascension she seemed to be slightly improving, but after your brother's arrest yesterday, she returned to her bed. She refuses to let me open the curtains and leaves her food and drink untouched. Your father was so worried last night that he sent Teodor for the doctor, who diagnosed melancholia. He let her blood, but I'm not sure it did any good. And your father couldn't pay the man. The doctor was none too pleased to have to await his fee, but your father said he would pay the moment his ship comes in." She whispered these final sentences. "I'm very sorry to bring you such ill tidings, Signora Justina."

I growled, angry at being unable to help my mother myself. "No, I thank you, Madelena. But you must return as quickly as possible to Mama and convey the message that she need no longer worry. Tell her that Papa's problem is taken care of." True enough, I hoped, and, regardless, it was what she needed to hear. "She will understand. And that I beg of her to eat something." Such soothing news would hopefully do much to allay Mama's fears and increase her appetite, even though I knew the matter would not be fully resolved until I spoke myself to La Diamante.

Madelena looked puzzled but nodded. "Of course, Signora."

I kept thinking. "Return here tomorrow afternoon. I should have word from Lord Cicogna about the notary by then. Then you can take Signora Benedetta back to the Zane palazzo to break the news. They may prefer their own midwife, but even Signora Zane will be unlikely to argue against Signora Benedetta, who delivered all my mother's children. And hopefully their joy at an impending heir will compel them to cover her cost. They would normally pay for their own midwife."

"Yes, Signora Justina."

"I suppose you have not seen Paolo since his arrest."

"No, just prior. As we were talking, the guards came to the palazzo. Your mother watched them take him away to the doge's prison."

"Oh, poor thing. She did not need to witness that."

She shook her head, her countenance pained. "When your father came home, he was livid, shouting all over the palazzo that Venice had bigger problems than a few wayward young noblemen. Not that your mother could do anything about it."

"I'm not surprised Papa is so angry. This is the last thing we all need. But apparently Paolo has a fine lawyer, so that is reason for hope." Though how we would pay for such legal counsel was another matter entirely, and one I could not even begin to contemplate. Hopefully the other young nobles' fathers would take care of that bill for the time being.

"Yes, hope." She gave Dolce a scratch behind the ears and stood up. "Hope would be helpful for your mother."

And me.

"I pray she will have it once you report my news to her. I also need you to procure a lock from my trunk." I gave her a few small coins, leaving even less to repay my family's debt. "That should cover it. Bring it to me when you return tomorrow."

"Yes, Signora Justina."

"Thank you for everything."

She curtsied. "Of course."

"One last thing, Madelena."

"What's that, Signora Justina?"

"Rest when you can. You look exhausted. We all rely on you so much; we need you to be in good health."

Her beautiful face contorted as she tried to staunch her tears. I trusted she knew not every slave engendered such compassion. "I appreciate your concern, Signora. I will try."

I hugged her, and we clung to each other a moment longer than was usual.

"Until tomorrow then," I said as she hastened out.

As my cell door clicked closed behind her, I thought of my mother crying at home. Of Paolo laughing in prison. Of Rosa hoping to get a good night's sleep. Of a courtesan's avarice. Of Father Hieronimo's sermon, and the pious monk in the San Zaccaria campo. Of the pope's army on the mainland.

Of Livia and Elisabetta, their many years together. Of Viena and Jacomo, and the sheer happiness my neighbour radiated.

I thought of God, and what sin was. Of what Livia said about God as love incarnate.

Of what she had said about discretion.

And then I made a decision.

Chapter 31

Just as the cook stepped out for a moment, I dashed into the kitchen to fill a basket with freshly baked goods for the poor, the Realtina bell signalling the end of curfew reverberating across the stone walls. The cook would not question me, long used to my sisters' conventual quirks, but I didn't need any unnecessary raising of eyebrows.

Back in my cell, after dressing in full habit, I counted my ducats. I had only twenty-nine in my possession, from Viena, Livia, and Elisabetta, plus the Carpaccio drawing that I thought might fetch a sum of five or so, although it was unclear who would buy it, and on such short notice. Paolo had the rest, who knew where at this point. Besides, he would need them for his own legal troubles, even if he were to avoid a fine.

I sighed. Today was La Diamante's deadline, and the amount would have to do. I dropped the coins into a small velvet pouch, then threaded the basket on my elbow and tiptoed through the empty parlour. With a backward glance, I slipped through the door. Technically I was not to leave the convent without permission, but since I planned to give food to the poor right in our square, there was little chance of punishment. If caught, I assumed Mother Marina would sternly chastise me, but also understand I was a new nun still becoming accustomed to the rules. I could even say I was doing penance for my brother's transgressions. All part of the truth I was finding increasingly bendable.

The campo sat mostly empty, the preaching monk absent, but a family huddled in the church doorway, children and father sleeping while the mother stared vacantly toward the wellhead. They were dressed strangely for Venetians, and I suspected they might be Jews from the Veneto, seeking shelter in our city from possible papal slaughter, as was being whispered.

With trepidation, I offered the woman some pastries from my basket. Her eyes focused warily on me, but she accepted, prodding her husband and children to arise. The kids sleepily stuffed the food in their mouths, while the father widened his eyes, I supposed due to never having seen a nun up close before. He thanked me as they packed their meagre belongings and hurried away, the children licking their fingers as they peered back over their shoulders longingly in hopes of more.

I waved goodbye just as Luca entered the campo, La Diamante on his arm. I swallowed hard at the sight of them. Luca eyed me carefully, while La Diamante smiled easily. She was dressed very well for so early, in a spotless red silk day dress with a dangerously low neckline, her hair swept up in those fashionable horns. No chopines, I assumed so she could manoeuvre herself easily without assistance. She had painted her face quite liberally, although close up I noticed that she'd been unable to fully mask the bags under her eyes. Given her profession, she must keep very late hours, and I wondered how Luca had coaxed her out so soon after sunrise, even if she did want to collect her money. A bribe, I thought wryly, given the courtesan's mercenary instincts. In the case of Luca, I hoped the bribe had been monetary and nothing more.

"My dear Sister! Soranzo, isn't it? La Diamante, as I'm sure you remember." She did not speak loudly but neither did she make any attempt to lower her voice, as if it were perfectly normal for a nun and a courtesan to converse openly in a square. I glanced around, hoping no one was around to overhear, and was rewarded with an empty square save for our unholy trinity. "I recall meeting you at the draper's shop a month or two ago. Such an interesting young woman." She appraised me critically. "Not as obviously beautiful as your sister, but a very appealing appearance nonetheless." She winked at me. Mortified at this display in front of Luca, I tried to quell my anger at the woman—her greed, deception, power.

Luca disengaged his arm from hers and stood beside me, his presence centring me and giving me courage. "Good morning, Signora Soranzo."

"Good morning." I closed the top of my basket. "I was just feeding the poor while I waited." I nodded my head in the direction of the church doorway. "A family slept there last night. Jews, I think." I added that afterthought to answer Luca's surprised expression. Venice did not usually have itinerants.

"Ah, I should inform the Council. We have heard rumours of them in the city. They are seeking safe harbour." He implored me with his eyes to begin talking to La Diamante. I was exposing myself to risk the longer I was in her presence. It would not do for me to be seen talking to such a woman in public and at such an odd hour.

La Diamante was looking up at the white and pink marble facade of San Zaccaria. "Many friends have told me I simply must visit this grand church. I've never had the time or inclination before, but now you and Lord Cicogna have given me the opportunity. We enjoyed discussing old times on the way over, didn't we, Your Excellency?"

Old times? Did I want to know more? Luca looked slightly abashed as he ever so slightly shook his head, but La Diamante just kept blithely smiling, her lips painted to be red. She was scented with perfume reminiscent of oleander, a lovely-smelling spider spinning her web.

I pushed down the urge to wipe the smile from her face and tried to decide what to say, wishing I'd rehearsed an opening line for this intimidating woman. "I believe my family has some unresolved business with your, um, establishment."

"Ah yes, true. In the last few days, I have received quite a few letters from your father, begging for more time." I felt some measure of relief that Papa at least had tried to save me, even if he had to resort to begging. "Once delivered by your family's gorgeous slave, but otherwise by your very handsome gondolier." Madelena hadn't mentioned such an errand and perhaps did not realize the letter's contents and its connection to me. And what must Teodor think?

As I reached into my basket, she laughed. "Are you to repay me with baked goods? I do hear San Zaccaria makes some of the best pastries in the city, but I doubt that would be sufficient."

I forced myself to laugh too, although Luca did not join in. "Of course not." I pulled out the velvet pouch and jangled it a little. "I have twenty-nine ducats here." Luca's eyes widened when I said the amount, and he looked from me to the courtesan, understanding dawning in his eyes as I felt myself blush at this crass exchange.

La Diamante looked at me patronizingly. "A dent in the debt, certainly, but you do know, Sister, that your father and brother owe me a hundred?" Luca's expression betrayed his shock.

My mouth went dry. "A down payment. I also have a drawing by Carpaccio in my room. A beautiful Madonna and Child. I believe it's worth another five ducats at least."

"And the other sixty-six?" She cast a hard eye upon me and reached over to finger my veil. "I've heard you have quite glorious hair. Did the abbess shear it all off or does she allow you to keep a little? That could be intriguing to the right man, with the heaviest purse."

Luca raised his eyebrows in alarm, clearly in full comprehension now. "Signora Soranzo, if I may?" he interjected, but I ignored him, if only to end my humiliation as swiftly as possible.

"I'm hoping you will let me repay the balance at a later date." I cursed the timidity in my voice, the war for waylaying my father's ship, and myself for bringing Luca into this. How could I have been so stupid?

"Unfortunately, no." La Diamante smiled as if she were truly sorry, and I felt both my virtue and Luca's esteem for me slipping through my fingers. Perhaps if I had a more commanding presence, like Mother Marina. I consoled myself with the idea that perhaps I could beg Luca to bid for me after all. "I need repayment in full—now. The war, you know. Much too risky to have outstanding amounts owing."

Luca pulled himself to his fully impressive height, and La Diamante finally paid him attention, looking up at him with open admiration. "Signora Spin, I believe there has been some misunderstanding, which can be easily rectified."

"The only rectification is payment in full." La Diamante certainly had a knack for steeliness, even while she flirted. "Lord Cicogna, I know your family understands such business arrangements. Your father has spoken to me often of his trading ventures and how he has increased his prosperity. I have listened well to his advice."

"Then I believe we speak the same language." Luca waved away my velvet pouch. "Signora Soranzo, you can put that away. You won't be needing it."

Did Luca mean to pay? In full and immediately? I reddened as I spoke. "Whatever do you mean, Lord Cicogna? I cannot have you pay my family's debt."

"We'll discuss the matter later. You had best go inside now." He looked at me as the first Marangona bell clanged. I could not decipher the meaning in his eyes. Luca, whose father's ship had recently come in, whose family had, as Paolo once said, the Midas touch. Who cared for me, even if he shouldn't—and perhaps was now regretting it. "In the meantime, I believe Signora Spin and I should visit my bank. It's not far. Shall we?" With a tight smile, he put out his arm for La Diamante.

La Diamante shrugged at our exchange, then took his elbow and leaned close. "Yes, let's. I don't care who pays me what I'm owed. And I do so prefer a bank to a church. Since I know I'm already headed straight to Hell, church seems like a waste of time, really." She had a hard beauty, an easy charm, and I was relieved to see her go as much as I felt the indignity of all my family's secrets laid bare before Luca. "It was lovely to make your acquaintance again, Sister Soranzo. You can pray for me. I need all the prayers I can get. That is, unless you sully your honour with unnatural fornication by your own choosing." She watched for Luca's reaction. His smile remained small, and she laughed. "If that happens, do visit me at my palazzo and tell me all. I should love to hear the particulars of that story."

They then walked away, leaving me with the velvet pouch still clinking with ducats and my mouth agape. Just after they left the square, the barefoot monk marched in and readied himself to preach, eyeing me with suspicion.

I forced myself to offer some pastries to him and his followers who straggled in, which they did not spurn despite their obvious disapproval of me. As the monk's full mouth started to boom out chastisements, I returned to the convent, wondering if I could ever again look Luca in the eye. That is, if I even saw him again after this utter abasement.

Back in my cell, I changed out of my habit and tried to untangle what had just happened. Luca was going to pay my family's debt of a hundred ducats, no questions asked. It was too much to fathom. I felt relief of course, puzzlement as to his motives, surprise at his generosity, and a large wave of gratitude. But I was having difficulty separating this from my abject humiliation.

He was to return later that day to report on Rosa, not to mention now La Diamante. I half hoped he would and half hoped he'd leave me to my disgrace. After replenishing my personal treat supply with the remainders from the basket, I ate two pastries for breakfast, then sat down to write it all out, though I kept coming back to my shame. How could I face him? If he even came.

Finally, a servant told me of his arrival with the mid-afternoon bells. My heart sped up at this pronouncement, and my hands felt sweaty.

I met him respectably in the parlour with my ducat-filled pouch in my pocket and my head dipped, unable to meet his eyes. I reddened as he spoke, his voice a low rumble as he described his successful visit to his banker. If he hadn't before comprehended the entire extent of La Diamante's demands and what he'd saved me from, he certainly did now. "Your virtue remains unblemished. La Diamante has agreed to remain quiet and not contribute to the Venetian gossip mill." That meant he'd paid the greedy strumpet even more for her silence. How much in all?

"Thank you." My voice was barely above a whisper.

He did not reply as I continued to stare at the floor.

"Will you not look at me?" His own voice was quiet.

I shook my head. "It will take me a long while to raise the funds I owe you, but I swear I will somehow. Just tell me the full amount. I will give you what I can now." I reached into my pocket.

He waved his hand. "It is entirely unnecessary."

"Please, I must. I cannot be your charity case."

"You are the furthest from charity, and I will not accept any money from you."

"You won't?"

"I will not. Not ever." He cleared his throat. "Moreover, you must know you have nothing to be ashamed of."

I glanced up to see him looking at me, and again I could not read his meaning. Could he really mean to never be repaid such a sum?

"You were trying to help your family, no matter the cost, and that takes considerable bravery. It in fact makes me admire you all the more."

I looked at him now in wonder. "Truly?"

"Truly."

"How can I ever thank you enough?"

He looked at me. "There is no need. I wanted to do it."

I shook my head. "Why?"

"You know why. I have the means, and then some. What better use to put it to than saving your honour? I could not live with myself otherwise. And you would do the same in return if you were in my position. I know that."

I searched for the right words to respond, which seemed beyond my capability.

He smiled tentatively. "I have other news for you, Signora."

We were not alone, of course, and our formal postures and interactions respected that. Several sisters sat murmuring with their visitors, little Santina among them with her mother and younger brother. She gave me her customary sticking out of her tongue now, for which childishness her mother chided her with a swat to her arm. Her brother watched with interest and stuck his own tongue out at his sister behind his mother's back.

I tried to ignore my diminutive nemesis as Luca relayed his success in locating the notary, learning the particulars from Paolo in prison, and going to the Zane palazzo to speak with Rosa.

"And Signora Zane let you in? Under what pretense?"

"No pretense. All the nobility knows what happened to your brother and the others, and I said I'd come as a family representative to brief your sister. Zane Elder and Younger"—that would be Zago and his father—"were at the doge's palazzo, and Signora Zane seemed grateful for further information." He noted my distressed look. "Do not fret—I only told her what is already widely known. Besides," he seemed reticent to add, "my great-aunt is the widow of Signora Zane's cousin, so there are distant relations to help grease the hinges of their door."

"I did not know your families were connected."

He smiled ruefully. "Such a tenuous connection, there never seemed a reason to tell you. You know how it is in Venice. Someday the Great

Council may allow unfettered access to the Golden Book, so we can verify all our interconnected relations as well as certify our noble blood. But I digress. Your family's notary drew up your sister's will to your brother's specifications, with her dowry to be given only to her surviving children or otherwise returned to the Soranzo family. Paolo has been named the executor and a Soranzo cousin is the substitute, in the event Paolo continues to have legal troubles." He seemed reluctant to admit the possibility that my brother's woes could continue longer than expected.

"Thank you for all this." An entirely inadequate sentiment for all that he'd done. "How did my sister seem?"

"She certainly was shocked to see me. I have not seen her since her wedding, and I was the last person she was expecting to visit. She seemed . . . thinner and paler than her wedding day."

"Ill though? Should I worry?"

"Midwifery is an area in which I sorely lack knowledge, but she assured me she was well, thanked me profusely, and asked me to send you her love. And so I do, with pleasure."

"Thank you, Lord Cicogna. I truly do not know how to repay you."

"As I said, there is no reason to repay me. And it is you I thank for allowing me to serve you. And your family." He added it as an afterthought, for decorum's sake, I thought.

His eyes slipped from mine. I glanced around the room as I gathered my courage, my heart sinking as I spotted Zanetta approaching Santina and her family.

Luca noticed her as well and stood a bit straighter. "Well, I must go. The Great Council is convening this afternoon, and soon. Please pass my regards to your aunt." He brushed invisible lint from his shoulder before lowering his voice. "I unfortunately know not when I will see you again. I hope you keep well."

My heart dropped at that prospect. I could not just let him leave without knowing when or if I'd see him. After all my worries over his respect for me, now that I knew he still possessed it, I could not just let him walk away. Never mind Zanetta, it was now or perhaps never. "Lord Cicogna, please wait a moment. There is one other matter we must discuss."

His brows rose, hope seeping into his countenance. "Of course."

I stood peeping up at him, then swayed, almost quite literally dizzy. Could I truly make this proposal?

His eyes widened in alarm. "You seem unwell. Please sit."

Agreeing this was a favourable idea, I settled myself on the closest settee as he spied a tray with a pitcher and brought me a cup of water. Zanetta appraised my situation with sneering interest before resuming her prattle with Santina's mother.

"Thank you." I took a sip along with a deep breath.

"Shall I call for aid?" He kneaded his hands together, his eyes flickering toward Santina and Zanetta. The last people I wanted.

I shook my head. "Please stay, just a moment longer. I know you must take leave."

"All right." He sat across from me, his long limbs folded gingerly under his seat, ready to spring into action should the need arise, his shoes tapping the floor.

The Great Council required his attendance, to help defend the sanctity of the Venetian Republic, and would note his tardiness. It was probably too late to avoid Zanetta's suspicions, although the Zane and Cicogna connection might serve there. I needed to muster my courage, and now. "Lord Cicogna?"

"Yes?"

I drained the cup. "Luca?" My voice was barely audible, but my heart-beat thundered.

He stared at me, frozen, his volume matching my own. "Yes, Justina?"

I had to do this. "I want to thank you properly. And before you tell me it is not necessary," for I saw him take a breath to speak, "I need to say it is partly for selfish reasons."

He looked intrigued and leaned over to catch my whispered words.

I inhaled deeply. *Say it.* "Let us have a day together."

He bit his lip. "What do you mean?"

What was I doing? I could not propose such a thing. Everyone would view me as little more than a harlot propositioning him, as immoral as if La Diamante had succeeded in selling my virginity, even if I stayed as chaste as the Virgin Mary. I started to shake my head. "Never mind. I should not have—"

"Yes."

And that one utterance changed everything. I forced myself to look directly in those eyes, the rich brown of olive wood.

He continued in a whisper. "A picnic on a lagoon island. I will arrange it all. Your birthday is soon, if I recall correctly. The twenty-ninth of June."

I could scarcely believe my ears, and I trembled.

"I must take my leave now, Signora Soranzo." Luca spoke loudly and bowed with formality.

Zanetta coughed just then and came over to greet Luca. Had she heard anything? I did not think it possible, as she had been conversing directly with Santina's mother, but I knew I risked much to make such an arrange-ment in the crowded parlour.

Zanetta and Luca exchanged pleasantries, she saying how very well he looked, and he mentioned having seen her mother earlier that day, for whose tidings she was glad, if a little curious. The whole time she studiously ignored me and did not engage me in conversation, which was just as well, as my heart was dancing in my chest and every ounce of strength compelled me to betray no emotion.

"Well, Signora Zanetta, I must rush over to make the final meeting of the Great Council this afternoon." Luca directed his statement to Zanetta, who smiled quite widely, perhaps even genuinely.

"Of course, Lord Cicogna." Was her friendliness simply due to their familial connection, however tenuous?

He bid us both farewell, bowing again, even kissing the back of Zanetta's hand. I felt a surge of envy and chided myself. But as he took my hand to do likewise, all jealousy was replaced with savouring the feel of his lips on my skin.

As he exited the convent, Zanetta looked at me, her green eyes intent. "What were you two discussing so intimately?"

I forced myself to arise, my own height topping Zanetta by a head, and instead of feeling gangly, I felt mighty. "Lord Cicogna was bringing me word of my family."

"Ah yes, of your disgraced brother and destitute father. How fare they?"

"Of my sister, who I may remind you is your sister as well."

"Your sister will prove her worth only when she bears a child, and a son at that."

I stayed silent. Zanetta would know soon enough about Rosa's baby, although I longed to throw the news in her face.

"I hope you don't also besmirch the good name of Cicogna, another relation of mine. Our families are close." She turned without another word, leaving me to sink back upon the settee, head back, eyes closed, trying to tame the fever that coursed through my body, not sure I could wait another month.

Not sure if I was condemning myself—and Venice—to eternal damnation.

And not sure I cared.

Chapter 32

June passed slowly but terrifyingly as I counted the days to my assignation, and I wavered between guilt and excitement, leavened with continual worry over Venice being sacked. The pope's army invaded Padua early in the month, and desperate people began flooding into Venice, chief among them frightened Paduans and terrorized Jews, the latter never having had permission to stay for longer than a few days in the history of the Serene City. So worried were the Great Council about imminent papal invasion that they even scaled back the Corpus Christi celebrations. The government banned women and children from participating, and armed men of all classes filled Piazza San Marco surrounded by hundreds of lion-spangled flags, ready to clash with the Warrior Pope should he storm between the columns of San Marco and San Teodor.

His Holiness didn't, and things settled back to the new normal state of edginess, which at least allowed for some movement within the city. The day after Corpus Christi, one week into June, Mama and Papa finally visited.

Papa updated us on governmental concerns over the Jewish influx as well as possible traitors in our midst. I was unsure how to feel at the sight of him. Anger certainly, and disappointment, but he was my father and thus I followed Moses's commandment. He did not mention La Diamante, but neither could he look me in the eye. I wondered if he knew Luca had covered his debt or thought La Diamante had just waived the amount owed. Regardless, he was clearly too ashamed to talk with me about the matter. His ship still had not come in and now there was talk of it being lost or sunk, but he had just been repaid another small outstanding loan, presumably allowing him to remit Mama's doctor's fee. In all, we had a pleasant if slightly awkward visit. Papa's farewell hug felt extra tender, and did I imagine him muttering a brief apology in my ear?

Mama stayed, the weight of the world clearly lifted off her shoulders since the government had blessedly released Paolo from prison the day before—in addition, perhaps, to the knowledge my honour had not been sullied. Accordingly, we had much cause for celebration, and she joined Livia and me for the midday service, followed by a meal in the refectory that she thoroughly enjoyed, giving her compliments to the cooks. She told us of her concern for Madelena's uneven health and was clearly thrilled at the thought of her first grandchild, but mostly she smiled more than I could remember. She left only when Teodor came to escort her home in the waning light.

Paolo briefly visited the day after that, confident the government would soon entirely dismiss his case, forming plans to meet with his fraternity, saying the city could use some levity and rueful that Luca could no longer join them as a married man. I tried not to blush at the name, our clandestine visit never far from my mind. But I also was annoyed at my brother's seeming selfishness and inability to learn a lesson.

Rosa came too, Signora Zane bringing her along on one of her visits to Zanetta. Rosa reported that her overnight situation with Zago had calmed down, along with her queasiness. "Although I do worry about Signora Benedetta. She keeps complaining of agita in her chest." Zago, finally displaying something akin to joy at the prospect of his heir, had readily agreed to pay for our midwife's services and presented Rosa with a small painting of the Virgin and Child by Titian, which she dutifully looked at each day, praying for a beautiful boy. She had even visited Mama a few times, Signora Zane's stubbornness softened by the idea of a grandson. In fact, Rosa reported the entire family was being much kinder, at least by their standards.

I had not seen Luca since making our hasty arrangement in the parlour, though he had sent me a brief note to formulate our plan, which I memorized, then burned in the fire. The Great Council was meeting regularly and with urgency, and Paolo's release meant there was no good excuse for Luca to come to the convent. He had breathed not a word of his role in paying La Diamante on my behalf to anyone, and Paolo did not even ask how we had found the money to satisfy the courtesan, likely assuming Papa had taken care of it while he was in jail.

Zanetta made it a habit to study my every move, and I shuddered every time I saw her. Realizing I could not be absent from San Zaccaria for an entire day without assistance, I revealed my plans to Livia, who was half-delighted, half-distressed. Even as she related the story of a San Zaccaria nun from the previous century who'd run off with her lover, she feared the danger in the wake of Celestia. Still, she seemed to understand my need. Reiterating the requirement of discretion, she contrived for me to "fall ill" after supper the evening before and be sequestered in my room, under strict instruction to be nursed only by herself to restrict possible contagion. At the ringing of the early morning bells, after the handful of our sisters who were awake before sunrise made their way to the church service, Livia escorted me from my room. Our destination was the water entrance on the Rio del Greci, but we only got to the hall near the refectory before we ran into Zanetta emerging from the kitchens, looking bleary-eyed. Her face lit up at the sight of me, and my heart stopped.

"I thought you, my dear sister, were ill and not to leave your room." She eyed us with suspicion, and I tried to look miserable, glad that despite the heat I had thrown on a dark cloak to cover my head and dress, which was making me slightly sweat.

Livia looked at her steadily, barely taking a breath before relating our agreed-upon fabrication. "My niece is feeling quite poorly this morning, so I am taking her to the infirmary."

Zanetta sniffed. "She seems able to walk without a problem."

"With all due respect, you are far from an infirmarian, so I prefer our sister Teresa diagnose her. We even discussed last evening that she may need to call upon one of the newly arrived Hebraic doctors, who of course would be unable to set foot through our hallowed doors. This has all been approved by Mother Marina."

Livia spoke as calmly as a canal surface in the dead of night, even though both Mother Marina and Teresa were ignorant of our plan. We hoped Zanetta's natural antipathy toward the two women would prevent casual inquiries.

Finally, Zanetta gave a curt nod and allowed us to pass without further interrogation, although I could feel her eyes on my back as we continued our brief journey.

As we passed the closed infirmary door near the water entrance, Livia sighed with relief. "That was lucky. I will need to keep track of Zanetta throughout the day to ensure she speaks to neither Mother Marina nor Teresa."

"I am sorry, Auntie. I do not envy you that task. I do not have to go." I forced myself to say the last. While there was nothing I wished for more, I could not endanger myself or my aunt.

She scoffed. "I told you our prison has its pleasant moments. This is one of the advantages of such a wealthy and prestigious convent as ours, a little freedom. I promised you that, as long as you exercise prudence."

"Auntie, I do not plan to . . . be with Lord Cicogna in the way you are imagining."

She just kissed me on both cheeks as we confirmed plans for my return that evening, when she would escort me back under the same pretense.

We stood for a moment, the brackish canal water teething at the stone, the last of the stars fading as the sky transformed from black to indigo. A pair of swans like large white clouds floated on the water, their heads tucked under their wings, as a gondola pulled up, a lantern on the prow, the gondolier on the stern, rubbing his sleepy eyes.

I, on the other hand, was acutely awake, as ready as I'd ever be, as the sun rose, the heat of the day rising as fast as the blood in my veins.

Chapter 33

Luca was inside the *felze*, curtains fully drawn, not the usual place for a man but wise in such a situation requiring the utmost discretion. It was quite dark behind the curtains, and he greeted me with an abbreviated bow before helping me settle myself, our hands touching in a brief, delicate dance before he sat, his long legs folding to the side like a grasshopper askew.

The closed curtains muffled the sounds of the awakening city: the screeching seagulls, the shouting boatmen, the clanging bells. The gondolier rowed us away from the city and further south, beyond San Giorgio Maggiore and its monastery, along the Lido and well into the lagoon. Everything became more hushed until all that could be heard was the lapping water and the *barcarolle* he sang to keep his strokes rhythmic. Luca and I were in a humid cocoon, the only two people on earth. I could hardly believe I was alone with a man in such a situation, let alone with this man in particular. I felt shy but also a level of trust I'd only ever experienced with a blood relative. I wondered how natural that was.

"Where are we going?" My throat felt dry and raspy, and he pulled a jug from the basket at our feet to pour us both cups of water.

"To an uninhabited island just west of Malamocco. It has fields and trees and crumbling old houses. It's peaceful and quite beautiful."

"Sounds heavenly. I've only really ever left Venice once before." I found my tongue had somewhat loosened. "When I was about six, we went to my grandfather's villa on the river Brenta. It was summer, and I remember running through the vineyards in my bare feet with Paolo and Rosa, playing hide-and-seek." I finished my water in a few gulps.

"I have similar memories of our family's villa. I look forward—" He stopped, turning to rummage through the basket again.

"What do you look forward to?"

"It's nothing." He took a cloth out of the basket and wiped his spotless hands. "I just wish I could go there again this summer. I know it's a childish desire these days."

"I don't think it's childish to yearn for a place that made you happy. But it is out of the question for now."

"I wonder if my family will even have a villa to go back to. A small matter when compared with sacked cities and fleeing residents, but still, it holds value for us, beyond the ducats." He briefly stretched his legs, clearly feeling a bit stiff from the cramped quarters. "Such a picturesque place, the Brenta. Why did you never return?"

"When my grandfather died a year later, Papa and his now late brother had to sell the estate to cover their father's debts."

"I'm sorry to hear it. I know your family has had financial . . . issues for some time."

I shrugged. "My mother used to say that my grandfather always acted like it was Carnival time, while my father has had to endure a long Lent. She once told Livia that the man was a mean old dotard. I don't think I was supposed to hear that."

Luca gave a short laugh, then apologized.

"No need, you don't offend me. I barely remember him, and not with any fondness."

The conversation lapsed back into nervous silence. I did not know what to say or how to act, and I suspected Luca felt the same, all confident appearance to the contrary.

"I have a gift for your birthday," he said, pulling a wrapped package tied with a ribbon from his basket and handing it to me. "Seventeen today."

I untied the ribbon to expose a flag fan. It took me a moment to find my voice. "A thousand thanks." I examined the ivory handle and delicate Burano lace. "It is beautifully crafted and perfect for today's heat." I started to wave it, grateful for its small breeze. Grateful to him.

"You are most welcome. We will arrive very soon." He wiped his brow with the back of his hand as we relapsed into timidity, knowing we were nearing our destination. The *felze* was fast becoming stifling as the sun rose higher. I was wearing a pale pink silk dress of Livia's that Elisabetta had altered and updated for me as a birthday gift after a consultation with her niece on the latest fashions, the heavy cloak already shed beside me on the cushion.

The gondola slowed, and the gondolier jumped out to pull the boat onto the rocky shore. Luca opened the curtains, and I was temporarily blinded by the brilliant sunlight bouncing off the azure lagoon, so calm and beautiful I could scarcely credit the ancient stories of the monsters that lurked within its deep.

Luca took my hand to assist me onto land, and I picked my way over the rocks in my slippers to the shade afforded by the trees along the shoreline. Luca and his gondolier followed with several large baskets, blankets, and a lady's parasol.

As my eyes adjusted to the light, I could see the gondola in full detail. Luca had not brought us in here in the regular Cicogna vessel. With its distinctive ornamentation, it would have been too recognizable. Instead, this one seemed to be rented or borrowed.

Luca instructed his gondolier to begin his return journey to the island when he heard the evening *compline* bells, which would afford us plenty of time before the curfew fires were lit. The gondolier nodded, smirking as his eyes raked over me fully.

I turned away, my face flushed, wondering if he'd remembered meeting me once and what he thought of me now. A naughty nun, bringing dishonour to the city? Or worthy of a risky affair for his young married master? Was he used to such trysts, with Luca or anyone else in the Cicogna family, or a former employer? Still, he treated Luca with only respect, bowing deeply before returning to the stern and giving a salute, and I remembered the old saying that a man could trust his gondolier with his life. I prayed it was true.

The gondola retreated northward until it was just a speck and then seemed to evaporate into nothingness. A few other boats were visible in the far distance, none coming close.

I turned to Luca, and he smiled at me tentatively.

We were alone.

The day was perfect. Hot, yes, but with a refreshing zephyr sidling in from the west. The lagoon was flecked with small islands, and beyond lay the more ominous mainland, the papal army camped somewhere on it.

But here, on this beautiful islet far from our usual universe, a warrior pope seemed a figment.

A few logs had washed up along the shore, and thereupon Luca was arraying fruit and pastries. He beckoned me over and bade me sit upon a blanket, offering me breakfast. I was hungry and took it gratefully, languidly fanning myself with his gift. We ate in peaceful silence as a flock of little stints splashed among the eelgrass-strewn rocks.

As we finished our meal, I extracted a small package from my reticule and handed it to Luca. "A present for you as well. To thank you . . . for everything."

He flashed me a quizzical smile, then unfolded the cloth wrapper. Inside were two white linen handkerchiefs edged with San Zaccaria lace befitting a man, on which I had embroidered Luca's initials. I had spent much time over the last month making them.

"Thank you. I shall treasure them." And he did seem most grateful as he looked boldly at me.

"You are very welcome."

"Shall we do a bit of exploring?" Luca suggested, tucking the handkerchiefs away for safekeeping and tidying up, placing heavy stones over the tops of the baskets to keep their contents safe from birds and animals. He removed his black robe, revealing a silk jacket, peplum, and colourful stockings from the Inamorati fraternity.

"Paolo would approve," he said with a gesture toward his legs. "It's too hot for my formal robe. But I had to wear it in transit, in case . . ."

In case he—*we*—were caught, his noble status might protect him, if he were able to think of a strong enough excuse for our being together, alone. But that was something I did not want to even consider.

He led me inland, through the stubby windblown trees and shrubbery into a more open field studded with red poppies. Although quite inviting, the grass grew long here, and I had trouble navigating in my dress and footwear, so Luca took my arm, sending a thrill through me, and we retraced our steps, deciding to stick with the shoreline.

We headed south in a silence that felt companionable, to me at least, although my heart hammered my chest and I was acutely aware of his closeness. We walked slowly, admiring the waterfowl, the flowers, the greenery, until we came to a small canal, across which lay a sister island. This twin contained some abandoned houses, the wayward stones interspersed with thick vegetation. One had a tree growing through the roof.

"I wonder who used to live there."

Luca gestured at the crumbling structures with his free hand. "These two islands were first settled over a thousand years ago. They flourished for centuries until Genoa captured Chioggia and everyone moved to the Giudecca for safety. No one has lived here for more than a hundred years."

"Why did they never come back?"

He shrugged. "Good question."

"Maybe once they'd made their new homes and livelihoods in the city, it was too much trouble to return to farming and fishing."

"I wish I could ask my old nurse, but she died when I was fifteen, soon before I left to study at the university in Padua. A good and kind woman. She told me about this island's history. Her ancestors lived here. When I was little, she'd commandeer the gondolier and bring me and my sister here every week on a fair day. Our adventures, she'd call them." He grinned at the recollection. "The two of them would lead us around on treasure hunts. We'd look for rocks and twigs and flowers and birds' nests and anything interesting like that, and then she'd feed us our midday meal before returning home."

I could not help but feel a little jealous. Beyond the one visit to my grandfather's villa on the Brenta, I'd been cloistered either in Venetian palazzi and gardens or at San Zaccaria. Rosa and I had taken a few picnics on the Lido, once with my father and Paolo when our mother was recovering from a rough stillbirth, and a few times with the nuns, but that was all.

Continuing our walk along the canal, we eventually came to a rickety old bridge. Luca inspected the connector, falling apart and far from safe to walk on. "Our gondolier would row us to the other island so we could explore there too, but I don't think we'll be doing that today."

A bit further along eastward, we spied the Lido in the distance, much closer than the mainland.

"I suggest we turn around rather than circling the island." He grasped my arm protectively, and I shivered.

"Are you chilled?" His brow furrowed with concern.

"Not at all. How could I be on such a fine day?"

His face relaxed. "It is indeed splendid." He turned us around, and we began the return journey. "Do you know why I felt we should go no further?"

"Why?"

He swallowed hard. "I did not want to risk anyone on the Lido seeing us, even from afar. Not only does it place you at risk—"

"What about yourself?"

He waved me away. "I can take care of myself. My concern is only for you."

Stopping for a moment, I looked up at him, and our eyes joined. "I am worried for you as well, especially after what happened to my brother." I felt slightly bitter at this intrusion of reality. It had been easy to slip into complacency, as if being alone together on this island were the most natural occurrence in the world.

"Do not forget he is now free. I am not sure how much the government actually cares about such transgressions with the pope's noose tightening round our neck. And we are just two people, not a full festa."

"True . . ." My voice trailed off. We both knew how reckless we were being and did not need to discuss it. My aunt's advice about discretion resounded in my head.

We resumed our stroll accompanied by the dulcet birdsong and softly lapping water, heading northward again on the west coast of the island.

"There is another less practical reason I do not want anyone to see us here." He ceased walking again, turning to face me. I shivered once more, and he gave a slight smile, clearly understanding this time it was not from any cold at all. "It is because this day is like a gift. Something I've wanted from the moment I met you. And I only want you"—he gently kissed my forehead—"and I to know about it."

I felt the same way, and I wanted to kiss him, desperately. But if we started, would we be able to stop?

What had I been thinking? Such a day alone with him would not conclude my feelings but further ignite them. And my determination to stay chaste would be impossible to maintain.

His eyes seared into me. "I know what you are thinking. I swear I will preserve your virtue."

I was not sure I wanted such a promise from him. "*Nothing deters a good man from what is honourable.*"

He smiled. "Seneca. Although I'm not certain how good a man I am."

"You are the best man I know. I am grateful to your nurse. She raised you very well, a true courtier."

He broke away, staring out over the turquoise waters, tiny whitecaps dancing on the surface. The dorsal fins of a small pod of dolphins broke through the surface, a veritable festa. "I am not honourable. I am greedy and selfish. If I did not have this day with you, I could not bear to go on with my wife. To never know true happiness."

"Do you worry it will make things worse? The longing?"

He raked his hand through his hair. "Of course I do. But as Virgil wrote, *A joy it will be to one day remember this.*"

I sighed. "I hope you are right."

"I do too."

The sun was now directly overhead and sweat crept down my neck. I'd left the parasol and the flag fan with the baskets, and I worried the sun on my skin would later give me away, even if I committed not a moment of true sin. "Upon reflection, I should never have asked you for a day. I am no better than La Diamante. I do not know what I was thinking."

"You're not that sort of woman at all. Do not let yourself believe that for one moment. Seneca would be proud of you."

I snorted in a most unladylike fashion. "I'm not sure I'm so honourable either. My mind betrays me in the eyes of Christ. He knows my unholy heart."

"What is in your heart, if not holiness?"

Lust, love. I believed it to be the latter, but it was quite entwined with the first and a sin in any event, no matter how much I tried to justify it.

He rubbed roughly at his eyes. "I beg your forgiveness, Justina. We have clearly made a mistake coming here. I wish I could call my gondolier back right now." He stalked away, back toward our picnic. He was angry, but I knew it wasn't with me.

I lagged, unsure of what to do. Comfort him, yell at him, kiss him, slap him. All of them and all at once, I felt.

Back at our logs, he removed the rocks from the basket tops and yanked out items for our midday meal, refusing to look at me, while I opened the parasol, grateful for its cooling shade and for keeping me busy. Finally he flung himself on a blanket, leaning back, legs outstretched before him, one colourful knee up, looking out over the water.

I sat down beside him and sipped some wine. "I believe we should forgive each other. And ourselves."

A seagull screeched overhead before diving into the water to snatch a fish.

"We are mere mortals, Luca, prone to sin. No matter, I'm glad I'm here." And I truly was, for it would be all I'd ever have.

He directed his gaze far into the distance. "There is an island to the northwest of here. I think you can just make it out." He pointed to a blemish on the water. "San Anzolo di Contorta. Do you know it?"

"There used to be a convent there. I've heard it mentioned a few times. Mama once spoke of it. Some scandal closed it a few decades ago."

"The pope formally shut it down in 1474. Do you know why?"

I shook my head. I'd heard whispers over the years but never knew exactly what happened, nor thought to inquire. I realized now there was only one reason Pope Sixtus would have gone to the extreme measure of closing a convent—deviant crimes.

"Affairs of the heart. The nuns with nobles and commoners alike. And children from those affairs."

I swallowed hard, preferring Luca's description over mine. *Affairs of the heart.* "Many of them, I presume, to force the pope to close the abbey entirely."

"Apparently. My uncles still talk about it sometimes." The corners of his mouth curved up. "With a bit too much fondness. His Holiness wanted the nuns to join a more, shall we say, *devout* establishment on the Giudecca, but some of the sisters protested, not wanting to leave their home, and he relented, allowing them to stay for the remainder of their lives. And then even more scandals occurred, for a few years at least. Eventually the gossip died down. But I imagine a few of them still live there. I have not heard otherwise."

I stared hard, trying to make out the shape of the island, to imagine an abbey on it, a church spire standing tall, but it was just a smudge on the horizon. "They must be quite elderly by now."

"Yes, I'd say so. I wonder if they still"—he cleared his throat—"entertain any visitors."

"If they're that old, they must not be very beautiful anymore and thus not much of an enticement."

"I guess not, but to men bonded by love, their appearance wouldn't really matter."

It was a lovely thought, a deep attachment and fondness developed over time, even if most of the couples around me did not seem to experience that. If that's what those Contorta nuns had, they were luckier than most, despite their ignoble status. No longer beholden to canon laws. So far away they were not even beholden to Venice. On their own miniature island of independence.

"Imagine the freedom." The idea came out involuntarily. Such privilege

I could scarcely imagine. But now it was there, in full view, a kernel waiting to sprout into full flowering.

"Yes, the freedom." Luca echoed my words, and I wondered how much his private meditations reflected my own.

I thought too of Livia and Elisabetta, who enjoyed their own brand of freedom. In Livia's cell, for a few moments at a time with the door firmly shut, they could be as free as the remaining sisters of Contorta. It was an intoxicating idea.

"My Auntie Livia recently told me a story. A long time ago, even before those scandals"—I indicated Contorta—"there was a girl living at San Zaccaria named Polisena, not yet a nun. A nobleman named Giovanni was visiting his sister at the convent, met her there, and fell immediately in love. But they could not work out the dowry, and she took her vows. Giovanni refused to give up and finally convinced her to meet him in the garden one night. He climbed over the roof and down the vines to her and proposed marriage. Of course she had to refuse. But Giovanni was persistent, and after several more moonlit visits, they consummated their love. He came to visit her regularly at night." I became immersed in the story as I remembered Livia telling it to me. Luca sat up and turned toward me to listen more fully, clearly absorbed in the tale. "Eventually, I guess inevitably, Polisena became big and gave birth to a son. But still, no one outside the convent knew. And that is presumably how it would have remained— except Giovanni would still not take no for an answer. He continued to return to the convent to visit Polisena, and now his child, and he was unrelenting in his desire to marry her. Finally, finally, Polisena agreed and ran off with him."

Luca exhaled slowly. "And then the world found out."

"Yes. The Council of Forty was required to prosecute Giovanni, who was sentenced to two years in jail plus a fine." Not unlike the punishment Paolo had faced. I glanced at Luca, but his expression was a mask. "But then something unexpected happened. The Forty overturned their own ruling and gave Giovanni the chance to make Polisena his wife and have the charges dropped. He had one month to do it, as long as he could provide a thousand-ducat dowry."

"I'm sure he raised the necessary funds." Luca spoke quietly but confidently. "I would in his situation."

"He did, and I'm certain you would too." I swiped the sweat from my brow. "Sadly, our circumstance is not the same."

"I know. Unlike Giovanni, I'm already married to another." He buried his head in his hands for a moment, before turning his face toward the sun and yelling an obscenity at it. He got up, took a rock in each hand, and hurled them at the sea, their vicious splashes startling the birds. He kicked at the ground, then ran from the beach toward the shelter of the trees just inland, leaving me blinking after him.

I'd never seen Luca lose his temper before. It was a most startling sight, to see a nobleman behave in such a way. And yet I could not blame him one bit. I felt the same way at the impossibility, the unfairness, of Venice expecting us all to dutifully play our parts.

I picked up a rock too and flung it out to sea. It dropped into the water close to shore with a satisfying thump, and I did it three more times.

I inhaled deeply, the briny air filling my nose and lungs. No, we could not have a lifetime together, but we could have this one day. We were already here, halfway through it, and we must not waste any more time. Besides, the pope's army was pressing closer, and who knew what the future would bring, how much of a future Venice or any of its citizens had left? As Paolo was fond of saying, *Eat and drink because life goes by in a flash.*

And not only eating and drinking . . .

If I were to do this, better for love than to the highest bidder. Better for love than to be violated by a mercenary.

I gathered my skirts and marched over to Luca, sulking in the trees. Before he could say a word, I encircled him in my arms, turned my face up to him, and kissed him, hard. His eyes momentarily widened before closing, and then he responded, kissing me back, hard. Pleasure ran through my heart, my belly, and lower, and I pressed myself as close to him as possible, feeling him through the thin fabric of my dress.

He moaned softly as he ran his hands along my face, his fingers along the pearls of my necklace, then lowered his head to kiss my neck.

I was breathing heavily now, and he eased my breasts out of the bodice to cover them with kisses too, before pushing the sleeves down from my shoulders. *Is this really happening?* I kept thinking over and over and over.

It is.

We both dropped to our knees, unable to stop, and then he gently laid me upon the pine needles and fallen leaves. He was over me now, admiring me between caresses. I had never felt so beautiful. I'd never really felt beautiful at all, but now I knew I had a face that could launch at least one ship.

One of his hands slid under my skirt and made its circuitous way up my leg, along the calf, the knee, the thigh, until I gasped in shock.

It was then that he withdrew his hand and lay upon me, holding me, panting, but most definitely stopping.

"What's the matter? Have I done something wrong?" I felt embarrassed and would have turned away if he hadn't been trapping me with his weight.

"No, nothing at all. You've done everything right."

"Then don't stop, please."

He groaned. With apparently tremendous effort, he rolled onto his back, eyes closed, face contorted in what looked like pain.

"Is something the matter? Are you hurt?" I sat up, then remembered I was half-naked, and hastily tried to reassemble the top of my dress.

He opened his eyes and put his hand on my arm. "Not yet. With your permission, I want to look at you." The dappled sunlight made a dreamy pattern on my skin. "I want to remember you just like this."

"All right." I felt self-conscious, confused.

He moved his hand to reverently touch my breast, tracing my skin. "There is nothing I'd like more than . . . But I will not soil your virtue. I promised to preserve it, and I intend to keep my promise, even if I am a barbarian in every other respect."

My breathing had subsided but not yet returned to normal. "You are a most honourable man."

"The colour of your eyes," he whispered. "Like the winter sea."

He looked for a long time before gathering me toward him, pulling me into an embrace, my head on his chest, my body pressed alongside his on our bed of pine needle and leaf. We lay there, not speaking, the rise and fall of our breaths in rhythm. I could hear his heart beating, smell his musky scent, and I revelled in this closeness. I'd never lain like this, never heard a man's heartbeat before, and it felt like a secret.

The sun pulsed down, shafts of light scattering between the leaves and branches, casting a warm glow over us like a fine lace veil, and the breeze blew in as sweet as his caresses. "This," he said, holding me securely, "this is . . ." He hesitated for a moment, and then we both said it together.

"Perfect."

I awoke as his fingers tenderly grazed my face and neck and heard him singing a song.

So nato a Venessia
So fio de pescaor
Par quindese giorni
Se magna el saor.

I'm a native Venetian
The son of a fisherman
For fifteen days
We eat the fish.

His voice was a melodious tenor with layers of richness and sweetness, and he sang with some expertise.

"I didn't know you could sing."

He brushed away a leaf that had blown upon my chest and smiled modestly. "My nurse taught me."

I gave a sly grin. "But while you are a native Venetian, you are the furthest thing from the son of a fisherman."

His smile turned to full-throated laughter. "No, definitely not. I learned that song from my nurse too. She was the great-granddaughter of a fisherman, the one from this island. My father never liked me to sing it, but she taught it to me in secret. He wasn't in the nursery when she put me to bed every night, so how could he stop her?"

We spent the afternoon trading folk melodies, church hymns, choir canticles, ancient Venetian songs, anything we could remember, sometimes singing alone, sometimes as an improvised duet. We talked about books in the San Zaccaria library and ones he had recently read, how he wished he had more time to spend at Aldine and the other presses.

With trepidation I told him about my latest writing, and he said it reminded him of a meticulous diary kept by Lord Sanudo. Swelling a bit with the sin of pride, I remembered my father mentioning the man, that Rosa should be glad she wasn't marrying him, and Luca chuckled. "He is a bit of a difficult character, with his incessant need to record. But it may yet become an invaluable record of the greatness of Venice. And yours could become the annals of a great convent."

"I hardly think my little jottings would be of interest to anyone but myself."

"I disagree. I'd very much like to read them."

I averted my eyes and blushed.

"It would be a true honour, Justina." He raised my chin to force my eyes up, looking at me with a kind of wonder. "I should love to see the inner workings of your mind."

I wanted desperately to look away, but he would not remove his finger, instead bringing me closer for a kiss.

"All right," I said. "I will consider it."

Finally, hunger called, and we returned to the beach. We sat on the blanket, our heads leaning together as the evening blessed us with a sunset to rival a painting by Carpaccio in its colours. The sky mutated from shades of ultramarine and azure to vermilion and ochre, then strips of violet and finally indigo. The moon was near full, so we didn't even need a torch as we reluctantly packed up. He donned his black robes as I placed my veil loosely around my shoulders, grateful for the additional layer of fabric as the evening cooled slightly and the wind picked up.

Our conversation slowed as the gondola approached to return us to reality, my heart sinking as the gondolier pulled the boat ashore.

Finally, it was time to board. The gondolier discreetly busied himself with loading our supplies as I took a final look at the island, our sanctuary and silent witness, the repository of what I knew would be my most cherished, bittersweet memories. Luca came to stand behind me, his arms encircling me, and I leaned upon his chest.

"No matter what I said earlier, I'm grateful we had today." He kissed the top of my head.

"Me too." I willed my voice not to break.

"I'll never forget it."

"Nor will I."

Luca led me across the rocks and into the boat. He again joined me under the *felze* and drew the curtains tight, back again in our cocoon, just him and me. I reclined on his chest for warmth and safety. He serenaded me with lullabies in that effortlessly clear voice, and with the rhythmic rocking of the rowing, I was nearly lulled to sleep. In that dreamy state, I wondered whether I'd heard right, whether he'd whispered *ti amo* . . .

I love you too, I thought, on that blade's edge between perfect happiness and complete despair.

The clanging of the curfew bell jostled me back to wakefulness, and I tipped toward despair.

"Justina, wake up, we're nearly there."

I opened my eyes to see him looking at me with anguish.

"I don't think I can do this," I whispered.

He shook his head. "We must. And you are strong."

The gondola glided to a stop, shuddering as it banged along the water entrance and the gondolier hopped out to tie it up.

Luca took my hand to help me up, kissing it as he did so. Before I could think of anything else, he exhaled and opened the curtain. He helped me onto the dock, handing me my cloak, dark as my grief, as the gondolier watched with curiosity. Livia stood in the entrance, wearing a tight smile as she peeked both ways along the canal to ensure no one was watching.

Luca bowed to her, quite formally, then to me.

I gave a quick curtsy, hastened into action by the worried expression on Livia's face. She did not let me stay to see the gondola leave, instead hustling me inside, and I could feel Luca's eyes on my back until she firmly shut and bolted the water entrance door with a decisive click.

Chapter 34

"Was it everything you'd hoped for?" she asked, but I could tell the question was perfunctory, and I grew alarmed.

"What's the matter? Does someone know I left, and why?"

She shushed me, shaking her head as she led me to my room. Conversation and laughter issued from behind several of the closed doors we passed, but none of them opened, and we made it to my cell unmolested.

Dolce greeted me with his usual enthusiasm, but I was shocked to see Madelena crying on my bed, her face mottled, her hands twisting a handkerchief into a knot, Elisabetta with her arm around her, trying to console her.

I flew over to her, the candle's flame flickering in my wake, and sat on her other side. "What's wrong?"

Sobbing, she was unable to speak. Elisabetta and Livia exchanged looks as I held Madelena, rubbing her back until her sobs finally turned to hiccups.

"Madelena dear, would you like me to tell Justina?" Livia knelt in front of her as Dolce nosed confusedly among our quartet.

She took several gulps of air before nodding.

Livia pulled up the chair from my writing table. "There is no easy way to say this, Justina, so I won't delay. Madelena is with child, and your parents have sold her."

I leaned back, stunned. "With child? Who's the father?"

Livia bit her lip.

"Mother of God, it's not Paolo, is it?"

Madelena nodded as fresh tears overwhelmed her again, and a surge of anger at the recklessness of my feckless brother frothed up. I'd seen this coming and yet had been powerless to stop it or protect my maid.

Livia stroked the woman's knee. "She says there can be no other. And I think your parents believe her. But she is a slave and not a servant, and even a very modest dowry to allow her to marry another of her class is out of the question with your father's financial situation. However, neither did they feel that they could keep her and not court scandal. Not surprisingly, they cannot abide a slave's bastard, even if it is their grandchild. So they have sold her quickly and for a pittance."

"To whom?" I whispered, seething, unable to come to terms with this new information.

Livia took a deep breath. "La Diamante."

My heart, already wounded, cracked in two at that revelation. "The courtesan? But why? If Madelena is with child, how could she . . . ?"

"Apparently, La Diamante was quite impressed with Madelena's beauty when your father sent her there recently to deliver a message. She feels a child is just a temporary impediment and she will be able to groom her well for . . . ah, future transactions."

Madelena wailed. I had never once seen her lose control of her emotions, always as calm as the lagoon on a summer's day, but clearly torrents churned beneath the surface, now allowed to burst forth.

"There, there." Elisabetta stroked Madelena's back with one hand and held her arm with the other. I sat utterly bewildered, my fingers tightened into fists as I smacked my thighs.

A soft knock came to the door, and we all froze while Dolce growled and Madelena sniffled.

Another knock, more insistent. "Justina, I know you're in there. I need to talk to you. It's urgent." Viena.

Livia sat for a moment, then came to a decision and let Viena in. "After all, she is one of us, and we need all our allies now."

Viena entered, eyebrows raised when she saw our unusual assembly at such a late hour. "Everything all right?"

I shrugged as I held Madelena's hand.

"I was worried about you," said Viena, her delicate face pressed with concern. "I'd heard you were sick and knew your aunt was nursing you. I thought it might be bad." She then gave a lopsided grin, her features slightly relaxing as she studied my visage. "But based on the sun you received today, I can surmise you're feeling perfectly fine."

I ignored her implication. "You said you'd something urgent to tell me. What is it?"

"Well," she said, looking around the room, her face resuming its uneasiness. "I was expecting us to be alone. But what I'm about to tell you will be common knowledge by tomorrow morning, so no need for secrecy."

My mangled heart grew even more twisted. I was not sure I could handle anything else. "Is the pope about to invade?"

Elisabetta sharply took in her breath. "A sacking?"

Viena shook her head. "No, nothing like that. In fact, the government has passed a new law in the hopes of keeping Venice pure and free from sin, to help prevent any such invasion. A law that affects, from what I can tell," she added, lightly touching my sun-kissed cheek, "you, not to mention a good many of our wicked sisters throughout our republic."

"Viena, you are talking in riddles."

"My father came to visit this evening, straight from the doge's palazzo." And she started reciting, as if from memory: "Those sacrilegious transgressors who traffic with nuns, within or without a convent, shall incur imprisonment, fines of up to five hundred ducats, and now perpetual banishment from Venice, nor can they hold any office. And if banished and found within Venetian boundaries, prison for two years and then exile again."

I involuntarily put my hand to my mouth, while Livia groaned. Madelena's reddened eyes grew wide, and Elisabetta crossed herself.

"There's more," Viena said soberly. "Any nun who leaves her convent shall be punished by the patriarch in such a way as to make her a significant example to others. Those who harbour them will be banished for up to five years, and those who transport them, such as boatmen, will be whipped from San Marco to Rialto." We were all too stunned by her words to react further, but still she went on. "Finally, nuns can no longer have secular servants but can hire only other nuns as servants."

Livia clucked at the last. "What a ridiculous notion. San Zaccaria has only noble nuns, so how could any of us be servants?" She started pacing the length of the cell, Dolce following her. "And as for the other laws, we've seen it all before. You know how it goes: *Venetian laws last but a week.* They keep making new laws because no one follows the old ones." She stopped. "Or enforces them."

Elisabetta looked doubtful. "But Livy dear, these new measures do sound quite severe. And now, due to the political situation, they may enforce them more thoroughly."

Auntie resumed her pacing. "True, the political situation is dire. Still, unless the government starts inspecting every convent corner and lagoon island, I don't see how it can have any better enforcement. Besides," the corners of her mouth curved up, "some of those very officials have been known to frequent a convent cell or two."

Another whimper from Madelena shifted the mood again. "As for Madelena," Auntie continued, "I propose we approach her new owner and arrange for her to stay at San Zaccaria until she recovers from her confinement. The baby will stay with us—Justina's niece or nephew, I might point out. Madelena can then do her duties for the courtesan. La Diamante will not be able to make use of her in her present state, and she will only become bigger with each passing day. What say you, Justina? She used to be your family's property, after all."

I searched Madelena's trembling face, looking for answers, and she gave the slightest nod. What choice did she have? It wasn't as if she could leave the city on her own. To travel alone as a woman had its own hazards, let alone during a war. I sighed. "Yes, Auntie, of course I agree. We will take good care of Madelena until her time comes, and then thereafter the baby, our own relation."

Madelena wiped at her cheeks to mop up the tears and nodded, but remained silent.

Auntie clapped her hands briskly. "Good, that's settled then. I will send a letter tomorrow, proposing our arrangement to La Diamante. I am sure she will look kindly on our sensible proposal, which preserves her ducats.

Then I shall ask Mother Abbess's permission for Madelena to stay with the maids and serve Justina until her time comes. I am certain of her response, despite these new edicts. The girl is not the first to come to us in such straits. However, Justina, I presume it is all right for Madelena to sleep here tonight? She's not appropriate in the guest house, and I'd rather not disturb Mother Marina so late."

"Of course."

Livia and Elisabetta departed with promises to apprise us on the morrow, and Madelena set to work making a nest for herself on the floor with a blanket and an extra pillow from my bed. Viena contributed another blanket from her room, then lingered for a moment as Madelena settled herself.

"Was it wonderful?" Viena asked me quietly.

I hugged myself. "It was. Though perhaps not in the way you imagine." Already my glow from the island was fading, feeling as if from another lifetime.

"You are in love. I can see the look in your eyes."

"Not that it matters. He's a married man." I exhaled. "And now with these harsh new laws . . ."

She gave a rueful smile. "That's part of my own worry. I think Angela Riva, Zanetta, and their confederates suspect me. And in this political climate, all they need is suspicion, not actual proof."

I gave her a sharp look. "Go on."

"I believe Santina realized something when she saw Jacomo come out of my room yesterday. They've been giving me pointed looks all day."

"That's not good."

"Not good at all. I'll have to warn Jacomo to stay away for a while. You be careful too." She ran her fingers along my cheek again. "With that sun-burnt face, you might do well to play ill a few days longer."

She gave me a hug, and I shut the door behind her. I glanced down at Madelena, who was staring up at me with sad eyes. I was unaccustomed to seeing her so bereft and helpless, like a kitten in a tree unable to muster the courage to descend.

"Bring up the bedding, Madelena." I patted my feather mattress, then I shed my pink silk and donned my nightclothes. After blowing out the candle, she slipped in beside me, sheltering us both with a thin blanket. I was hot, my skin afire from the sun, but she was shivering.

"I'm so very sorry that you are in this predicament, Madelena."

I could feel her chest quivering. "It is I who am sorry, Signora Justina. I have brought dishonour to your family."

"No, it is Paolo who has done that, but he won't face any consequence for it."

"It is hard for me to blame him, as I went to his bed willingly enough."

"How willingly? Paolo can be quite charismatic and persuasive and, moreover, is"—I swallowed—"*was* your master's son."

I could feel her nod in the dark. "That is true."

I sighed. "And you with little choice in the matter."

A long silence. "That is also true."

I knew I was too overcome for sleep to come quickly—my day with Luca, worry over the new laws, concern for Madelena, anger at Paolo. So I huddled close to my now-former slave. She took my hand over her side and had me cup the slight bulge of her belly, as Dolce jumped on the bed and curled up at our feet.

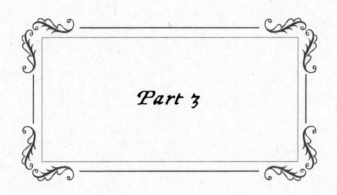

Part 3

Chapter 35

I walked numbly through the following days. I'd had my time with
Luca and held it like a rare relic on a feast day. I was unsure if I
regretted my impulse, whether it might have been better never to
have met at all, to quench my passion rather than fuel it, but it was done,
and I did not feel the need for contrition.

It was, however, futile to believe we could meet again, not with the
new laws circulating so furiously through the city, not with Zanetta
nosing around, not with Paolo released and safe and Mama finally at
peace, although the gossip about our house lingered. When I would
catch the eye of Carpaccio's Virgin hanging on my wall, I wondered if
I should defy Luca and sell it to help reimburse his money, to weaken
the bond between us, but he had been so adamant. Thus, she continued
to hang on my cell wall, cautioning me, the flag fan he had given me as a
birthday gift propped up next to it.

I kept busy. There were the matters of settling Madelena among the convent servants, of Livia negotiating satisfactory terms with La Diamante, of listening to Viena agonize about Jacomo. They had decided to lay low until the initial scrutiny died down, but she wanted to discuss him every chance she had, and I was her only confidante. It was another secret to keep from the purview of Zanetta and Angela Riva, who seemed to appear whenever my group broached such delicate topics, their eyes narrowed, crossing themselves piously. My strategy became avoidance, and I advised Madelena to do the same, for her unexpected presence was much discussed and commented upon, and her condition would soon be apparent.

All of Venice was on edge, continually wary the Warrior Pope would break through the defences at any moment, sail across the lagoon, and invade the city. Madelena's descriptions of the Sack of Constantinople were never far from my mind, and the extensive pillage and rape histories of other cities, towns, and villages were frequent topics in the refectory, along with chatter about Paolo, the other young wayward lords, and the wicked and unholy nuns of Celestia who were damning Venice's very existence.

Around the Feast of San Benedetto, a sweltering day of much subdued rejoicing for our Benedictine establishment, Elisabetta became unnaturally tired. Livia, worried it was due to the excessive heat, took to bringing meals to her room and conferring frequently with Mother Marina and the infirmarian Teresa. Teresa prescribed a diet of meat, eggs, sage, rosemary, and fresh fruits and vegetables, but the food seemed to little avail, given Elisabetta's suppressed appetite, and Livia began frantically writing every doctor in the city.

I found myself frequently alone in my room, grateful for its coolness, flipping through the books I had brought from home and the one Luca had given me, or sitting at my desk, writing, musing, about what was happening in our convent—my own thoughts on my position in society as well as those of the women who surrounded me.

I did not at first read what I wrote, just put down page after page of scratches, so absorbed I did not notice the bells ringing and was often late for meals. I wrote in the vernacular, for while I could read Latin fairly well, writing it was an effort, and I felt the need to set down the words quickly. I took much solace and pleasure in the endeavour—work simply for work's sake, the only activity that made me feel fully alive and whole.

After a few weeks, I sat down to read what I had written and found it better than I had hoped. The pages needed more structure and depth, but I thought there might be something in them, more than just daily diary entries of conventual happenings and my own thoughts on them, though that in itself had some value. The manuscript did not fit any category of which I was aware. Something more, a treatise perhaps or some sort of political work, although not purely political as the spiritual was an integral part. However, I did not know with whom to verify this instinct. Under normal circumstances Livia would be best, but so consumed was she with worry about Elisabetta that I could not consider asking her. Not Rosa or Paolo or Mama, and certainly not Papa, due to the potentially heretical content. Viena did not have the correct faculties, and I did not feel close enough to any other nun to bare my soul in such a way. Perhaps Mother Marina had the right mind, but I worried about her reaction, not to mention she was always engrossed by conventual affairs.

And then it came to me—Luca. I turned this thought over in my mind for several days, trying to untangle my base desire to connect with him from my need for honest commentary from the appropriate sort of intellect. His words from our day on the island kept returning to me, saying how much he wanted to read it.

I therefore wrote a letter in my best hand, asking him for his unvarnished thoughts, begging to keep our correspondence in the strictest confidence, reminding him he was under no obligation if his myriad other family and governmental duties took precedence. And forcing myself to include a sentence that under the present circumstances it would be unwise for him to visit.

I sealed the missive, wrapped my pages, and with trepidation instructed Madelena to deliver them.

23 July 1509

To Signora Justina,

Thank you for your unexpected but welcomed letter, and I hope my own finds you in excellent health.

I was delighted to receive your manuscript. I had hoped you would send it, but you seemed so reticent that I dared not expect it. I read it as soon as I had a moment to myself and, as you requested, I provide you with my critique, hoping you receive it in the spirit in which I give it, that is, with the utmost respect.

I found your pages most illuminating. I believe you have the kernel of a profound idea in the page exploring the prominence of Jesus's female disciples. Your manuscript would benefit from further expansion upon this, perhaps by creating a stronger parallel to our own era, particularly in light of the new, stricter laws governing conventual life, as well as the necessity of female education.

This last notion is certainly heretical to many patrician fathers.

Interestingly, I see the most tolerance not from the nobles but from the rich merchants of the citizen class, who are preparing their daughters to help their future husbands increase their collective wealth and see no reason to keep them confined to Plato's cave. Know too that if this patrician ever has a daughter she will be an inheritrix of such an education. Your own father has been a man ahead of his time.

Thus I send you, along with the return of your pages, my copy of Plato's Republic published by the Aldine Press. Please keep it as long as you require.

You will have heard by now of Padua returning to Venetian control. Such a gratifying victory, especially after the worries about adequately funding the military, has been uplifting not only to Paduans but to all of Venice. I hope the joy—as well as relief—has found its way behind the convent walls.

As I know of your admiration of books, I must tell you about a copy of the Hebraic Bible our friend Lord Sanudo has acquired for his personal library from one of the newly arrived Jews. When I heard about it, I asked to see it. He obliged by showing me his entire rather impressive collection along with the Bible, which is simply exquisite. I so wish you could have held it in your hands as I did.

I will bid you farewell now and look forward to any new pages you wish to send. Please convey my greetings and wishes of robust health to your aunt and the other company you keep. I also hope your mother and sister keep well. I saw your brother recently at a festa and he is the same as always, although he did take me aside to tell me his unexpected news. I was most surprised to hear it and now understand the unfortunate rumours that have circulated regarding your house. I *sometimes meet your father during sessions of the Great Council and always find his manner most dignified.*

You asked after my family, and I can tell you that they all keep in good health. I appreciate your continued prayers for them and myself.

Luca Cicogna

His response brought me such secret delight that it was difficult to contain amid the continuing strife of friends and family. Viena brooding over Jacomo and his dearth of visits, so close and yet so far. Livia stewing in worry over Elisabetta, who continued to eat less and sleep more, which obviously had nothing to do with the weather. Madelena trying to hide her sorrows as her belly expanded. It was easy enough to share late-night pastries and wine with Viena and listen to her woe, but Livia rebuffed any assistance as she tried to come to terms with the undeniable circumstances of Elisabetta's condition, and I knew not what to say to Madelena.

All these things brought me sadness too, and yet I felt akin to a lark as I read and reread Luca's letter. To see his script, to know it was he who had pressed pen to page. His confirmation of my manuscript's direction. And a new book of Plato from Aldine Press. It was much to take in.

I continued to spend the deep-heated summer days mostly in my cool cell, reading Plato and making notes, emerging for raids of the kitchens, meals in the refectory, and visits from family, or to pray by Elisabetta's bedside, where I could only stare and think of her unholy alliance with Livia as the infirmarian let her blood.

Papa and Paolo came infrequently, but Mama did so weekly, with reports of Rosa but never Rosa herself, to my dismay. Each time, she would take Livia aside to speak privately. Did Mama know or suspect the truth about Livia and Elisabetta? I could only imagine so, as her jaw always tightened whenever someone mentioned Elisabetta, although I never did see them argue.

On the day before the Feast of the Assumption, Mama told me of Papa's attempts to procure a post for Paolo that would allow him to be closer to the front, which I knew to be code for a legitimate reason to exile him for a time. Paolo was not keen on an end to his merrymaking, professing his wish to always be preparing a mummery. Mama was clearly fearful, but parroted Papa's reason that Paolo's character needed moulding. I was inclined to agree, despite any worries I had over his safety. It was quite strange to be living through a war, simultaneously duller yet more constantly disquieting than I had ever imagined.

On the Assumption, I sat through the service beside Livia and Viena, still unable to raise our voices in praise of the Virgin due to the never-ceasing interdict. My mind could not stop thinking about refinements I wanted to make to my text, the Divine Mother's invulnerability and redemption inspiring me to reconsider the role of women in today's Church. But I worried I was indeed entering heretical territory, as dangerous and deadly as the battlefield.

And yet I felt compelled to keep writing. I spent the following week refining my ideas and revising my pages, followed by another letter to Luca asking for his judgment on the matter of potential heresy, along with the usual niceties and news of conventual and familial happenings. I enclosed both the manuscript and his Plato.

As I capped the bottle, a hard rain beating outside, I was unsure of what I wanted from my growing pile of paper. It might never be read beyond myself and Luca, and that might be enough to satisfy me. But in the event it were, I did not wish to bring scandal upon San Zaccaria or further infamy upon the house of Soranzo. Even though I was supposed to be beyond such earthly concerns, I could not ignore the embers of gossip that had not been entirely extinguished, fed by a continuous stream of air from the bellows known as Zanetta.

"What's that?" Zanetta hissed at me as I left my cell to search for Madelena, Dolce stalwartly at my feet. My manuscript, letter, and the Plato were wrapped up in a cloth bag tied with string. "And to whom are you sending it?"

"I'm not sure it's any of your business." I clutched the parcel protectively to my chest, trying to continue down the corridor, but Angela Riva stood like a bulwark behind her and Santina stuck her tongue out at me.

"Anything that affects this convent is my business." Her green eyes flickered toward my cell and then Viena's, and not for the first time I wished our doors had locks. "We cannot risk another Celestia-like scandal. And Mother Marina turns a blind eye to the deviance in our midst. That would not have happened under Angela's reign."

"The vote for abbess happened before I took the veil. I had nothing to do with it."

She smoothed back her blond hair, and I noticed a few strands of grey mixed in it, hard to see unless up close, which I uncomfortably was. "As if you ever would have voted for Angela. You would just follow your aunt's lead like an unthinking lamb."

That was true. I would have voted for Mother Marina had I been here, but not because of Livia, or at least not just because of her. My own antipathy toward Zanetta and Angela had grown strong as I'd gotten to know them. Moreover, I found Mother Marina, despite my initial fears, to be an excellent and compassionate leader.

Recalling Livia's advice to ignore them, I took a breath and a step, but so did Zanetta.

"Off to find your aunt? We all know she will be in Elisabetta's room, pining away."

The flare of anger I felt was so violent I nearly swatted her with my parcel. *Breathe*, I told myself. I could not let her realize how she affected me. And how much did she know or suspect about Livia and Elisabetta? I thought I was the only one with confirmation of the full truth.

I thus forced myself to display a beatific smile while wishing desperately for an escape. "They are dear friends, and Elisabetta is not well. I'm sure you would feel the same if Angela fell ill."

Zanetta rolled her eyes just as Viena opened her cell door, cradling her cat. "I thought I heard voices out here. Everything all right, Justina?"

Dolce emitted a few barks while Leo watched him placidly, safe in his mistress's arms. Taking inspiration from his feline example, I nodded with as much serenity as I could muster. "I was just about to take Dolce out." Better to not mention Madelena or Livia.

Viena nodded. "Zanetta, what brings you to our corridor? None of your relations or friends reside here, and your own cell is on another level entirely." She acted wide-eyed and innocent, but I knew she was being shrewd.

Zanetta raised herself to her full height, still short beside me, and sniffed. "Just stretching our legs. The gardens are soaked. You should bring a towel for your little beast, Justina."

"Thank you, Zanetta," I said, grateful for the change in subject, "for your excellent advice."

Viena, Leo, Dolce, and I watched Zanetta walk toward Angela and Santina, and the trio departed, Santina limping behind the older women and giving me the fig hand behind her back.

Viena exhaled. "I know it is a sin, but I hate them so."

I giggled with relief. "Me too. Thank you for rescuing me."

Viena scoffed and gestured toward my parcel as Leo escaped her arms and ran under her bed. "Shall I take Dolce out to the garden while you fetch Madelena? Lucky for her the rain seems finally to be letting up."

&

31 August 1509

Dear Signora Justina,

I trust this letter finds you still hale. However, I am very sorry to hear that Signora Elisabetta is ailing. I have added her to my daily prayers, along with your most esteemed aunt and yourself.

Although your brother is my dear friend, I concur with your father and with you. Paolo has much potential. I imagine it is disheartening to a father to see it squandered.

I have studied your new pages. Thank you again for entrusting them to me. I found particularly intriguing the idea of how free your mind is, despite the limitations of the convent walls, and feel this warrants further explication. I am neither priest nor biblical scholar nor theologian, but do not feel your words have stepped over the line into heresy, although they will cause many a raised eyebrow among our more conservative thinkers. I know you have no plans to do so, but if you were to consider publication, and it is something I urge you to at least consider, I suggest publishing anonymously or pseudonymously.

I would be pleased to be your agent in such matters, whatever name you use. I hope you may do me the honour. But if you refuse, I still shall prevail upon you to continue to read your unpublished work. I spend so many hours in affairs of government, trade, and family that it is a true privilege to engage in matters of the mind. Outside the presses and the palazzi of certain women of our mutual acquaintance, people rarely discuss such ideas. Venetians prefer being merchants to philosophers.

There are reports of French and papal troops joining forces with the Holy Roman emperor on the way to Padua. This is no secret as the rumours are rife throughout the city. Please have your sisters pray to preserve the fate of our Most Serene Republic. The various governmental bodies meet constantly about what to do, and I do not commit treason in saying the doge's uninspiring behaviour has been difficult to witness.

At the assembly yesterday, I introduced myself to your brother-in-law Lord Zane and congratulated him, suggesting it might aid the health of his unborn child for his wife to visit her sister. I do pray he duly received the message and that you may forgive my impudence. It is one small thing I may do.

I also enclose my copy of Dante Alighieri's Commedia from the Aldine Press. I trust you will find Alighieri's opinion of the female sex to your liking. Beatrice, his ideal woman, makes a most inspiring guide through Heaven.

I close in haste to ensure you receive this missive today.

Pray for us all—Luca Cicogna

❧

Rosa finally came to visit on Marymas, bringing a basket of apples as a gift on a brilliantly sunny afternoon, the sky as blue as the Virgin's robes. I was delighted to see her and her ripening shape, and silently grateful to Luca for his effective intervention. She looked well and plump and almost content. "Zago has been mostly heeding the midwife's advice, and I sleep well at night," she confided on the way back to my cell after saying a rosary by Elisabetta's sickbed. "He likes to put his hand upon my belly and imagine our son's future. He is finally contented, I think. And I can feel the child move now, like a new bird unfurling its wings."

"How lovely." I certainly felt joy for my sister, but was that a hint of jealousy as well, for something I would never experience? A babe within my womb, and its father's pride? I glanced at the infant in the Carpaccio drawing and saw him for the first time not as the divine Jesus but as a human baby, one who felt hunger and slept and spit up.

The picture reminded me too of my unpaid debt to Luca. I could still not quite put it out of my mind, even though he had assured me more than once it was unnecessary. But perhaps by doing so I would feel less attachment to him. "Do you think Zago might help me find a buyer for that drawing?"

She stood closer to examine it. "Why ever would you want to sell it? It is such a beautiful rendition of Virgin and Child."

I had never told Rosa about La Diamante and what had almost transpired last spring. That was the first secret I had ever withheld from her. My day on the island with Luca was the second. My continuing feelings for him the third. The fourth, my manuscript, something that could be my life's true work, was locked in my chest. I shook my head slightly, a pang of grief for the end of our childhood settling uneasily beside that sliver of jealousy.

"I supposed I might help Papa with some of his debts." It was all I could think of to reply, and half the truth anyway.

"I shall ask Zago then. He knows so many people, both patricians and citizens. He certainly may be aware of an interested party."

I gave a wry smile. "Zago is starting to seem almost courtly."

"Sometimes." The ghost of a memory crossed her face before she sat on my bed. Dolce hopped up beside her and put his head in her lap. "I am forever grateful to Signora Benedetta. She reminds him at her every visit to treat me delicately and hints always at a boy."

I sat beside them both and petted Dolce's ears. "She is a wise woman, in more ways than one."

"I do worry about her though. She is growing very aged and rather slow, for all her wisdom." She looked askance at me. "I am no longer her sole mother-to-be. Even though she said her midwifery days were over, she has made another exception. Someone you know."

"Ah, who may that be?" I asked, trying to remember who of our acquaintance had married in the last few years.

Rosa cleared her throat. "It is Lord Cicogna's wife."

My heart dropped. "Luca's wife is with child?" Of course she was. Did I truly expect him to be a chaste husband? It was his duty, and he was a young man. For all I knew, he took pleasure in it. "I am pleased for them. A baby is always joyous news and a blessing from God."

Rosa was silent for a moment. "A blessing from God." She took my hand, her eyes so blue, her face so young, midway between girl and woman.

"Are you sure you are all right, Justina?"

"Yes, of course. Why wouldn't I be?" I looked back at the Virgin and Child. "Please don't forget to ask Zago about a buyer."

❧

25 September 1509

Signora Justina,

I owe you many apologies as well as the unadorned truth. First for not telling you myself the news of my unborn child. I have suspected since late June, and indeed Signora Benedetta has since confirmed it. My immense joy at an heir in the new year is only matched by my misery in separation from a certain sister. I did not know how to tell you, nor whether it was necessary to make this revelation. It would not change anything. I know this. And yet . . .

Being in my own kind of Hell, far worse than Dante's imaginings, I have confessed repeatedly to my priest. I have prayed to the Blessed Virgin for purity of heart and clarity of thought. The priest says I must stop writing letters.

But I find myself at my desk again, as the evening light turns rosy gold, with my window facing south into the lagoon toward a certain island, reminding me of a summer sunset only a few months ago, begging for your pardon and understanding for the delay. As you have doubtless heard, Padua is under siege. Some Paduans have straggled into Venice and are being scrutinized as to their loyalties. The meetings are long, the atmosphere tense. But I am having difficulty concentrating on state affairs.

I know you have discouraged it, but will you relent and allow me to visit? I could procure more pages from you, strictly as a matter of business. Have you agreed that I may be your agent? To publish your work, anonymously? I could even translate it into the Latin myself if you did not wish to use the vernacular, allowing for a wider readership. I feel it my duty to assist you as I can, to let people know what it is to be a nun, forced into a convent against one's will. It is not something that the patrician fathers who put their daughters there have ever considered. As a man soon to become a father, I am in fact now fearful of having more than one daughter.

I enclose again the Commedia. I want you not only to read it, but to have it. As a token of my good will and respect for what you are writing, if nothing else.

How fares Signora Elisabetta? I pray she has recovered.

You know you need not repay me the ducats from earlier this summer. I will never accept reimbursement from you. It is the smallest thing I can do for you. A gift.

With prayers you will forgive me,

Luca Cicogna

10 October 1509

Dear Signora Justina,

I dare to write to you again, praying you are in good health. I am concerned that the illness that has waylaid Signora Elisabetta may have spread. Does she fare any better? Have any others fallen sick? I have not heard so, and your brother assures me you are well, but still I worry.

Have you written any more of your treatise? I include a ream of paper, new quills, and several bottles of ink, having utter faith you will put them to excellent use.

I have been blessed with fortunate news. I have been voted into my first government post, an advocate in the civil court. My term will begin on the first of December.

Between sessions to accommodate the Paduans newly resident in our city and meetings to discuss my forthcoming duties, I made time to visit the Aldine Press to procure their edition of Plutarch's Moralia. I found his essay called "Tranquility of the Mind" to be a great salve in these turbulent times, an important reminder to tame one's passions and utilize reason. I have read it several times to glean all I can from it.

While at the press, I took the liberty to speak to Ser Manutius about your work, omitting your name but including your position in society. He was most intrigued by your ideas as well your sex, and although he made no promises, he did ask I keep him apprised of your progress and send him any pages when they are ready. What say you?

With prayers,

Luca

Postscript—sometimes I find myself humming a certain fishing song . . .

Chapter 36

After I read the *Commedia* twice through, I realized how invaluable the role of Beatrice was to my work. It was she who led Dante out of Hell, she who was the direct connection to God. I returned to my manuscript with Beatrice shaping my words, her spirit guiding my hand to form the letters.

Upon rereading this new section, I knew I would be forever obligated to Luca for the connection. I would treasure his book always, not only in its own right as a precious vessel of knowledge, but also as a token of his recognition for who I was becoming.

I looked anew at his two most recent missives. I wanted to believe him. His words felt true. I could sense his anguish, the wildness of his mind. He wanted to honour his vows, but the heart was not in alignment with reason.

I knew exactly what he meant, because I felt the same.

I ran the tip of my finger over his signature. Touching it felt as intimate as the kisses we'd shared nearly four months ago. I imagined him blowing the ink dry and could almost feel his breath upon me.

I felt pride for his advancement, that he was being recognized more widely for what I already knew about his uncommon character, despite his extreme youth. The city fathers would not be disappointed in him. I knew in my bones that he had the potential to be doge half a century from now, and a good one.

I felt the sin of pride in myself, that I was stirring in him such loyalty to my work and such willingness to possibly endanger himself on my behalf. I did not think he offered that lightly. He knew exactly what he was doing and thought me worth the risk.

And I forgave him. Of course he did not know how to tell me that his wife was with child. He had no idea how to broach such a subject with me, of all women. Not after what had transpired between us. I did not like it, but eventually I understood it.

So, on the morning of All Souls' Day, I wrote him back, thanking him for his gifts of paper, quills, and ink, but most of all for the *Commedia*.

With a deep breath, I gave him permission to act as my agent with Ser Manutius. If both men thought my work worthy, I felt it my duty to publish it, albeit anonymously, for myself, for my sisters, and for the future daughters of Venice. Seeking publication was audacious, but these uncertain times were making everyone bolder.

I told him I prayed daily for him, his family, and his unborn child. I hoped his wife was progressing well and that he had found a measure of his own peace.

I wished him such peace, just as I wished the same for myself. And I meant every word.

Sometimes I found myself humming a fishing song too. The song conjured an azure sky above a verdant island in the lagoon, lying together in a field of poppies, his palm cupping my breast, my ear pressed against the beating of his heart, the warmth of the day covering us like an embrace. The remembrance brought me delight and misery in equal measure. I considered asking to borrow Luca's Plutarch, for I could have used advice on the tranquilization of my own mind, or at the very least on acceptance.

It was no longer summer. The weather had turned: the sky now a gunmetal grey, the air damp, the fog frequent. Every day it seemed possible the pope would invade the city, and yet we somehow became accustomed to the constant threat. The happenings closer to home seemed more frightful and real. Elisabetta was on her deathbed, her flesh wasted away from some sort of disease, and Livia mad with grief. Madelena had grown rounder and more reticent, and I had now seen Rosa three times since Luca had spoken to Zago. Luca's wife too would be growing big, although a few months behind them. I had what I thought was almost a complete first draft of my manuscript, and I was compelled to share my musings with the world, to see how they would be received.

Perhaps the only thing unchanged was Viena and Jacomo's attachment. True, they had exercised great prudence by avoiding each other for months in the wake of the new laws, given the suspicions of Zanetta and her ilk—whose behaviour had not changed either—but they had recently resumed their clandestine liaison, unable to stay apart. Viena had told me breathlessly a few days before, and I had to admit they had been doing a most impressive job of discretion. Her undercurrent of happiness was a welcome counterbalance to Madelena's subdued sadness, Elisabetta's sickly state, and Livia's breathtaking sorrow.

As I finished my letter to Luca, Madelena returned from Dolce's walk, both damp from the morning mist. Dolce jogged over for a nuzzle before curling up on the foot of my bed. I urged my maid to sit down when I saw her rubbing her lower back. Two months until her time, and she was clearly uncomfortable. La Diamante, relieved she did not have to deal with this inconvenient stage in her new slave's life, had Madelena visit her palazzo about once a month to inspect her, ensure she was in good health, and familiarize her with her new duties, with plans for her to start work before Carnival's end. The babe would remain at San Zaccaria, where perhaps Madelena could visit her child, if La Diamante would allow her. I did not know what Madelena thought about any of this for she never discussed the future. But she seemed grateful to be serving me alone in the convent, despite Zanetta's frequent insults and constant needling over who the father was. Madelena remained silent on this point, for which I was grateful.

I often wondered about Paolo. So far he had succeeded in convincing Papa to keep him here in Venice rather than send him to the front. He visited me every few weeks, always in lively spirits, never too worried about anything. Recovered from his brief spell in jail, he was his usual self, full of gossip and tales from festas, mummeries, and gatherings that seemed to occur with increasing frequency, a frenzy of pleasure perhaps to avoid any thoughts of impending doom. When he saw Madelena, however, a tenderness crept into his voice, although he did not specifically refer to her burgeoning condition. She would not look him in the eye and departed as soon as it was prudent to take leave of a lord, her fingers absently caressing her belly. After she left, he would reassure me that he would keep an eye on the child as he grew up.

Would he? Or would he be content to forget all about it? Some patricians took care of their mistresses' bastards, but I knew of no such children with a slave for a mother. If the baby were a girl and if Mother Marina allowed it, she very well might spend her entire life confined to the convent, forgotten and ignored. If a boy, barred from the nobility by his mother's ignoble status, we would need to find him a trade and apprenticeship. With any luck, my father and Paolo would discreetly assist their unacknowledged kin to find a station in life. If not, I vowed I would any way I could.

I stifled a sigh as I dashed off my signature, capped the ink bottle, and wiped the quill, finally assembling the dried letter and manuscript into a cloth bound with a leather thong. I smoothed the top of the fat package with my ink-stained fingers and handed it to Madelena.

"After you have rested, please take this to Lord Cicogna." I did not need to give any further instructions; she was well versed on the location of his palazzo, just a few moments' walk from San Zaccaria, not to mention well versed in my feelings for him. She knew I was working on something of import, something that lengthened with every delivery, but I had not told her what. I trusted her completely to fulfill her duty and not gossip or show anyone the package's contents.

"Of course, Signora Justina." She made to rise, but I patted her shoulder and she resettled herself in the chair. She poured herself a cup of watered wine from the pitcher on my desk while I rummaged through my chest to extract some *fave*, small rose-coloured pine-nut cookies that the convent kitchens had been churning out for the last two days. I'd filled my cell stores with several dozen of the sweet treats just the night before.

"Thank you. I am always hungry these days." She wiped pink crumbs from her lips. "I only broke my fast a few hours ago."

I laughed. "Rosa told me the same thing at her last visit. And if she doesn't eat, she feels queasy. It seems normal for your stage."

After thanking me again, Madelena staggered to her feet, took the package, and opened my cell door, only to meet Viena at the threshold.

"Come quickly, Justina. Your auntie wants you. It's Elisabetta. Bring your rosary. The priest just left."

Chapter 37

Elisabetta lay on the bed in her cell, her breath coming in ragged rasps, the dreaded death rattle. Over the preceding months, she had wasted away, her skin now tightly covering her angular bones. She drifted in and out of consciousness, her eyes flitting open when I entered, a smile flickering across her lips.

Livia, her cheeks stained with tears, was by her side holding her hands, entwined with a rosary. "Thank you for coming so quickly, Niece."

Elisabetta blinked in acknowledgement of my presence, and I kissed her pale forehead. So often in the last few months she had burned with fever, but today she was cool to the touch.

I knelt at the foot of her bed and began to say the rosary in a low voice, as Livia murmured to her. I tried not to listen, tried to focus only on the prayers, but my aunt's words were inescapable.

"I thank the Lord every day, my love, that I entered this convent. I met you on the day we both took the veil, age fourteen, and I think I fell in love with you at first sight, although it took me many years to admit it. You were so beautiful, even with your hair cut short, and always so very kind. Such a contrast to me, with my sharp tongue and wicked ways, but you never seemed to mind. You made me good, Betta. You made me a better person—a better woman and a better nun—and you and the Lord know best how that has transpired."

I kept reciting the rosary by rote, my knees aching, my eyes flitting between the two women, Livia with the tears undammed now, flowing down her cheeks and splattering the blanket, Elisabetta with her eyes still closed but a beatific expression on her face, her chest unhurriedly rising and falling, rising and falling, ever slower. Which was better, which worse? To have had a long love spanning decades, like Livia and Elisabetta, or never allowing love to blossom, as with Luca and me? Which was more pain, which less?

Pray for our sins now and at the hour of our death . . .

"It should be me, not you, in this bed, ready to greet Christ. God should not punish you this way. I will never understand God's ways, never, never. You are too young, too good. I would gladly carry your pain, as Christ carried the cross for our sins. So many sins . . . I did not have long enough to love you. I did not love you well enough, as well as you deserved." Livia sobbed for a moment. "But you are to meet Him soon and then the pain will leave. Will you watch over me from Heaven? I need you to watch over me, please. I love you so much. Only God knows how much."

Elisabetta opened her eyes just then, staring straight at Livia as if she could hold her with her eyes, and I stopped praying. A look passed between them of what I could only describe as the purest devotion, and I knew then which was worse.

Ever so delicately, Elisabetta exhaled, and Livia and I watched, waiting, waiting, for the next inhalation.

We waited for a long time.

But it never came.

Eyes still open but no longer looking at anything, Elisabetta had drawn her last breath and rendered her soul to her celestial husband.

... now and at the hour of our death.

"No," Livia whispered. "No, please God, no," she wailed and climbed into bed next to her beloved, holding her, hugging her. "No no no no no no no ..." Her words dissolved into quiet agony.

I stayed on my knees, rosary clutched betwixt my steepled hands, staring at them both, the woman departed held by the woman not ready to say goodbye. It had happened before my very eyes: this strange, unnatural, sinful, beautiful connection, sundered forever.

Chapter 38

The next week passed in a haze of mourning, as thick and disorienting as the unrelenting fog that crept over the stones of Venice each morning. Livia was in the first hours inconsolable and then grew withdrawn and silent, but she could not display the extent of her pain. Most of our sisters did not suspect anything untoward between the pair, just a very close friendship built over decades. Many of them had similar deep relationships, ones of either amity or enmity, from living in such close proximity. Perhaps only I and Madelena knew the truth. Viena may have guessed it but was too enraptured in her own romance to comment. Or perhaps that enchantment was what enabled her to understand. Either way, she kept quiet. I was unsure what Zanetta truly knew, but she did not crow about it in the immediate aftermath, as if perhaps sensing that would cross some line, or maybe plotting her next chess move. Whatever the reason for her reticence, I was grateful.

Over the course of the next few days of vigils and funereal rituals, abbreviated due to the interdict, I prayed for Elisabetta, that her soul had been welcomed into Heaven, that perhaps God had some sort of understanding for such earthly love, but my stomach twisted in worry that perhaps her judgment would be much harsher, for God of course saw all, even a forbidden love that to me seemed of loyal constancy.

More heretical imaginings, but I could not banish them, instead scribbling additional pages of my treatise as I tried to untangle my colliding thoughts.

Selfish ones too flitted through my head and heart. What was the point of it all? Venice was on the verge of a papal sacking, at which soldiers and mercenaries might very well forcibly take my virtue, and I could not be with my chosen lover. Outwardly, I was serene and prayerful and supportive of my aunt, while inside I shrieked louder than a Venetian seagull, as stricken as the day I took the veil.

Out of the depths I cry to you, O Lord.

The days passed, and I felt as if I were watching everything submerged under brackish, filthy canal water. Bone-deep tiredness and despair, from grief over Elisabetta, pity for my auntie's loss, anguish at my own situation, and a sharp, deep ache for the life I might have had.

Lord, hear my prayer. Why are you not hearing my prayer?

Finally the burial day arrived along with a bright sun, blue skies, and the cold bora wind driving in from the north, and our dear Elisabetta was laid to eternal rest in the convent cemetery.

Eventually, the bora still blasting, the church bell rang, signalling the end of the official mourning period and the return to our regular duties.

Livia did not emerge from her cell for two days more, and I fretted her absence, giving her the space she so clearly wanted but often hovering outside her door to ensure I still heard signs of life beyond Enrica's subdued clucking. A sneeze, a clearing of the throat, a shuffle across the floor, each sound was a small miracle that allowed me to breathe more easily and go about my business. This consisted mainly of picking at meals, worrying over Angela Riva and Zanetta's increasingly suspicious chatter about Livia, praying for the soul of Elisabetta, writing new pages, and wondering about my manuscript's reception at the Aldine Press.

My heart pulsed with pain over Luca, which I interpreted as a grief for what could never be. *Which is worse*, I tormented myself as I had at Elisabetta's departure, *to be Livia and have loved long and deeply and feel such pain, or to be myself, to have briefly experienced paradise, only to have it snatched away forever and given to someone else?*

And then I would chastise myself. Luca was alive, well, thriving. On the Great Council before the usual age, chosen for his first governmental position, at the start of a long, illustrious career, soon to be a father and pass on his lineage. I should thank God for His mercies, not lament the disappointment of my indulgent and childish wishes.

By the next evening meal, I felt it imperative to bring Livia with me to the refectory. Her absence was becoming glaring, the talk more insidious, and even Mother Marina seemed slightly piqued. So to Auntie's cell door I went, knocking and calling her name.

The door creaked open as she let me in, looking haggard, avoiding my eyes.

"Auntie, you must come with me to the meal. There is gossip."

"What does it matter? Nothing matters anymore."

I enveloped her in my arms. "I know, Auntie. But you still must live here. You will need to face them. You desire yet to be the next abbess, do you not? You have worked so hard through your time here to position yourself.

You cannot give them the satisfaction of confirming wrongdoing in their eyes." Her brow arched ever so slightly, but she did not correct me. "And I need you. You're my aunt. My only family here. If not for your own reputation, then for my sake."

She did not reply but allowed me to wash her face and brush her hair into a simple plait as Enrica preened her feathers in a corner. Then I helped her disrobe and put on a laundered dress in a subdued blue. Auntie had lost quite a bit of weight over the last few months, her ribs visible, her hip bones nearly poking through her skin. The dress was loose, but she looked presentable enough.

Steering her from Zanetta and Angela, who eyed her a bit too inquisitively, I seated her facing the wall, her back to those less inclined to pity and more to prattle. Viena warmly welcomed her, and sympathetic if unsuspecting friends quickly surrounded her. She managed to eat a roll with a generous pat of butter washed down by a half glass of wine, then begged our pardon at not joining us for the entire meal, scurrying into the hall.

I let out a sigh, and Viena patted my hand, bringing her head close to mine so we could speak softly but frankly. "Give her time. As is written in the Psalms, *The Lord is near to the disconsolate and saves the smashed in spirit.*"

"I hope you are right, and that God does not forsake her."

"Jesus was merciful and loved the sinner."

I nodded. Livia was a sinner. I could not deny it. So was Elisabetta. And Viena. Would I add myself to that immoral roster? Half of me shied away from the very idea, while half relished the thought of putting myself into such a state.

"Jacomo and I sometimes pray together."

"Do you?" I could not disguise my surprise at such an intimacy. Was that a flare of envy I felt, at what she and Jacomo had, and Luca and I did not? I immediately reprimanded myself for that trespass.

"Ours is not just a corporeal affair. It is of the mind, of the spirit, and of faith. He is my husband in all but name."

I could not keep my lips shut even as I half envied her. Perhaps that envy was why I continued speaking. "That is a sin. Not to mention he is a commoner."

"What does it matter that he is a commoner when I am a nun? And I know it is a sin, but is it not a sin to force us to become nuns in the first place? I don't know about you, but I said my conventual vows with my mouth and not my heart. My parents demanded I come here, and when I protested my father beat me." Her fingers flew to her cheek as if the memory of the blows was still fresh.

She had summed it up perfectly: with her mouth and not her heart. Like me. Like Rosa too, compelled to marry Zago. Who among our sisters had taken the veil due to a true calling? I could name only one or two. "Me too," I whispered, my mind already working on ways to revise a key passage of my manuscript to encompass forced monachization.

Did that coercion to take the veil make our vow less binding, as Viena intimated? Did that in turn allow a tiny space for my love with Luca to flourish?

But the stakes, so high now for any man who consorted with a nun, were even higher for Luca than for the common Jacomo. As a nobleman, Luca had much more to lose.

And what would be the punishment for transgressing nuns such as Viena and me?

Viena must have assumed my long silence to be censure and so shot me a glare. "*Let he who is without sin cast the first stone.* You should confess your own sin from the summer." Viena fairly hurled her words at me. I had never known her to be angry.

I pushed back from the table, no longer hungry, my food only half-eaten. "We did not sin."

"All the worse for you then. Everyone would assume it, and yet you didn't even have the pleasure."

I scuttled out of the refectory, feeling inflamed. But not by Viena's harsh words and tone. By the fact that she was right.

I wished I had sinned, wished I did need to make a confession. It was indeed all the worse for me that I hadn't.

Chapter 39

I stayed up late, slept fitfully, and roused early the next morning, assisted by the aromatic smell of roasting chestnuts emanating from the kitchen as the cooks prepared for San Martino the following day. I was working on the idea Viena had given me about saying our vows with mouths but not hearts. Madelena stopped in to advise me on Livia, who had broken her fast at the refectory and seemed bewildered at my absence. I dismissed her with promises to make it to the midday meal, knowing I was shirking my duties as a niece but anxious to jot down the words before they disappeared into the mists of my mind.

Eventually spent of thought and overcome by frequent yawns and brewing hunger, I blew the pages dry, locked them in my trunk, and decided to take Dolce for a quick walk.

The air in the courtyard was warm, the scent of rain heavy on the scirocco wind that now tumbled up from the south. The last of the cyclamen blossoms danced, and my skirts whirled around my ankles as I took a turn in the garden, chickens clucking in every direction at Dolce's enthusiastic approach. The garden was nearing its seasonal end, filled with greens and root vegetables, including some pumpkins, the seeds recently brought from the New World, and I marvelled at their orange strangeness as a few fat drops punctuated the stones.

I was ostensibly praying though really letting my mind meander when Madelena found me, her eyes wide. "You have a visitor. Lord Cicogna." My heart lurched with unexpected anticipation as she grabbed Dolce's leash with one hand, her other cradling her stomach, as was her recent habit. I followed her inside and headed to the parlour, half with trepidation, half nearly skipping.

On the threshold, I smoothed my hair and collected myself. The parlour was empty, my sisters thankfully all at the refectory, aside from Luca in his black robes, looking hesitant. Feeling heady, I took the risk of shutting the door for privacy. I had not seen him in nearly five months. He never failed to entice me, like a queen bee drawn to her hive.

"Signora Soranzo." He came over to kiss my hand, and a shiver went through me.

"Lord Cicogna, it is so very good to see you." Why he was here, I wasn't sure, but I also wasn't sure I cared about the reason.

He released my hand with obvious reluctance. "Before all else, please accept my sincerest condolences on the passing of Signora Elisabetta. I was quite saddened to hear the news and pray for her eternal soul."

"Thank you. That means much."

"Do you fare well?"

"Well enough, I suppose, considering the circumstances. However, my auntie is quite distraught, having been close with Elisabetta for many years, and I worry for her." I knew he would not understand my true meaning, yet hoped I was able to convey the depth of their bond.

He frowned, compassion etching his expression. "I am sorry to hear your aunt is in such pain. It is very difficult to lose a dear friend."

My eyes threatened to overflow. "Thank you again."

"Perhaps what I say next will bring you cheer. I felt this news did not belong in a letter, that it was better to dare tell you in person." He gestured behind him to the package on the table. My manuscript. I put my fingers to my lips as his smile broadened. "I brought your pages to Ser Manutius as soon as I read them, and he too fairly devoured them. He sees great publication value here. This is not his usual fare, as you know, since he primarily focuses on bringing ancient texts to the present, but he has a small budget for special original projects such as yours."

"Truly?" I could not believe my ears.

"Truly. He is not without commentary, which he has kindly noted for you. I believe the revisions represent a fair amount of work on your part, if you are willing."

"I am more than willing. I am in fact already working on additions and amendments." As I wondered what Luca would think of them, another thought struck me: Luca too had taken his marital vows with his mouth but not his heart. He had not wanted to marry his wife. I suspected even Zago had felt the same, not that I had much compassion for him.

"One other item of import. He agreed that anonymous publication would be most suitable, to protect the interests of your family and convent and given the current political climate. Such a text will likely ignite a firestorm of debate in Venice, and you should be protected."

I nodded slowly, giddy, barely able to take it all in. "I want no harm to come to my former and current homes, especially with war ever present."

"Then it is settled. He knows you will need some time for modifications but is hoping to move rather quickly as rumours are circulating that the printing presses may be forced to close."

"I will complete them before we celebrate Our Lord's birth."

"If you would permit, when the manuscript is ready, I would be happy to reread it to let you know my thoughts before passing it on to Aldine Press."

"Yes, please." I went over to the table and untied the string on the package, peeling back the cloth to reveal the top page, my own script interspersed with the handwriting of Aldus Manutius. "Luca, how can I ever thank you?"

He came to stand beside me. "Calling me by my Christian name again is a good start. Justina."

I had not even realized I had done so. It marked a certain intimacy, one I both feared and welcomed. "I apologize." But I could not help it. Around him, I was like a flower opening to the sun.

"There is no need." He turned to face me, and like that heliotrope, I mirrored him. "I could not stay away any longer anyway." He tipped my chin up, and then, right there in the empty parlour of the San Zaccaria convent, he leaned down to kiss me, his breath scented faintly with clove, and I drank in the sunshine, enjoying every moment of what seemed dawn, dusk, and a summer's bright afternoon.

As our lips almost touched, a throat cleared and we jumped apart. What had we done so unthinkingly, and within hallowed walls? I turned to face my judgment, expecting Zanetta and feeling immense relief upon spotting

Viena. An ally certainly, although we had not parted on good terms the previous evening.

Luca looked at her with a certain steel in his eyes, drawing himself up to his full patrician height. He did not know her thoughts at all and could not easily ascertain if she were friend or foe.

She broke the silence. "If you're going to partake in such pleasure, I recommend much more discretion." Her smile was as uncanny as her cat's stare.

I exhaled. "Viena."

"Enjoy your goodbyes with Lord Cicogna, then meet me in my room. I have something to tell you."

"Thank you, Signora Viena." Luca spoke calmly, but I knew him well enough now to detect the relief in his voice.

She gave a brief nod, then slipped out the door, closing it firmly behind her.

"That was lucky," Luca said, reaching out to hold my hand.

But I would not allow him this time. "Luca, believe me when I say there is nothing I want more. But this is folly. You are married; I am a nun. The laws are much stricter now."

"But not well enforced, from what I have discerned over the last few months."

I swallowed hard, screaming *yes* within my heart and my body. But I was being selfish. What if it had been Zanetta or Angela who entered? Or not even an enemy. "It is only a matter of time before they make an example of someone, and here we are in the public part of a holy house, where someone much less sympathetic than Viena could walk in at any time. I don't want that example to be you. To lose your new government post, to pay a substantial fine, not to mention face banishment from Venice. I do not even know what my punishment would be. It is not worth it." I forced myself to continue. "I am not worth it, not with your wife big with your heir. It was a risk for you to come to the convent today at all. You are not my family, nor a relation of anyone at San Zaccaria."

"There is my family's connection with the Zanes, and Signora Zanetta always seems willing to converse. Besides, you and I have legitimate business. Let me decide what risk I am willing to bear."

"But to what end? We cannot be together in any case. It is hopeless, and we torture ourselves." I turned away, my marble facade starting to shatter into a million shards. "I think you should leave now."

He said nothing as tears streamed down my cheeks and I swiped them away with bare fingers, the taste of salt on my lips. Finally, he strode around to face me, extracting a clean cloth from his robes. It was in fact one of the handkerchiefs I had made him so many months before. "I have not yet given up hope. But for now, I will honour your request to leave. I will write soon to inquire about your progress on the revisions. If nothing else, I have faith this treatise will end up in the proper hands, that it might even change some influential Venetian minds, and so I must see it through to publication."

I dabbed my face with the handkerchief, sniffling as I nodded. What we had did originate as a meeting of the minds, at the very least.

He touched the birthmark on my forehead, as intimate as a kiss. "Keep that handkerchief, and I its mate. When you hold it, I hope you think of me as much as I of you. Goodbye for now, Justina." Then he pivoted on his heel and strode to the exit.

I watched him go, holding the fabric to my lips, the scent of him embroidered into it as I had his initials.

Chapter 40

My stomach growled as I headed to Viena's cell, having missed both breakfast and now the midday meal. Auntie and Madelena would be wondering what had happened to me. The convent air was redolent with rain and sugar, the cooks having moved from chestnuts to cookies in further preparation for San Martino, and I passed a maid lugging a crate of wine bottles, presumably from one of San Zaccaria's own island vineyards. The rain fell in heavy sheets, and I hoped Luca would not be too drenched by the time he reached his palazzo. I hugged the cloth package to my breast, grateful Aldus Manutius's advice was not dissolving into illegibility.

I locked the manuscript in my trunk on top of Luca's letters, tucked the handkerchief under my pillow, and then warily knocked on Viena's door. She answered almost immediately and welcomed me in, offering roasted chestnuts she'd snagged from the kitchen along with a cup of wine, both of which I accepted with appreciation.

"I am sorry about last night, Justina. I was impertinent." She held out her elegant arms to me. "Will you forgive me, my dear friend?"

"Only if you will forgive me too." We embraced hard, then both laughed a little before I helped myself to some chestnuts. "Thank you, I'm starving."

"There's more where that came from, as I know you are well aware from your own kitchen raids." She laughed again before her expression sobered. "Justina, seeking your forgiveness was not the only reason I wanted to speak with you."

"Oh?" She sounded quite serious. I gulped the rest of my wine and sat down, Leo jumping onto my lap. "Tell me."

Sitting beside me, she took an enormous breath. "I'm with child."

I whistled. "Are you sure?"

"Quite. I've missed my courses for three months and show all the signs."

I nodded, thinking of the closed convent of Contorta in the lagoon and San Zaccaria's own past transgressions, about which Livia had told me. "Well, it's not as if this convent has never had a pregnant nun. It will cause some scandal, and Zanetta will undoubtedly be difficult to bear, but I'm sure Mother Marina will minimize those effects. She is a strong leader. And if it's a girl, you can raise her here. If a boy, I'm sure Jacomo will find an excellent apprenticeship for him with his carpentry connections. Have you told him yet?"

"Yes, he knows. But I'm not going to tell Mother Marina."

Leo purred as I stroked his back. "Well, maybe not yet, but it will be obvious soon enough. How has Jacomo taken the news?"

She shook her head. "Justina, I am not making myself clear." Her voice livened. "I'm running away from the convent. Jacomo and I are leaving Venice together."

If I was surprised by her initial revelation, this latter pronouncement struck me almost dumb. "Leave Venice? When?" I could hardly speak the words.

"Tonight. I have a bag packed. We've been planning this for several weeks now." She laid her hand along her still-flat stomach, much the way Madelena did of late.

"Tonight?" Her news still stupefied me, my mind not working properly, and I stopped petting Leo, who meowed his displeasure.

"Yes, but I did not want to leave without saying goodbye to you, my dearest friend here. You know what they say: *Better one true friend than a hundred relatives*."

"Where will you go?"

"Anywhere Jacomo can get carpentry work. Far from here, beyond the Veneto. Elsewhere in Italy. If he faces banishment anyway, better I'm banished with him."

"But what about the war?" The danger was unfathomable, and even in peace the thought of leaving Venice, our home, our patrimony, especially with noble blood in our veins and duty in our hearts, was almost unbearable to me. How could she consider such a thing?

"Perhaps Greece then. Jacomo is very good with his hands, a master craftsman. He'll be able to make enough ducats wherever we wind up, I have no doubt. His talents are wasted here at San Zaccaria."

"What about your family? Your mother?" Leo gave up on me, jumped to the ground, and began licking his paws.

"She will be extremely upset, and I feel very badly about that. I will miss her terribly. Not my father so much." She shrugged. "I'll write to her when we are settled, to let her know I'm safe. That her grandchild is safe. But I must go. I never wanted to come here." She gestured at the stone walls. "I have already lost everything by taking the veil. And now I am a pregnant patrician nun in love with a commoner. Could it get any worse? I have nothing left to lose, so why not try gaining another life as a mother and the wife of a carpenter?" She patted my arm ruefully. "And do not worry about the hereafter. I will go to confession. Jacomo too. And as soon as we can find a willing priest, we will ask him to marry us. God is merciful and will forgive us."

My face was in my hands as I tried to absorb what she was telling me, my breath ragged. She was leaving her home and divorcing everything she knew and held dear. The same things I knew and held dear. And she could not have looked any more pleased.

"Justina." She removed my hands from my face and clasped them in her own, looking me right in the eye. "It was the death of Elisabetta that finally made up my mind. Jacomo had been urging me to come away with him, but I resisted, for all the reasons I know you are thinking. But as she was wasting away, and then after she died, the reaction of your auntie . . ." Her eyes flicked away for a moment before locking again on mine. "I know about Livia and Elisabetta. I know you do too. Don't worry, I never breathed a word to anyone else. And while in some ways I cannot comprehend their sin, in other ways I cannot help but admire their audacity. Their easy proximity to each other. And their bond. I want that too, and more."

"Oh, Viena, I just worry about what will happen to you. It will be so much harder than you think. We've both lived such sheltered lives."

"Jacomo hasn't. He's had a hard life. He's rowed on the galleys, travelled to other places, worked since he was a boy. And I'm willing to take the risk." She let go of my hands and smoothed her skirts. "Justina, I'm going to write Signora Teresa at the infirmary that I'm nursing a cold and will rest in my room for a few days, so as not to pass on any potential contagion. In a day or two, though, someone will come looking for me and discover I'm gone. If they ask you about it, you can deny you know anything, but if they press you, tell them I'm a sinner and good riddance. Tell them my departure is good for Venice, so her convents will be pure, and we can win the war."

Thinking I probably would not say anything at all, I put my arm around her shoulders. "I'm going to miss you."

She cleared her throat. "I will miss you too. But know that Jacomo loves me and will take care of me and our baby. Know that I am happy. Know that I am free."

Chapter 41

I saw Auntie at the evening meal, my attempt to appear normal clearly failing when she asked if I was all right. I nodded vaguely. Though I excused myself after the meal on the grounds of exhaustion, I stayed awake in my cell a long time into the night, thinking, waiting, holding Luca's handkerchief between my hands like a holy object. What would Viena's leaving mean? After the loss of Elisabetta, and with Livia half out of her mind, I was going to be lonely, for one thing.

When would my sisters discover Viena's absence? Would they question me? Would her departure ruin San Zaccaria? Would the scandal get out? Would it bring more oversight and enforcement? Would it cause Venice to lose the war to the pope? Aside from these more serious considerations, I could not help but wonder selfishly if it would ruin any prospects for myself, literary, romantic, or otherwise.

Try as I might, my ears straining far into the dark, I could not identify the moment when Viena and Jacomo left. I heard whisperings in the corridor and doors opening and shutting, but these were not unusual midnight melodies.

As sleep continued to elude me, I lit a candle and tried to at least read the commentary from Manutius, but I could not concentrate. The rain continued to fall hard, this time sweeping in from the mainland to the west on the *libeccio* wind. The moon was near to full, and although I was not a gondolier keeping track of the tides, I knew Venice was ripe for an *acqua alta*. I hoped Viena and Jacomo would be long gone by then, wet and windblown but no worse for wear.

With a grunt like that of a trapped pig, I flopped onto my bed and stared at the ceiling. It must be San Martino already, and I first murmured, then sang out the irreverent song about the saint that Paolo had taught Rosa and me as a child. Luca had sung it too on the day of our picnic.

San Martino went to the attic
To meet his lover
His lover was not there
And he fell to the ground ...

In this house there are two little girls
Both very curly-haired and beautiful
With delicate faces
They look like their father.

Paolo used to tease that those girls were Rosa and me. As I sang the lyrics now, I began to wonder if Luca were San Martino, miserable, with his lover missing: me, bereft, trapped behind thick stone convent walls.

Imagining Luca was with me in my bed, I finally fell asleep near dawn, my dreams interlaced with the feel of his hands upon my body.

A rap at my door a few hours later followed by Dolce's yaps startled me awake, and I blushed at the memory of my vivid visions.

As I further came to my senses, anxiety jolted through me, and I feared my sisters had already found Viena's room empty. I smoothed my hair, straightened my nightgown, and donned a dressing robe as another knock came on the door.

Madelena stood smiling outside with a basin of water for my ablutions. "You will be pleased to know your sister has arrived for a visit. Shall I help you dress?"

Yes, I was pleased indeed to see Rosa again, and quite relieved Viena's escape was not yet detected.

"Why don't you have her come directly to my cell?" I wanted some privacy, and no one would deny a blood sister's visit. "Perhaps you could bring a tray of breakfast?"

"Very well, and then I'll help dress you thereafter."

She rekindled the coals in the brazier before leaving, and I tidied up my cell as I waited, stacking the pages of my annotated manuscript into a neat pile at the back corner of my desk, weighed down with a rock from the garden, wiping the quill tips, mopping up tiny ink spills, corking the open bottle. I splashed my face with the water Madelena had brought, cleaned my teeth, and brushed my hair, now longer than my shoulders, then made the bed, tucking Luca's handkerchief, which I normally kept under the pillow, into the pocket of my dressing gown. As I straightened Carpaccio's Madonna—I did so admire her devoted beauty—I was glad I had not resorted to selling it, even though Zago had found a potential buyer.

At another knock, I opened the door, and a damp Rosa was hugging me tightly, her belly a taut balloon between us. "How fares baby Rosa?"

"Baby Zago, I pray, and I hope you do too." She flashed me a pleading look as Madelena took her wet cloak and hung it by the brazier, then went to procure breakfast.

Rosa sat on my bed awkwardly, and Dolce leapt up beside her, his tail wagging furiously as his former mistress petted him. "I fear this may be my last visit to you. I am most uncomfortable, and given the unrelenting rain, Signora Zane did not want me to come. Zago seemed genuinely alarmed for my safety, saying an *acqua alta* is imminent. But Papa stopped by last evening and convinced them both that a final visit to my sister would be good for my spiritual health heading into my confinement, and they finally agreed, seeing how my past visits to you so uplifted me. Signora Zane is here visiting Zanetta as well. We cannot stay long." She stroked a contented Dolce, smoothing back his white fur. Then she noticed her old doll that I still slept with, picking it up to inspect it, smoothing its little dress. "I forgot about this."

"How are you, Sister, truly?"

"Soggy. The winds are blowing the rain in every direction. Otherwise, I feel I'm about to burst like a firecracker at Carnival." I laughed, then pulled her into another hug as her brave front crumbled.

"Whatever is the matter, Rosa?"

"When Papa visited yesterday, he told me Paolo will be heading to the front lines in the next few days, near Este, or possibly to Ferrara. It's an administrative role, but I fear very much for his safety." She clasped Dolce to her bosom. "Papa asked me to tell you that he will visit you as soon as he can. I imagine Mama will too, after the weather improves."

"Although not unexpected, that is worrisome news about Paolo." Events seemed to be turning lately in Venice's favour, but it was clear this war would not end soon. And our brother, although he liked to keep his hands clean and his skin soft, was an impetuous young man inclined to bravado. My heart contracted at the prospect of losing him.

When Madelena returned with a silver tray laden with San Martino biscotti, I wondered if his departure would have any impact on her. It would certainly make things harder if she had a son and Paolo was gone, unable to place him in an apprenticeship. I was not at all sure what my father would do.

I inhaled heavily. I should not let myself get ahead of matters. It would be many years before the child's future need be determined, and Paolo would be long returned.

Madelena did not stay long, and Dolce squirmed out of Rosa's arms and followed the maid out the door.

"I will pray that God keeps our brother safe and out of harm's way."

"I will too. Will you pray for me as well, to keep me safe and out of harm's way?"

"Oh, Rosa, I already do! Daily. Auntie Livia does as well." At least she used to, but perhaps she was so consumed by grief she had forgotten. I would have to remind her.

Rosa took a deep breath. "How is our auntie? I will see her before I leave. The gondolier is returning to fetch Signora Zane and me before the Marangona bell for the midday meal."

I was not sure what to say. Rosa did not know the truth of the matter between Livia and Elisabetta. "She is sad at the loss of her friend. You may be surprised by her appearance. She is thinner and pale."

Rosa nodded. "I wish I had a friend at the Zane palazzo. Do you remember when Papa told me I was going to marry Zago, how I said I was scared? I still am. Scared to deliver a child. Scared I will die. And now I'm scared the baby will die."

"Oh, Rosa. You have Signora Benedetta. You know how good she is."

She shook her head. "She is getting so old and frail now. You have not seen her in a long while. I am not sure she is still capable. When I saw her last week, her breathing was strange."

That was an alarming bit of news. But even if Zago were indifferent to or just ignorant of women's matters, would the astute Luca allow the same enfeebled midwife to aid his child's mother? "Could you ask your mother-in-law to switch to the Zane midwife?" Surely Signora Zane would be more in tune with such womanly issues and would not want anything to harm her grandchild. And Signora Benedetta had largely already served our purpose.

"But I always imagined Signora Benedetta would be there for me. I've known her my whole life. She delivered all of us. I don't want a new midwife!" She looked like a scared little girl, and I had to remind myself that she was not even fourteen, her birthday the day after the Epiphany. With all that had gone on of late, I myself was feeling considerably older.

I gathered her in my arms. "There, there, it will be all right. We'll figure something out. We can ask Auntie what to do. She always knows. You must calm yourself. It's not good for the baby." I kept murmuring what I hoped were soothing words, and eventually they seemed to have a palliative effect. "Come, have something to eat."

"I already ate this morning." She hiccupped.

"Sit with me then, for I have not yet broken my fast, lazy nun that I am."

She acquiesced, and together we shuffled the few feet across the cell and sat in the chairs by my desk, my manuscript still in the corner. I covered it with a napkin to keep it clean, with the idea of resuming work on it the moment Rosa departed. "And you might be persuaded to have a biscotto."

"I do find the sweets hard to resist."

I smiled. "I know." I placed an almond fennel biscotto on a small plate and handed her a cup of watered wine before serving myself.

She dipped the biscotto in the wine, then took a nibble, visibly relaxing. "The San Zaccaria cooks are much better than the one at the Zane palazzo."

"They are known as some of the best in the city. A small recompense for being here." I bit into a second biscotto with a sigh. There was a reason I so frequently raided the kitchens and stockpiled their delicious bounty.

She polished off her second breakfast and sat back, both hands resting on her belly, tracing small circles on either side.

"You look healthy, Sister," I said, as I admired her rosy cheeks and swelling bosom. "That bodes well for the babe."

She merely nodded, not looking happy but neither seeming sad now. Far away, a church bell pealed, and I idly wondered why.

I closed my eyes for a moment as I savoured the last few bites of biscotto. When I opened them, Rosa was sitting up straighter, her eyes wide, her face stricken.

"What is it, Rosa?" I leaned over in alarm as more church bells joined in the cacophony.

She looked at me in horror. "I think my waters just broke."

Chapter 42

Madelena returned within moments of Rosa's revelation with a startling pronouncement of her own: "An *acqua alta!*" An incoming high-water crisis explained the now wildly clanging bells.

"It's too early!" Rosa rose to her feet, the back of her skirts soaked.

Madelena seemed puzzled at first, then immediately comprehended, her face returning to a mask of calm. "Shall I fetch Signora Benedetta?"

"Can you, if the water is rising?" Likely the crypt of San Zaccaria was already almost full, well beyond the watery membrane normally found on the stone floor, and the lagoon would be creeping into the convent's water entrance on the canal side. Such was the insidious nature of an *acqua alta*. I kept a tight grip on Rosa, who was breathing loudly. "You have your own condition to consider."

Madelena watched with grave concern as Rosa doubled over her belly. "I'll try."

I nodded. "Do be careful, and turn back straightaway if it's too much. I'll bring Rosa to the infirmary and meet you there. Signora Teresa must have delivered a few babies during her years as infirmarian at San Zaccaria."

With a querying look, Madelena dashed out as I threw a cloak over Rosa to cover the wet stains on her dress. "Can you walk?"

"Yes, I can manage." She shuffled forward as I, still in my dressing gown, supported her through the doorframe, along the corridor past Viena's closed door, down the stairs, and then along another corridor, now overlain with a film of canal water, to the infirmary, ignoring any stares as we tried to maintain our dignity and appear inconspicuous.

The infirmary was empty save for Signora Teresa, who frowned when we told her what was amiss. She helped Rosa onto a bed before hurrying to shut the door and shove linens along the bottom to stem the tide.

She then took me aside. "I am very concerned your sister has not yet reached full term, not to mention her own youth. This will be dangerous."

I would have felt immeasurably better if Teresa had delivered more babies. As experienced and trustworthy as I knew Teresa to be in curing maladies for the old and infirm, she'd brought only a few babies into the world, the illicit children of the nuns who'd become pregnant during her decades as infirmarian.

"I did send my maid for our midwife. They shouldn't be too long." I hoped this was true.

"If they can manage the *acqua alta*. And isn't your maid big with child herself? Pray for your sister." Then she went to prepare as the water began to breach the ineffective linen barrier and slither under the door.

I seated myself beside Rosa, my slippers and the hem of my robe wet. "Squeeze my hand as hard as you want when the pains come. Transmit to me all your misery, and I shall bear it for you."

She looked at me pleadingly as her body shook, not just from Eve's curse but also from terror.

I was desperate to alleviate her suffering. "Let us pray. We will say the rosary together."

I took out the one I kept tucked in my dressing gown pocket, alongside Luca's handkerchief, and together we started reciting the decades, my voice unerring whenever Rosa had to endure the unrelenting afflictions.

As we finished the third decade, Madelena ran in, completely soaked, shaking her head. "The water is coming in too fast. It's already up to my knees outside."

And up to our ankles inside.

Rosa gripped my hand as a contraction overtook her. I intoned my thirty-first Hail Mary as Madelena looked on in consternation.

"Signora Rosa, do not despair," Madelena said as the pain ebbed. She looked bedraggled and pale, her eyes knotted with uncertainty, so I beckoned her to speak privately.

"Madelena, you do not look well. Has your labour started?"

She shook her head. "It's not labour, I'm in no pain, but I am exhausted. I am so sorry, Signora Justina, I hate to not help you, but I do think I need to lie down now."

"Of course." I nodded, thinking quickly. "But can you manage one errand first, within the convent? Please find Auntie Livia, Signora Zane, and Signora Zanetta. Ask my aunt to come here straight away, but please tell the Zanes we will keep them apprised of the matter. Their presence will not be a comfort to my sister. Then, get dry and take that well-deserved rest. Do not worry. I know Signora Teresa is up to the task." I prayed I was correct, but I suspected that I lied.

Madelena splashed her way out of the infirmary, sending more water surging in when she opened the door, and I thought of Noah, helplessly watching the rising waters. Would San Zaccaria prove a worthy ark, in more ways than one?

I surveyed the scene. Teresa was standing in water to her ankles looking overwhelmed. My sister was clearly in pain and seemed as helpless as a newborn kitten.

I could no longer stand by idly murmuring ineffectual prayers. Instead, I took a deep breath and smoothed my dressing gown. "Signora Teresa, where is your habit?"

She turned to me, confused. "My habit? Whatever for?"

"I'm leaving the convent to find a midwife."

Six hours grows, six hours falls. That was the conventional wisdom for how long it took for an *acqua alta* to have its say. That meant the highest water would probably occur around *vespers* and be gone by morning, leaving mud and chaos in its wake. Although sometimes nature did not follow conventional wisdom.

Without Mother Marina's permission or even knowledge of my whereabouts, I stood in the empty San Zaccaria campo with the water above my knees, the bottom of Teresa's unfamiliar and too-short habit soaked and clinging to my calves. I was also wearing a pair of her ill-fitting shoes, and a misty rain had quickly dampened the black cloak draped over my shoulders and head. I looked around, trying to decide where to go, feeling utterly alone and nervous to be so.

Signora Benedetta lived somewhere in Dosoduro, not far from our palazzo, but I did not know exactly where, and I could not even get close to home without a gondola. I had no money with me for a *traghetto*, even if I could find one in the deserted city. I thought about begging La Diamante, who must know a midwife or two, but alas I did not know her residence either. Not for the first time I cursed myself for being a woman.

The doge's palazzo was not far, and I knew I could find my way there. But what were the chances a midwife was anywhere near that bastion of men, and moreover during an *acqua alta*? And while it was possible that Teodor might be waiting if Papa had a meeting, most likely they and everyone else were home.

Should I just knock on a random door and hope the resident took pity on a frantic nun?

And then it came to me, a place nearby where at least a few women would be, one of them with child. And at least one man I knew.

Under normal circumstances, one could walk to the Cicogna palazzo in the time it took to say a few rosary decades, but I underestimated how difficult it would be to wade through the insistently rising water. I forced my legs forward, heading toward the lagoon step by laborious step, praying that Livia was now holding Rosa's hand in my stead, that Mother Marina would forgive my bold decision, that Luca would be home or that he would not be home, I could not decide which.

Finally I made it to the desolate *fondamenta* that ran along the lagoon, although it was now impossible to see where the cobblestones ended and the lagoon started, given how high the water had risen. The undercurrent threatened to knock me down. I had no idea how to swim and hoped I did not accidentally slip in over my head. I clung close to the stone wall of a white palazzo until I looked up and recognized the terracotta-coloured one that was Luca's.

My heart thudded as I beat upon the big wooden double doors. An angel was carved into the white stone lancet arch above, and I beseeched her that someone at the Cicogna palazzo would be able to help.

One door swung open, sweeping me and a rush of water into the ground-floor entrance. I lost my balance and became entirely drenched as I struggled to regain my footing.

Luca himself, clearly shocked at my presence, helped me up. "Justina! What are you doing here? What's wrong?"

"Luca, who's there?" A feminine voice called down the staircase, and I could see voluminous rose-coloured skirts.

I spoke softly, unsure if it was his wife or mother. "It's Rosa. I need a midwife. She's gone into labour at the convent much too soon. I didn't know where else to turn."

A swishing of skirts, and Luca's wife inched down the staircase in full resplendence. She was followed by a diminutive woman with piercing blue eyes wearing plain dark clothes and a red scarf, black wisps of hair peeping out. I could not guess who she was. She did not seem to be a regular kind of servant or maid, nor even a Venetian.

"Who has come in such weather?" His wife sounded half scared, half angry.

Luca stared at me with wide eyes as he escorted me to the drier portion of the enormous ground-floor room near the bottom of the stairs, where a bewildered manservant came striding in, and I came face to face with Elena Paruta. I could not help but notice the modest swell of her belly as well as the scowl upon her slightly bloated face.

"A nun? How may we help you, Sister?" She was not exactly friendly.

"I'm from around the corner at San Zaccaria, Signora." She nodded as I continued in as devout a voice as I could summon. "My sister, that is, my blood sister, came to visit me this morning. She is big with child and unexpectedly went into labour and then the *acqua alta* started. She cannot make it to her home, we cannot reach her midwife, and as you might expect, my spiritual sisters are not experienced at delivering babies." This half lie rolled off my tongue rather easily.

"And you think we might happen to have a midwife here at our palazzo?"

"I knew you were with child too, Signora."

She raised an eyebrow and her tone. "Oh? And how might you come to such knowledge? Do I know you? I do not recognize you."

I realized I had made a blunder. I could not admit I was in correspondence with her husband. What would she think or suspect? I had not thought this plan through.

Luckily Luca seemed to have found his voice. "Elena, darling, I recognize this nun as the sister of my dear friend Paolo Soranzo. You remember him, from my Inamorati fraternity? Always jesting. He attended our wedding and you have met him a few times." He spoke crisply and confidently. "I told Paolo our happy news months ago, and he obviously informed his sister. And of course the Cicogna palazzo is well known throughout the city and very near San Zaccaria. Naturally she would come here, given the circumstances."

I could only nod along, grateful for Luca's political smoothness. Elena seemed only partially placated, even this reminder of her lofty position in society not enough to soothe her.

He went on, and I glimpsed the doge he might very well someday become. "Signora Soranzo, God indeed moves in ways unbeknownst to us, for you have miraculously come to the perfect place. My wife has just today engaged a new midwife, as sadly Signora Benedetta is too old and ill to deliver babies anymore." He gestured to the slight woman with the red scarf, who I noticed now was holding a large bag. "We were just deciding whether the good signora should stay until the *acqua alta* subsides or whether our gondolier should take her home. Although I had not realized how high the water had already risen until I opened the door for you."

"I am happy to assist any mother in need." The midwife spoke with an accent I did not recognize. "Just lead the way. It sounds close, so we can walk."

"Or swim," I added ruefully.

The midwife looked perplexed. "Alas, that is not something I ever learned."

"It is not far. I will escort you both." Luca nodded to his servant, who dashed off.

"Luca." Elena spoke petulantly. "You cannot leave me alone."

I knew Luca well enough now to see him work to maintain his composure. "My dear wife, I will be but a short while, and you will not be alone. My mother and father are both upstairs and would be pleased to care for you. San Zaccaria is very close, and these women should not be unaccompanied, especially in these weather conditions."

"Send your servant in your stead." She glared at me as the midwife lowered her head and descended the stairs toward me, clearly wise to the ways of bickering husbands and wives.

Luca gave a small bow to the midwife, then to me. "Signora Soranzo, if you and the midwife could just make your way to the door, I'll be but a moment. My man is fetching my cloak."

"A thousand thanks, Lord Cicogna. Signora Cicogna." I dipped my head toward them both, not daring to look Elena in the face but desperately wishing to catch Luca's eye. He astutely avoided it as he took his wife's elbow.

"You called her by her Christian name," she hissed. "*Justina.*"

He murmured something inaudible as the midwife and I sloshed toward the front doors. She asked me some details about Rosa's condition, and as I finished describing it Luca joined us wearing his cloak.

"Shall we?" He opened the door and another surge of water cascaded inside. He shook his head. "I hope the damage will not be too severe. The perils of living right along the lagoon. Here, let me take that." He gestured to the midwife's bag, hoisting it on his shoulder, and I realized it must hold the tools of her trade.

He had me go first, creeping back along the palazzo walls, the midwife right behind me, and he closely bringing up the rear, his long arm protectively stretched out beside us both. I gripped his hand in mine, grateful for his firm touch. I was truly frightened now, the water nearly up to my waist, and even higher on the tiny midwife. It was rising much faster than I had anticipated. Luca had to nearly shout over the rush of water and continuously clanging bells. "I hope you will excuse me both, for the closeness. I do not want to risk either of you being swept away." It seemed a legitimate concern.

We made our way to the street that led inland toward the convent, our progress slow but steady, the water lowering somewhat until finally we were at the convent door. I was still holding Luca's hand and reluctantly let it go after he gave mine a final squeeze.

The midwife looked wide-eyed at the convent walls and church but remained silent as Luca returned her bag and bid her farewell.

Then he turned to me. Every parting was pure agony, but we had no choice. So I simply thanked him and hoped my eyes signalled to him all the words I could not voice. "I do not know how I will repay you yet another kindness."

In his eyes, I read his own unvoiced thoughts. "I pray your sister and the babe are all right."

I nodded and opened the door, and together with the midwife I crossed the threshold, more water pouring inside. I hoped we were not too late.

The parlour was in chaos, the rugs removed to save them, the furniture hoisted on racks to try to keep it dry, servants running around with towels and rags. None of them stopped to speak to us, or even seemed to notice us, and we made it to the infirmary sopping wet but unmolested.

There, we found Livia at Rosa's side and Teresa busy at work. She looked up. "Justina! You found a midwife?"

I had never even asked the midwife her name, and I turned to her expectantly.

"If you please," the woman said in her strange cadence. "I am a wise woman, what you call a midwife, new to the city. My name is Esther di Bassano."

I gaped at her name. Now I understood her accent. I had brought a Jewish woman into San Zaccaria.

Chapter 43

Teresa looked at me questioningly, and I shrugged, my eyes only on my sister. She seemed as limp as a rag, clearly spent from the unrelenting pains. It was well known that Jews fleeing the war on the mainland were settling in Venice, and they would have as much need for midwives as anyone else.

Teresa made a sign of the cross. "Clearly it is God's will. Both of you change out of those wet clothes first, then we will talk." She handed the midwife a dry nightdress she kept for patients and me the dressing gown I had been wearing before and allowed us to swiftly change behind screens before hanging up our drenched garments by the big brazier, thankfully not yet flooded with lagoon water.

Then she addressed the midwife. "How many babies have you delivered?"

"A few hundred? I've lost track." Esther had removed her scarf as well, her dark hair pinned up, and was already prodding Rosa's belly.

Teresa glanced at me with a raised brow, and I nodded. An experienced midwife, even if of the Jewish variety, was truly a godsend. Livia crossed herself.

Esther had one hand on Rosa's belly and the other between her legs. "This baby is stuck, and the mother is exhausted." Rosa in fact seemed to be barely conscious, every contraction racking her body as if it had a mind of its own. Esther frowned. "We have no time to lose."

She rummaged through her basket and brought out a small pot that smelled of herbs and animal grease. She rubbed this concoction liberally on Rosa's belly as we all watched, wide-eyed. "For the pain. If you could sit by the mother's head to assist her?"

Livia and I, spurred to action, took seats on either side of Rosa and resumed saying the rosary. Esther briefly looked at this spectacle with interest, then began manipulating Rosa's belly, clearly trying to shift the baby's position in the womb, all the while muttering in a language I had never heard. Rosa whimpered and squeezed our hands in a death grip.

Livia's eyes filled with tears. "How proud your mother will be of you." Rosa smiled weakly at this pronouncement before the pain again consumed her.

These ministrations went on for some time as we prayed, our feet cold and wet, although the water had finally seemed to stop rising. I was shivering uncontrollably, and Teresa threw a dry blanket over my shoulders. I thought I might fall over from exhaustion and could not imagine ever giving birth myself, for the child of Luca or any man. And if I were this tired, I could only imagine how Rosa must feel. Esther, however, was unflagging in her energy, splashing around as if she had spent her whole life delivering babies during *acque alte*.

Finally, soon after evening fell and Teresa lit more candles, Esther announced, "It is time." She instructed us all as to how we could hold Rosa's torso and knees to get her in the correct position, then gave Rosa smelling salts to rouse her.

Terrified at the thought of losing my sister, I lost track of how many times Rosa pushed, but Esther kept up an encouraging commentary. "The hair is black. Ah, the hands were holding the head, which explains a lot." Teresa was beside her, assisting, and I saw the old nun glance up at me with an inexplicable expression on her face that speared further fear into my heart. Was the baby dead? Deformed?

"It's a girl." A ribbon of thrill ran through me. Esther cut the cord before Teresa whisked the baby away to clean her up, and I realized I did not hear the baby's telltale lusty cry. That was not good. I knew that from Mama.

But Esther clearly had no time to worry about that. "Now it's time to save the mama." She did not stop moving, massaging Rosa's belly to help expel the afterbirth, blood soaking through copious amounts of linens. So much blood, so fast. Livia kept praying, unrelenting, as if by sheer force of will she might keep her niece alive, clearly unable to contemplate the thought of losing another so dear to her.

But I just stared at my nearly unconscious sister, her face so white. She looked impossibly young. I was going to lose her, my dear Rosa, my sweet girl.

How would I ever tell our mother?

How could I go on living myself?

Just then, Teresa splashed over to me with the swaddled newborn. "I'm so very sorry," she said, gently transferring the bundle to me. "She's gone." She made a small sign of the cross over the infant's covered face. "I cleaned and baptized her. She is with God now. It was His will." She glanced over at Rosa, her expression still inscrutable.

I took my niece into my arms, cradling her close. As I rocked her, I kept looking from the covered baby to my sister. Esther had not yet given up on Rosa, as resolute as when she had first entered the infirmary, and that provided a glimmer of hope.

I removed the handkerchief that Teresa had placed over the baby's face to look at the tiny girl, too small. She had not stood a chance, born much too early.

I could not process what I was seeing.

She was beautiful, no doubt, in the way that all freshly born babes are. Her hair was black and fine. So different from the very fair Rosa and Zago.

And she was dark-skinned. Not like anyone in our family, or any Zane. Not like a Venetian. Nor even like Madelena, of Byzantine blood.

Her father must have been black.

Teodor.

I studied the infant, then my eyes flickered over to Rosa again, pale as the clean linens before her unrelenting blood had drenched them, then back down at the baby, eyes closed as if asleep, two long fringes of black lashes lying across her cheeks. I shivered anew as I thought back to a beautiful dry spring day, the trees newly tipped with green.

Teodor, our gondolier, the father.

When had it happened?

Before Zago had exerted his marital authority upon Rosa, before the wedding? Had she slipped out in the night to meet Teodor, to have one taste of gentle and mutual affection? It had to have been then. Teodor, handsome and mysterious, closer to her in age, who clearly desired her.

I knew her so well, and yet I had missed this. How could I have been so blind?

Rosa had played with fire and could very well burn for it. A patrician woman not only consorting with a commoner but betraying her lawful noble husband.

And that husband's mother and sister within the very same edifice as we were.

I was at a loss for what to do. I just stood there ankle-deep in the intruding lagoon, watching the diluvial scene of blood and birth, wishing the metallic-scented infirmary were the true ark and would be tightly shut up for another forty days, until I could make sense of it all. I prayed to the patron saint of children, San Nicolò, some of whose bones were relics here in Venice, that Rosa would live and that the baby's paternity would stay hidden forever. I silently thanked Luca for helping Rosa write her will, for bringing Esther here, for all he'd done for me and my family.

Please God, do not let Rosa die . . . Please answer my prayers . . .

Finally, finally, Esther straightened up and wiped her brow. Rosa's eyes were still closed, and she was as unmoving as her daughter. I was frozen by the thought that Esther had stopped working because there was nothing left to try.

But she said something in that unknown language—a prayer?—and breathed a sigh of relief before turning to Livia, clutching her rosary as she spun through the decades. "She will live."

Livia stood up, joy in her eyes, and hugged Esther, who smiled tiredly.

Teresa inspected Rosa with interest, then approached Esther. "Signora Bassano, you saved this girl's life. I could not have done that. Thank you."

Esther dipped her head. "It was one of the more difficult births I have attended. I am not sure she will be able to have children again. And I was too late to save the baby. But the mother will live." She smoothed the sweaty blond hair on top of Rosa's head. "A child herself."

I nearly fell on my knees in watery gratitude before the wise woman, joyous I would not lose my sister and my mother would not lose another child.

But as I held the little one, a daughter, granddaughter, and niece, lost, not just for the Soranzo family but also the Zanes, I could only gape at Rosa. An adulteress with a dead baby, a fornicator with a commoner. If she were unable to conceive again, then she would be incapable of giving Zago an heir, the only feature about her the Zanes seemed to find worthy.

At that moment, I alone realized the life Rosa would be returning to could possibly be worse than death.

"Justina." Rosa's voice sounded rusty and hoarse. "I'm alive." She had finally roused as I agonized over her predicament.

Livia, Teresa, and Esther gave me space and started putting the room to rights as I came over and took one limp hand. "Yes, my dear Sister, and thank God for that."

"The baby?" Her eyes indicated the bundle I held. "I don't hear him. Is he sleeping? Is it a boy?"

I shook my head, willing back the tears.

"It is not a boy?"

"No, it is not a boy, and I'm so sorry to tell you, Rosa, but your girl died during the delivery. You were right—she was born too soon."

Rosa remained dry-eyed, as if she did not believe me, and she feebly gestured at the bundle in my arms. "Let me see her."

"Are you sure? You are still weak." If Rosa did not learn the truth, would I be able to limit the secret to the women in this room?

"I am her mother, Justina. My breasts are already filling with milk. I can feel it." She sounded steelier than I'd ever heard her, although she struggled to sit up. I propped a few pillows behind her back and head, and then handed over the swaddled infant.

She took the babe into her arms, her expression as beatific as the Madonna. When she removed the handkerchief covering the baby's face, her eyes widened.

She looked, unmoving, for a very long while until she finally spoke, her voice still raspy. "She's beautiful."

"Yes, very."

"She looks like a doll."

I cleared my throat. "Is that all she looks like?"

Rosa did not move, her eyes still drinking in the sight of her dead daughter. "I told you I did not want to marry Zago." With her fingers she traced the lines of nose, cheeks, chin. "I wanted to know what love felt like." Then she ran her fingertip over the delicate lips. "If not love, then passion."

I had no reply to that. I had the same desire. Love, passion—whatever it was, I wanted it too.

"It was my only chance, Justina. So I took it. I never expected . . . this."

"Do you still think about him?"

"I try not to. Sometimes I allow myself the memory, like removing the precious relic of a saint from its gilded case on a feast day."

I knew something of what she meant but had to focus on practical matters. "We need to figure out what to do. Signora Zane and Zanetta are awaiting news of you and will want to see their new relation."

She nodded, but I could not discern if she'd registered what I'd said. "If it was a girl, Zago wanted her named after his mother."

"Of course, that is to be expected."

She kissed the babe's sweet forehead. "But in my heart, my baby girl will always be Teodora."

I could only nod.

"I want Teodor to see his child."

"Rosa, I do not know how we can arrange that." The *acqua alta* had started to subside, but movement would still be very difficult. I could understand her impulse though. The first thing Mama always wanted to do was show Papa his babies. I would feel the same.

Rosa's voice was barely audible. "Find a way, Justina, please. And I want to stay here at the convent. That is what I wanted from the beginning. If I cannot have love or even just peace, at least I can have my sister and aunt. I will not go back to the Zane palazzo."

Defying the Zane family? "I don't know, Rosa."

"You'll think of something; you always do." Rosa's lids drooped, and her voice was barely a whisper. She was exhausted and had much healing to do. I left my baby sister holding her own baby as she drifted to sleep.

"There is a problem, yes?" It was Esther. She briefly checked Rosa and seemed satisfied. "The father is not the father. Am I understanding this correctly?"

I shook my head. "She had to marry him. You know how it is. And his mother and sister will be here soon to see the baby. They are in this very convent right now."

"Well, the baby is gone and sadly nothing can be done about that." She looked over at Rosa, her blond lashes light upon her pale cheeks. "I have been a midwife now for ten years and have seen much. We women have much in common, regardless of our faiths." She took a deep breath. "We don't need to show the baby's face."

"I'm sure they'll want to see it."

"Yes, naturally, but we can tell them the baby was deformed by the delivery, that I had to do that to save the mother's life. That's not strictly true in this case, but I have done it before. It is necessary sometimes, when the fetus is known to be dead, and the mother's life is at imminent risk."

I considered this proposition. We would still bury the baby, of course, but we could do it here, at the convent, and soon. That was a comforting prospect. And praise God the baby was not a boy whom Zago would insist upon burying with the Zanes. A girl, so much more dispensable and undesirable to a patrician father, could be more easily protected by us nuns. My spirits perked up at this solution, then lowered again. "They will blame you, Signora Bassano. A woman of the Jewish faith, a foreigner to Venice, brought into a holy convent, who desecrates a baby during delivery. The Zane family might accuse you of blood libel."

Esther's eyes widened at this, then she sighed and started resolutely packing her bag. "It is our fate as Jews to be misunderstood wherever we go. Venice certainly won't let my people stay if they suspect blood libel."

"We cannot put you in danger." I would have to think of another way.

Teresa came over. "I do not approve of Rosa's sin, but Christ died for our sins and pleads with us to be merciful."

Esther put a final tool in her bag. "Our prophet Ezekiel would agree."

Theresa nodded resolutely. "We will say I delivered the baby, that Esther arrived too late to help the child but that she saved Rosa. No one will question me." She glanced at me and Livia. "Well, I always did find our sister

Zanetta quite peevish, and Heaven help this convent if Angela Riva had become the abbess."

Livia rolled her eyes as I nodded in agreement. Esther thanked her and went to change back into her damp dress.

That was settled then, but how to summon Teodor?

Just as I was contemplating another unsanctioned foray outside the convent walls, Esther announced she was leaving.

"By yourself?" Livia asked. "Shall we send a servant to escort you?"

Esther shook her head. "Best to not draw attention that I was here. Maybe no one will even know if I go now, and that would be best. Besides, the water has started to fall, and midwives are allowed out after curfew. Babies come when they want. Even the doge knows this." She gave a rueful smile.

A nascent plan formulated in my head. "Do you know your way home?"

Esther gave a decisive nod. "From my work, I have gotten to know this maze of a city fairly well already, and I have always been good at finding my way. A necessity of the trade, one might say. My husband and I are staying in Dosoduro with his parents and brother's family. I am sure he is frantic with worry. He was not expecting me to stay out all night, and we have never experienced an *acqua alta* before, being from the mainland."

"Of course." My plan took shape. "Where exactly in Dosoduro?"

As she described the location of her rented house, I realized how close it was to the Soranzo palazzo, and she readily enough agreed to pass a message to Teodor. Most likely he was not even sleeping, given the high waters and worries about the gondola.

"God's will," Teresa said not for the first time, and Livia made yet another sign of the cross.

"I'm ready." Esther threaded her bag on her arm and arranged the red scarf over her head. "Let the mama sleep as long as she wants. When she wakes, give her beef broth, then red meat for a few days. After that, she can eat whatever appeals to her. Signora Teresa, you will need to stop the milk. I'm leaving some herbs that should help. She should stay here in the infirmary until you deem her ready to go. It will be a while."

Or longer, if I could do anything to fulfill Rosa's wishes.

"Of course." Teresa stood uncertainly, her hands steepled before her. She seemed compelled to bless Esther but also to realize this would be inappropriate. "Thank you, Signora Bassano. You are very good at what you do. I learned much today."

"Yes," Livia added, "thank you for saving my niece. We will be forever grateful." She pulled out a small purse and the ducats within to pay Esther, ducats we had not needed to repay Luca, God bless his generosity. "The less the Zanes interact with you, the better."

We all nodded sagely as Esther counted the coins. "This is double what I expected."

Livia smiled sadly. "For your troubles."

Esther curtsied. "Thank you, Signora. My family will put this to good use."

I followed her to the door with a candle, compelled to talk more privately. For an idea had started forming in my mind, so tempting I could barely allow myself to contemplate it. "I will show you the way out." She nodded her assent, and together we sloshed through the darkened corridor toward the parlour as quietly as we could. The curfew bells had long ago rung, and the convent was thankfully asleep.

"Signora Bassano, let me echo what my aunt said. Thank you for saving my sister. I'm not sure what I would do without her." My voice quavered at this admission. The thought of losing Rosa was too much too bear.

She patted my arm with her free hand. "I understand. I am very close with my sister too."

"Thank you too, for delivering this urgent message to the gondolier. We would not be able to manage it otherwise."

She sighed. "It is an exceedingly difficult situation. I must admit that I usually side with the mother. A midwife often knows too much."

I summoned my courage. When else would I be able to ask such a question? "Signora Bassano, may I ask of your knowledge on a personal matter?"

We entered the empty parlour, the furniture still raised and in disarray. The water remained a few inches deep here, but the candlelight cast a warm glow around the damp room. She turned to face me, looking expectant.

My eyes were downcast in embarrassment. "How does one prevent becoming with child?"

Her expression turned curious. "You are a nun, are you not?"

I nodded, flushing at her inquiry.

"And nuns, if I understand correctly, never marry. They are married to your God. And chaste for life."

Again, I nodded sheepishly.

Her voice softened. "But that does not mean they stop loving, yes?"

A tear sprang unbidden to my eye. "Yes."

She appraised me with those intense blue yes. "It is also a sin in our faith to fully know someone outside marriage, but I will not lie by saying it doesn't happen. As I mentioned, we midwives know too much." She glanced around to ensure we were alone, then whispered, "We Jews have ways to assure conceiving a child, and thus ways to prevent it. The most important is to never have congress after the eleventh day after your first day of bleeding and never before the twentieth day."

I thanked her as I digested this information, as valuable as gold from the New World.

Esther seemed about to add more, but she kept her counsel and instead pulled her cloak more snugly around her.

"A midwife knows too much . . ." I said softly as I hugged her. She had been in our lives for just a few hours but could not have done more.

She patted my back. "But if she is truly a wise woman, she knows when to keep her mouth shut. And now I should take my leave."

Chapter 44

As the early *matins* bells rang, Teresa gently retrieved the infant from Rosa's limp arms and wrapped her even more securely, so it would be impossible to view any part of the body or face without completely unwrapping her. Then, exhausted, we all slept until just after the *prime* bell at sunrise, when a knock came at the door: Madelena, who declared she was feeling much better and ready to help. We asked her to wait at the water entrance for Teodor, to keep his presence a secret. We then slept for a little longer before Signora Zane and Zanetta arrived, fully dressed, to greet their new relation, even though we had not summoned them.

Livia and I once again groggily roused ourselves as Teresa opened the door, walking gingerly through what were just puddles now. The *acqua alta* had fully receded, although the lagoon and canals were likely still high. But the imminent threat was past.

"Where is my grandson?" Signora Zane breezed in with Zanetta, her shadow in fair appearance.

Teresa told her the baby was a girl, then related our story, mostly true. Despite my antipathy toward the pair, I had to admit they both looked overcome. "It was a very difficult delivery. Sadly the baby's body had to be defiled to save your daughter-in-law. The baby was already gone. I am so sorry." Teresa spoke with both compassion and authority. She did not add that said daughter-in-law, still asleep, might have been rendered barren from the ordeal.

"Was she baptized?" Zanetta asked, her expression mournful.

Teresa nodded. "I did it myself."

"I still should like to see my grandchild." A few tears trickled down Signora Zane's cheeks.

Teresa went to fetch the bundle and placed it in Signora Zane's arms. The woman held it close to her bosom, stroking the linen and whispering something to it. A blessing? It was to have been her granddaughter—of course she would grieve her.

Zanetta crowded next to her mother and enveloped both females in her arms. It was a surprisingly tender scene, and I thanked God that He saw fit to give me compassion for the Zanes, to remind me to love my enemies. Even Zago would feel distress at the loss, however common such tragedies might be.

I looked at Rosa, who was now awake and watching the trio with alarm. I caught her eye, then placed my index finger to my lips, and she blinked acknowledgement.

Teresa noticed Rosa was awake too and came over to smooth her furrowed brow as she addressed the Zanes. "Your daughter-in-law will need to stay in the infirmary until she is well enough to travel. It may be a few weeks. As I said, the delivery was exceedingly difficult."

Signora Zane broke out of the circle, still embracing the bundle. "Then we will take the baby to be buried with the Zanes."

"No!" Rosa nearly shouted this as she looked around wildly for help. Her exclamation was for the baby, but also, I knew, because of Teodor. Also for herself, as the mother.

Livia came over to strengthen the human bulwark with which we encircled my sister. "There, there, Niece. No one will take your baby from you before you are ready." She spoke to Signora Zane with sympathy. "I'm sure you can remember what was like when you had your children. My own sister has described the intense attachment. A mother does not want to let them out of her sight for a moment. Pray let Rosa say her goodbyes in her own time."

Noticing Rosa's distress, Signora Zane agreed to this, and her voice softened slightly. "All right. I do know how you feel, Rosa. I too lost a few babies many years ago. It is indeed difficult." She took a deep breath as if perhaps reburying her memories. "Now that the *acqua alta* has subsided, I will return to my palazzo. I know Zago will want to come later and see both you and the child. We'll take the baby then."

Rosa's eyes widened at this pronouncement, and Livia and I each placed a hand on one of her shoulders.

Zanetta nodded at us, her expression unreadable, then turned to her mother. "Mama, let us break our fast in the refectory and ready you before the gondolier returns."

Signora Zane seemed to notice me only for the first time. She handed me the child. "I am sorry for your loss, Signora Justina."

"And I yours. It is a blow to both the Zane and Soranzo families."

She bobbed her head. "Indeed. But Rosa is still young. There will be more children." She did not say this harshly, more with resignation. Then she left, Zanetta shadowing her exit much as she had her entrance.

Teresa closed the door firmly behind them and exhaled. "Now what?"

Rosa began sobbing, the first time she'd done so since the delivery, and Livia held her. "There, there, child, let it out. We will not allow any harm to come to you."

"They want me to have . . . more children . . . I don't want to go back . . . I can't . . . Teodora . . ." Rosa hiccupped her way through these disparate thoughts, with every right to enumerate her miseries.

"It's all right, dear." Livia continued to soothe her, more like herself than I had seen in many months, and for that I was relieved. "You can stay here. I will talk to Mother Marina. San Zaccaria will be your sanctuary for as long as you need."

Teresa chimed in. "Your aunt is right. You must calm yourself. You must allow yourself to recover and not become agitated."

I wrung my hands. When would Teodor arrive?

So many secrets, that now other people knew. Could I truly keep completely hidden what I was hoping—against hope—I might be able to do?

Another knock on the door, and we all looked at each other. Signora Zane back already?

Teresa slowly trod over to the door and opened it with great hesitation. Madelena was there. And behind her stood Teodor, twisting his cap.

He glanced around as if God might smite him on the spot for penetrating the inside of a convent, let alone one housing all patrician nuns.

Teresa ushered him inside. "Thank you, Madelena. Please break your fast and ask the kitchen for some beef broth for Rosa."

Madelena curtsied and left as Teresa gathered the bloody sheets. "I'll just take these to the laundry." And she slipped out with a full basket.

Livia cleared her throat, then kissed Rosa's forehead. "I will take my leave as well and freshen up. Rosa, I promise I'll return soon. Justina, you stay here." It was not a suggestion as much as a command. "And bolt the door behind me."

I did just that, then laid the bundle beside Rosa and began unwrapping it.

Teodor looked at me, then at Rosa trying to control her breathing, then me again, completely unsure of what to do.

Finally, Teodora emerged from the white linens, a rose carved out of ebony from the far east. Her limbs were rigid now, her legs curled up to her tummy, her arms bent, her hands next to her ears, as she had been in the womb.

Teodor stepped closer, staring at her with wonder. "She is beautiful." He took a long finger and ever so gently touched her cheek.

"She is," Rosa whispered. "She is our daughter."

Teodor shook his head in disbelief. "Never did I think so." He began stroking the baby's arms and legs. His only chance to make her real.

I edged away, to give them a measure of privacy, this unlikely and doomed family. But try as I might, I could not help but eavesdrop upon their conversation.

"I am sorry," Teodor ventured.

"It's always been you, Teodor."

"You are so very young, Signorina Rosa." His fingers froze. "I mean, Signora. You will change your mind about me someday. What we did was wrong. I should have known better. I realize that now. The trouble you could get into. My livelihood . . ." He trailed off.

"I'm sorry about that part." And she not only looked but sounded like a child, not much older than the baby, although I imagined she herself felt ancient. "But we will not let you be punished. No one will know. The baby's looks will remain a secret."

"But how? Won't Lord Zane want to see his child?" He tucked the linens snug around the baby's body as if she might catch a chill. "Just like I did?"

He was right. I knew he was right, in my bones. And Zago would come this afternoon. I wasn't sure how long it would take us to dig a grave in the convent cemetery. The labourers who worked at the convent would be very busy cleaning up after the *acqua alta*, and they were down a man, with Jacomo having fled alongside Viena, although they might not yet know that. Besides, they would be more people to tell, more chances for the secret to escape.

"We need to bury her right now." I approached the bed. "Teodor, I will need your help."

He peered up, alert. "Where, Signora Justina?"

"Right here at the convent. We'll say Rosa could not bear to have the baby away from her. The Zanes will be angry, but they would never desecrate a grave. To protect both you and Rosa, let alone Teodora, we must bury her right now."

His eyes misted over. "Teodora?"

"Yes," Rosa whispered. "Not officially of course. But that is how I will remember her."

His voice was no louder. "Me too."

I again tightly swaddled Teodora in what was to be both her receiving blanket and shroud, covering her cherubic face, then handed her to Teodor, who brought her to his chest, and I had a flash of what Luca would look like holding his firstborn. One who would never be mine. I sighed. "I'll need to find a shovel. We must be discreet."

"I will follow your lead." He could not tear his gaze from his daughter.

I stood uncertainly aside to allow them to say goodbye.

"Take good care of her, Teodor." Rosa sniffled. Teodor came over and lowered the baby to her level so she could kiss the linens.

"I will, Signora."

"Call me Rosa. Please." She caressed the bundle one last time, then closed her eyes and turned her head away.

"Goodbye, Rosa." They would see each other from time to time, but only in passing, with formality, and perhaps this moment would seem like a dream.

"Goodbye, Teodor. Take good care of yourself too." Her voice was barely audible.

He looked down at her. "And you as well." He took a step back, hesitated, then returned to Rosa, leaned over, and brushed her lips with his.

Then with an uncertain nod to me, he put his cap on, cradled the baby in his arms, and unbolted the infirmary door as Rosa rotated onto her side, her shoulders shuddering. I put my hand upon her elbow and told her I'd be back as soon as I could. She did not respond as I followed Teodor and their daughter out of the ark of the infirmary, like Noah in his drunken, naked misery, looking in vain for the rainbow.

Chapter 45

Stagnant puddles lined the hallways as our trinity wended our way toward the cemetery beside the church. The convent was, as I had suspected, still mostly slumbering. A few noises here and there, but we didn't see anyone. The labourers would likely start to clean the church first, if they had even yet arrived from their homes.

Dark clouds still covered the sky, but dawn light was seeping into the sky. The small enclosure that held Elisabetta and my other departed sisters was thick with mud. The workers would have much work to do to set things right throughout the convent and its grounds.

The flood had forced open the door to the small shed that held an array of tools, which lay scattered nearby. Teodor handed me the baby and grasped a shovel, looking at me expectantly. My feet were already muddy and my dressing robe odoriferous, so I trudged through the sludge to indicate the spot next to Elisabetta's final resting spot, careful not to slip.

Teodor began to dig, silently, grimly. I held the baby and stood watch over the sepulchral setting. Grey clouds scudded along in the strengthening breeze, and the air was fresh with the scent of salt. My mind drifted again to the creation of this child in my arms, my niece.

I'd had a sense of something brewing between Rosa and Teodor, and yet I had not pursued it, had not adequately protected my sister. Anger flared in me at the man digging, and just as quickly tapered off. I could not be bitter with the gondolier. The attraction between them had been mutual, and they were both young and, I had to admit, foolish. And yet, as much as my training and station in life cried out in protest at their actions and the subsequent result, I did not begrudge them their fleeting moment of happiness.

Just as with Viena, I might even be jealous at their decisive action.

Either I mused for a long time or Teodor made short work of his task, whether in shrift for his sins or maybe simple fear of being caught. Before long the gondolier reported that the gravesite was ready, a tiny, watery, rectangular hole about the depth of his leg, a pile of mud beside it. Mud caked the man's costume, and I hoped he had another clean one ready at the palazzo, for his own sake.

Just then, the door to the cemetery scraped open. I looked up in alarm at the sound. There was nowhere to hide and nothing to explain Teodor's presence. I pleaded a quick prayer; I would just have to make things up as I went along.

When Livia entered, I breathed a sigh of relief that it was not Zanetta or Santina. The hem of Livia's dress was soon soiled, but she didn't seem to care. "Rosa told me where you were. She didn't want you to be alone and asked me to say a blessing, to give my great-niece a proper departure with as many relatives as feasible. It's not as if we can have a proper funeral mass anyway, with the interdict."

Both Teodor and I nodded. It felt odd to know the family gondolier was my niece's relation. I transferred the child to him, and Livia took that moment to rest her hand on Elisabetta's headstone, a bit crooked now from the flood.

Teodor cradled his daughter one last time, tears running freely down his face. Eventually, he kissed the blanket, now streaked with the mud from his hands, knelt, and very tenderly placed his daughter at the bottom of her final resting place, as Livia came to my side and threaded her arm through mine.

Teodor straightened up, slipping slightly, picked up his tool, and threw the first shovelful of mud onto his shrouded daughter. Then another, and another, until a tidy mound curved atop her, and he patted it smooth with the back of the shovel. Finally, he staked the tool in the ground and came to stand beside us.

Livia made a sign of the cross, which Teodor and I echoed, before saying a few prayers. A ghostly wind blew, parting the clouds, and a ray of sunshine fell across the grave, as if a benediction from our heavenly husband. Not a rainbow but still a sign. *Thank You for Your mercy . . .*

"It is done then." Teodor glanced around the courtyard, clearly nervous. He was quite tall and graceful in stature and exceedingly handsome, with compassionate eyes and smooth dark skin. So opposite Zago in every respect, including the one that mattered most: noble blood. "Signora Justina, I must take my leave. I need to wash up and change. I'm sure your father will be wanting me to take him to the doge's palazzo as soon as possible." Yes, he was a good man, an honest man, but just a gondolier, and no amount of patrician love would change his station in Venice.

"Of course. The end-of-curfew bell will ring soon." I did not know what else to say.

He dipped his head, then, without another word, he was gone, with Livia and I staring after him, the breeze swirling the mud-heavy skirts around our ankles.

"Dirty already." I pointed at the brown streaks on the bottom of her black gown. I felt drained, my shoulders slumped.

She shrugged. "No matter. I'm glad I was here to bear witness. And that Elisabetta will take care of Rosa's baby."

"Me too. And now we must think how to explain this hasty burial to the Zanes."

She sighed as we re-entered the convent. We took care to remove our slippers and hitch our skirts to not leave a trail of mud in our wake, and walked barefoot through the corridors, holding the backs of our slippers with the tips of our fingers. The wet floor was cold on my naked soles, and I felt as if I were sleepwalking. I was shivering by the time we arrived back at the infirmary.

Rosa had thankfully fallen asleep again, well blanketed, and Teresa was there with fresh linens, food, and news.

"Have you heard? Our sister Viena has run away with Jacomo the carpenter." She shook her head and tsked. "And to think she told me she feared a contagious disease. I just hope this disease isn't catching. Lice breeds lice, and sin breeds sin."

Chapter 46

Livia gaped at her, and I played ignorant. In truth, I was so tired and hungry I could barely think, although I did wonder what Teresa would say if she knew about my island excursion with Luca or Livia's affair with Elisabetta. I respected and liked the woman, but she was of a different generation and more set in her ways.

She was also kindly and attentive. At her insistence, I wolfed down a pastry. I hadn't eaten since the late breakfast I'd had the morning before with Rosa.

Teresa folded the clean linens and stacked them neatly in a cupboard. "I don't want to gossip, but it's all over the convent now. Angela Riva, Zanetta, and Santina saw to that." She shook her head. "This is the biggest scandal to hit San Zaccaria in several decades. And on the heels of Celestia! If word gets out, only the Lord Himself knows what our punishment will be, let alone Viena's when she is discovered. We of course know Jacomo's punishment."

Avoiding my eyes, perhaps with my picnic in mind, Livia dropped into the chair beside Rosa and tucked the blanket over her more securely. "With the present political climate, the penalties could be very steep. The government will be looking to make an example after Celestia. We can't have this revelation now."

I took a sip of wine. "But what if they've left Venice and can't be found?" The thought of Viena's unknown punishment was overwhelming. Would they allow her to return to the convent, or impose something much more dire? As I devoured another pastry, I realized I was rooting for them.

"Well, I guess they would be relatively safe as they have effectively banished themselves, but they could never come back." Livia eyed me sharply. "How do you know they've left Venice entirely? There's a war on. Travel is dangerous. And we've just endured an *acqua alta*."

Trying to slow down my chewing, I worked to achieve a calm expression. "I'm just speculating."

Livia and Teresa shared a look. "Niece, clearly you know something. We won't tell, unless it's information that can help Mother Marina manage this crisis. Right, Teresa?" Teresa nodded, her eyes round.

I tapped the ground with my cold bare foot, my slippers still unwearable.

"Justina." Livia sounded for a moment just like my mother, with me the petulant child. Then her voice softened. "You know I liked Viena very much. She was becoming part of our group. We must protect her if we can."

I groaned, too tired and hungry to resist. "All right. Yes, she told me she was leaving with Jacomo two nights ago, just hours before she left. And that she was big with Jacomo's child."

It was Teresa's turn to groan, but Livia just nodded sagaciously. "I suspected as much."

"They wanted to be together and live as man and wife. She never wanted to become a nun."

"Young people today." Teresa shook her head and began to sort through some of her medical instruments. "I wonder how they left Venice and where they were going. I cannot even imagine how they will manage."

I could not either. To leave Venice felt as foreign as flying to the stars. "That I don't know, but I pray God grants them safe passage."

Livia crossed herself. "Viena is a soft patrician girl who doesn't know how to keep house or mind a child. She will have a hard life with a carpenter."

"She loves him," I whispered. "And he her."

Livia brushed away the tears that sprang to her eyes. "I can understand that, truly. But nothing in her upbringing has prepared her for what's to come. Sometimes life is too complicated for love. I don't always agree with the strictures Venice places on us, but now that I am older, I can see the reasons for many of them. I just hope she is strong enough to live this new spartan life she has chosen."

"And that her midwife will be as good as Signora Bassano." Teresa touched Rosa's forehead. She did not seem worried about the temperature as her hand fell away.

"I will pray for that too." I took a clean blanket and wrapped it around me, trying to quell my shivering. I had to admit they were right, and I wondered how fully Viena and Jacomo had thought out the possible consequences. But then again, had Rosa?

Was *I* worried enough about such consequences? The direction my thoughts had lately turned seemed suddenly quite reckless.

At Teresa's insistence, I left with a third pastry to return to my room to rest and freshen up. I'd been mostly awake since yesterday morning with more physical activity than I'd ever had, and I was stumbling from exhaustion. In my room, I quickly stripped and washed. I had no idea where Dolce was; presumably Madelena had taken him, but I was too tired to worry. I threw on fresh nightclothes and crawled under the blankets.

My sleep was heavy and dreamless, but I woke to pounding on the door. Bleary-eyed, I opened it to find a very disturbed Madelena.

"Signora Justina, you must come quickly. Lord Zane is here and wants to see Rosa and the baby right now. I told him to wait, but he is very angry and pacing around the parlour."

"Help me dress, Madelena. My black dress, for mourning." I forced myself to clear the cobwebs in my head as I threw a black lace shawl over my hastily styled hair and then shot out the door. "Find Livia, to help me."

I glanced at Viena's room as I headed down the corridor. Her door was open and Angela Riva and Santina were sorting through her remaining belongings. Looking for clues to her whereabouts, no doubt, if not further damning evidence, and to scavenge for themselves. Normally when a nun died, she left a will specifying her intentions, but Viena hadn't died and this was not the normal situation.

Zago did not seem pleased when he saw me enter the parlour as the *vespers* bell struck, and Zanetta, beside him, had her usual vinegary expression, their matching frowns making them look like dour near twins.

"Will Signora Zane join us as well?" I asked after swallowing my pride and greeting my brother-in-law.

"She was too fatigued to return." Zago spoke in his usual clipped manner. "Please take me to see your sister. I am here to bring both her and the child home."

I aimed to stall him for as long as possible. "I am so very sorry for your loss."

He looked at me, startled perhaps by my compassion. "And you as well." He gave a rough nod. "My wife, if you please."

"As you may have been told, it was a very difficult birth and Rosa will need time to recover."

"I will be the judge of that."

Poor Rosa. She was too weak and ill to make it to the parlour, let alone to return to the Zane palazzo. Under usual circumstances a man could not enter beyond the parlour, even if his blood sister were a nun. But these were not usual circumstances, and I felt I had no choice.

As I slowly led him and Zanetta to the parlour door, Auntie Livia and Mother Marina herself saved me. Livia blinked at me, but it was Mother Marina who spoke, calmly and with much patrician and spiritual authority.

"Lord Zane, welcome to San Zaccaria. I understand you are here to see your wife."

Zago had a patrician authority of his own and was unused to being denied, although he was clearly attempting to modulate his temper. "As you may imagine, Mother Abbess, I am anxious to bring my wife home after her ordeal."

Mother Marina nodded sympathetically, raising her rosary-clad hands to her breast. "Indeed, it has been a terrible trial. I understand from our infirmarian that your wife still requires much recovery and is unable to even walk yet. And of course, we all mourn the loss of your dearly departed daughter, may she rest in peace." She crossed herself with much deliberation.

"Thank you. Now, if you will just lead the way." Patrician though he was, he was not about to go barging past the abbess into her convent. He knew the rules. Zanetta looked at Mother Marina fiercely, perhaps feeling her own position in the convent engendered some latitude.

Mother Marina was a paragon of peace but also quite firm. "I'm very sorry, Your Lordship, but that is not possible."

"What do you mean? She is my wife, and I have the right to see her at least."

Mother Marina shook her head sadly. "Your wife has sought refuge here. She has asked for shelter at San Zaccaria to preserve her honour and safety. And I as the abbess have granted her such sanctuary for as long as she requires it."

"Pardon me?" Zanetta was indignant. Zago looked stunned. Livia slipped her hand into mine and squeezed.

"This is ridiculous," Zago sputtered as he went to walk around Mother Marina, who strategically blocked the door. He dared not touch an abbess, but his face turned red from suppressed rage. "You will not allow me entrance?"

Mother Marina shook her head again. "I will not. You know very well it is a convent's right to protect laywomen in need. With the hope of reuniting a marriage where feasible." She said this last part very carefully.

Zago flexed his hands into fists, then slowly uncurled them. "Then let me have my child." His voice was still angry but edged now with grief, and I felt a twinge of sympathy for him, despite myself. "I want to bury her with the rest of the Zane family."

Mother Marina glanced sidelong at Livia, who spoke up. "I'm afraid that is not possible either, Your Lordship. Rosa asked us to bury the body here, today. She did not want her daughter to leave the premises, since she intends to stay."

"This is a travesty!" Zanetta exploded.

Mother Marina took over again. "Signora Zanetta, I'm sure you of all people can see the appeal of having the babe interred here. San Zaccaria is a sanctuary for anyone who needs it. We are pleased to serve God in this way, to look out for even His very youngest adherents. The benefit of course is that you, as aunt, can visit the child's grave any time you wish and represent your family."

Zanetta went to say something more, but Zago put a hand to her elbow. "Sister, let us not waste time here. We will immediately consult our lawyer."

Mother Marina smiled tightly. "You are welcome to do that, Lord Zane. Though I don't think I have to remind you that as abbess of San Zaccaria I have complete control over what goes on inside these convent walls."

"Then perhaps I'll visit the Venice patriarch." Zago bowed very stiffly and formally. "Good evening."

He gave Zanetta a perfunctory kiss on the cheek and departed the parlour, all of us watching him, my heart beating wildly.

Zanetta turned to Mother Marina. "How dare you?"

"Are you challenging my rightful authority as abbess of San Zaccaria?" Mother Marina was not tall, but her presence loomed large. "One I have obtained by a valid election of all who live here?"

"A very close election, I might remind you, and its validity in doubt." Zanetta shook her head petulantly. "But you hardly have *complete* control over what goes on inside these convent walls."

Livia squeezed my hand hard as Mother Marina replied, "Is that a threat?"

"I will be sure to let my brother know about our dear sister Viena's hasty departure with the carpenter. He would be all too happy to inform the members of the Forty." She flounced toward the door, pointedly waiting for Mother Marina to let her by. "And Patriarch Contarini too. The Zanes are quite close with his family."

Mother Marina glared at her while moving aside. "Signora Zanetta, you do what you must, and I shall do the same. Before you go, however, I will remind you that you took vows to this convent. It is your home and family now, and you owe it your loyalty. Think twice before you sully your home's reputation, for you will also suffer any punishments handed down."

Zanetta did not reply to this but left the parlour with an exasperated sigh.

Mother Marina sighed and closed her eyes for a long moment. When she opened them again, she had composed herself. I admired her mastery of her passions, realizing this ability was likely the cause of her election as abbess as well as an inspiration to Livia. I was indebted to her for her help with Rosa and her firmness with the Zanes.

"Mother Marina," I said in a small voice as she turned to leave with a heavy step. "Thank you for allowing my sister to stay. To give birth here. To bury her child here. I know you have risked much."

She smiled wearily, then blessed me. "I am only doing God's work. As the Apostle John wrote, *Little children, let us not love in word or talk but in deed and in truth.*"

Livia crossed herself. "Do you think Lord Zane will inform the patriarch?"

Mother Marina gave a rueful shake of her head. "I do not believe so.

I believe his pride will prevent him from admitting that his wife has left him."

As she exited the parlour, saying she would give special dispensation to Rosa's father and brother to briefly see her in the infirmary when they next visited, relief entwined with guilt and grief washed over me. Mother Marina had risked so much for Rosa, Livia, and me. Allowed a Jewish woman into her convent, for surely she knew that now. Stared down a powerful patrician. Turned a blind eye to the forbidden love of Livia and Elisabetta. And I had not told her what I knew of Viena, or of my own summer sojourn. I was too scared to be honest with her and knew I must add the sin of lying to my growing list for confession. I would have to force myself to forgo further transgressions, which likely meant not finishing my manuscript for the Aldine Press. I could not further jeopardize the reputation of San Zaccaria.

Clearly sensing my feeling of defeat, Livia hugged me and suggested we visit Rosa on our way to the refectory to tell her about Zago's aborted visit. My stomach grumbled at this suggestion, as I had long ago digested my three-pastry breakfast.

Before we could leave the parlour, however, a new visitor burst into the room.

"Justina and Auntie! How fortuitous to meet you!" Paolo. "I just met our brother-in-law Zago in the campo. He was indignant and could barely bow to me, and I cannot understand for what reason."

"Are you here to visit Rosa?"

"Rosa? No, why? Is she here? I thought he had been here to see his sister and how she fared with the *acqua alta*."

Of course, my family had no knowledge about Rosa, the birth, the burial. There was much to report. I wondered how my mother would take the news of the death of her first grandchild and her daughter finding sanctuary from her husband in a convent. Let alone my father's reaction. And how was Teodor faring?

However, before I could tell Paolo anything, he went on evenly, "I'm here to see Madelena."

Chapter 47

After absorbing this stunning announcement, Auntie and I told him our own news. Paolo was of course saddened to hear of his niece's demise, but echoed Signora Zane in reminding us that Rosa was not yet fourteen and would have other children. He did seem taken aback when we informed him that Rosa intended to stay at San Zaccaria for the foreseeable future and said he would convince her otherwise. "No wonder for Zago's distemper." I tried to keep from rolling my eyes but knew that Papa would probably arrive on the morrow to do the same, so Rosa might as well sharpen her arguments.

We thus decided that Livia would escort Paolo to briefly visit Rosa in the infirmary. He raised his eyebrows in mischievous delight at being able finally to enter the convent beyond the parlour, although she reminded him she would never leave his side and that Mother Marina had given such permission only to blood relatives due to Rosa's immobility. While they visited, I would find Madelena and bring her back to the parlour to see Paolo. And forewarn her, although I did not say it aloud.

I went up to the servants' quarters, empty at this hour but for Madelena, who greeted me with surprise. I had never come to find her in all the months she'd been living at the convent. She was such a good servant, always anticipating my needs. I would miss her sorely when she left after her baby's birth in a few months, and I felt yet another pang about her destination and the separation she would have to endure from her child. I prayed we would not need Esther di Bassano but likewise felt comforted to know we could call upon her if required. Although perhaps Teresa had learned a few things.

"Is everything all right, Signora Justina?" She was carrying a basket filled with my mud-streaked clothes.

I suddenly did not know how to tell her about Paolo. What did he want with her? I was so caught up in Rosa's predicament that I had not thought to probe him. "How are you feeling, Madelena?"

She smiled, still uncertain. "Well enough, thank you. Did everything go all right between Lord Zane and Signora Rosa?"

I told her about Rosa taking sanctuary at San Zaccaria, Zago demanding to see her, Mother Marina's intervention.

She was wide-eyed. "Your father will not be pleased by any of this."

I shook my head. "Very true, although of course we won't tell him everything. And my mother will be quite distressed. But that is not why I am here."

She took the news of Paolo wanting to see her fairly well, although she did blanch. "I suppose I cannot refuse a lord?"

"You don't want to see him?"

"I know he is your brother and my child's father, but honestly, no. I have made my peace. I have nothing to say to him. I will have this baby and then I will start my new life at La Diamante's. Remember, Signora Justina, that I am a slave. But La Diamante has offered me a way to buy my freedom over time. Perhaps then I will have some choice over my destiny. But never with a nobleman, not in Venice."

"Has she?" I was surprised to hear of La Diamante's offer. The woman was shrewd as well as generous, knowing that in allowing Madelena to free herself, she had also bought her loyalty.

She bobbed her head. "I hope you don't think me out of place, but when she told me that, I was glad your father had sold me. I had not contemplated freedom until then."

Freedom and free will, things Viena had wished for and acted upon. Even Rosa had the impulse, although she was paying dearly for it. I remembered too the Contorta nuns in the lagoon, with their own kind of sovereignty. That was something I wanted as well, although such a desire seemed increasingly foolhardy and further from reach. Was there any chance my manuscript might lead to such freedom for women of my kind? Luca had said it might ignite a firestorm. And while I fretted about the effect it would have on San Zaccaria if I were found out as the author, as well as how Mother Marina might react, I could not suppress a shiver of excitement. Could I dare hope for change in my lifetime? Even in the next few years? It was impossible not to contemplate.

"It is clearly an enticing prospect for you." Of course it was, but not once had I considered Madelena's desires before. She knew me and my family so intimately, and yet we knew nothing about her. Was it so for every one of our class?

"Yes." She sighed as she pinched her cheeks to redden them. "I suppose I must face your brother at some point. Will you stay with me while I speak with him?"

I looked at this lovely woman on the precipice of a new life through fresh eyes. "If you would like, then yes, of course."

"I'm ready then."

Paolo was not pleased at my determined presence by Madelena's side, but he eventually accepted it. I wondered if he construed my behaviour as disloyal to him and our family, although that was not my intention.

"How was Rosa?" I asked since Paolo was uncharacteristically quiet, and Madelena awaited with her head bowed.

"She seemed quite stricken with grief and did not look well, I must admit."

"It was an exceedingly arduous birth." When he did not respond, I felt compelled to add, "An arduous marriage as well."

He raised a brow. "I still contend she is young and will become accustomed to it. Did not our mother? I would say she is content. And our aunt Leonarda. Most of the older married women I know seem satisfied."

"I'm not sure I agree with you about Mama, although I do not intend to disparage our father. She seems more resigned, I would say."

"I am not here to split hairs with you over our parents' marriage and Venice's ancient customs. That was the way of our ancestors, and the way it is now. It may change someday, but not as far as I can foresee."

I shook my head, too depleted to argue. What was the point? He was likely right anyway. "Why are you here then, Brother?" Madelena straightened her back, thrusting her belly out slightly, but did not meet his eyes.

Paolo cleared his throat. "As mentioned, to see Madelena."

"And what do you wish to say to her?"

He cleared his throat. "I want to tell her I am departing on the morrow to join the army on the mainland. There is talk of a potential battle near Ferrara. I am to assist the generals, help with correspondence, that sort of thing—an unofficial governmental aide-de-camp. Papa arranged it all, training for me to join the Great Council, he said." He puffed up his chest slightly.

My heart clamped. Exasperated as Paolo could make me, he was still my dear brother. "I do not like the idea of you being in danger."

He scoffed. "Hardly. The generals direct the action but do not participate in it. I will be well protected." Then he hastily added, "It is an honour to have been placed in such a prestigious position."

I eyed him skeptically, impressed by my father's acumen in giving his son something honourable to do rather than just lazing around planning festas and mummeries. "Then it sounds like congratulations are in order."

He gave a merry little bow, a vestige of his old self. "Thank you, Sister." Then he took a deep breath and turned to Madelena. "I would like Madelena to accompany me."

We both looked at him in shock as I spoke. "But she is big with child."

Paolo shrugged. "There are surgeons in the army, and midwives in Ferrara too, I would wager. It is a unique opportunity to be together, away from the prying eyes of Venice." *And its ancient customs*, I thought. He shuffled his feet. "Which is something I would like very much."

I turned to Madelena questioningly. Perhaps this was something she would like too. A different kind of freedom, one that might allow her some sort of love.

"You want me to be your army whore, Your Lordship?" Madelena spoke hesitantly, her surprising words harsher than her tone.

Paolo looked piqued. "That is not how I would put it. I never thought of you in that way, Madelena, never." He glanced down at her protruding belly. "Not to mention you are carrying my seed. It is my responsibility. *You* are my responsibility."

Never did I think my brother would utter those words, *my responsibility*. Was he growing up? Or just afraid to be alone?

"This child will be your bastard, and you have not in all these months seemed concerned about him." Madelena seemed to be gathering confidence with every word she spoke, having clearly overcome her reluctance at conversing frankly with a nobleman. "And what about when the war is over? What then?"

He seemed taken aback. "I don't know. But I won't shirk my responsibility, that I can promise. Nor you." He added the last two words with clear affection, and I began to realize the depth of fright my brother was feeling about being dispatched to the front.

"With all due respect, My Lord, you are a noble, and I am a slave. But not for long."

"What do you mean?"

"I mean that my new owner has offered me my freedom, in time. And I intend to take her up on her offer."

"I would set you free too," Paolo whispered.

"Unfortunately, you don't have the right. You don't own me."

"I will pay La Diamante for you."

"With what money?" Madelena knew better than most the ugly truth of the Soranzo coffers.

He shook his head. "Not now, but I will earn my ducats as soon as I am sent afield. I will arrange for the Council to pay La Diamante directly. The money will never even leave Venice."

Madelena stopped to consider this. Paolo watched her intently, no trace of a smile on him. He was the most serious I had ever seen him. Did he truly love Madelena and would he keep her as his mistress when the war was over? She could never be his wife unless Paolo relinquished his nobility, something my parents would never allow and Paolo himself would never want. But being the mistress of a patrician was nothing to sneer at, especially for one of such humble origins.

A thought struck me then. Even if I could contemplate betraying Mother Marina's trust, how would I feel as Luca's mistress? Would my noble pride allow it?

Madelena reached out and took Paolo's hand. He was surprised when she laid his palm across her belly, pressing her own hand on top of his. He concentrated, then looked up with delight. "The baby kicks."

She looked up at him keenly, not moving their layered hands. "With your sister as our witness, do you acknowledge this baby as yours?"

He stared directly in her eyes. "I do."

"Do you swear, throughout your life, to look after this child, and if it is a boy, to find him an apprenticeship? I realize of course he can never join the Great Council, being a bastard with a slave for a mother, but I still want him to have a good life."

"I do swear it. And if a girl?"

She glanced at me. "Then I want her to enter San Zaccaria and be with her aunt, with you providing the requisite dowry."

I was not sure what Mother Marina would say to this, San Zaccaria rarely admitting non-noble girls to its ranks, but she might make allowances.

"I swear it."

Madelena released his hand, and he let it linger for a moment on her stomach before bringing it to her cheek. "The lovely Madelena. Will you accept my offer? It would please me so."

She reached up to his hand and stroked it gently for a moment before removing it and inhaling. "I will not. I will have this child and then take La Diamante up on her offer. I am very sorry. But I trust you will honour your sworn word."

She did not look again at him or me, but left the parlour, a stunned Paolo staring after her. I wondered if this was the first time a woman ever had spurned him in his so-far golden life.

After a moment, his gaze settled on mine as his fingers absentmindedly stroked his cloak. No tears filled his eyes, but his expression was the most bereft I had ever seen. Just for a moment though, and then it was gone.

He smirked. "You know the expression? *Fritters are like women: if they are not round and a bit fat, they are not good.* Madelena was certainly very good. Anyway, I must be going. I'm glad I had the chance to bid both you and Rosa farewell before I leave for the front." His hand went to his hair, which he rakishly combed with his fingers. "I do wish I had the chance to visit with that beautiful new sister of yours, but duty calls. What's her name, Viena? One of God's more enchanting creatures." He grinned, but I knew it was not genuine, and I was relieved that word of Viena's departure had not travelled along the canals—yet.

He hugged me, and I returned the affection. "Be safe, Paolo. Don't do anything stupid. Think of Mama." He would always be my brother, even if he never had the solemnity I so appreciated in Luca.

"Me, stupid? Never." He smiled briefly before turning serious. "Take care, Sister, until we meet again."

Chapter 48

Mama and Papa visited the next day, Papa as predicted to convince Rosa to return to her husband, Mama to see after the health of her daughter and mourn at her granddaughter's grave. I had to give Rosa credit. She was very firm with Papa. It helped that she was still barely walking and Auntie Livia and Mother Marina herself were standing by her side for courage and reinforcement. Papa did not seem convinced her cloistering would last, but finally he acquiesced. "For the time being. When you recover, we will revisit the topic." Mama cried a lot, but Rosa appeared indifferent, or perhaps hardened was a better word.

This hardness served her in good stead when Signora Zane returned, Zanetta at her side, both dressed in black, to persuade her to return to Zago. She refused, then refused to see them again. Zago either had the good sense or enough pride to not return, although he did write her letters. After reading the first, she burned the rest unopened. He even sent me two letters, which were much less threatening than I had anticipated. He mainly wanted to know if Rosa was all right and to ask me to convince her to honour her marital vows. Out of loyalty to Rosa, I did not reply, and the letters ceased.

After several days, Signora Teresa deemed her well enough to leave the infirmary. While moving to the convent's guest house would have been the natural progression, Mother Marina gave her special dispensation to move into Viena's empty cell, next to mine. "I think it would serve her well to be right beside her sister."

It was not like old times, however. My sister had changed, I feared irrevocably. Rosa insisted on sleeping by herself. For the most part, she said her sleep was dreamless. Dolce stayed with her, pleased with all the attention she provided him, and I felt it gave her good purpose to look after him, take him for short strolls, see to his food. He grew a bit fatter in those weeks.

Soon after Dolce's departure from my cell, Viena's cat Leo decided to take up residence with me, and I appreciated his quiet presence whenever I sat down to work on my manuscript's edits, which I felt compelled to finish despite some misgivings.

Livia also spent quite a bit of time with Rosa. She never told Rosa the whole truth about Elisabetta, but they gave each other much-needed comfort, regularly visiting the graveyard together. Mama too came with more frequency, although as much as possible she avoided Madelena, whose time was growing nearer.

Paolo sent a few letters, regaling us with stories from the front, his impressions of the generals ("Don't tell Papa, but I am not at all impressed with Angelo Trevisan"), accounts of beautiful women he'd glimpsed, and a few complaints about how many hours he had to spend writing and how cramped his hand was getting. I could only smile, since I could relate. I was becoming increasingly motivated to finish shaping my ideas on paper, thinking vaguely that I could pen my way out of my pleasant prison.

I also continued my correspondence with Luca, thanking him for his assistance with the midwife and telling him some about Rosa. Every time a letter from him arrived, I would scrutinize it for hidden meaning, but he only dared to write about the revisions and upcoming publication, expressing much anticipation in seeing the final form, and I reciprocated likewise. I could only assume he had renewed his marital dedication, which cracked my heart although I could not blame him. This was one area where I could not match him, feeling no further commitment to my conventual vows.

After November elapsed, the weeks marched through Advent, and the weather grew colder and damper. My father stopped by more often, both missing Paolo at home and enjoying the practicality of being able to visit his daughters together. Sometimes Papa walked from the nearby doge's palazzo, or Teodor rowed him as close as possible, but Rosa never mentioned the gondolier, although once Livia told me she had glimpsed him peering through the iron fence of the graveyard. Every visit, Papa attempted to persuade Rosa to return to Zago, mentioning several times the disapproval of Auntie Leonarda, but she remained steadfast in her refusal, and so he would accede until next time, then switch to news of the government and war as well as any information he could provide as to Paolo's whereabouts. The Great Council indeed anticipated a battle near Ferrara, but Papa seemed confident in Venetian victory.

My trepidations finally banished, I gave myself the goal of completing my manuscript before the Eve of Christmas. I had tentatively titled it *Women's Pleasant Prisons*, although I was open to suggestions. Luca wondered if, to provide for wider readership, something less initially confrontational might be in order. But I had thought of nothing better or more accurate, and so I decided to stick with it unless Aldine Press preferred otherwise.

I became lost in my work for hours at a time, exploring the plight of women in all strata of society. If the pain I felt at my circumstances had not disappeared, it had at least become manageable, perhaps because I was able to pour some of my emotions onto the page in as logical a form as I could conceive.

As the bells struck *vespers* two days prior to Christmas, I wrote the last sentence of my manuscript with a satisfied flourish and blew the ink dry, then sat back with gratification. It was complete, and I could focus on my conventual duties and family for the upcoming feast day and Christmastide.

After subsisting on treats swiped from the kitchens for the last several days, I was looking forward to the evening meal at the refectory with Livia and Rosa, who always studiously avoided her sister-in-law. They, along with Madelena, knew I was writing something, but I did not tell them much and they did not inquire, perhaps too consumed with their private griefs. Better to keep quiet anyway, since I knew the text was very likely to court controversy and I preferred that Mother Marina never realize I was the author. As I capped the ink bottles, straightened the pages on my desk—a satisfyingly thick, book-length pile—wiped the quills, and tried to clean my ink-stained fingers to no avail, a knock came at my door. It was Madelena, who was so large now she seemed ready to burst.

"Feeling all right?" I asked with a smile.

She dipped her head in acknowledgement. "Big and clumsy, but otherwise all right. But that is not why I've come. His Excellency Lord Cicogna is here to see you in the parlour."

"Oh!" A happy if complicated surprise. I had told Luca my anticipated deadline and thought he might have come to see if I had met it and even to celebrate my manuscript's completion. I hurried to tidy my appearance, giving up on my stained hands, and threw my lace veil over my hair. I still wore black for my niece.

I flew to the parlour, wishing I had thought to procure a bottle of sparkling wine and two cups for celebrating, but I was impatient. Save for Luca, the room was empty, all my sisters in the refectory to dine.

He was there in his black robes and rose at my arrival, his face so grim I knew immediately his visit had nothing to do with my manuscript.

He gathered my inky hands to his chest, uncaring if anyone saw us. "It's your brother."

"What about him?" Fear gripped me, and Luca held my hands even tighter.

He looked me in the eyes with enormous sadness. "Justina, I am so sorry to have to tell you this, but Paolo has died."

I stood stunned, as if a brick had just hit me in the chest.

"I am terribly sorry, Justina."

"What happened?" I could only whisper.

"The Great Council this afternoon received word of a great Venetian loss at Polesella, near Ferrara."

"But Papa anticipated a victory."

He slowly shook his head. "The outcome was certainly not what we forecast. Our magnificent fleet, dozens strong, was on the River Po, waiting to attack Ferrara, with our mercenaries making small attacks on land. You might not know that the river around there is usually low with high banks. But there was much rain and snow in the hills. The temperature rose, as did the water, very high, and our galleys with it, until the decks were level with the riverbanks, where the enemy had congregated quietly and unbeknownst to us. Early yesterday morning, well before dawn, the Ferrarese made a surprise attack." His voice caught, and I gripped his hands just as hard. It was as if we were holding each other up, and for either of us to let go was for both to fall to the floor. "It was utter carnage. Many of our ships were sunk. Soldiers and sailors were massacred or drowned. So few of them knew how to swim. Hundreds of casualties at least, maybe thousands."

"And Paolo?"

"The officer he was working for saw him slain with his own eyes and was able to include him in the initial list of casualties."

I exhaled heavily, feeling dizzy. Mama would be distraught at such news, Rosa and Livia too. And Papa devastated by the loss of his only son. "Does my father know?"

"He was heading immediately to your mother. He is quite concerned about her reaction. I think he has lost his own sensibility for now. He asked me to tell you, as Paolo's friend and as a favour to him. He will come as soon as he is able, when he feels your mother is stable, but he is unsure when that will be exactly and did not want to delay your receipt of the news. Your sister and aunt too, of course. He felt you would be best to tell them."

And Madelena. How would she feel?

Charming Paolo, the one who could always make us laugh, jovial, convivial, merry. My brother, whom I'd known my entire life. The thought of him gone was inconceivable.

I became overwhelmed. Luca dropped my hands and entwined his arms around me, holding me securely, letting me sob quietly into his chest. "I am so sorry," he whispered, over and over again, for what might have been brief moments or many hours, I had no sense.

Finally, my tears spent, I pulled back and extracted a handkerchief from my pocket. His handkerchief, the one I had made for him and embroidered with his initials, its twin still in his possession. A hint of a smile came to his face when he saw it. "You carry it with you?"

I wiped my tears, my voice thick. "Always, Luca, always."

He patted his robes, his voice sombre. "And I its mate. Always."

Anger shot through me. Not at him, of course. But at all else. "Why? Why Paolo? Why us? Why any of this?"

"I do not know."

I did not know either. All I knew was that losing Paolo before his prime felt like one too many of God's trials. Viena having to sneak away with Jacomo. Rosa hiding from her husband. Madelena forced to harlotry. My separation from Luca. All of it. "What is the point?"

"To fulfill God's will, I suppose."

"Ecclesiastes says, *Two are better than one, because they have a good return for their labour: If either of them falls down, one can help the other up. But pity anyone who falls and has no one to help them up. Also, if two lie down together, they will keep warm. But how can one keep warm alone?*"

Luca looked doubtful and spoke with care. "I am not in holy orders, of course, but the Bible says many other things as well."

"Yes, all the sins we commit. Such as adultery. I know them well." I stuffed the handkerchief in my pocket. "And I no longer care."

He stared at me. "You no longer care?"

I tore myself from his gaze, stalked a few steps away, and put my head in my hands.

I stood that way for a few moments before he came behind me and put a tentative hand on my shoulder. "Justina, what are you saying?"

I twirled around. I knew my face must be blotchy, my eyes puffy, my hair a mess, but I did not care. All I cared about was my dead brother. My mournful sister. And the man who stood before me.

"I'm saying I want to be with you."

"It is the grief talking."

"It may be. But I've struggled to tame this feeling for many months now. Ever since I met you. We were supposed to marry. We would have had such a good marriage, you and I. I did not want to become a nun. You did not want to marry Elena Paruta. What if you or I were to die tomorrow, like Paolo? What if the pope sacks the city and the papal army rapes all the nuns? The vows I took mean nothing to me anymore. I have tried to stay true to them, but for what reason? God does me no favours. I'm seventeen years old. I will likely live for many more decades in this place." An eternity, the realization almost unbearable. I waved my hand around the parlour. "The risks are great, but I cannot wait any longer. I want to be with you."

His eyes widened. "How?"

"Come tonight at the curfew bell. Over the convent roof and meet me in the courtyard nearest your palazzo."

I did not think his eyes could get any rounder, but they did. He stared at me for a long while, and I could tell he was weighing the decision in his mind. "Yes."

As soon as he said it though, I balked. "Even though if we're caught, you could risk loss of your office and perpetual banishment?"

"Did you not risk your own banishment when you left the convent with me in the summer, right when the Council passed their edicts? And do you not risk some unknown punishment now?"

I nodded slowly.

"I'm well aware of the risks. Do you not think I have considered them all? I have, again and again and again." He raised my chin with the tip of his fingers, and I trembled. "And I'm willing to take them. I have tried to stay true to my vows too, but in my mind, I have already sinned with you. I may as well make it true. I have not even heard of any arrests, but regardless, we will exercise the utmost discretion."

"You are sure, then?"

"Yes. As sure as I've been about anything. More than the day I asked for your hand so many months ago, more than the day of our picnic. Through our letters, your manuscript, these past few months, I know you in a whole new way, a better way. I wish I could do it all over again, defy my father and take you as my wife. It is something I've regretted every single moment. Sometimes I have so much regret I feel as old as the doge, although I'm not quite twenty-five." He slightly shook his head. "Are *you* sure?"

I inhaled then exhaled deeply. "Yes."

He brought my face closer, then brushed his lips against my own. I tried to keep from shaking as he leaned his forehead against mine.

"I am so sorry about your brother. I wish I could take away your pain."

"And I yours. He was your dear friend."

He nodded. "I'll see you just after curfew tonight." He kissed the top of my head and with obvious reluctance left the parlour.

I watched him go, then stood there motionless, partly in keen distress at the news of Paolo's death, partly in shock at what I had set in motion. These events were linked to me. Too many died too young, too soon, before having fully lived, before having truly loved. It was a common enough story.

Luca, just a few years older than Paolo. My heart's desire, to be fulfilled, sin be damned. There would be time for confession later.

Chapter 49

I made my way toward the refectory in a sort of trance. I had to tell Livia and Rosa about Paolo. I was no longer hungry, my insides a messy mix of grief, fear, and anticipation. I vowed not to breathe a word of Luca's clandestine visit to anyone, not even my most cherished ones. It was too perilous, and even though I wanted to meet him with every fibre of my being, I knew we were being audacious and impulsive. Had Polisena, the San Zaccaria nun from half a century before, and her beloved Giovanni, who'd climbed over the roof to meet her, felt the same way?

Just outside the door, though, I changed my mind. I could not tell them about Paolo yet. How would they take such horrific news? Both had already endured so much loss. Why rush to tell them and start their grieving anew? It would still be horrible, whenever I told them. They would be distraught. And they would want to be with me, possibly all night. I felt a stab of guilt—never had I kept anything of such importance from my sister or aunt, and deception was not in my nature. It felt wrong, as if I were tearing off a limb. And while I consoled myself with the thought I was delaying the inevitable sear of pain, I knew my motives were selfish.

But for once, I would do what I wanted—no, needed—for myself. Not for my family, not for San Zaccaria, not for Venice, not even for God. Not telling them for one night would not harm them, nor would it change anything. Paolo was dead, and still would be tomorrow. I would tell them as soon as the sun rose.

Best to avoid them for now, to commit the lesser sin of omission. I could say I was mad with grief and needed to be alone. It wasn't so far from the truth. To have to speak aloud such terrible news, to make it real, was nothing I relished, nor could truly face. So I diverted to the kitchens and loaded one plate with dinner and another with dessert, enough for two people.

When I returned to my room, I found Madelena had been busy while I'd been in the parlour with Luca, leaving behind a bucket full of warm water, the clean laundry she'd done for me the day before, and fresh linens on the bed. She'd also lit coals in the brazier to ward off chill.

I forced myself to my knees to say a prayer, an unofficial penance, but gave up halfway through and turned to my beautification efforts. My eyes were red and kept swelling with tears—nothing I could do about that. But I did wash from head to toe, then cleaned my teeth and brushed out my hair, now well past my shoulders, until it was almost dry. Nothing like its former glory, but a hint of it.

As the *compline* bell rang, I debated what to wear, finally settling on my prettiest nightgown and robe. Actually they were Elisabetta's prettiest nightgown and robe, which Livia had given to me a few weeks before. Elisabetta had done the lacework and embroidery herself. Feeling awkward at the thought, I could not help wondering if she had lain with Livia in it. I finished my ensemble by donning my silk slippers, from which Madelena had meticulously cleaned all mud. Silently I sent thanks to Esther, for doing her calculations gave me confidence there was low risk of a child.

Throughout my ministrations, I took care to keep quiet and was thankful for the presence of silent Leo rather than yappy Dolce. My sisters would be making their way toward their own beds, and I knew my cell had to be as mute as an empty church, so everyone would believe me already sleeping.

And then I waited for the rich deep chimes of the Realtina bell, the curfew clang for all of Venice. I tried to read some of Luca's gift, the *Commedia*, but could not concentrate. I spent my time gazing at the Carpaccio drawing and the Barbari map, reminiscing about Paolo: us as children playing hide-and-seek in a Veneto vineyard and more recently him dressed up as Helen of Troy. Remembering his mischievous smile and the contagion of his laughter, trying to absorb this most horrific of news, which felt unreal. Luca's handkerchief became quite damp.

When the Realtina bell, my signal to shed all regulations, finally stopped reverberating, I poked my head out my cell door, Leo escaping into the night. The corridor was silent as the crypt, quieter even, as there was no dripping noise. Likely everyone had retired early, in anticipation of the morrow's Christmas Eve festivities. Tomorrow the cooks would arise even earlier than usual to prepare the fishes fresh from the convent's lagoon grounds, and the nuns would stay up very late for the service at midnight, although still not an official mass due to the interdict that carried on without end.

With luck my cell was the last door by the second stairwell, so I slipped down the stairs like a phantom, not daring to take a candle, having added my black cloak over my white ensemble to be less conspicuous as much as for warmth. I wondered what Paolo would have thought. He likely would not have minded a common woman sneaking out to meet a nobleman for an assignation, but his patrician nun of a sister? He had contrived for Luca and me to share a few secret kisses, so part of me felt he'd be at least a little proud of my boldness, and that thought comforted me.

I slithered through the corridor that led to the first courtyard and eased open the door, wincing when the hinges creaked. A blast of cold wind greeted me, and I forced myself outside, shutting the door behind me so as to not attract attention with icy air or unexpected noise.

I stood under the arcade and peered into the night. The sky was clear with a nearly full moon and smeared with stars, including a very bright one, perhaps the very one that had brought the Magi from the far east to the Christ Child. I said a small prayer to Jesus, asking for His forgiveness and understanding. The star winked just then, and I half-madly took this as His assent, although I knew it was heretical.

"Luca?" I whispered. Had he come? Or had fear prevented his arrival? Or far worse: Had he been caught?

"Justina, is that you?" The voice I dreamt about, a sweet whisper from the darkness. Joy rippled through me.

"Over here." I scanned the courtyard, a little easier to see now that my eyes had adjusted to the moonlight, and from behind the dormant fig tree emerged Luca. He dashed over, and we embraced with fervour.

"Oh, Justina," he breathed into my hair, and then he kissed me deeply. I responded in kind, his lips so warm in the cold night. His hands roamed under my cloak, and mine under his, until he finally caught my fingers. "Not here, Justina. We must do it right."

"Did you have any trouble getting in?"

"None. The roof tiles were dry and sturdy, and the wisteria vine provided good footing." And he kissed me again, before breaking away, his breath heavy. "Lead the way."

I turned toward the door back into the convent, spitting on the hinges before opening it even more slowly this time. Barely a creak rewarded my efforts. My head inside, I looked both ways to ensure the corridor was empty, then beckoned Luca.

As silent as the fog that rolls in overnight, we crept back toward my cell, my hand holding his, his large and comforting. At the top of the stairwell, just outside my cell, I checked again for other prowlers, but all was clear, so I hurried to open my door and shoo him in, the candlelight flickering from our passage.

We both giggled quietly from the nerves and fear, before facing each other, the night before us. Finally alone.

Chapter 50

"So here we are." Luca tore his eyes from me to glance around the cell, from the Carpaccio and flag fan he'd given me to the thick woven rug on the floor. "Warm and comfortable. But not exactly as I'd imagined."

"How had you imagined it?"

"A bit more austere, I suppose. But knowing patrician women, I guess I'm not surprised to see such comfort and luxury in a noble convent."

"I'm not that extreme compared to some of my sisters. I hear that Angela Riva has solid-gold candlesticks and Zanetta Zane a full-length mirror from Murano."

He smiled. "I'm also not surprised to hear of the vanity of Zanetta Zane. She is not your favourite person, I deduce. I cannot blame you. I met her at a Zane family function when I was sixteen and she about seven years older. She was quite friendly with me, and truth be known, I was rather flattered by her attentions. Then I later learned she'd already been a nun for at least a decade, so it all became rather odd."

"How well do you know her?"

"Not very. We met perhaps five or six more times until this year, when I've seen her more than any other. She is always friendly, always mentioning our family connection and how she thinks I'll do well on the Great Council. I would consider her kind and witty, if I didn't know better."

"That's quite surprising." It was difficult for me to imagine Zanetta any other way than nasty, caustic, and spiteful, but I supposed everyone consisted of multitudes, even members of the Zane family.

He smiled shyly. "I certainly did not come here to talk about Zanetta Zane." His eyes alit on the manuscript upon my desk, the *Commedia* beside it. "Ah, there it is! Complete?"

I nodded. "I'm swelling from my own sin of vanity."

"You are justified to feel proud, Justina." He flipped the top few pages before replacing the rock I used to weigh down the stack. "But there will be time to read this later." He turned to me. "How are you, regarding Paolo?"

My eyes filled. "My heart is bereft, but I believe I have not yet fully absorbed the finality of it."

He nodded sympathetically. "I have an inkling of how you must feel, although only as a friend. His loss is almost impossible to comprehend and thus does not feel real. It is comforting to be able to talk to one who knew him so intimately. Is there anything I can do for you?"

I shook my head and forced the tears down. Not now. There would be plenty of time to cry later.

"Please let me know if there is." His voice turned husky. "For I would do anything for you. And I cannot believe I am really here with you."

"Nor I."

He took a step forward, and his voice lowered even further. "Or that you are really here with me."

I matched his step, and the candlelight flickered.

My cell was not large, and we stood only steps apart. After what seemed like an eternity, Luca closed the distance, but only to remove both our cloaks and hang them on the pegs next to my door. He turned to me. "You are truly the most beautiful woman I've ever seen."

I did not know what to reply. Quivering from nerves, I fiddled with the lace on Elisabetta's robe. I only ever felt beautiful in his presence.

"Are you still sure you want to do this?" He did not come closer, a tantalizing distance away. "We do not have to do anything you do not want."

I knew how to answer that. "Yes." No second thoughts, no regrets. Sin now, contrition later. Life was too brief. "You?"

He smiled in bittersweet relief. "I've been wanting this ever since Paolo introduced me to you." He reached to untie my dressing gown, ever so gently disrobing me and laying it over the back of the chair.

Standing there in my nightdress, I watched as Luca started to remove his own clothes, his eyes not leaving me. I could not help but stare as he exposed more skin, a natural olive shade. He noticed my admiration of his lean physique with a small grin. "Would you like to help?"

I nodded with timidity, in utter disbelief at what I was doing, giggling a little as I assisted him in removing his hose. His body was unmarred by scars, save for a well-healed one on his forearm. I touched it gently. "I was burned as a child. Too close to the fire looking for sweets from the cook."

When he was just in his woollen undergarment, he brought my hands to his bare chest, and I ran my fingers over the whorls of brown hair upon it.

Then he lifted my nightgown off and looked at me with his own kind of wonder, as if he truly did believe I was the most beautiful woman in the world.

He brought his hands to my cheeks and lowered his head to kiss me. I could not help but respond, my hands moving from his chest to his shoulders and up into that hair that I always longed to run my fingers through. He smelled faintly of sandalwood and manliness.

Entwined, we stumbled over to my bed, unable to keep our hands off each other. He only stopped to remove his underclothes, and my eyes widened. I had never seen a man, just little boys, and I swallowed hard at the sight.

He smiled again a little shyly. "You still sure?"

I swallowed again. "Yes."

He caressed my face. "I don't know how much you know, but oftentimes, for a woman, the very first time, well, it can hurt."

Both Madelena and Viena had told me something of the sort, so I simply nodded.

"I'll be as gentle as possible, but anytime you want me to stop, just tell me, please. The last thing I want to do is cause you pain."

I nodded again as he held me close. I had thought I was ready, but not for this exactly, for no amount of telling could truly describe it. His touch was delicate as he took a leisurely tour of my body.

When a soft moan escaped my lips, he looked up at me with silent laughter. "Unfortunately, we must remain quiet."

I blushed. "That is turning out to be much more difficult than I anticipated."

"Well then." He kissed me full on the mouth and then carried on.

What an awkward ritual lovemaking was. The potential for so much embarrassment. Painful and horrible for so many women, but as Viena had told me, in the right hands it could be beautiful.

I thanked God I was in such perfect hands.

Far too soon, Luca brought my head to his chest, covering us with the blanket to create a nest of warmth underneath it.

"It wasn't too awful, was it?" he whispered.

"Luca, how can you say that?"

He sighed. "I'm glad. I'd hate to think it will be a terrible memory for you."

I shook my head. "The opposite. The most wonderful. I never want this night to end."

"Nor I." He sighed again. "Justina—" He stopped when we heard a brief creak.

"Just the wind," I said. "It's not unusual to hear. Or maybe some festive mice."

He smiled before his expression wavered between the bitter and the sweet.

"What is it?" But I could tell from his expression exactly what it was. It felt cruel to experience such fleeting joy, to know it would not last. "I understand, of course. But must it be just this one night? Dare we dream of spending more time together? I know it is risky, with the potential for harsh punishment, but I feel my heart might be equally at risk if we say never again." I could not believe my own fearlessness, or perhaps temerity, but this was what I wanted to my core.

His eyes sparkled at the prospect. "If we are exceedingly careful, then yes, perhaps we may dare dream. It would give me such joy."

I propped myself up on one elbow and boldly leaned over to kiss him. He matched my fervour, his hands roaming all over me, my body falling so easily into him. It was as if a fever had overtaken us, our skin hot to the touch, him kissing me deeply to keep me quiet.

For I was having a very difficult time remaining quiet this time.

Until finally we lay, our chests heaving, our bodies melded together, unable, nay unwilling, to disentangle or let go.

Chapter 51

W e slept lightly until the early morning *matins* bell roused us both awake.

My eyes fluttered open as he tickled my face with kisses. "I suppose that's my signal to go."

"I hate to admit it, but I think so, especially if we want the chance to do this again."

I could feel his cheeks rise into a smile against my hair. "I would very much like to do this again."

I returned the smile. "Me too." I turned my head to look up at him. "Tell me something. Is that . . . usual?"

"Is what usual?"

"You know." I glanced away with embarrassment as he grinned.

"You mean enjoying yourself with complete abandon?"

I felt a fool but had to know. "Be honest."

"Well." He cleared his throat. "Well, I would say it is unusual. My . . .

wife . . . tolerates it, for the duty of procreation. It's hard to tell with courtesans as they are such excellent players. You are the first woman I've been with who seems to have experienced honest, true pleasure."

I considered this, inwardly pleased to know his wife did not enjoy it very much.

He stroked my face. "I think you experienced it because it is not just duty or bodily pleasure, but rather love."

"Love?"

"Yes. You know that by now, don't you, Justina? That I love you. More than Petrarch could have loved Laura, for he may never have even known her."

"I love you too. More than I love Jesus, and I know that is heretical to say."

He brushed the hair that fell in my face behind my ear. "I would classify everything we are doing as heresy, or certainly sin."

I thought of something Viena had said. "I must tell you something, Luca." He looked expectant. "I said my convent vows with my mouth but not my heart." His expression turned quizzical. "I did not mean them. I am not certain they are binding."

He smiled mournfully. "Binding enough, I suppose. I said my marriage vows with my mouth but not my heart too, but unfortunately I do not think that makes my marriage invalid."

"But what if it did? Not before the Church or the government, but before us?"

He sat up, and I did the same. "You mean, we could marry each other? At least unofficially?"

I nodded.

He held my hand. "We could start by taking each other's hands."

I squeezed it hard. "We have no gifts for each other, so I give you my body."

"And I give you mine."

"We have no feast either, but I do have some sweets I swiped last night." The plate full of pastries was within reach, and I balanced it beside us before taking an almond cookie and feeding it to him.

He polished it off in two bites. "I'm famished. I really worked up an appetite." I fed him another cookie before he did the same for me in turn. We then washed it all down with some wine.

I took both his hands. "And now the vows."

He cleared his throat. "I promise to love and to honour you, Justina Soranzo, for better or for worse, until death us do part."

"And I promise to love and to honour you, Luca Cicogna, for better or for worse, until death us do part."

He leaned over to kiss me, his breath cookie-sweet. He closed his eyes, but I kept my eyes open to look at him. His lashes were long, and a lock of brown hair curled on his forehead.

"Shall we consummate it now?" he asked slyly.

Closing my eyes, I kissed him in reply.

This time, there was no sleeping or cuddling in the aftermath. It was well past *matins* and paramount that Luca leave undetected. We both hurried to dress, intermingled with kisses and suppressed laughter. I had truly never been so joyous in my life, and Luca whispered assurances of the same.

Finally, it was time for him to slip out the way he had come. I insisted I would take him as far as the courtyard door to ensure he did not get lost, and he agreed only reluctantly, not wanting to put me in danger.

Taking a deep breath, I eased open my cell door to see if the corridor was clear, Luca right behind me—only to find Zanetta Zane on the threshold, arms crossed, fingers drumming, green eyes flashing in triumph.

Chapter 52

I froze, and Luca put a reassuring hand on the small of my back.

Zanetta's mouth curved into a malicious smile. "Well, well, well. What have we here? Or should I say, who? Lord Cicogna, I'm very sorry to see you." Her smile disappeared, replaced with dismay.

Luca and I said nothing, his hand touching me more firmly. We were fully clothed, perhaps the only factor in our favour. How much had Zanetta heard through the door?

"Are you not even going to invite me in, my dear sister in Christ?"

I glanced behind me at Luca, and he gave a slight nod. So I stood back to usher Zanetta in and shut the door with haste. It was better not to waken our slumbering sisters and attract further attention.

"I guess I can't say I'm surprised," she said, eyes sweeping from our faces to my unkempt bed and the crumbs on the dessert plate. "I thought I heard something in the middle of the night, so I got up to investigate." Although her cell was on a different floor, I did not feel it my right to argue the point. "And yes, I did hear quite the unholy earful."

"Please, Zanetta." The plea was out of my mouth before I could stop it.

"Please, what?" she snarled. "I've had just about enough of you and your family and ilk. Your aunt and her sinful connection with her *friend*, Elisabetta." Luca raised an eyebrow. "Yes, I know about that. Your slave, who it is clear granted her practice to your noble brother"—the very mention of Paolo was like a sword in my side—"and then parades around this convent serving you while she is about ready to burst with a bastard, before leaving us to ply her trade for a courtesan. And your neighbour Viena, whoring herself with a common carpenter, for the love of God. At least you have the decency to sin with a fellow noble, although he is married." She appraised Luca, and her expression was inscrutable. "And your sister, deserting my brother, defying our family and their marriage contract. Yes, I know it all." My thoughts could not help but turn to Teodor and the small grave in the cemetery. *Not all, Zanetta.* That secret still hidden gave me a tiny coil of hope.

She went on. "Even though it is the greatest city in Christendom, Venice is a small village when it comes to gossip, the patriciate even smaller. You are all sinners, protected by our weak abbess. It disgusts me. Angela Riva never would have allowed such transgressions during her tenure. No, she would have been strict and run the convent with a tight hand, an abbess beyond compare."

"Signora Zanetta, if perhaps we could come to some sort of private arrangement," Luca ventured. "In the name of our families. Such a long, illustrious, entwined history between them. And our personal connection."

She snorted. "It's always business with you noblemen, isn't it, Lord Cicogna? But this is the business of San Zaccaria we are talking about, the very business of the Venetian government too, I might add. I will not be

bribed with coin. What were those laws they put into place in the aftermath of Celestia? For you, Lord Cicogna, it is looking like imprisonment,
a hefty fine, loss of your new office. Too bad, such a promising career. And,
oh yes, perpetual banishment from our Most Serene City. That will make
it difficult to continue your congress with a bride of Christ, at least a Venetian one. Although I do feel for your wife and unborn child. I'm sure you
are hoping for an heir."

Luca remained stoic, his breath even, taking the measure of Zanetta,
although his hands had bunched into fists.

"And for you, my loving sister." Zanetta turned to me. "Not only tonight.
Didn't you also leave the convent right after those laws were passed? To
spend time with him, I presume?" She flicked her head at Luca. "Your punishment is a little more open-ended and up to the abbess. I don't expect
much from her, although you do employ a secular servant. Can't say I
blame you there. It's not as if *I* would be your servant. But perhaps Patriarch Contarini should be informed. The Zane and Contarini families are,
as you know, very tight." Her eyes flickered over to my table, which held
quills, bottles of ink, the blotter, and—I realized with great pain—my precious manuscript. I had become much too casual about not locking it up.

Zanetta was unrelenting. "And then there is that stack of heretical filth.
Women's Pleasant Prisons. You've left your manuscript lying about the last
few weeks, Justina, ever since your sister gave birth here. When I was helping clean up Viena's empty cell, I decided to look inside your room, and
what did I find but that offensive blasphemy? I could not believe my eyes.
I've read the additions since, and they make me sick."

"No." This from Luca. "No, it is neither heresy nor blasphemy. It is brilliant."

"You've read it?" Zanetta's voice filled with surprise and contempt. "And thought it brilliant?"

"Yes, I have, and I do. And I'm going to help her get it published." He inched toward the table.

"What?" Zanetta was clearly shocked, and he took the opportunity to snatch up the manuscript and clutch it to his chest, like a helpless babe in need of protection. She stabbed a bayonet glare in my direction. "You dare to bring more scandal to San Zaccaria, Justina? First your auntie's unnatural affair, then your sister, then Viena, then your own whoring, and then your apostasy published for all of Christendom to read?" She shook her head. "It's high time Mother Marina was fetched. And don't think I'll go the whole way to her cell and allow Luca to escape unnoticed. No, I think I'll wake my sister-in-law, Rosa, right next door, and ask her to summon the abbess for me. It seems like just punishment for her to witness her sister's downfall. And Mother Marina will hardly be able to deny what is in front of her very eyes."

"Zanetta, why do you hate me so much?" My voice wavered, but I willed back the tears. This was all happening too fast. I had to keep her talking, change her mind. My entire world was falling apart, a glass vase shattering into a thousand pieces, unable to be fixed. My brother dead. My aunt and sister in danger. And just when I had Luca, to lose him forever, for Venice to perpetually banish him and force him from his new position. It was all too much.

"Why do I hate you?" She stood still, as if considering the question for the first time. "I think it's having to look at the smug faces of first your aunt and then you all this time. Always getting what you want. Yes, you had to take the veil, but you all certainly have made the most of things."

She glanced at Luca. "You think I wanted to become a nun? No. I too have loved a man—" She broke off, perhaps realizing she was revealing too much. "I took my vows at the same service as Livia and Elisabetta. They could have been my friends. But they were not interested, a few years older than me, which they never let me forget. And eyes only for each other, from that very first day. I think I knew even then what they had was perverse, but I could not have named it. Only when Elisabetta died did I truly see it for what it was. The grief of a lover." She spat on the ground. "And your aunt's political ambition. She hopes to be abbess someday. Over my dead body. And then you, and Rosa, getting everything your way. The abbess of the great noble convent of San Zaccaria in sympathy with you. Allowing a laywoman to stay here in a cell and not the guest house? As if my brother were some sort of abuser? Our fathers legally arranged that marriage, and it should be honoured, like all the ones before it. What makes Rosa so special? Does she have something to hide?" Her eyes widened as the wheels turned in her head. "Another lover, perhaps? Yes, that must be it. What else could it be? My brother will be most interested to learn that piece of news. Is that why you did not allow us to see the child? Because she looked nothing like Zago?"

Luca watched her soliloquy in wonder, clearly trying to puzzle it all out, his hands protecting the manuscript.

She turned to Luca, her eyes slightly misting. "Lord Cicogna, I do feel sorry for you and your parents, although perhaps I'm doing your wife a favour. I sincerely regret that you are the collateral damage as I achieve even more than I'd hoped for." She seemed as if possessed by the devil. "The downfall of Livia, Rosa, and Justina, in one night, and the further humiliation of Mother Marina and the house of Soranzo. And your father a senator, Justina. I wish I could see the look on his face as the Senate reads the charges against his daughter, just months after his son was arrested. Even better than I anticipated as I stood outside your door, witness to your disgusting carnal sins."

Chapter 53

As Zanetta stalked toward the door to rouse Rosa, I found my voice. "Wait."

Both she and Luca turned to me, her face curious, his pleading with me not to capitulate. But what choice did I have? I could not ruin all these lives: Luca's, my sister's, my aunt's, that of the entire convent.

"Zanetta, you are right." Her face softened slightly. While I wanted to discern evil in her expression, what I really detected was misery, and while I hated her for what she was doing to me and my loved ones, I pitied her as well. She too had those she loved, a brother she wished to protect, and, as her gaze kept slipping toward Luca, I began to wonder about the nature of her connection to him. "There has been too much sinning. I am sorry for it, and I will make my penance." I bowed my head.

"Justina." Luca's voice brimmed with emotion. He clearly realized what I was about to do.

"That is a start," Zanetta sniffed. Her eyes flickered to me, then toward the manuscript Luca still held to his chest. "But not nearly enough."

"I will also try to persuade Rosa to return to Zago. I know her proper place is by her husband's side."

She grimaced, but perhaps it was a smile. "You must more than just *try*. My brother takes his vows very seriously. He has been quite troubled about the death of his daughter and Rosa not returning to him."

I nodded. Even I had seen some glimmers of Zago softening.

"What about Livia? She must never be abbess."

I made my own grimace. "No, she will never be abbess." This was not difficult to promise: it was the only realistic outcome. Other sisters besides Zanetta would surely have come to their own conclusions on the essence of Livia's grief. I would have advised my aunt the same in any case.

"And?" Zanetta was unrelenting, but what choice did I have?

"And I promise Lord Cicogna will never enter this convent again." I could not bear to look at him as he stifled a groan. "For the price of your silence. For the honour of San Zaccaria, and the glory of Venice. We will do our duties, he to his wife and to our republic, I to my heavenly husband."

She nodded her approval as she levelled her gaze at Luca, an expression on her face I could not decipher. "Almost there, Justina. There is just one more bit of business to discuss, and then our arrangement can be concluded." She pointed at the papers he held.

"Do not, Justina." Luca's voice broke, just as my own heart was finally torn into pieces and thrown on the floor like lacerated petals after a windstorm. "Your work needs to be published and read widely. It is for her benefit too. She asks too much."

"Hush," she hissed at him. "It must never see the light of day. It must be burned. San Zaccaria's very own bonfire of the vanities."

I nodded, my head bent, Eve enduring God's wrath in the garden. "It was vain of me to write such a thing, and prideful too. I will burn it now and confess to Father Hieronimo."

Zanetta nodded. "All right, if you do all those things, then I will remain silent. For the honour of San Zaccaria and the glory of Venice." Although I knew it was not pure selflessness on her part. I remembered Mother Marina reminding Zanetta that she should not soil the very place she herself lived in. She too would have to live with any dishonour attached to our nunnery if word got out. "We must all do our part to ensure our Most Serene Republic wins this war and our convent appears pure." She made a sign of the cross. "And for my brother, so he will not have further scandal attached to our name through your sister. And now it is time to say farewell, Lord Cicogna. I'll allow that. Perhaps your biggest sin, besides fornication and adultery of course, was the impetuousness of youth, and so I will be charitable. In honour of our families' entwined histories, as you say. After all, Jesus teaches us to be merciful and to love those sinners who transgress." She looked as if she wanted to say more, then shut her mouth into a grim line, and I pondered how easily she had decided to save Luca's honour.

Luca swept over to me. He held me close, my manuscript pressed between us like a third beating heart. I could not believe this would be the last time I would ever touch him, speak with him, be with him. A second death I would have to mourn, along with Paolo.

I cannot do this, I thought. But I could not allow the words to escape my lips. I needed to be strong, for Luca. Venice could not banish him or make him an example. He was to become a father. He had a most promising future. He could be doge someday.

And I could never be the dogaressa.

I could feel his gaze on me, but I could not meet his eyes as I whispered, "You saved me, my honour, my family. Now it is my turn to save you and yours."

He stroked my cheek, his touch a flame upon my skin. "Remember our vows, Justina," he murmured, and I tried to memorize every nuance, the musicality of his voice as well as the words he uttered. "To love and to honour, for better or for worse, until death us do part." I still could not look him in the eye, but I nodded and felt his kisses all over my head, every one sending me teetering between despair and elation. "I said those vows with my heart, not just my mouth. Do you hear me? Do you understand?"

I nodded again, and he cupped my chin, forcing our eyes to meet, his own beautiful brown ones questioning, clearly needing to hear my answer. "Yes, for me as well. Until death us do part."

"Do not forget. Someday, we will find a way." His voice breaking.

I wanted to believe him, but it was too difficult to do so.

"Enough now of these lovers' musings." Zanetta snapped her fingers to hurry us along. "Soon the bells for *prime* will ring and the sun will rise."

Slipping a few pages of my writing into his cloak, Luca took my face in his hands and kissed me one last time, hard enough, I thought, to bruise my lips, so that I would feel his imprint on me a long time to come. I attempted to do the same. But it would never be enough.

Zanetta angrily cleared her throat, our signal to break apart, and the rest of the manuscript pages fell to the floor like dead autumn leaves. "You will write again," Luca whispered as Zanetta opened the door. She peeked out while Luca straightened his cloak and slashed his fingers through his hair.

I gripped the back of the chair as he exited, not looking back. Zanetta followed him as far as the stairwell, then he was on his own. I prayed he made it to the courtyard and over the roof unmolested.

I, too, was now on my own. Zanetta returned to face me, but I felt disembodied and part deaf as well.

She would not let me mope or even sit. "Come now, help me pick this filthy heresy up."

I forced myself to move, to gather the sheets and make a messy pile, all the pages out of order. What did it matter anymore? Did I write all this? I could scarcely remember. It already felt like someone else's work.

Zanetta scooped up the disjointed manuscript and beckoned me to follow. I did so in a daze, down the stairwell and toward the kitchens.

A lone cook was already stoking the fire, watching us enter with a curious yawn. She bobbed her head at us, but Zanetta ignored her and grabbed the poker from her pudgy hand. The woman shrugged and walked to another part of the kitchen to begin her preparations for the Christmas Eve feast.

Without delay, Zanetta took a few pages and tossed them on the fire, the flames flaring up and consuming them within seconds. With a satisfied smile, she added more and more until it seemed something out of Dante's inferno, the last page going up in a puff of smoke as thick as Venetian fog in January.

I did not cry, I did not wail, I did not wring my hands. I just stood there, stupefied, like some sort of Grecian statue. I could feel nothing except the heat of the fire. Savonarola would have been proud.

"I cannot believe Luca helped you with this drivel."

I did not answer her. What was there to say? She did not have the mind to truly understand it.

"Such a handsome, smart man. Why would he ruin his prospects for the likes of you? He must stay true to his wife, for the good of his family name, for the glory of Venice, and in the eyes of God." She had a faraway look in her eye, and I realized then she'd called him by his Christian name.

A memory came of her flirtation in the parlour. I thought of her quick willingness to let him return unmolested to his family and wife. And the strange, indecipherable looks she gave him.

Zanetta loved Luca. She loved him and would not be the cause of his downfall.

How she had come to love him or when exactly, I could not speculate. I felt slightly repulsed. He was her fantasy escape from this prison, if only in her own mind.

But if she could not be with him, she would ensure I could not either.

Zanetta slapped her hands together to brush away any soot, then yanked my arm, the cook watching us go with wide eyes. The bells for the *prime* service rang. "It's not too early to speak to your sister."

Chapter 54

Rosa opened Viena's door, dull-eyed, clearly startled to see me standing beside Zanetta Zane and at such an early hour. "Is everything all right, Justina?"

I turned to Zanetta. "Would you let me speak to my sister alone? You can stay in my room right next door with the door open, so you know when we're finished."

Zanetta's eyes narrowed, but she relented and allowed me to enter by myself. Rosa shut the door, Dolce dancing at our feet.

"What in Heaven's name is going on, Justina?"

We sat down on her feather bed, and I looked around the room as Dolce curled back up on the floor next to the glow of the brazier. The crucifix was Viena's and the art on the walls too. Rosa had not really changed anything, as if she had known the cell would never truly be her own.

"Justina, you are scaring me. Why is Zanetta allowing you to do anything? Tell me. Is it Paolo?"

Paolo. I had not yet even told her about him. And as heartbreaking as that news was, it might not be even the worst thing I had to tell. "Yes, but not just Paolo."

"Is he . . . dead?"

I wiped the tears from the corners of my eyes. "Yes. There was a terrible defeat near Ferrara. Many losses."

Her face crumpled. "Our poor brother. Did Papa come? How is Mama? Are they still here?"

"Oh, Rosa. There's that and there's more. I cannot comprehend it all . . ." The tears ran fully now. I could do nothing to stop them, try as I might.

Rosa hugged me and stroked my head. "I cannot believe it about Paolo. Are you sure? Tell me, Justina. What else is there? I will help you now. It is my turn." That announcement just induced more tears. She did not know the half of it. Bewildered, she continued to hold me, pulling my handkerchief from the pocket of my dressing gown.

I took it from her and dabbed my cheeks, my breath sputtering until it reached a semblance of calm. I unfolded the handkerchief, smoothing it on my lap, running my finger along the lacework, my lacework, and then along the stitching I had embroidered, Luca's initials.

"I've never seen that before." She admired the handiwork. "I don't think I've ever seen you make one so beautiful. You clearly spent a lot of time on it." She traced the initials: *LC*. "Wait a moment. Is this Lord Cicogna's? Luca? Did you make this for him?"

She stared at me. I could neither answer nor look at her.

"You did. You still love him, don't you? After all this time. And I have been too wrapped up in my own problems to even notice or inquire. I am sorry, Sister."

Her apology compelled me. Zanetta was waiting right next door. I could no longer delay. "It is I who must apologize."

"For what?"

"I may have ruined your life, and Livia's too, with my greed and indiscipline."

"Whatever do you mean?"

"I knew about Paolo last evening because Luca, Lord Cicogna, came to tell me. Papa was hurrying home to Mama, and he asked Luca to convey me the message, to avoid delay. And I waited to tell you, planning to do so this morning at first light." I sniffled and dabbed at my face again with the handkerchief.

Rosa looked puzzled. "Why would you wait to tell me such news of our brother? You could have awoken me."

I gulped. "Because of my lust and selfishness and pride. My love for Luca has grown so much over the last year, and I daresay his in return, despite his marriage, that Paolo's dying spurred us to take action."

Her eyes widened. "What sort of action?"

I took a deep breath and dropped my hands. "He sneaked into San Zaccaria and spent last night with me."

"What?" Shock painted Rosa's face.

"And Zanetta caught us."

Her hand went to her mouth. "Mother of God."

"But that is not the worst of it. She threatened to tell the Senate— and Papa a senator! To have Luca dismissed from his government positions and banished from Venice. She never wants Auntie Livia to become abbess. Of course she wanted to tell Mother Marina, saying I had sullied the good name of San Zaccaria right on the heels of Viena doing the same, and bring about her downfall too."

Rosa kept shaking her head in utter disbelief.

"Rosa, there is even more."

She looked at me, stricken. "What else could there be?"

My sweet, dear little sister. My heart could not take any more breakage, so thoroughly smashed already. "She hates that you have taken sanctuary at San Zaccaria and not returned to her brother, to whom you are quite lawfully wedded. She intimates that Zago does care for you and is deeply in grief due to your absence." I shuddered. "And she seems to have deduced that perhaps you had a lover and that the baby was not Zago's."

She cried out. "How could I ever have thought I'd have true sanctuary, with that awful woman here as well?"

I gripped her hands. "I admitted nothing of the sort, of course, but we knew burying Teodora so furtively might not be enough. I begged Zanetta not to say anything, but she was ready to shout the news from the campanile in San Marco." My lips quivered. "And to tell her brother of her suspicions."

Rosa leaned back, limp. "What will happen to me, a noblewoman who had an affair and a bastard with a common servant? Imprisonment and banishment, just like Luca. We could go together. I do not know how I would survive otherwise."

I bit my lip so hard I almost drew blood. "It turns out Zanetta is not entirely cold-hearted, Rosa. She has agreed to remain silent, to preserve her brother's reputation and the Zane name and even that of San Zaccaria. Although she has demanded that I persuade you of one thing."

Rosa's eyes were on the ceiling, and her voice was suddenly devoid of emotion. "To return to my husband."

Another exhalation, and I nodded. "I am so sorry."

"And that will save you and Luca, as well as me?"

"In a way. She has asked for other provisions, including my never seeing Luca again. We will escape official punishment." But not the daily internal agony. And I did not even tell her about my manuscript. I ran my hands through my hair, my head feeling as if it might split in two.

She sighed. "I will admit I've already been starting to wonder if I should return to Zago anyway. How long could I truly have stayed here?"

For a long while, she continued staring at the ceiling, unmoving, and I wondered if she had suffered some sort of apoplexy. When I was on the verge of running out to summon the infirmarian, Rosa finally spoke, her voice surprising me with its calmness and strength. "I will do it."

Chapter 55

I moved numbly through the rest of that day, within my body, but without it. As if I were watching players in a mummery, me the main player.

Livia took the news of her ambition cut short stoically, saying she was already coming to that conclusion and vowing it was more important to protect the reputation and good name of Elisabetta. She cried much for the loss of Paolo, her favourite nephew.

Madelena was silent at the news of Paolo's death, and I dismissed her for the day, leaving her in her room with her hands upon her belly.

I told Zanetta about Rosa and Livia, and she reiterated that she would remain silent. I asked her even to swear on a Bible, which she begrudgingly did—as long as I did the same. As I made the pledge, I could not help but think I was doing so with my mouth and not my heart.

Zanetta sent a maid to summon a gondolier to return Rosa that very afternoon to the Zane palazzo, pleased that her brother would have his wife back before the holy feast celebrating Christ's birth.

Livia and I helped Rosa pack her few belongings. We were mostly per-functory in our conversation, speaking little. I insisted she take Dolce with her, and she seemed somewhat heartened by the thought of his company. Her old doll, she refused to bring. But she swore she'd visit the convent weekly, to see me and Livia and pray by Teodora's grave.

Livia kept shaking her head over Zanetta, wondering how she had pieced so much together, although she had not guessed Zanetta's attach-ment to Luca. "I underestimated her. I never thought her particularly intel-ligent." She let out a long exhalation. "I knew she wanted to be our friend, from the very beginning when we took the veil together, but I was having none of it. She was several years younger than us, and awkward. I despised her from the start. Elisabetta always counselled patience on my part, and while she made me a better woman, she could not penetrate that evil sliver within myself." She turned to me and gave me a hug. "I am so sorry about Luca, Niece, so deeply sorry. I know you love him." She rubbed her chin with her thumb. "Perhaps there is a way."

I shook my head. "I promised Zanetta. The stakes are too high for everyone for me to renege." I said this mechanically, not letting myself feel anything.

Papa came to the parlour after the midday meal, which I could not eat. Mama was distraught and unable to join him. He hugged Rosa and me both hard. He was pleased to hear that Rosa planned to reunite with Zago and said he'd accompany her back to her marital home. "I will also have a word with my son-in-law. What say you, Daughter? Some fatherly advice on marriage? Ensuring too you are able to visit your mother and sister as often as you wish."

She thanked him, saying she'd already decided she would insist on seeing her family more often, and he clasped her to him again. He eyed me over her head, and I watched my father as he displayed his love for his daughters and mourned his son. His aged eyes were misted with distress, his hair even whiter than I'd recalled, his lined face more haggard. He was a complex man who brooked no dissent but had also insisted we be educated, one of the few patrician fathers to ensure his daughters learned Latin and read widely. He had me enter a convent because he thought I would appreciate the opportunity for scholastic pursuits. He was my father, and he loved me the best way he knew how. I did likewise.

Finally came the time to say goodbye to Rosa. We would see each other again very soon, within a week, and that provided a measure of relief.

After Rosa departed, I returned to my cell. I still had not tidied up from last night, and evidence of Luca was everywhere. I lay on my bed and curled the sheets and blankets around me, Luca's handkerchief in my hand. I could still smell him, us. In my mind, I relived every moment, and nearly gasped out loud at the memories. They were all I could hold on to, and I clung to them as tightly as my rosary when I prayed. I was not sure when I would pray again, though.

I fell asleep, so tired from the night, from the day, from my sorrow, and Luca laced my unhallowed dreams.

I woke with a start to a knock, trying to cling to the last vestiges of my dream, unsure if it was a comfort or a misery. Livia was at the door to escort me to the refectory for our fish feast. I begged off. I was not ready to eat or be with people, to face Zanetta, Angela Riva, Santina and the tongue she always stuck out at me.

Livia was understanding. "I will be there for you, just as you were there for me, make no mistake about that, Niece. I will help you bear this."

I nodded, unable to cry anymore. I was empty now.

After Livia left, I continued to lie on my bed, looking first at the flag fan from the summer, then at the Carpaccio. As I studied the Madonna's beatific expression, wondering if I ever again might feel a fraction of such happiness, another knock came at the door. I ignored it, but the knocker persisted until finally I sighed and padded over.

It was Madelena, her eyes red, a letter in hand. I snatched it, wondering if it could be from Luca, but I did not recognize the hand or the seal. Of course it would not be from him. It would be too raw to receive anything from him, and I could only assume he would feel the same.

Upon opening it, I scanned immediately for the signature. "It's from Viena."

"Oh? I hope she keeps well, and her unborn child too." Madelena stroked her belly.

"Not too much longer for you now."

"No, just a few weeks. Signora Bassano saw me yesterday. She said I am progressing well. She is predicting a girl."

I could not help but smile. "My niece. I should like that very much." I could give her Rosa's old doll as a reminiscence of her aunts and the women who would always love her.

"I would too. I know she would be in the most loving of hands, yours and your auntie's."

"And you could visit any time you wished."

Madelena smiled sadly. "I will continue to pray then for a daughter."

"I will as well." And I reached out and hugged my maid, both of us clinging to each other, as much for our missing men as to comfort each other, the babe wedged between us like a small bundle of what I could only call hope.

Chapter 56

After Madelena left, I read Viena's letter, which she had written a month ago.

Dear Justina,

I pray this note finds you well. Jacomo and I recently arrived in Rome, and I am able to enclose this missive in an ambassadorial pouch on its way to Venice. My maternal uncle is one of the ambassadors, newly returned to Rome in the hopes of making peace with the pope, and while he was none too pleased at my fall from grace and sinful state, he did agree to put my mother's mind at ease with a letter and shrugged when I asked to enclose a second to you.

My uncle took further pity on me by giving Jacomo odd jobs to do around the ambassadorial palazzo. As you know, Jacomo is very skilled with his hands, as well as hardworking and agreeable, so he has quickly made himself useful and indispensable. I too am earning a bit of money doing lacework and embroidery, alas for a few Roman courtesans. My position delightfully scandalizes them, and they are quite thrilled to procure San Zaccaria needlework—the convent's reputation in this regard has spread far beyond Venice.

Speaking of which, I do pray fervently that the convent's reputation has not fallen too far with my departure. Mother Marina was nothing but good to me, and to Jacomo too, and I hope she, my sisters, and the convent do not suffer. My uncle has not heard tale of any such news, and that brings me comfort.

Rome pales in comparison to Venice. It rains constantly, the warren of streets teems with mud and refuse, and the buildings are unremarkable. Even the Vatican, that holiest of places, is an unimpressive edifice of no grandeur that constantly threatens to fall. His Holiness Julius II has grand plans (if he could ever cease his warring), having hired many talented artists and architects, but truly I do not think he will achieve his ambitions. Have no doubt, Venice will be the most excellent and serene city for millennia to come.

I keep well. The child within me has grown big and although I accordingly grow uncomfortable, I feel energized.

Justina, I am happy. My uncle saw that Jacomo and I were married as soon as possible, so now I can call him my true husband. We rent a cozy little room, and Jacomo is carving a beautiful cradle in his spare time, while I make the layette. I have never felt more grateful to God. I go to confession and Mass often—it is so comforting to be in a city that is not under interdict and excommunication—and that has helped me achieve some reconciliation and peace.

I pray that God too holds you in His hands, that you may find mercy and happiness, if not with your beloved lord, then at San Zaccaria.

> *Please give my love to your aunt and our friends and tell them*
> *I fare most well.*
>   *Viena*

I reread the letter several times, unable to fully comprehend how Viena had achieved such a state. Despite my own circumstances, I was happy for her. The fallen angel, already back in God's grace.

Chapter 57

I opened my chest to put Viena's letter inside and was reminded of the cache of paper, ink, and quills that Luca had given me a while back. He had sent so many supplies, I had been unable to use them all. The dried rosebud he had given me so long ago for San Marco was there too, infusing a faint floral scent to the paper. His letters were there as well, but I would save them for another time, when I felt stronger.

I also readied the lock that I'd had Madelena procure for me many months before, ensuring it still worked properly.

I looked up again at the Carpaccio, the Madonna's eyes so peaceful, then glanced at the Barbari sketch of Venice in Luca's hand. I might never again venture outside these walls to the world that lay beyond, and I sighed before pushing away the thought. I cleared the clutter off my table and put the little pile of dirty dishes outside my room in the corridor. As I did so, Leo sauntered up and meowed at me.

"Come inside already." I scooped him up and closed the door. He allowed me to hug him for a moment before wriggling free, jumping down, and licking his belly.

As he settled into a furry purring mass near the brazier, I laid out a few sheets of paper and an ink bottle. I took my penknife and sharpened a quill.

Before I settled myself, I took the blanket from my bed and wrapped it around my shoulders like an embrace. I stroked Luca's handkerchief in my pocket.

Then I sat down and began to write.

We are the bones of this city, the heart, the womb. The hidden structure and architecture behind the beautiful facades. We are unseen yet leaned upon, vessels yet not empty, the home for our families. The hopes of our city are thrust upon us, and we will be punished if we fail.

Who sees us? Others of our kind. Mothers, daughters, sisters, both bloodline and spiritual. Maids, because they must and because they are even more forgotten than us.

Precious few others. Our sons, when they are babes. Our brothers, as playmates. Our fathers, on their deathbeds. Our husbands, in the quest to produce an heir. Our lovers, in the throes of passion. Our priests, in the confessionals. God, when we do penance.

One year from now, a decade, a century, half a millennium, will things be different? Dare we dream it? When we are seen for ourselves, not just as the conduit of progeny, heirs, lineage, not just as beautiful objects to be protected, inspected, appreciated, but for who we are at the core . . .

Epilogue

Venice, September 1513, Feast of the Birth of the Virgin Mother

He is so soft!"

Little Paola sat with her legs splayed on the floor of the San Zaccaria parlour, petting Dolce's white fur and smiling the impish grin that reminded me so much of my brother. Her favourite doll, Rosa's old one, lay beside her, faded and worn from so much love.

"Dolce has grown unusually tolerant in his old age," Mama remarked as she held a sleeping baby boy curled to her breast, his hair so blond he looked nearly bald. "I hope he still has a few more years in him so that Zordan has a chance to play with him too."

Rosa reached over to caress her son's forehead with an indulgent smile. "At the moment Dolce hides every time he sees Zordan crawl toward him."

Livia chuckled. "Zordan has gotten to be quite the fast crawler. Rosa was like that, wasn't she, Chiara?"

Mama nodded with a smile before freezing at the sight of Zanetta Zane walking over to us, her green eyes narrowed. The rest of us just stared, always unsure what to expect from her.

Zanetta forced a pleasant look onto her face. "I heard my nephew was visiting. He's grown so big since the last time I saw him."

Rosa inhaled. "Hello, Sister-in-law." She spoke very evenly. "Would you like to hold him?"

Zanetta's expression grew more genuine. "Very much so."

Mama stood with a forced smile to transfer the baby to Zanetta, who was now smiling herself. He slightly roused before she jiggled him back to sleep, then nuzzled his head as she wandered to the other side of the parlour, out of easy hearing.

Livia patted Rosa's knee. "That was very gracious of you."

Rosa shrugged. "I have finally made my peace. Zanetta is his aunt and blood relation. Zago is pleased with his son, and we have reached a truce. Although Signora Bassano said on her visit last month that she is certain I will have no more children now."

"Did she?" Mama looked dismayed. Rosa was her only hope for further grandchildren. Mama never acknowledged Paola as such, of course, but she had softened considerably toward the child over the years, a link to her beloved son.

Rosa nodded. "I know that is disappointing for you, Mama. But there is an added benefit."

Mama brushed away a small tear that had escaped. "What is that, darling?"

Rosa's eyes took on a mischievous look. "She told Zago this too. And he has not bothered me a single time in the marriage bed since. I have never slept better."

Mama looked slightly scandalized as Livia cackled. "Let him pay for his pleasure then. It is a treaty worthy of the Ottomans. You are indeed looking well, Niece. Very well rested." We all attempted to control our giggles.

"What's so funny, Auntie?" Paola looked up from Dolce at Livia with her big brown eyes and that Paolo smile. In her looks she favoured her mother's Turkish beauty, but in her amiable nature she was all her father.

"Come here, my little chicken." Livia held out her arms and Paola ran into them with glee. "That is old lady talk, not fit for little girls' ears." Paola squealed with delight as Livia tickled her and Mama joined in, and we all broke into laughter.

Zanetta glanced over at us for a moment before returning her gaze to the infant. Was that jealousy I detected in her eyes?

Rosa took my hand. "Sister, will you walk with me a moment?"

"Of course. Would you like to visit Teodora?"

She nodded as Mama and Livia resumed their chatter. We linked elbows as we left the parlour and headed into the corridor that led to the cemetery. Leo brushed past my ankles companionably on his way to the kitchens.

"So rarely are we able to talk alone anymore." Rosa rested her head momentarily on my shoulder.

"Yes, and I miss it. We should do this more often."

We entered the graveyard, where the flowers were in full splendour as Enrica pecked around hopefully.

"Good thing Leo is not out here." I smiled. "Livia would never forgive me or him if a single one of Enrica's feathers were harmed."

Rosa did not reply, her attention turned to the little headstone beside Elisabetta's.

We stood there for a long while with our heads bowed, and Rosa whispered some prayers. Finally, she crossed herself, then took my arm again before sitting on a stone bench.

"Does Madelena still visit regularly?"

"Yes, La Diamante gives her permission to visit Paola every week. Although as the child grows up, it is becoming increasingly difficult to explain who exactly Madelena is. And of course, when she can buy her freedom, who knows what she may do or where she may go." Or whether she'd take her little daughter with her, something I did not want to contemplate.

Rosa reached into her pocket. She pulled out a folded pamphlet on cheap paper. "Zago brought this home the other day. I thought it would interest you."

I took it in hand, unfolded it, and read the title aloud. "*On why the noble fathers of Venice should properly educate their daughters.*" I scanned the rest of the text, which expounded all the reasons why this should be. I was in disbelief. It was almost as if I had composed it. No author was listed. "Anonymously written, it seems."

"Zago says it has ignited quite the discussion in the Great Council. Another reason to be glad we had a son, so we won't have to argue about it."

I read through the page again. Did Luca have this pamphlet printed based on the pages of my manuscript he'd spirited out all those years ago? I did not know which pages he'd taken, chosen at random. Until now. It seemed plausible. I scrutinized the words again. No, it seemed probable. Those were my ideas and phrases, edited by a practised mind to be more concise and even stronger. I sat there, stunned.

Did Rosa suspect the same author? I'd never told her of my first manuscript, or my literary correspondence with Luca, or his willingness to play my agent.

Finally, I sighed, refolded the paper, and put it in my own pocket. "I will always be grateful to Papa for educating us." *And to Luca,* I silently added,

for his bravery in daring to have my ideas printed. For his remembering me
behind the forgotten walls of the convent.

She nodded, then cleared her throat. "Any news of Lord Cicogna?" Ah, she must have suspected Luca's authorship.

It took me a further moment to compose myself at her question. I had largely reconciled myself to reality and had no regrets. I had never confessed our liaison to Father Hieronimo when he came a few days after Christmas, despite my promise to Zanetta. When she asked if I had, I'd lied and said yes, then confessed that. But I still was troubled thinking about Luca. I had received no letters or messages from him over the past years, nor had I sent him any. I no longer carried his handkerchief around with me all the time, but I did sleep with it under my pillow, touching it in the night as I allowed myself my memories.

"Nothing beyond the usual Venetian gossip and Papa mentioning him in ordinary conversation. The last I heard is that three months ago he was promoted to Lord of the Night Watch for the Castello *sestiere.*" The same *sestiere* where San Zaccaria was located, and I recalled how he'd once said he would caress the stone of the convent as he walked by and imagine it was my skin.

Rosa nodded. "Yes, and Zago says he is doing an excellent job. He mentions him sometimes too. He believes Luca has a bright future ahead of him."

I swallowed hard to eliminate the lump that had developed in my throat, and patted my pocket. "Something Zago and I can agree on."

The lump slowly dissipated, and we sat together in comfortable silence, watching Enrica inspect a flowering shrub.

"What a lovely day." Rosa raised her face to the late summer sun, wispy white clouds scudding dreamily along with the warm breeze. The air was scented with freshly turned earth. "Have you been getting out at all? Or too busy with your manuscript?"

"I am in the middle of a section that requires much contemplation." I was focusing more purely on monastic life, rather than women in Venetian society generally, as I had in my original manuscript, writing this time in the more difficult Latin rather than vernacular. "Hard to do along with teaching the foundlings and boarding girls, looking after Paola with Livia, and making time to finally tackle Greek. But I do so enjoy it all. I don't want to sacrifice anything."

"I hope you will let me read it someday."

I smiled evasively. I knew I could enjoy Rosa's support no matter what, but Livia was the closest intellectual companion I had nowadays and I hadn't even let her read it, although on occasion I tried out ideas on her. I most wanted to discuss it with Mother Marina, but I did not wish to put her in a difficult position, especially as far as Zanetta was concerned. I was also scrupulously careful about locking my manuscript away any time I left my cell. I sometimes wondered what the new pope, Leo X, a member of the Florentine Medici family famous for his artistic patronage, might make of it. Would he find it heretical? Evidently His Holiness was quite urbane and scholarly, so different from the now deceased brutish Warrior Pope.

But I felt no compulsion to find out what His Holiness or anyone else thought about my project. It was for me alone. Nor did I feel a rush to complete it. I had a lifetime to think about it and to write it.

And as I had once written Luca, despite the convent walls, when I was writing, my mind was free.

Author's Note

I could not have written this novel without the work of many academics, researchers, and writers. While not an exhaustive list, the following sources have been especially valuable in shaping my novel, although all errors remain my own:

Virgins of Venice: Broken Vows and Cloistered Lives in the Renaissance Convent, by Mary Laven; *Marriage Wars in Late Renaissance Venice*, by Joanne M. Ferraro; *The Boundaries of Eros: Sex, Crime, and Sexuality in Renaissance Venice*, by Guido Ruggiero; *Venice, Città Excelentissima: Selections from the Renaissance Diaries of Marin Sanudo*, edited by Patricia Labalme and Laura Sanguineti White; *Information and Communication in Venice: Rethinking Early Modern Politics*, by Filippo de Vivo; *Venice: Pure City*, by Peter Ackroyd; "Visible Lives: Black Gondoliers and Other Black Africans in Renaissance Venice,""Power and Institutional Identity in Renaissance Venice: The Female Convents of S.M. delle Vergini and S. Zaccaria," and "Elections of Abbesses and Notions of Identity in Fifteenth- and Sixteenth-Century Italy, with Special Reference to Venice," all by Kate Lowe; *Ciao, Carpaccio!: An Infatuation*, by Jan Morris; *Women and Men in Renaissance Venice: Twelve Essays on Patrician Society* and "Political Adulthood in Fifteenth-Century Venice," both by Stanley Chojnacki; *Art and Life in Renaissance Venice*, by Patricia Fortini Brown; *Michelangelo and the Pope's Ceiling*, by Ross King; "Nuns and Their Art: The Case of San Zaccaria in Renaissance Venice," by Gary M. Radke; "The Regulation of Domestic Service in Renaissance Venice," by Dennis Romano; "Wives, Widows, and Brides of Christ: Marriage and the Convent in the Historiography of Early Modern Italy," by Silvia Evangelisti; "The Foundation of the Ghetto: Venice, the Jews, and the War of the League of Cambrai," by Robert Finlay; "The Legal Status of the Jews in Venice to 1509," by Benjamin Ravid; Alexander S. Wilkinson's review of Rosa Salzberg's *Ephemeral City: Cheap Print and Urban Culture in Renaissance Venice*.

As much as possible, I hewed closely to the dates of actual events, mostly taken from the diaries of Marin Sanudo, and used as much of the real geography of Venice as I could glean from maps of the era, including Jacopo de' Barbari's famous woodcut map made in 1500. I also consulted paintings of the period, particularly those created by Vittore Carpaccio (c. 1465–1525) and Titian (c. 1488–1576). As well, in the course of several visits to the city, I went to the church of San Zaccaria, the crypt, and adjacent buildings open to the public. The site of the San Zaccaria convent now operates as a police building. Aldus Manutius founded the Aldine Press in 1494, and it was instrumental in Venice's printing industry and bringing classical Greek and Latin texts to publication as well as publishing some contemporary works.

Pope Julius II really did impose an interdict on Venice in 1509. An interdict was essentially the excommunication of an entire jurisdiction, which meant that except for Penance, all religious sacraments could not be performed, including marriages and baptisms as well as Mass. For Catholics, being under interdict was an untenable position, which is why the threat of such papal action spurs my patrician fathers to have their children properly settled, not knowing how long the interdict would endure. In this case, it lasted less than a year.

I greatly compressed the ceremonies related to marriage, which really took place over several days. It was routine for noblemen in their thirties to marry girls in their mid-teens. Rosa's age of thirteen is very young, but within the realm of possibility. I took the idea of Zago sleeping with Rosa before the wedding night from a mention in Sanudo's diary. Noblemen before marriage did have much freedom, and many such young men joined fraternities that staged mummeries and hosted parties. The "Baggy Pants" fraternity was the name of a real fraternity as mentioned by Sanudo.

Similarly, the process of becoming a nun would unfold over several years, but I compressed the ceremonies into a single day for plotting purposes. Additionally, the political structure and hierarchy of a convent was quite complicated, with different levels of nun based on class, so I simplified that into ordained nuns and lay servants. There is some circumstantial evidence of lesbianism in nunneries, as related in Mary Laven's book.

The lagoon island convent of San Anzolo di Contorta (or della Polvere) was a real place. Pope Sixtus IV shut the profligate convent down in 1474, forcing most of the nuns to move to a more pious convent in the Giudecca but allowing the few who refused to stay for the rest of their lives. They lived there until the last one died in 1518. The island is now uninhabited and difficult to travel to. The incident of the noblemen being caught at the Celestia convent is straight from Sanudo, while the true love story of Polisena and Giovanni at San Zaccaria is from *The Boundaries of Eros*.

Before 1514, the nuns of Venice had quite a bit of leeway in their interactions with the outside world. They were able at times to visit outside the convent, and the metaphorical wall separating them from the rest of the city was quite porous. However, after the horrific loss at the Battle of Agnadello specifically and the War of the League of Cambrai generally, at the time this novel takes place, the authorities began to crack down on the city's nunneries with a very heavy hand. In 1514, officials tried to literally wall in the "naughty" nuns of San Zaccaria, but the sisters threw stones at them to keep them away. Officials eventually built a wall in the parlour but conceded to the construction of windows.

It is unclear where the nuns buried their dead in 1509. Possibly some of them are in the crypt, where eight doges are also laid to rest. There is evidence of graveyards in Venice, although burying the dead in Venice proper was outlawed at the beginning of the nineteenth century, due to the watery and thus unhygienic conditions (Venetians have buried their dead for the last two hundred years on the nearby island of San Michele). I chose to locate the final resting place of less important nuns in a small fictional San Zaccaria cemetery for plotting purposes.

The island on which Justina and Luca enjoy their picnic is known today as Poveglia. It has a notorious reputation now due to its history as both a plague island and the site of a mental hospital. However, in 1509, it had been abandoned by farmers and fishermen for over a century and its haunted reputation was still far in the future.

Because the political structure of the Renaissance Venetian government was highly complex, I simplified as much as possible for clarity and ease of reading. One item of note is that only the noble class could rule and govern the republic, and all men verified to be of the noble class joined the Great Council at age twenty-five (some, like Luca, obtained special permission to join at a younger age). From that assembly, in extremely complex voting rituals, were chosen the Council of Ten, the Council of Forty, the doge, and other governmental posts.

Venetian society was very rigidly class based. Below the nobility were the merchants and bureaucrats of the citizen class, who were often very wealthy, and below that was everyone else (labourers, servants, etc.). To mix classes via marriage was very rare. For a noble to marry or have children with someone below the patrician caste was to give up all rights of the nobility—and, moreover, considered a betrayal of the republic. Many rules and laws governed dowries and marriages of the patrician class, which I tried to make as straightforward as possible.

Most of my characters are fictional, although I used real noble last names. My inspiration for the character of Justina was the proto-feminist ideas and works of Sister Arcangela Tarabotti (1604–52). Mother Marina and Angela Riva were actual nuns who in 1509 vied to be the abbess of San Zaccaria. Mother Marina squeaked out the win in a very close and contentious vote, which I used to influence the behaviour and actions of my nuns.

I made up the servant Teodor, but black gondoliers and labourers from beyond Venice, like Madelena from Constantinople, were far from unheard of (see Carpaccio's *Miracle of the Relic of the True Cross*, painted circa 1496). Slaves could be people of any colour, and they often had the opportunity to work their way out of bondage (like Madelena). Our modern conceptions of slavery and race are not applicable to this time, as it was well before the era of the African slave trade. Fifteenth- and sixteenth-century Venice was truly a crossroads of the world, and it was quite usual (at least for men) to interact with people of different races, religions, and origins. What mattered most to Venetians was maintaining one's place in the rigid class hierarchy, adhering to strict societal rules and codes, and protecting the reputation and status of women, particularly women from the patrician class (unmarried noblewomen wore almost burka-like veils in public).

In 1516, the Jews who had begun coming to Venice from the mainland in 1509 during the War of the League of Cambrai were forced to live in a controlled section of the city that became known as the Ghetto, likely from the Venetian word for "foundry." Visitors can still see the distinctive architecture of this area today.

Acknowledgements

First, thank you, reader, for reading my novel!

I also would like to wholeheartedly thank the following people. Some did translations, others gave information or ideas, and many provided much-needed moral support: the BBC's *In Our Time: History* podcast, Kerry Clare and her blog school, the Crazy Group, my aunt Camille DeSimone, Professor Alberto Galasso, Avi and Rachel Goldfarb, Theresa Lemieux, Marilyn Meditz, Jodi Miller, the *Our Fake History* podcast, Andy and Marian Ruston, Elly Sheahan, M.K. Tod and her blog *A Writer of History*, Professor Barbara Wall, Jacke Wilson and the *History of Literature* podcast, and Erla Zwingle's blog *Venice: I am not making this up*.

Thank you so very much to those who read drafts and provided vital feedback: Rebecca Batley, Nili Benazon, Iyana Browne-Gordon, Nicole Campbell, Denise Deakins, Judith Dean, Kate Jewell, Vanessa John, Tracey Madeley, Kate Newton, Andrew Noakes of *The History Quill*, and Veronica White.

I would like to give a shout-out to Janice Kirk. During our long and fruitful co-authorship, we created and matriculated in our own little MFA program, learning much about the craft of writing. Enrica the chicken is for you.

Thank you to my agent, John Pearce, who has been a stalwart presence in my writing life since 2004. Thanks as well to Chris Casuccio and the entire staff at Westwood Creative Artists.

Much gratitude to my lovely editor Jennifer Lambert. I so appreciate your enthusiasm and editorial acumen. Thanks also to designer Laura Klynstra for the gorgeous cover, production editor Canaan Chu, copyeditor Sarah Wight, proofreader Catherine Marjoribanks, as well as everyone at HarperCollins Canada.

Thank you very much to the Canada Council for the Arts for their financial support.

Thanks to all my fellow historical fiction authors. I love reading your work and learning about writing and history with every novel I devour.

To all my family for their ongoing support over the years, especially my dad, my brother, all my in-laws, my nephews and niece, Nym for his fuzziness, and my children, who I'm thrilled to say have both become huge readers. Big A, you can read this one now. Little A, you might have to wait a few years.

To my husband Ajay, for your love, support, integrity, creativity, intelligence, patience, and so many things you would be embarrassed to read upon these pages. You are a true gentleman.

My mother died somewhat unexpectedly of cancer complications during the writing of this book, and I had Elisabetta die of lymphoma, just like her. Mom only knew I had finished the first draft. Ever since I was a little girl writing poems and stories in notebooks that she bought for me, she was my biggest fan and cheerleader, always telling her friends and family about my work, setting up book club sessions and readings every chance she had, and unfailingly asking about my progress. She was also the repository for my matrilineal family's stories. I hope she's proud of my first solo novel. I miss you so much, Mom.

Book Club Questions

1) While the novel is from Justina's point of view, it is also about other women: Rosa, Livia, Viena, Madelena, Esther, Zanetta, La Diamante, Mama, Elisabetta, Mother Marina, and others. Which woman do you most identify with? Which woman did you like the most? Why?

2) Would you consider any of these women to be feminists? Why or why not? For their time, could they possibly be considered feminists?

3) What do you think of the men in this novel? Luca, Paolo, Papa, Zago, Teodor, and others. Who did you like or not like, and why?

4) How much do Venetian society and rules influence the characters in the novel, both women and men? How does that influence compare with other periods in history, including today?

5) How much does the War of the League of Cambrai influence both Venetian society and the characters in this novel? What about the interdict?

6) How much do religion and faith influence both Venetian society and the characters in this novel?

7) Do you think Justina made the right decisions at the end of the novel? What do you wish she had done differently? What would you have done in her situation, back in 1509? What would you do with the benefit of modern-day information?

8) This novel was meant to bring forgotten women's stories to the contemporary reader. Which other character would you like to see have her own novel and why?